Julian

The Burkes: Book #2

By

KIMBERLY RAE JORDAN

THREESTRAND PRESS

A CORD OF THREE STRANDS IS NOT EASILY BROKEN.

A man, a woman & their God.
Three Strand Press publishes Christian Romance stories that intertwine love, faith and family. Always clean. Always heartwarming. Always uplifting.

This is a work of fiction. Names, characters, places, and incidents are a product of the author's imagination. Locales and public names are sometimes used for atmospheric purposes. Any resemblance to actual people, living or dead, or to businesses, companies, events, institutions, or locales is completely coincidental.

JULIAN/ Kimberly Rae Jordan. -- 1st ed.
ISBN-13: 978-1-988409-90-0

Therefore, if anyone is in Christ,
he is a new creation;
old things have passed away;
behold, all things have become new.
II Corinthians 5:17

Therefore, if anyone is in Christ,
he is a new creation;
old things have passed away;
behold, all things have become new.
II Corinthians 5:17

CHAPTER ONE

"Kiara Reynolds?"

At the sound of her name, Kiara looked up from the book she was reading on her phone. A woman stood near the reception desk with a warm smile on her face.

Getting up, Kiara approached her, hoping her nerves didn't show too much.

"Kiara?"

At her nod, the woman's smile grew. "I'm Janessa. Nice to meet you."

Janessa led her down a hallway, then stopped by an open door. "Here we go. You said when you called for an appointment that you're pregnant?"

"Yes," Kiara said with a nod, clutching her hands together. "I've had a positive pregnancy test at home."

Several of them, in fact. It had been hard to believe that the first one was right, so she'd taken more over the days that followed. All of them had been positive.

Janessa asked her a few questions, then had her go into the bathroom to pee in a cup. Kiara didn't think there was any doubt she was pregnant, but she did as requested.

When she came out, Janessa took her weight and her blood pressure before taking her to an examination room. "Doctor Misha will be with you in a few minutes."

"Thank you."

It had taken longer than it probably should have for her to make an appointment to see a doctor. But since she was heading towards the end of her first trimester, she knew it was necessary. As soon as she'd realized she might be pregnant, she'd read up on what was good and what was bad for pregnant women.

Not drinking hadn't been a problem. She hadn't touched a drop of alcohol since the night she'd spent with Julian. Consuming less coffee hadn't been great, but she'd managed to cut back to a cup every couple of days.

There was a light rap on the door, then it swung open. A woman wearing a forest-green pantsuit stepped in. She was a beautiful Black woman with a warm smile and kind eyes.

"Hello," she said as she approached Kiara. "I'm Doctor Misha."

"I'm Kiara Reynolds," Kiara said as she shook the hand the doctor held out to her.

Doctor Misha sat down at the desk and turned her full attention to Kiara. "So, you are, as you suspected, pregnant."

Kiara nodded. "I figured it was either that or I'm dying."

The doctor's eyebrows lifted at that. "So where are you at with this? How are you feeling?"

"Miserable."

"Physically? Emotionally?"

Kiara gripped her hands together. Did she dare to be honest? "Both."

"I see." There was no judgment in the doctor's expression, only compassion and concern. "Why don't you tell me a bit about the circumstances of your pregnancy?"

Kiara pressed a hand to her stomach as it gave a lurch. She breathed through the feeling, then exhaled heavily.

"I got pregnant after a night of drinking with a man who is the brother of my adopted sister."

Doctor Misha's dark brown eyes widened. "That sounds complicated."

"It is." Kiara hesitated, then said, "Can I trust you?"

"Yes, of course," the doctor said. "Whatever you tell me stays between the two of us."

Kiara took a deep breath and plunged in, explaining everything, glad that the doctor didn't seem rushed. She gave all the details, without giving actual names. But apparently, that didn't matter.

"Are you talking about Annie's sister?" Doctor Misha asked. "Is her twin your adopted sister?"

Kiara stared at the woman. "You know Annie?"

"Yes. Her boyfriend is my brother-in-law."

"Cole?"

Doctor Misha nodded. "I'm married to his brother, Jay." She reached out and laid her hand on Kiara's arm. "But that doesn't mean I'll reveal anything you've told me to anyone."

"Thank you," Kiara said, relieved. "I just... I'm a bit overwhelmed."

"So you don't have a relationship with the baby's father?"

"No. I'm not even sure I'd consider us friends at this point."

"How does he feel about the pregnancy?"

"He doesn't know." And Kiara wasn't sure how to tell him. Or if she even wanted him to know.

"What are your thoughts about the pregnancy?" Doctor Misha asked.

"Like how it's making me feel?"

"Do you want to keep the baby?"

Reflexively, Kiara spread her hand across her stomach. "I don't want an abortion."

"Good," Doctor Misha said. "I believe strongly that there are better options for an unplanned, and perhaps unwanted, pregnancy."

"Adoption?"

"Yes. There are lots of wonderful families willing to adopt babies whose moms aren't able to keep them."

"I have no reason not to keep the baby," Kiara said. "I have enough money to support us both."

"There are more than just economic reasons that a woman might decide she can't keep her baby. Maybe she's not in a good place mentally or emotionally."

Her emotions might be all over the place, but Kiara knew with certainty that she wanted to keep her baby. She wanted a connection with someone of her own. Someone she could love and be loved by. Someone who needed her, especially now that Angie didn't.

"I want to keep the baby," Kiara said.

Doctor Misha smiled at her. "Well, now that that decision is made, let's see what we can do to help you feel better."

By the time she left the doctor's office, Kiara had instructions for what prenatal vitamins to buy and a prescription for her morning sickness. She also had a requisition for bloodwork. But best of all, she left with a recording of her baby's heartbeat.

"Ready to go?" Lucy asked as they got back in the car.

"Not yet. I need to go to the lab and then to the pharmacy."

Kiara wasn't sure why she still needed to have a bodyguard. Her adoptive father Jim was no longer a threat, thanks to Jude's quick thinking. However, Jude, in his role as the head of security, wasn't hearing any of her arguments about not needing a guard.

She hadn't argued too aggressively as yet because she still needed someone to drive her around. At some point she'd get her license, but right then, she had other things to focus on.

Once everything was done, Lucy drove back to the estate and let her off at the back door to the main house. Kiara detoured to the kitchen to grab some crackers and cold ginger ale before going to her room.

Up in her room, she took the medication the doctor had recommended, ate some crackers and drank a little of the ginger ale before crawling into bed. She was once again very tired.

Between the exhaustion and the morning sickness, Kiara wondered if she'd ever feel normal again. Both were so unlike her that she didn't feel like herself. Was that how the whole pregnancy was going to be?

As she considered the remaining months of the pregnancy, Kiara knew she couldn't keep it a secret for much longer. Not for the first time, she contemplated leaving the estate, going somewhere else to have her baby and raise it on her own.

However, her nausea deepened at the thought of being away from Angie. From the moment they'd first met as children, they'd been inseparable. But Angie didn't need her the way she once had. Jude was her protector now. Her motivator. The role Kiara had played in Angie's life had been taken away, and she didn't know what that meant for their relationship.

Her hand drifted to her stomach. This little baby hadn't asked to be born, especially to a single mom who wasn't sure if she'd be a good mother.

Kiara hadn't had the best examples of motherhood growing up, and the reality of becoming a mother worried her. All she could hope was that since she knew what hadn't been good about how her birth mother and Sandra had related to her and the other children in their care, she could figure out how to be different in how she mothered this little one.

Despite her tough upbringing, she knew how to love. If it hadn't been for Angie, she might not have known that. But having her for a sister—a sister who needed her—had taught Kiara how to love and care for someone.

"It's you and me, little bean," Kiara whispered. "I'll love you with all my heart, and I hope that you'll love me too."

She'd always hoped that one day a man would love her like the men loved the women in the books she read. For a short time, she'd wondered if Julian could be that man for her. He'd seemed to enjoy the time they spent together talking. But then had come the night when, in an alcoholic daze, things had moved beyond just talking.

Kiara hadn't been as intoxicated as Julian that night, but she'd been no less impaired when it came to the decision she'd made to allow things to progress the way they had. Looking back now, she could see that a misguided hope that she and Julian had been forging something real had caused her impairment.

It was only in the days following that night, when she realized he didn't remember what had happened, that the hope that he might have feelings for her had died. It had been foolish of her to think that someone of Julian Burke's caliber would ever look at someone like her as anything other than a passing fancy.

Having a man choose to love her had seemed to be a lofty dream even before she had a baby as part of the equation. Now, they came as a package deal, and the prospect of raising a child that wasn't theirs might turn men off.

"You and me, bean," Kiara murmured. "You and me."

Kiara swallowed against a sudden wave of nausea and closed her eyes, not bothering to fight the exhaustion that drew her into oblivion.

Kiara woke with the feeling that she was going to throw up. Scrambling out of bed, she bolted into the bathroom. Thankfully, by this point, she had plenty of practice making that particular trip.

Once it was over, she rinsed her mouth, then washed her face. When she looked in the mirror above the sink, she winced at her appearance.

She looked like death warmed over. Dark circles shadowed her eyes, and her skin was pale, even beneath the light tan that was her natural skin color. And to top it off, her dark curls were a tangled mess.

"This is worth it," she reminded herself, gently touching her still-flat stomach. "We're going to be okay."

A soft knock sounded at her bedroom door, and Kiara froze, hoping it was Angie. She wasn't ready to face anyone else yet, especially not looking like this.

"Kiara? Are you in there?" It was Angie's voice, soft and concerned.

"Just a minute," she called, quickly splashing more cold water on her face and running her fingers through her tangled hair.

When she opened the door, Angie looked at her with concern. "Were you sick again?

"Yeah." Kiara turned away from the door, leaving it open as an invitation. "Same old, same old."

"How did your appointment go?" Angie asked as she followed Kiara to the bed and settled beside her on it.

"It went well." Kiara plucked at the fabric of the comforter she'd drawn over her legs. "The doctor asked me if I wanted to keep the baby."

"She was offering you an abortion?" Angie asked, her tone incredulous.

"No. She was suggesting adoption," Kiara corrected.

There was a long moment of silence before Angie said, "Are you considering that?"

Kiara shook her head. "I know not every adoptive family is like ours was, but having the experience we had with Jim and Sandra... Well, I can't take the risk."

"Oh, I'm glad," Angie said. "You won't be alone. I'll be with you through all of this."

"I just hope I'm going to be a good mom," Kiara said, voicing the one big fear she had.

Angie reached out and grabbed her hand. "You've been a great big sister to me. You've always cared for me and protected me. You'll be a great mom."

"I wonder if I should leave," Kiara said.

Angie's grip on her hand tightened, almost painfully. "Leave? Why?"

"I just think it's going to be hard to raise a child here, knowing who the father is."

"You need to tell him," Angie said. "He should take responsibility for his part in what happened."

Kiara shook her head. "He doesn't remember. He might not believe me."

"That's what a paternity test is for. If he doesn't believe you, he'll probably want a paternity test. Agree to it."

It was so much more than just getting Julian to accept that he was the father of her baby. He was a man known for dating beautiful women. She doubted that he would want the world to know that he'd been with her.

"It's just an option," Kiara said. "I haven't decided."

Angie frowned. "I don't like that it's an option."

"It's not like I'd disappear completely," Kiara assured her. "I just need to have a little distance from... here."

Angie let go of Kiara's hand and wrapped her arms around herself. "We've never been apart."

"I know," Kiara said. "But you have Jude now. You don't need me around."

"That's not true," Angie protested. "I want you close. Jude isn't replacing you in my life."

"I know that," Kiara said. "We'll always be sisters, but Jude can protect you now. He can help you."

"I still don't want you to go," Angie murmured.

"Nothing is for sure yet," Kiara said, trying to head off the emotional reaction that was sure to come if they continued down this path. "We'll talk about it later."

Angie stared at her for a long moment, her blue-green eyes holding sadness. "Just promise me you won't make a decision without talking it through with me first."

Kiara held up her hand. "I promise."

Angie didn't look completely convinced but had obviously decided to let the subject drop for the time being. "Are you going to come down for dinner tonight?"

Kiara would have preferred not to, but she felt like she needed to give Angie something after she dropped the bombshell about possibly moving away.

"Yeah, I'll be there."

Angie smiled. "Good. I'm going to get ready for dinner, then go see Jude. I think he'll be joining us too."

Though she did feel that Jude had replaced her in Angie's life, she didn't hate the guy. He had saved Angie from Jim, and Kiara was forever grateful to him for that.

Once Angie had left, Kiara went to the bathroom and tried to work her curls into some semblance of order, then applied a little bit of makeup to hide the dark circles under her eyes.

She changed into a dark knee-length skirt and tights and paired it with an oversized sweater. So far, her clothes all still fit, but maternity clothes were definitely in her future.

Down in the dining room, it was just her, Angie, Jude, Duncan, and Elizabeth. They were spaced out around the table, which had been shrunk down to its smallest size.

As usual, the food was delicious, but she was careful to eat only small amounts because she didn't want to risk triggering her stomach. Dessert was the most tempting, as it was a warm blueberry crumble with vanilla ice cream, and she had a fierce sweet tooth.

"Ready to get back to your room, love?" Angie asked, probably having noticed that Jude had only eaten half his dessert before putting his fork down. He was still staying in the medical suite in the basement of the house where the doctor Duncan had flown in helped with Jude's care, since he hadn't wanted to stay in the hospital in Coeur d'Alene.

"Yeah. I think so."

Kiara watched them go, then focused on the remainder of her dessert. Eating more than she probably should have, but it tasted so good.

"Kiara, I'm glad we have a moment to speak," Duncan said when it was just the three of them.

She looked up at him, concern growing inside her. "Um... okay?"

Duncan glanced at Elizabeth, whose brow furrowed. "We've been concerned with your recent illness. Are you feeling better?"

Kiara didn't want to lie. "A bit."

"Is there any chance you could be pregnant?" Elizabeth asked, her voice gentle. "Because the way you've been sick lines up with how I felt when I was pregnant with Benji."

Kiara's heart pounded as she was faced with having to reveal her secret. She wished that Angie was still there. But she was on her own, and it was a secret that was going to come out eventually. So maybe this was the best way.

"Yes. I am pregnant."

The older pair exchanged a look, apparently able to communicate with just a meeting of the eyes.

Duncan looked back at her, his gaze unreadable. "If you don't mind me asking, who is the father?"

"I'd rather not say," Kiara replied. She had no idea if that was a secret she'd keep forever, or if she'd talk to Julian about it eventually.

"Is it Julian?"

Kiara hoped her shock didn't show on her face. Why would Duncan come to that conclusion? There were other men on the estate that she'd been around. Derrick, who had helped her at the shooting range, as well as other security guards.

Was there something in particular that had led him to that conclusion?

"I'd rather not say."

For a moment, Duncan's expression tightened, but then it relaxed. "I know the two of you were spending a lot of time together in the evenings. I thought perhaps it had led to something more."

Kiara just stared at him, not sure what to say to that. "Yes. We did spend time talking."

"I hope you know that we would welcome any child that becomes part of our family," Elizabeth said. "And we'd like to support you as best as we can."

"Have you seen a doctor?" Duncan asked.

"Yes. I went to the clinic in Serenity Point. Apparently, the doctor I saw is married to Cole's brother."

Duncan nodded. "However, if you want a different doctor, let us know, and we'll find one for you."

"I'm happy with her," Kiara told him.

"That's good," Elizabeth said. "It's important to feel comfortable with your doctor."

Kiara was a bit surprised that neither of them asked her if she wanted to keep the baby. She appreciated that, especially now that she'd made up her mind to do just that.

"I do feel that the father bears some responsibility for this baby," Duncan said. "So keep that in mind."

Kiara nodded, because what else could she do?

She took another bite of her dessert, wondering how much time needed to pass until she could make her escape. Thankfully, distraction came as Benji, who had stayed at school to work out with some of his friends, arrived and sat down at the table to eat a late dinner.

Once she'd greeted him, she excused herself and hurried upstairs to her bedroom, afraid that the emotional turmoil that had resulted from the conversation she'd just had would cause physical turmoil. And she didn't want to be anywhere but her bathroom should that happen.

In the sanctuary of her room, Kiara sank down on her bed and took several deep breaths. What would happen if Duncan approached Julian to ask him about the likelihood of his being the father of her baby?

The best-case scenario would be if Julian didn't remember that night—which seemed to be the case—and then denied there being any chance of that being true. If that happened, then she could make the decisions she needed to in order to figure out the future for her and her baby.

CHAPTER TWO

The humid Singapore late afternoon air followed Julian Burke as he walked into the Asian headquarters for Burke NeuroTech. He paused, taking a moment to look around. This was his favorite of the Burke NeuroTech locations.

Beyond the floor-to-ceiling windows of the building, Biopolis, Singapore's biomedical hub, glowed in the night. It was a landscape of glass and steel towers with honeycomb patterns of illuminated windows. To Julian, Biopolis at night felt like a beacon of progress, alive yet serene, a center of science and ambition.

With Anthony, his bodyguard, at his side, Julian approached the elevators and used his security credentials to take him to the floor where the R&D labs were located. He leaned back against the elevator wall, watching the numbers pass. He was tired but also energized.

The flight from New York City to Singapore had been over nineteen long hours, but at least he'd traveled first class, which meant his seat had fully reclined into a bed. Still, he never slept well on those long-haul flights. So, while he might have gotten some sleep, it hadn't been overly restful.

He and Anthony arrived around four p.m. local time, and after a brief stop at his hotel to freshen up and grab a bite to eat, they'd headed to the lab. He had been eager for an in-person update from the head of R&D, and thankfully, that eagerness was slowly edging out the tiredness he'd landed with.

As they stepped out of the elevator, Julian was immediately plunged into a space that thrummed with innovation. Illuminated computer screens, murmured conversations, and the faint hum of equipment filled the large open area.

With Anthony at his side, Julian navigated the sleek lab, his shoes silent on the polished floor. His anticipation grew as he approached Sean, who was bent over a large workbench. The man, wiry and focused, looked up, his glasses reflecting the room's lights.

"Julian," he said, pushing his glasses up his nose before holding out his hand with a smile. "Good to see you again."

Julian gave his hand a firm shake. "Good to see you again, Sean. I'm eager to hear how things are going with the trials."

Sean nodded with enthusiasm. "This is bigger than we hoped. We're not just competing with TENS units, we're rewriting pain relief for women."

When Sean had initially approached the Burke Foundation to see about getting a grant for his research on a pain-relieving device specifically for women, the premise had intrigued both Duncan and Julian. After several meetings, Duncan had hired Sean and set him up in the lab in Singapore.

Julian wasn't a scientist, but he'd gotten caught up in Sean's passion for the project. Sean had come up with the idea, spurred on by his mother's battle with chronic pain caused by endometriosis. With such a personal motive, Sean had devoted many hours to developing the product.

Sean picked up a small metal plate that had a flesh-colored square on it. "The Health Sciences Authority's fast-track program gave us early feedback, and our latest trials are showing incredible results for this stage in the development."

Julian leaned closer to look at the small device. "Give me the numbers. What's new since last week?"

Sean put the plate down and picked up a tablet from the workbench. He pulled up an image that Julian didn't understand. "This is a holographic model of pelvic nerve pathways. This is data from our phase one trials. We had forty women with endometriosis, right here in collaboration with KK Women's Hospital. They showed a significant reduction in chronic pelvic pain after three weeks."

"Sean, that's phenomenal."

Sean nodded, excitement sparkling behind his glasses. "They needed no drugs, and they registered no side effects. The AI crunches the biofeedback, including heart rate variability, skin conductance, menstrual cycle data from the app. Using that, it tailors the pulse patterns to each woman's neural signature."

"So you're having success with a personalized response and not just a generic pulse like a TENS machine would give someone?"

Sean nodded. "It's being tailored for each woman individually using the biofeedback gathered by the patch."

Julian stared at the data on the tablet, already envisioning the impact across worldwide healthcare markets. "What's driving the jump?"

Sean's eyes lit up. "Two big wins. First, we optimized the electrode array, focusing on micro-scaling, flexibility, and targeting specific nerves with precision. Second, the AI's predictive model, which was trained on last year's datasets from global pelvic pain studies. The more it learns about a woman's physiology, the more accurately it anticipates her pain and works to block it."

Julian let out a low whistle, running a hand through his hair. "Predictive pain relief? That's a game-changer."

He had never thought he'd become so interested in something that was focused on women's health, but Sean's passion for the project had been infectious, especially after the man had shared how lacking research into women's health issues was.

"Exactly," Sean said, holding up the metal plate again. "Non-invasive, reusable, rechargeable with a 48-hour battery. If the woman wants, the app can sync with telehealth platforms, meaning women's doctors can see real-time readings. We're also seeing stress levels drop, better sleep. The biofeedback is teaching women to manage triggers, not just pain."

Julian's grin widened, his mind racing with possibilities. This could be the start of a rise in future research into women's health issues. He tapped the workbench. "Timeline for phase two? Can we scale trials across the region?"

Sean adjusted his glasses, his tone cautious. "We're ready for a larger test group—two hundred women—and expanding beyond endometriosis to include patients with PCOS and interstitial cystitis. We've had interest expressed from hospitals in Bangkok and Seoul."

"That sounds great," Julian said. "What's holding you back?"

"We need funding to scale production. The flexible electronics aren't cheap, and we're optimizing the battery. Six months to a year, we could be ready for the first steps in trying to get FDA approval."

"I'll handle the funding," Julian said, already mentally pitching this to Duncan. He doubted that funding would be a problem once he presented the latest developments of the FemPulse. "This little patch... it's going to disrupt Big Pharma's grip on pain meds."

Sean nodded but lowered his voice. "One thing, though. The data—pain patterns, cycle info, stress markers—it's gold, but it's sensitive. In Singapore, data privacy laws are tight. We need top-tier encryption, especially if we're sharing with regional partners and beyond."

Julian's expression sobered, but his enthusiasm held. "Got it. I'll loop in our cybersecurity team. No leaks, no compromises." He clapped Sean's shoulder. "You're doing brilliant work, Sean."

"I appreciate your support with this, Julian," Sean said, his voice taking on a sincere tone. "We wouldn't be here without the support of you and your dad. I'm so grateful that you saw the possibilities and took a chance on the FemPulse."

"When you first shared your vision with us, the lack of products geared specifically for women's health surprised me. Even things being marketed for women seem to be created using non-gender specific research."

Sean nodded. "It's what spurred me on to pursue this."

"Well, I'll be back tomorrow to hear updates on the rest of the ongoing projects," Julian said. "I'm exhausted, but I was excited to hear about these developments."

"We'll be ready for you."

"And let's plan for dinner tomorrow night," Julian said.

Sean smiled. "Sounds good. I can have my assistant make reservations if you'd like."

"That would be perfect." Julian shook Sean's hand again, then headed for the elevator with Anthony, resisting the urge to stop and chat with other researchers in the lab.

He needed some solid sleep, so he'd be ready for the back-to-back meetings the next day.

Julian was so glad for the break from the heavy emotions back at the estate. He'd stayed there out of respect for Angela, and to some extent, his dad. But he was glad for a reason to escape, and for something that he was passionate about to distract him.

When they got back to the hotel, he told Anthony that he was in for the night, so the bodyguard went to his room in the suite they were sharing. He was no doubt as exhausted as Julian was.

Julian tossed his suit coat over the arm of the couch, then loosened his tie as he walked to the bar. After pouring himself a drink, he wandered to the window and stared out at the stunning Singapore skyline.

As he stood there draining his drink, thoughts flitted through his mind. There was no way he was going to be able to sleep with his mind whirling the way it was, his thoughts spiraling.

They were strange, disconnected thoughts.

The meetings the next day. Angela's return. Her dating Jude. The report he'd need to give Duncan. Debating whether he should go back to the estate or just stay in NYC after this trip.

But the thought that kept popping up as he stood in front of the window drinking was about Kiara. They'd spent a lot of time together, talking in the library. Drinking. It had been nice not to drink alone, even though Kiara hadn't indulged as much as he had.

There had been nights when Anthony had come to find him and get him to bed so that Duncan wouldn't discover him passed out on the couch. Kiara had already been gone when Anthony had woken him up.

But those evenings in the library had petered off, and it had seemed that Kiara had started to avoid him. Maybe she'd just decided she was done drinking with him, especially when he didn't remember much of what they talked about after a few drinks. He couldn't fault her for that, but he'd missed having someone to hang out with. Drinking solo was never fun, but if the alternative was not to drink at all, he'd do it alone.

Julian went back to the bar and refilled his drink. It took four drinks to finally get him to the point where he thought he could fall asleep when he got into bed.

Thankfully, he wasn't getting to bed too late, so he'd have plenty of time to recover from the hangover in the morning. He was a pro at that these days.

Pro or not, the next morning was rough for Julian. He should have remembered that drinking and jetlag did not go well together.

He dragged himself out of bed and into the shower, where he stood for a long time, hoping the hot water would wash away the tangle of cobwebs in his brain because of his overindulgence.

Once he felt a bit more human, he got out and prepared for his day. After blow-drying his hair, he got dressed and then went into the living area of his suite. Anthony was already there, having ordered coffee and some food for them.

The bodyguard traveled with him exclusively and had done so for many years. He didn't even make a comment about the fact that Julian looked a little rough.

“Here you go,” Anthony said, holding out a cup of coffee.

Julian gave him a nod of thanks as he took it. The coffee was perfectly made, but then Anthony was well aware of how he liked the beverage.

Over the breakfast that Anthony had ordered and was eating the most of, Julian reviewed his schedule for the day. It was going to be a long day, and he hoped he had the stamina to get through it.

This was the most important trip he'd taken since Angela's return to the estate, and he wanted to make the most of it.

The first meeting of the day was with the engineering team, and Julian arrived ten minutes early, hoping the extra time would help him focus through the lingering headache. Unfortunately, the conference room's bright lights felt like needles in his eyes.

"Mr. Burke, can I get you anything else before we begin?" asked the assistant who had shown him in.

Julian forced a smile. "A cup of coffee, please. And maybe dim these lights a touch?"

As the room filled with Burke NeuroTech's top engineers in Singapore, Julian straightened his posture and pushed the discomfort aside. This was what he'd come for–to be immersed in the work, not in his personal issues.

The engineering lead, Dr. Ava Lim, walked him through their latest developments with a precision that demanded Julian's full attention. Julian took notes, asked questions, and gradually felt his mind sharpening as he engaged with the material.

By late morning, the familiar rhythm of technical discussions had worked its magic. Julian's headache had faded to a dull whisper, and he found himself genuinely engaged in the information that was being presented.

As the engineers filed out at the end of the meeting, Julian allowed himself a moment to appreciate the clarity that had returned to his thoughts.

This was what he loved about the Singapore operation. The team's dedication reminded him why he'd been drawn to the neurotechnology side of Burke Pharmaceuticals in the first place. Here, surrounded by innovation and progress, the weight of family expectations felt manageable rather than oppressive.

The rest of his meetings proceeded with similar success. Julian found himself settling into a familiar cadence, the technical discussion providing a welcome distraction from the emotional turmoil he'd left behind at the estate. Thoughts of Angela and Kiara drifted to the back of his mind. Not gone entirely, but not demanding his attention the way they previously had.

By late afternoon, he was back in his hotel room, feeling more like himself than he had in weeks, though jet lag was still wearing on him.

A quick shower washed away the day's accumulated fatigue, and as he dressed for dinner, Julian caught his reflection in the mirror. The smudges were still there under his eyes, but the shadows had retreated from his gaze.

Not forever, he knew. But for a few hours, he'd gained some distance from the things that haunted him.

The restaurant Sean's assistant had chosen was tucked away in Clarke Quay, overlooking the Singapore River. Julian and Anthony arrived first, and the hostess led them to the private dining room that had been reserved for their dinner.

Dr. Lim would also be joining them, and Julian was looking forward to the meal with the two most impactful people working at Burke Neurotechnology's Singapore lab.

Anthony would join them at the table, though he wouldn't take part in any of the conversations. He never did. He was a silent witness to most aspects of Julian's life. Unless it was a safety matter, the man shared his thoughts with Julian only when it was just the two of them or if they weren't in a professional setting.

Through the wide windows, Julian watched the river's dark surface shimmer with reflected lights from the surrounding buildings. The warm glow of the restaurant provided a welcome contrast to the sterile brightness of the lab. His headache had finally subsided, replaced by a pleasant anticipation for the evening ahead.

Sean arrived first, dressed in a casual blazer rather than his lab coat, looking more relaxed than he had the previous day.

"Julian," he said, extending his hand. "Hope you haven't been waiting long."

"We just got here," Julian replied, gesturing to the untouched water glass in front of him. "This looks like a nice place. I've never been here before."

"They have a set menu for the private dining rooms," Sean said. "So I hope you like it."

"I'm sure it'll be fine," Julian said, settling back in his chair. Though he was very much in his element there in Singapore, there was a part of him that missed the estate, but he couldn't exactly pinpoint why.

"The chef here is incredible," Sean continued. "He trained in Seoul for fifteen years before coming to Singapore."

Shortly after Dr. Lim joined them, the food was brought out, starting with a selection of banchan, which the server said was the name of the small appetizers that filled the center of their table with vibrant colors and aromas. The rich scent of marinated meats and spices filled the private room, making his stomach growl in anticipation.

The conversation wandered from the technical to more personal as Sean and Dr. Lim—Ava—shared bits about their lives in Singapore.

Dr. Lim was a beautiful woman—just the sort he usually chose to spend time with—but he didn't fish in the company pond. He might not place many restrictions on his interactions with women, but married women and women he worked with were among those restrictions.

But there was something in him that balked at the idea of flirting with any woman, and it wasn't just because of his personal standards. He thought of the time he'd spent with Kiara, and the lighthearted conversations they'd had. It had been different from how he usually spent time with a woman.

He'd actually really enjoyed their time together, but apparently Kiara hadn't felt the same way. He wondered if he'd said something that had offended or upset her. Maybe he should talk to her when he got back to the estate, just to make sure he hadn't done something while he'd been drunk that had caused her to back away from the time they spent together.

As the meal wound down, Julian was pleasantly full and more relaxed than he'd been in recent months, with the exception of the time he had spent with Kiara. He took care of the bill, then the four of them left the private dining room.

Standing outside the restaurant, Julian said good night to Sean and Ava, promising he'd see them the next morning before heading back to New York. He'd thought about spending more time in Singapore, but there was really no reason to, now that he'd had the meetings to get caught up on everything. He had no skill in research and development, and he didn't want to hang around the labs getting in the way.

Back in the hotel suite, Anthony went to his room while Julian poured himself a drink and settled down with his laptop at the desk by the large windows that looked out over the city. Using the notes he'd taken, he typed out a report for Duncan.

After Duncan read through it, he would no doubt ask for clarification before sending it on to the board. Julian expected to receive either a lengthy email or a phone call from the man.

As if on cue, his phone dinged with an alert for a text. Picking it up, he saw a message from Duncan, even though texts weren't his usual form of communication. The message, however, didn't pertain to the report he'd just sent him.

Duncan: *I know you were thinking of staying in New York on your return from Singapore, but please come back to the estate.*

Julian frowned at the message, wondering what was going on. *Why?*

He knew Duncan wasn't going to be pleased with that one-word response questioning him, but he really wanted to know why he wasn't able to make the decision for himself.

Duncan: *There is something I need to discuss with you in person.*

Julian sighed. And of course, Duncan couldn't fly to New York to discuss it with him.

I'll be there.

Duncan: *I'll have the plane waiting for you in NYC.*

Julian was glad that after his long flight from Singapore, he wouldn't have to still take commercial flights to Idaho.

As he was staring at his phone, another text message came in. One that suddenly made him glad Duncan had demanded his presence in Idaho.

Mom: *Please make arrangements for us to have dinner when you get back from Singapore.*

Julian hadn't talked to his mother much since the disastrous meeting with Angela and Kiara. But from the few brief conversations they'd had, it was apparent that she'd washed her hands of the twins.

As soon as she'd realized that things weren't going to be a walk in the park with Angela, she'd apparently decided she wasn't interested in pursuing a relationship with her.

Julian wondered if he made things too challenging for her, that at some point, she'd let him go too. Perhaps he was going to find out.

I'm sorry I can't do dinner this time around. I need to get back to the estate.

There was no response, but Julian hadn't really expected one. He hadn't catered to her request, so she wouldn't say anything more to him. At least for a while.

Which was just as well. Apparently, he had something to deal with back at the estate.

CHAPTER THREE

It was nearly midnight—after almost twenty-four hours of travel—when the helicopter finally set down on the helipad at the estate. Julian stepped out into the night air, which was considerably cooler than what he'd left in Singapore.

He and Anthony grabbed their bags from the luggage compartment, then made their way to a waiting UTV. It was a short drive to the house, where they dropped him and his luggage off before Anthony and the driver continued on to the security building.

The house was quiet, and Julian already knew that Duncan wasn't waiting up for him, so he headed straight for his room. Although he did make a detour by the library to grab a bottle of his favorite whiskey.

As Julian stalked down the dimly lit hallway to his room, the long day of travel and the upcoming meeting with Duncan weighed heavy on him. He almost wished he could have stayed in New York and dealt with his mother instead.

Duncan rarely summoned him for personal reasons, and the summons for business reasons were usually to the offices in New York. This... he just wasn't sure what to expect. And that unknown drove him to fill his glass with whiskey... more than once.

The next morning came too soon for Julian's liking, but Duncan would expect him sooner rather than later.

He dragged himself out of bed, into the shower, then dressed in a white, long-sleeved, button-down shirt paired with a Loro Piana Bespoke Suit in navy and his favorite Berluti Alessandro Démesure Leather Oxfords. Normally, he wouldn't wear anything so expensive at the estate, but Julian felt like he needed some armor.

For some reason, his gut told him that he wasn't going to like the reason Duncan had demanded this meeting.

Once he was ready to face the day, though he was still dealing with a headache and fatigue due to jetlag, Julian entered the breakfast room with his shoulders back and his head held high. To his relief, the only people there were Jude and Angela.

Julian forced what he hoped was a casual smile as he stepped into the room. "Good morning."

Jude looked up from his coffee and gave him a curt nod. "Julian."

Angela glanced his way and smiled. "Good morning, Julian. When did you get home?"

Home? He wasn't sure he considered the estate home.

The familiar pang of guilt twisted in Julian's chest as he looked at Angela. Twenty-four years, and he still couldn't shake the weight of what he'd done. And what he'd failed to do.

He moved to the sideboard, where a spread of breakfast foods waited under warming lamps. The smell of bacon and fresh biscuits should have been appealing, but his appetite remained nonexistent. Still, Julian served himself a small portion of scrambled eggs and a single slice of toast, knowing he needed something in his stomach before facing his father.

"We got in about midnight," he answered Angela belatedly as he took a seat at the table. "It was a long day."

Angela nodded sympathetically. "Singapore is quite far. Did everything go well with the meetings?"

"Very productive," Julian replied, forcing himself to take a bite of toast. He had to follow it with a sip of his coffee to wash it down. "The projects there are making remarkable progress."

He noticed Jude's arm was still in a sling, a reminder of the injuries he'd sustained protecting Angela. The security chief was watching him with that unreadable expression he always wore.

Julian had never been able to determine whether or not Jude liked him.

There was a five-year difference in their ages, but sometimes, Julian felt like Jude was closer to Duncan's age. He wondered if it had to do with Jude losing his dad when he was a young adult. The man had had to learn to take care of himself. Meanwhile, at that age, Julian had been partying at college.

"How are you doing, Jude?" Julian asked.

"Better than I was," Jude said. "But still have a little way to go."

Angela reached out to lay her hand over his. "He is chomping at the bit to get back to work."

That didn't surprise Julian. Jude was nothing if not devoted to his job.

"Where's Kiara?" Julian asked.

Angela and Jude exchanged a look similar to the one Duncan and Elizabeth shared when they communicated without words. He was still trying to get used to the idea of Angela dating Jude. Most surprising was how Duncan had accepted the relationship between the pair.

But right then, the look between the two had him curious. "Is she okay?"

"She's... fine," Angela said with another glance at Jude. "She just hasn't come down yet."

There was something in the air that validated the feeling in his gut that everything with Kiara wasn't fine.

"Well, I'd better not keep Duncan waiting," Julian said as he finished the small amount of breakfast he'd taken. He drained the last of his coffee, then left the breakfast room.

As he walked to Duncan's office, Julian smoothed his tie. He had to stop himself from running his fingers through his hair, since he didn't want to appear disheveled when he met with the man.

When he reached the office, he knocked on the door. Julian heard Duncan's voice call out for him to enter. The deep baritone carried the same authority it always had, and Julian straightened his shoulders one final time before turning the handle.

Duncan sat behind his massive mahogany desk with papers spread before him. The morning light streaming through the tall windows cast sharp shadows across his face, making his expression difficult to read.

He looked up as Julian entered, and those familiar gray-green eyes—so like Julian's own—studied him with an intensity that made Julian's stomach clench.

"Have a seat," Duncan said, gesturing to one of the leather chairs positioned in front of his desk.

Julian settled into the chair, working to keep his posture relaxed despite the tension coiling in his shoulders. The whiskey from the night before had left him with a dull headache that pulsed behind his temples, and he hoped it didn't show on his face.

"Thank you for coming back."

The formality in his father's voice made Julian's stomach tighten. He settled into the leather chair, fighting the urge to fidget with his cufflinks. "Your message made it sound urgent."

Duncan leaned back slightly, his penetrating gaze fixed on Julian's face. "I received your report from Singapore. Excellent work. Sean's progress with the FemPulse is impressive."

"Thank you." Julian waited, knowing that wasn't why he'd been summoned.

"However, that's not why I asked you to come back." Duncan folded his hands on the desk. "I need to discuss a personal matter with you."

Julian tensed. Personal discussions with his father rarely went well. The last one had been about Angela's return, which had been fine, but before that... well, he preferred not to think about those conversations. They usually turned into lectures about the choices he made regarding who he dated.

"Is everything okay with Angela?" he asked, even though he knew the answer since he'd just left her.

“Angela is fine," Duncan replied, his expression unreadable. "This concerns Kiara."

Julian's heart skipped a beat. He hadn't expected that. "Kiara? What about her?"

"She's pregnant.” Duncan studied him for a long moment, as if measuring his reaction. “And I believe you may be the father."

The words hit Julian like a physical blow. He blinked, certain he'd misheard. "I'm sorry... what?"

Duncan's expression didn't change, but Julian caught the slight tightening around his father's eyes. "I understand this is shocking news. But I need you to think carefully about your interactions with Kiara over the past little while."

Julian's hands gripped the armrests of his chair as fragmented images swirled through his mind. The library. Kiara's laugh echoing softly in the dimly lit room. The burn of the alcohol on his tongue. But the memories felt like looking through frosted glass—shapes and shadows without clear definition.

"It's not possible," he said, his voice sounding distant to his own ears.

But maybe it was? He didn't have clear memories of the time they'd spent together past a certain number of drinks. Plus, it might explain why she'd stopped spending time with her. Had he...? He couldn't even stomach the thought that something had happened between them that she might not have wanted.

"I... we talked," Julian said slowly, his voice hoarse. "In the evenings. But I don't remember..." He trailed off, the implications making his stomach churn.

"You don't remember what, exactly?"

The question hung in the air. Julian pressed his palms against his temples, trying to force clarity through the fog of too much alcohol and too late nights. "I don't remember anything happening between us that could have led to... a pregnancy."

Duncan's expression hardened. "Julian, I'm not asking for details of your intimate life. I'm telling you that Kiara is pregnant, and the timeline aligns with when you two were spending evenings together."

Julian ran a hand through his hair, disregarding his earlier concern about appearing disheveled. "Has she said I'm the father?"

"She hasn't confirmed it, but she hasn't denied it either." Duncan leaned forward slightly. "When I asked her directly if you were the father, she said she'd rather not say."

The implication hung heavy in the air between them. Julian's mind raced, desperately trying to piece together what might have happened. Surely he would remember if something physical had happened between them.

The headache he'd woken with that had been a dull throb suddenly sharpened into something more vicious.

He thought of the looks that Angela and Jude had exchanged in the breakfast room. If there was anyone that Kiara would have confided in about who the father of her baby was, it would have been Angela.

Julian's hands clenched into fists on his thighs. The hesitancy in Angela's eyes when she'd said Kiara was "fine" suddenly took on new meaning. She knew. Of course, she knew.

"I need to talk to Kiara," Julian said, his voice barely above a whisper.

Duncan's expression remained impassive. "I thought you might say that. However, I wanted to speak with you first, to make a few things clear."

"Clear?" Julian's voice cracked slightly. He cleared his throat, trying to regain some composure. "I don't even know if it's true yet."

"But you're not denying the possibility."

Julian's stomach twisted. The honest answer was that he couldn't deny it—not when there were entire evenings that existed in his memory as nothing more than hazy impressions and black holes.

"No. I guess I can't deny it."

Duncan nodded. "Still, in the event that it is confirmed, I want you to understand the expectations I have for you."

"Expectations?" Julian asked, feeling shellshocked but trying to brace himself for what was still to come.

"Once we've established that the baby is yours, you're going to marry Kiara."

"Marry?" Julian tried not to choke on the word. He had never envisioned that for himself. "You want me to *marry* her?"

"If we determine the child is yours, yes. It's time for you to settle down."

"And you think Kiara is the person I should do that with?"

Duncan nodded. "Yes. We know she's not after your money, since she has plenty of her own now. And I think it's time you took responsibility for someone besides yourself."

"I don't love her," Julian said. "I barely *know* her."

"View it as an arranged marriage and then commit to making it work. You need to take responsibility for your actions, and you need to offer Kiara and the baby the stability of a family."

Julian stared out the window beside his dad's desk, trying to keep hold of the pieces of his life that were slipping away from him.

"One more thing."

Duncan's tone of voice had gotten even more serious, and Julian dragged his gaze back to him. This time, there was something more in his dad's expression. Something more emotional.

"I haven't wanted to do this, but this latest situation with Kiara has forced my hand." Duncan heaved a heavy sigh. "After you and Kiara get married, I want you to go to rehab."

The shocks just kept on coming. "Rehab?"

"Clearly your drinking has gotten out of hand, and it now has the potential to impact our company."

"What do you mean? I never go to work drunk."

"But you're drinking to the point where you don't remember what you're doing," Duncan said. "You are in possession of sensitive information. Confidential information. The competition might decide to send someone to try to get some information out of you. Your lifestyle... your drinking... is no secret. It makes you vulnerable, and someone might take advantage of that."

Julian wanted to argue that that wasn't possible, but he knew it was. "I'll stop drinking as much."

Duncan shook his head. "You're going to rehab, and if you resist, you're going to be removed from your position. Removed from the company."

Shock froze Julian. "You'd fire me?"

"I would. For your sake, first and foremost. Drinking the way you do isn't healthy for you. If you can't see that, then I need to step in. I need to do this for the sake of the business as well. You've invested too much time and energy into the neurotechnology projects to risk endangering them."

Julian was speechless. His whole world had been rocked. Knocked off its axis. It felt like everything was crashing down around him.

"I've found a place for you, and once we've got things sorted out with Kiara, you'll check into the treatment center."

A suffocating pressure settled on Julian's chest as the word *rehab* echoed in his mind. His vision narrowed until all he could see was his father's stern face, the rest of the room fading to gray. This couldn't be happening. Not to him. Not now.

"I don't have a problem," he said, hating how defensive his voice sounded. "I've never missed a meeting. My work in Singapore was exemplary—you said so yourself."

"And yet here we are," Duncan replied, his tone maddeningly calm. "Discussing a child you may have fathered during a night you can't remember."

Julian's jaw clenched so tight he felt a twinge of pain. He wanted to argue, to storm out, to do anything but sit in this chair feeling like a teenager being reprimanded. But his father's words had planted a seed of doubt that was rapidly taking root.

Had his drinking really spiraled so far out of control? Julian stared at his father, searching for any sign of exaggeration or manipulation, but found only grim determination in his steely gaze.

"I need to talk to Kiara," he said finally, his voice rough. "I need to hear this from her."

Duncan nodded once, the gesture curt and businesslike. "Of course. She's likely in her room or with Angela. But Julian..." His father's voice hardened. "This isn't a negotiation. If the child is yours, you will marry her. But regardless of the outcome of that situation, you will get help with your drinking. The alternative is losing your position with the company."

Julian rose from his chair, legs unsteady beneath him. The walls of his father's office seemed to press in around him, the air suddenly too thick to breathe properly.

And more than anything, right at that moment, he wanted a drink.

"I understand," he managed, though the words tasted bitter in his mouth.

He turned toward the door, desperate to escape the suffocating weight of his father's expectations. Each step felt leaden, as if the Persian rug beneath his expensive oxfords had turned to quicksand.

"Julian."

He paused at the threshold, hand gripping the brass doorknob so tightly his knuckles went white. Looking over his shoulder, he saw that his father had risen to his feet behind his desk.

"I know this is difficult," Duncan said, his voice softer now. "But it's time to step up. To be the man I know you can be."

Julian didn't trust himself to respond. He gave a nod, then yanked open the door and stepped into the hallway, closing it firmly behind him. The click of the latch echoed in his ears like a prison door slamming shut.

The hallway stretched before him, suddenly feeling endless. His breathing came shallow and quick as he loosened his tie with fingers that didn't want to function.

As he walked away from the office, his gaze went to the open doors of the library. The pull to just pop in there for a quick drink was strong.

So strong that he came to a stop in the doorway. Just one drink wouldn't get him drunk. His tolerance for alcohol had risen over the years. But one drink might help him deal with the situation.

He took a step into the library, then paused. Would taking that drink prove Duncan right?

That thought was enough to make him turn from the temptation. He had to do this with a completely clear head.

When he neared the stairs, he changed directions and headed for the breakfast room.

As he'd hoped, he found Angela and Jude still there. Angela was carrying a mug to the table and glanced over as he walked in, her eyes widening. "Hey, Julian. Do you want a cup of coffee?"

Being offered a cup of coffee in the midst of his life falling apart felt a bit ridiculous. Unfortunately, he didn't think he could stomach anything right then. Although he would have made an exception if she'd been offering him alcohol.

"Not right now," he said. "Is Kiara in her room?"

"Uh... yes, I think so." Angela glanced at Jude, then back at Julian. "Why?"

"Why?" Julian lifted his brows at her. "I just came from talking to Duncan, and now I need to speak with Kiara."

"I don't know if that's the best idea," Angela said, gripping the mug she held in both hands.

"Maybe not," Julian agreed. "But if I *am* the father of her baby, I need to know."

"Oh." Angela's shoulders slumped. "Can I go talk to her first? Just to make sure she's feeling okay?"

"Sure." Julian was happy for a reprieve, however brief it might be.

Angela set her mug on the table, then scooted out of the breakfast room, leaving Julian with Jude.

"How are you doing?" Jude asked. His tone was measured, but surprisingly, it didn't seem to hold any judgment.

Julian walked over and sat down at the table. He shrugged out of his jacket and laid it on the chair next to him.

"I'm not sure, to be honest," he confessed. "It's not every day one finds out they might have fathered a baby."

"I'm kind of surprised you haven't had it happen before now," Jude said.

Julian gave a huff of laughter. "My exploits have been exaggerated."

"Have they?" Jude asked. "Really?"

"A bit. Ask Anthony. He'd tell you."

"Do you think Kiara's baby isn't yours?" Jude asked.

"I don't remember being with her," Julian admitted. "But I can't deny that we spent a lot of time together. And that time wasn't just spent talking. We drank more than we should have."

"Kiara remembers," Jude said. "So I don't think she was drinking as much as you were."

Julian shifted on the chair. It felt weird to know that someone had memories of him that he didn't share.

"So she told you I'm the father?" Julian asked. "Duncan said she wouldn't confirm either way with him."

"She told Angela that you were," Jude said. "And I don't think she'd lie to her. She'd have no reason to."

Julian wasn't entirely convinced of that, but he agreed that Kiara would tell her sister the truth.

As Julian watched the man, he mused over the change in him since he'd fallen for Angela. He'd always assumed that, like him, Jude wasn't interested in a serious relationship, let alone marriage. But there was no way that his dad would be on board with the pair dating if Jude wasn't serious about a future with Angela.

What had changed for Jude? What was it about Angela that made the man abandon his bachelor lifestyle?

Though Jude had never embraced being single the way Julian had, still Jude had willingly given up his single life for Angela. Julian, however, was being forced to give up his, and because of that, he could never see himself happily embracing domesticity the way Jude had.

He'd lived his life on his own terms for over thirty years, and now he was being reined in and forced onto a different path. Whether or not he liked it, change was coming to his life, and he had no choice but to accept it.

CHAPTER FOUR

Kiara tapped the screen of her tablet, watching as the virtual page turned to the next one in the book she was reading. The exhaustion and sickness that had arrived with her pregnancy had kept her in her room—close to her bed and her bathroom—for a big chunk of her time, so she'd been reading more than ever.

Reading had always been an escape for her. Through books, she'd experienced life beyond the homestead and then later, beyond Briar Hollow. And the stories she'd enjoyed the most had featured love as a main theme.

Not just a romantic love, though that had definitely been her preference. She'd also enjoyed stories that had featured close friendships and families who loved each other, even when things got tough.

She hadn't had much love in her life, and she'd so desperately wanted more of it. The only person she'd felt loved by had been Angie, and she was so grateful she'd had that.

Though she'd experienced romantic love through the books she read, Kiara had never truly expected to find it for herself in real life. Now, with a baby growing inside her, she wondered if that dream was even more out of reach.

As a wave of nausea rolled through her, she tightened her grip on her tablet. She took slow, measured breaths, willing her stomach to settle. The medication from Doctor Misha helped, but it wasn't a cure-all. Some days were just harder than others.

A soft knock at her door made Kiara tense. She knew that Angie was spending time with Jude, so she didn't know who else it could be.

"Who is it?" she called, tucking an errant curl behind her ear.

"It's me," came the muffled reply.

Kiara exhaled with relief. "Come in."

The door opened, and Angie slipped inside, her expression tense. She closed the door quickly behind her.

"Julian's here," she said as she crossed the room to sit on the loveseat beside Kiara.

"He's back?"

She'd known he'd be back eventually, but she hadn't expected him to return so soon. In some of the conversations they'd had, he'd spoken about how much he couldn't wait to get back to New York and away from the estate. Though he'd left the estate for short periods of time, she'd expected that this trip would keep him away longer.

Angie nodded. "He's back, and he's looking for you." She reached out and grabbed Kiara's arm. "He knows."

Kiara's stomach twisted with something worse than morning sickness. She set her tablet down, fingers trembling slightly. "Duncan told him?"

Angie nodded, her blue-green eyes filled with concern. "He wants to talk to you."

"Of course he does," Kiara muttered, pressing a hand to her stomach. She'd known this moment would come eventually, but she'd hoped for more time. Time to figure out what she wanted. What was best for her baby.

"How did he seem?" Kiara asked, not entirely sure she wanted to know the answer.

"Shocked." Angie squeezed her arm before moving her hand down to intertwine her fingers with Kiara's. "But he didn't seem mad."

That was something, at least. Kiara had been bracing herself for anger, accusations, demands for proof. Shock she could handle.

She'd been shocked herself when she'd first realized she was pregnant.

"I don't know what to say to him," Kiara admitted, her voice barely above a whisper.

The words she'd practiced in her head over the past few weeks suddenly seemed inadequate. How did you tell someone they'd fathered a child during a night they clearly didn't remember?

Angie's grip on her hand tightened. "You don't have to say anything you're not ready to say. But Kiara..." She paused, her expression growing more serious. "He has a right to know, doesn't he? About the baby?"

The question hung in the air between them. Kiara had wrestled with it countless times, especially during the long nights when sleep eluded her and her mind refused to quiet. She'd gone back and forth so many times about it. In some ways, it was a relief to have it taken out of her hands.

“I keep thinking about what's best for the baby," Kiara said finally. "Julian doesn't even remember that night. What if he thinks I'm lying? What if he wants nothing to do with us?"

"Then that's his loss," Angie said fiercely. "But what if he surprises you? What if he wants to be involved?"

That possibility terrified Kiara almost as much as the alternative. Julian's world was so different from hers—expensive suits, international travel, beautiful women who graced magazine covers. She couldn't imagine how a small-town girl and an unplanned baby would fit into that life.

Another wave of nausea hit, stronger this time. Kiara pressed her lips together and breathed through her nose, willing it to pass. The stress wasn't helping her morning sickness at all.

"I guess I don't have a choice anymore," she said when the feeling subsided. "I have to talk to him."

"Do you want me to stay with you?" Angie asked, concern etching her features.

Kiara considered it for a moment. Having Angie there would be comforting, but this conversation needed to happen between just her and Julian.

"No," she said finally. "This is something I need to do myself."

Angie nodded, though reluctance showed in her eyes. "I'll tell him he can come up, then."

"I think I'd rather meet him downstairs," she said. "Maybe in the solarium if no one is using it."

"I'll check, then send you a text if it's empty."

"I need to freshen up," Kiara said, glancing down at her oversized t-shirt and leggings. "Tell Julian I'll meet him in the solarium in fifteen minutes."

"Okay." Angie leaned over and gave her a hug. "Let me pray for you."

Kiara sagged against her, drawing on her sister's strength, which was different from how their dynamic usually was. She was used to being the strong one. The one taking care of everything.

"Heavenly Father, we thank you for the gift of life and this little one You've given Kiara, regardless of the circumstances that have led to this point. I pray You give her strength and wisdom as she navigates the road ahead with Julian. Also open Julian's heart and mind to this new life he's been a part of creating. I ask that You reveal Yourself clearly to Kiara and Julian in their current circumstances. I love Kiara so much and want the best for her. In Jesus' name, amen."

Kiara had never embraced faith in God the way Angie had, but she appreciated the prayer and hoped that God would hear and answer her sister's prayer.

Angie gave her a tight squeeze, then released her. "Okay. I'm going to see if the solarium is free. If it's not, where do you want to meet?"

Kiara knew where she didn't want to meet him. "I don't know, but not the library."

Angie stared at her for a long moment, then gave a single nod. "Maybe the living room."

"That would work."

Sliding off the bed, Angie said, "I'll text you in a couple of minutes."

When Angie closed the door behind her, Kiara hurried to the bathroom. After emptying the contents of her stomach, she splashed water on her face.

A glance in the mirror told her that she wasn't looking her best, and unfortunately, makeup probably wasn't going to help much. Still, she dabbed a bit of concealer under her eyes.

When the text from Angie came in, letting her know that the solarium was available, Kiara's stomach lurched again. She got a ginger candy from her nightstand and popped it into her mouth, hoping it would help quell the nausea a little.

She swapped her T-shirt for a sweater and a new pair of leggings—the only really comfortable pants she had. It took a few minutes to pull her hair back into a ponytail and then put product in it to try to control the frizz a bit.

Her curls weren't tight, but they had a tendency to go frizzy if she didn't take special care of her hair.

All through her preparations, she gave herself a pep talk.

"You've got this, Kiki," she murmured as she stared at her reflection in the mirror. "You survived years with Jim. You can do this. You're not alone. Angie is there for you."

She rested her hand on her stomach. It was still flat. Well, not flat, because she'd always had a bit of a belly to match her curves. But even though her belly hadn't yet grown noticeably, there was a presence that was relying on her to protect it. To plan a future for them.

And the first step in doing that was to have a conversation with Julian, and whatever that entailed.

She took a steadying breath and made her way downstairs. Each step felt heavier than the last, her legs unsteady beneath her. The ginger candy helped with the nausea, but it couldn't touch the knot of anxiety that had settled in her chest.

The solarium was tucked away at the back of the house, its glass walls offering a view of the estate's flower garden. Kiara had always loved the room—it felt separate from the rest of the house somehow, more peaceful. She hoped that tranquility might help her get through this conversation.

When she pushed the door open, Julian was already there. He stood with his back to her, hands clasped behind him as he stared out at the garden. He wasn't wearing a suit jacket, and his shirt sleeves were rolled up, making him look less intimidating than she'd expected. Still, her heart hammered against her ribs.

He turned at the sound of the door opening, and Kiara's breath caught in her throat. His green eyes met hers across the room, and she saw her own uncertainty reflected there.

"Kiara." His voice was rougher than she remembered, strained in a way that made her stomach clench.

"Julian." She stayed by the door for a moment, suddenly unsure of her legs. The ginger candy dissolved on her tongue, leaving behind a sharp sweetness that did nothing to calm her nerves.

He gestured toward the wicker seating area near the windows. "Would you like to sit?"

She nodded, not trusting her voice, and made her way to one of the cushioned chairs. Julian settled across from her on the loveseat, leaving a careful distance between them. His usually perfectly styled hair looked disheveled, as if he'd been running his hands through it.

The silence stretched between them, filled only with the soft hum of the solarium's climate control system. Kiara twisted her fingers in her lap, trying to find the right words to begin.

Julian cleared his throat. "Duncan told me you're pregnant," he said finally, his tone and expression both neutral.

Kiara nodded, her mouth suddenly dry. "Yes."

"And he believes I'm the father."

The directness of his statement caught her off guard. She'd expected more dancing around the subject, more hesitation. But Julian got right to the point.

"You are," she said softly, meeting his gaze directly despite the tremor in her voice. Her heart thudded painfully against her ribs.

Julian's expression tightened, a muscle working in his jaw. He leaned forward, elbows on his knees, hands clasped together so tightly his knuckles whitened.

"I don't remember us..." His words trailed off, and he didn't attempt to pick them up, leaving Kiara to fill the silence.

"I figured as much," she said. "When you acted like nothing had happened the next day."

"I guess I drank a little too much."

Kiara nodded. "You were drinking a lot."

"And you weren't?" he asked.

"I drank enough to kind of give me a bit of a buzz," she said. "When I stopped, you kept drinking."

He looked down at his hands, and Kiara could see the strain in his profile.

"So you weren't as out of it as I was when we..."

Again, his voice trailed off in a way that felt so unlike the Julian she'd known up to that point. The directness of just a few minutes ago was gone now that he had confirmation of his role in her pregnancy.

"What do you mean?"

He looked up then, his gaze holding wariness. "Our time together. Was it consensual?"

For a moment, Kiara could only stare at him. As the strain grew on his face, she quickly said, "Yes. It might not have been a good decision, but it was one we both made, even if our judgment was impaired."

Relief crossed Julian's face. "Okay. As long as you're telling me the truth."

Kiara struggled with being the only one who had memories of that night. She wished he didn't have to rely on her word because he might have doubts until the baby's paternity could actually be determined through a DNA test. "I am telling the truth."

"Duncan wants us to get married."

Shock jolted through her. "Married?"

The word hung in the air between them like an actual physical thing. Kiara's chest tightened, and she struggled to draw a proper breath. Marriage? To Julian Burke? The idea was so far from anything she'd ever imagined for herself that she couldn't form a coherent response.

"That's his solution," Julian continued, his voice strained. "For the baby."

Kiara pressed her palm against her stomach. "I don't... I wasn't expecting that."

Julian ran a hand through his hair, leaving it even more disheveled. "Neither was I, but my father was very clear about his expectations."

The way he said "expectations" made Kiara's heart sink. There was something cold and formal about it, like this was a business arrangement rather than a life-altering decision about their future—and their child's.

"I'm not expecting you to marry me, Julian. That's... that's not why I kept the baby."

He angled a look at her, his expression still unreadable. "Why did you keep it?"

The question wasn't accusatory, just curious, but it still stung, and for a moment she wondered if he would have preferred she end the pregnancy. Kiara swallowed hard against the sudden lump in her throat.

"Because it's my baby," she said simply. "And I... I've always wanted a family of my own."

Julian's eyes softened slightly at that, and he looked away, staring out at the garden. The morning sunlight caught the highlights in his hair and gave a glow to his skin. He was truly a handsome man. More handsome than she'd ever imagined her future husband being.

Kiara had always figured she'd end up with a down-to-earth man who spent his days working with his hands. She would have assumed that a man like Julian would be completely out of her league.

But alcohol had stripped away all of their differences, reducing their interactions to a physicality that hadn't cared that they wouldn't have made a good couple in real life.

But it was more than just the alcohol. Loneliness, coupled with a desire for a love of her own like Angie had with Jude, had created a situation where she hadn't been thinking rationally. When Julian had kissed her, she'd assumed that he'd felt something for her. That he too was looking for a connection.

She couldn't have been more wrong.

Whatever he'd been looking for that night, it hadn't been a lasting connection. And since he couldn't remember that night, he'd likely never be able to tell her what his motivation had been.

She might not know what his motivation had been that night, but she certainly knew that this marriage proposal wasn't being driven by his attraction to her or his desire to be married to her. No, it was Duncan who was dictating things now.

“So, are you agreeable to getting married?” Julian asked.

Kiara frowned. “You're actually on board with the idea?”

He didn't answer right away, his gaze distance. “I think it's probably for the best.”

That surprised her. "But... how would it work?"

"I think we just need to stay married until the baby is born," Julian said. "Then we can get a divorce."

It hurt Kiara's heart to be talking about divorce before they'd even gotten married. What would happen if she said no to getting married?

Would Duncan accept her answer if it was no? Would Julian?

Julian cleared his throat as his head bent forward. "One other thing. Duncan is insisting that I go to rehab for my drinking."

Kiara was shocked once again. "He is?"

"Yes. He says it's become a problem," Julian said, then gave a humorless laugh. "And in light of our situation, I can't exactly argue with him."

"And you're going to go?"

"I don't really have a choice," Julian said. "If I don't go, I'm out of a job."

"Duncan would fire you?"

"He said he would." Julian shrugged. "And he's usually a man of his word."

"I'm surprised."

"I was too, but such is life." He sounded very resigned.

"I'll be leaving for rehab as soon as we get married," he said. "Provided you agree to the marriage."

Kiara had a lot of thoughts tumbling through her mind. But there was one question that kept coming to the forefront.

"Do you lose your job if we don't get married?"

The hesitation before Julian responded hurt more than it should have. "He didn't say that specifically. His focus was on the rehab."

"Do you want me to say no?" she asked. "To tell Duncan I don't want to get married?"

Julian's eyes widened slightly at her question. For a moment, he looked almost... relieved? The expression vanished so quickly that Kiara wasn't sure she'd seen it correctly.

“I'm not asking you to say no," he said carefully. "I'm trying to do the right thing here."

Kiara twisted her hands in her lap, the pressure of the decision weighing on her shoulders.

Marriage to Julian Burke. It was surreal–like something from one of her romance novels–but she couldn’t allow herself to view the situation that way. This was obviously something that was being forced on Julian, and he clearly wasn’t happy about it.

"What will happen to the baby if we don’t get married?" she asked, her voice barely above a whisper.

"I'd still support the baby financially. I'm not going to abandon my responsibility.”

The irony was that she didn’t really need his financial support. Thanks to Duncan’s generosity, she had plenty of money to support herself and the baby.

Maybe she should have left the estate as soon as she found out she was pregnant so that she could have avoided all of this. But she hadn’t done that, so now she had to deal with the situation and Duncan and Julian’s attempt to address it.

Silence was heavy between them as her thoughts went to the baby.

What would be best for them?

In this particular case–since Julian was a good man–it would be better for the baby to have two parents in their life, regardless of what path they took. But would it be better for them to know that their parents had been married when they were born, even if they divorced later, than for them to have never been married at all?

Deep down, Kiara didn’t want to have to tell her son or daughter that they’d been born as a result of an alcohol-fueled bad decision.

She'd rather they think they'd been conceived in love, even if the marriage hadn't ended up working out.

Maybe that was delusional reasoning, but she didn't want her child to have any reason to feel unloved or unwanted.

She thought of the prayer Angie had prayed with her not that long ago and wondered how this scenario fit into God's plan, and which decision would be an answer to that prayer.

In the end, she had nothing to go on but what she thought was best for the baby.

"Let's get married."

CHAPTER FIVE

Once the conversation had died off between him and Kiara, Julian left the solarium. Not wanting to have another conversation with Duncan, he'd sent him a message to let him know the wedding was a go, and that he was dealing with jetlag and needed to take a nap.

What he really wanted—besides a nap—was a drink, so he headed for his room.

After being given the rehab ultimatum, he'd known that Duncan would have had all the alcohol removed from his room. What the man didn't know, however, was that Julian had always kept a private stash, just in case something like that happened.

He opened the large, locked chest in his walk-in closet, where he'd hidden a plentiful supply of his favorite whiskey, and pulled out a bottle. Just holding the bottle helped ease a little of the anxiety his conversation with Kiara had caused.

Though he'd planned to just have one drink, in the end, he consumed enough to help him pass right out.

And over the next three days, he had to drink more each night in order to quiet his mind enough to sleep.

Having Angela back should have been the happiest time in his life, but it had made the memories that had haunted him over the years become even more vivid. Which was no doubt why his alcohol intake had increased the way it had. Every time he closed his eyes to sleep, memories flooded in from that horrible time.

And now, he was faced with losing the one thing that had helped him cope. He was dreading rehab even more than he was the upcoming wedding.

But in order to secure the future he wanted for himself, he had to deal with both.

"You can do it," he murmured as he struggled to fasten his cufflinks.

Though he had the money to strike out on his own, he wouldn't be able to have the impact he had leading Burke NeuroTech. He enjoyed working alongside people whose passions and intellect allowed them to create truly innovative things to help people in the future.

A knock on the door had him glancing over at it. "Come in."

The door opened to reveal Anthony. "I was told to come check on you."

"Making sure I haven't escaped out a window?" Julian asked as he turned his attention back to the cufflink.

"Something like that." Anthony approached him. "Here. Let me help."

When Duncan had told Julian that he'd need to choose someone to stand up with him, he'd initially thought about asking one of the guys he'd stayed in contact with after college. However, he wasn't sure any of them would understand what was happening.

Instead, he'd chosen the man who had been with him nearly every day, protecting him and making sure he got where he needed to go safely. Anthony was probably a better friend to him than any of those guys were, if he was honest.

"Thanks," Julian said when the cufflinks were in place. "Is everything a go?"

"Kiara hasn't backed out, if that's what you're asking."

Julian nodded. "I guess it's time then."

There would be no guests aside from family present. And once the ceremony was over, he'd be leaving on a plane for the rehab center his dad had chosen for him.

There was a pit in Julian's stomach as he and Anthony walked down the hallway to the stairs. The civil ceremony was going to take place in the solarium, where just four days earlier, he and Kiara had decided to take this step.

Or rather, Kiara had decided to take this step. He hadn't had a choice.

What was happening began to really sink in as he and Anthony walked down the stairs together. Julian gripped the banister, grateful for something solid to anchor him as he felt like his world tilted on its axis.

The whiskey from the night before had left him with a dull ache behind his eyes, but it wasn't enough to drown out the surreal nature of what was about to happen.

In less than an hour, he'd be married to a woman he barely knew, who carried the child that he couldn't even remember creating.

"You doing okay?" Anthony's voice cut through his spiraling thoughts.

Julian forced his shoulders back, straightening his spine the way his father had taught him years ago. He smoothed his tie, the silk feeling like a noose around his neck. "Just peachy."

The sarcasm felt familiar on his tongue, a shield he'd perfected over the years.

As they approached the solarium, Julian could see through the glass doors that Duncan and Elizabeth were already there, along with Annie, Benjamin, Angela, and Jude. A man he didn't recognize–presumably the officiant–stood near the windows with a small leather portfolio in his hands.

And then there was Kiara.

She stood beside Angela, wearing a cream-colored dress with a full skirt that didn't quite reach her ankles. In her hands was a small colorful bouquet.

Anthony stepped ahead of him and pulled the door open. With a deep breath, Julian stepped into the solarium. All eyes turned toward them, and Julian gave a slight nod as he made his way to where Kiara stood.

Duncan's gaze was on him, but his expression was unreadable. Elizabeth offered a gentle smile that didn't quite reach her eyes. Julian wondered what she truly thought of this hastily arranged marriage.

His own mother knew nothing about what was going on. He didn't need a lecture from her about what he was doing. Even without talking to her, he knew what her opinion would be, and he didn't need to hear it.

After a few brief pleasantries, Julian and Kiara took their places in front of the officiant.

The gray-haired man with wire-rimmed glasses cleared his throat. "We're gathered here today to join Julian Burke and Kiara Reynolds in matrimony."

Julian stood stiffly beside Kiara, acutely aware of the small distance between them. She smelled faintly of vanilla and something floral he couldn't quite identify.

He wondered what she was thinking at that moment. Was she feeling as conflicted as he was?

The officiant continued with the ceremony, his words washing over Julian in a haze.

The sunlight streaming through the glass walls felt too bright, intensifying his headache. He blinked against it, trying to focus on the words being spoken.

They had chosen to go with simple vows rather than writing anything personalized, and thankfully, they just had to repeat them after the officiant rather than try to memorize them.

"Julian, do you take Kiara to be your lawfully wedded wife?"

The question hung in the air. Julian swallowed hard, his mouth suddenly dry. He could feel everyone's eyes on him, waiting. The silence stretched until it became uncomfortable.

"I do," he said finally, the words scraping his throat raw.

The officiant turned to Kiara. "Kiara, do you take Julian to be your lawfully wedded husband?"

Julian risked a glance at her. Her face was pale, but her voice was steady when she answered. "I do."

"The rings?"

Julian's stomach dropped. In all the rushed preparations, he hadn't even thought about rings. He started to turn toward Anthony, panic rising in his chest.

But Duncan stepped forward, extending his hand. Two simple gold bands rested in his palm.

"Here," he said quietly.

Julian took the smaller ring, his fingers trembling slightly as he reached for Kiara's left hand. Her skin was soft and warm, a stark contrast to the cold metal he slipped onto her finger.

When she placed the larger band on his finger, her touch was gentle, but her hand was no steadier than his. The ring felt foreign and heavy against his skin.

"By the power vested in me by the state of Idaho, I now pronounce you husband and wife." The officiant closed his portfolio with a soft snap. "You may kiss the bride."

Julian's breath caught. He hadn't considered this part either. He turned toward Kiara, meeting her wide hazel gaze. The uncertainty he saw there mirrored his own.

He leaned down, gently cupping her shoulders as his lips brushed hers in the briefest of kisses. Her lips were soft and carried a light taste of strawberry that lingered on his lips even as he pulled back after just a second.

Julian stepped back, his hands falling to his sides as polite applause filled the solarium. The sound felt hollow in the glass-walled room, echoing off the windows and plant-filled corners.

Nodding stiffly at the small gathering, Julian accepted their congratulations with mechanical responses that felt disconnected from his body.

"Congratulations," Duncan said, stepping forward to shake his hand. His grip was firm, businesslike. "I'm proud of you for doing the right thing."

The right thing.

Julian's jaw tightened at the phrase, but he managed a nod. Elizabeth embraced both him and Kiara with genuine warmth, though Julian caught the worry in her eyes when she looked at him.

Angela hugged Kiara tightly, whispering something in her ear that Julian didn't catch. When she turned to him, her smile seemed forced, strained at the edges.

"Take care of yourself," she said quietly, and Julian knew she was referring to more than just the rehab.

He knew her loyalties would always be with Kiara, and he couldn't blame her for that, but he appreciated that she was expressing care for him too.

"Thank you," Julian managed, his throat constricting around the words.

Benji approached them with his usual good humor, seemingly oblivious to the tension in the room. "Congrats, bro! And welcome to the family officially, Kiara." He pulled Julian into a quick hug, slapping his back with enthusiasm that felt jarringly out of place.

The small reception that followed felt like an exercise in endurance. The most awkward social event he'd been to in years.

Julian accepted a glass of sparkling cider—not champagne, he noted bitterly—and stood beside his new wife as they made stilted conversation with the small gathering. His fingers kept finding the unfamiliar weight of the gold band on his left hand, twisting it unconsciously. The gold band felt like it was burning into his skin.

"We should leave soon," Anthony murmured, appearing at his elbow. "The plane is scheduled for departure from Coeur d'Alene in an hour."

Julian nodded, relief washing through him at the news. He needed to escape this room, this moment, this entire situation.

He set his untouched cider on a nearby table, then walked to where Kiara stood with Angela. The sunlight caught in her dark curls, highlighting strands of auburn he hadn't noticed before. She turned as he approached, her expression guarded.

"I need to leave for the airport soon," Julian said, his voice low enough that only she and Angela could hear.

Kiara nodded. "How long do you think you'll be gone?"

"Thirty days minimum." The number hung between them, a measurement of the strange limbo they now occupied. "Maybe longer, depending on... how things go."

Kiara crossed her arms. "And after that?"

Julian hadn't thought beyond the rehab. The future stretched ahead of them like an unmapped territory, full of decisions they'd have to make about custody, living arrangements, and their strange marriage.

"We'll figure it out when I get back," he said, the words feeling inadequate even as he spoke them. "Also, I won't be able to call or text for the first little while. So just know that's why you aren't hearing from me."

"Okay."

He searched for the words to say. "Take care of yourself. And the baby."

Kiara gave him a small smile. "I will. Take care of yourself too."

For a moment, they stood there in awkward silence, two strangers who happened to be married, connected by an unplanned pregnancy and a hasty ceremony neither had truly wanted. Julian felt the weight of all the things, all the decisions that still needed to be made.

"Goodbye, Kiara," he said finally, the formality of the words hanging awkwardly between them.

"Goodbye," she replied, her voice soft.

He hesitated, then leaned forward and pressed a brief kiss to her forehead. The scent of vanilla was stronger up close, mingled with something floral that reminded him of spring.

As he stepped back, Julian caught Angela watching them, her expression unreadable. He gave her a nod before turning away, his shoulders stiff under the cut of his expensive suit.

Anthony approached him. "Your bags are loaded into the helicopter, so we can go whenever you're ready."

"Thanks. I just need to speak to my father."

Anthony nodded. "I'll wait for you in the mudroom."

It was weird to think that in addition to leaving his job and life behind, he'd be without Anthony for the time he was away too.

It was probably the longest they'd been apart since Anthony had been assigned to him. But the treatment center had its own security since it catered to the wealthiest of the wealthy, so Anthony wasn't needed.

At the sound of his name, Julian turned to face his dad.

Duncan stepped closer and spoke to him in a low voice. "I know this isn't how you envisioned your life unfolding, but you're taking the right steps."

Julian's jaw clenched. The right steps?

Everything felt manipulated and forced into place like chess pieces on his father's board. He wanted to argue, to push back against the narrative that painted him as some wayward son finally coming to his senses.

"The facility I've chosen has an excellent reputation," Duncan continued. "They specialize in high-functioning professionals who need to address their relationship with alcohol without derailing their careers."

High-functioning. Julian almost laughed at the irony. If he was so high-functioning, why was he standing here married to a woman he couldn't remember being intimate with?

"I realize you won't be able to call or email, at least at first, but once you're able to contact us, I wouldn't mind an update."

Julian didn't want to update him on the torture he was about to undergo, but he nodded. Maybe he'd feel a little different once he had some distance from this turbulent time.

"I'll keep that in mind," Julian said, forcing his voice to remain level despite the turmoil inside him.

Duncan clapped him on the shoulder, his grip firm. "This will be good for you, son. You'll come back stronger."

Julian nodded again, not trusting himself to speak further. His father's expectations pressed down on him like a physical force.

He turned away, desperate to escape the solarium with its bright sunlight and the eyes of his family—his new wife—watching his every move. "I need to go. The helicopter is waiting."

After a quick wave to the others in the room, Julian left the solarium and made his way through the house to the mudroom.

Anthony was waiting by the door as promised, his expression neutral but his eyes watchful. "Ready?"

"More than ready," Julian muttered, following his bodyguard out the back door.

The early spring air hit his face as they stepped outside, cool and fresh after the stifling atmosphere of the solarium. Julian loosened his tie, gulping in deep breaths.

A UTV was waiting for them, and Anthony climbed into the front row beside Derrick, another of the security team members, while Julian settled into the second row.

All too soon, the UTV reached the helicopter. Julian and Anthony boarded, and Julian settled into a seat next to the window.

He slipped on the headset that Anthony handed him, though he had no desire to talk. Thankfully, Anthony knew him well enough to understand that conversation wasn't welcome right then.

As the helicopter lifted off, Julian watched as the estate fell away, growing smaller and smaller until they left it fully behind.

The twenty-minute flight to Coeur d'Alene passed quickly, then they were boarding the plane that would take him to his new home for the next month or more.

The plane had internet, so as soon as it took off, he opened his laptop to do a little work. Mainly, it was writing emails to a few people to let them know that he'd be unavailable for the foreseeable future and to address any issues with Duncan.

The letter to Sean was the hardest to write because he knew he'd be unable to be kept abreast of the latest developments for FemPulse. He didn't give details about his absence beyond stating that he was dealing with some health issues.

As he sent each email, anger grew inside him. It started out burning strictly for his father, but soon, it grew to encompass himself as well.

He wanted to lay the blame for his current situation on Duncan being unreasonable and demanding, but in his heart, he knew that it was his own actions that had led to this point. He'd chosen to drink as a way to cope with stuff that he didn't want to deal with. And that drinking had led to him making some not so great decisions. Not the least of which was sleeping with Kiara when he was too drunk to remember it.

By the time they'd landed at the airport in Aspen, Julian was resigned to his fate. After retrieving his luggage, Anthony took it to the car service that was waiting for them.

The treatment center was a little way outside of Aspen, and Anthony would be accompanying him there before returning to take the plane back to Coeur d'Alene.

Julian watched the scenery rush by the car window, mentally preparing himself for what was to come, and wishing fervently that he'd been able to have at least one drink during the flight. But his dad had had all the alcohol removed from the plane, just like he had from the estate.

Nerves were fluttering wildly as the car paused at the gates of the treatment center. Anthony took care of identifying them so that they could enter the property.

Once inside, the car made its way along a meandering driveway up to a large building that looked more like a fancy hotel than what Julian had imagined a treatment center would look like.

The driver pulled up under the port cochere and came to a stop. As soon as they did, a man stepped through a set of large glass doors and approached the car.

He opened Julian's door and greeted him. "Welcome to Crystal Haven Wellness, Mr. Burke."

"Thank you." Julian climbed out of the car and turned to see Anthony working with another member of the center's staff to transfer his suitcases from the car to the rolling luggage cart.

"Please follow me," the man said. "Your luggage will be taken to your room."

And that was that. The end of the road.

"Just one moment," Julian said and walked to where Anthony stood. "Thank you for coming along. I guess I'll see you in a month or so."

"I look forward to it," Anthony said, holding out his hand. When Julian took it, he gave it a firm shake. "I hope that everything goes smoothly."

"Thanks."

With a final nod at Anthony, Julian turned to follow the man in a suit up the stairs and into the building.

The Crystal Haven Wellness Center's lobby reminded Julian of the five-star hotels he frequented on business trips—all polished marble floors, tasteful artwork, and discreet luxury. Except unlike those hotels, there was no bar in sight.

"I'm Marcus Delaney, the intake coordinator," the man said as he led Julian past a small seating area. "We'll start with some paperwork and then get you settled in your room."

Julian followed Marcus down a hallway to a warmly lit office. The walls were painted a soothing sage green, and a plush leather chair waited across from a large desk. A framed diploma hung on the wall–Northwestern University, Julian noted.

As Marcus delved into the setup of the center, Julian tried to pay attention and ignore the desperate longing he had for a drink. He clenched his hands into fists to curb the slight tremor in them.

He wanted to tell the man that he actually wasn't an alcoholic. That he didn't have an alcohol problem, and that he could quit at any time. And he would have if Duncan hadn't held his job over his head.

So he would go through the motions, do what they required of him, and then leave the treatment center as soon as he could.

CHAPTER SIX

The next couple of weeks passed slowly for Kiara. It was an endless cycle of nausea, occasional vomiting, and exhaustion. She had hoped that the end of the first trimester would bring her relief, but she wasn't too confident that would be the case, unlike how it was for so many other women.

Though Kiara no longer took part in the self-defense training or target practice, Lucy took her out driving two or three times a week. She was still determined to get her driver's license at some point, but the overwhelming need to get it had definitely subsided. The unmoored feeling that she'd been dealing with since coming to the estate had also lessened now that she had her pregnancy and impending parenthood to focus on.

As the weather warmed and the snow started to melt, she tried to get out for a walk each day. Sometimes, Angie would join her, but her sister still had self-defense training and target practice taking up her time. Kiara wasn't sure Angie's focus on those things was because she wanted to improve. It likely had more to do with spending time with Jude.

Her feet scuffed on the asphalt road as she left the parking area behind the large house. She shoved her hands into the pockets of her light jacket as she headed down the road.

As they did most days, her steps took her in the direction of the house that was being built for her and Angie. It was going up at a rapid pace, more rapidly than she'd initially imagined it would.

She'd heard Jude and Duncan discussing it, and Duncan had said that he'd requested longer working hours on the house without concern for the increased cost.

As the house came into view, Kiara's steps slowed to a stop. She gazed at it, wondering if she'd get a chance to live in it. She had no idea how things would unfold for her and Julian when he returned from the treatment center.

Duncan might have forced the marriage, but at least to her knowledge, he hadn't insisted they live together. It was entirely possible that she'd move into the house with Angie as planned, and Julian would return to his home in New York. That wouldn't be the worst way for things to pan out.

Kiara pulled her left hand from her pocket and stared down at the ring Julian had put there. It was a simple, slender gold band. There was no matching engagement ring, specially chosen for her by a man who loved her and wanted to spend the rest of his life with her.

She curled her fingers into a fist and shoved her hand back into her pocket, removing the ring from her sight.

Even two weeks later, she still wasn't used to having the ring on her finger. There were moments when she forgot it was on her hand and that she was married. But far more frequent were the moments when the ring felt like it was made of the heaviest metal known to man.

Kiara walked on, following the winding road toward the construction site. She needed to keep moving. Doctor Misha had said exercise was good for her, though on some days even getting out of bed felt like climbing a mountain.

Workers in hard hats moved across the property like industrious ants, the steady rhythm of hammers and the whine of power tools filling the air. She kept her distance, not wanting to be in the way, but she was close enough to observe the progress. The foundation was complete, and the framing had gone up quickly. Soon, they'd be working on the roof.

She rested her hand on her stomach, which had only just begun to swell, a gesture that had become second nature. As she stood there, she tried to imagine herself living there with a baby. The idea of leaving the estate was no longer a consideration since marrying Julian.

Her child would have such a different upbringing than she and Angie had had. He or she might live in a rural setting, but the estate was a far cry from the homestead. And it wasn't just a better home that she could offer the baby. Kiara was determined to raise her child comfortable in the knowledge of their mom's love and care for them.

There would be no abuse of any kind heaped on the child the way it had been on Kiara. And fear wouldn't have a starring role in the child's emotions.

Angie would likely say that Kiara had been brave and protective, but that didn't mean Kiara had felt no fear during their years at the homestead. She'd just chosen to shift her fear for her own wellbeing to Angie. Knowing she had to take care of her younger sister and protect her had given Kiara a bravery she might not have otherwise had.

Unfortunately, it had resulted in a more... stressful life for Kiara. She didn't regret having protected Angie the way she had, but it had made things more difficult. There was no doubt she'd also protect her child in the way she'd protected Angie, but living on the estate, she didn't think it would be necessary.

Turning from the construction site, Kiara continued her trek along the road. She passed Annie's house, then headed back in the direction of the main house.

By the time she reached the back door, she was ready to get off her feet. She stepped into the mudroom and removed her jacket and shoes before heading further into the house.

"Kiara."

She turned to see Duncan coming from the direction of the breakfast room.

"How are you doing today?"

Whenever he saw her, he asked that, concern on his face. He'd wanted her to be seen by the doctor he used for family medical concerns, but Kiara was quite happy with Doctor Misha. The woman was gentle, and any concern she had was for both Kiara and the baby. She wasn't just concerned about Kiara for the baby's sake, like it felt Duncan was.

"I'm doing okay. Just enjoyed a nice walk."

Duncan smiled. "That's good. Did you go by your house?"

"Yes. They're making great progress."

"They are," Duncan agreed. "I'm hoping it will be ready a couple of months ahead of the original schedule. Have you been making decisions about the interior work?"

Kiara nodded. "Yes. The interior designer has been sending Angie and me lots of options. Almost too many."

"It can be overwhelming, so if it's too much, just tell her. Perhaps she can narrow things down a bit more for you. By the way," Duncan said as he held out a white envelope. "This came for you."

Taking it, Kiara looked down at the front of it. Her name was scrawled in bold black ink. There was no return address, which concerned her.

"I believe it might be from Julian," Duncan said. "The postmark is from near where he is."

"Julian? Really? I didn't think he was allowed to contact anyone."

Duncan nodded. "I think he's limited on access to a computer or his phone, but writing and receiving letters is permitted."

"Oh." Kiara pressed it to her chest, not certain if she was excited or anxious about what it might contain. "I guess I'll go read it."

"Uh... listen." Duncan shifted in a way that made him seem so unlike himself. "I don't need to know the contents of the letter, but will you let me know if you have any concerns?"

Kiara had understood why Duncan wanted Julian to get help. It was clear to anyone who spent any sort of time with him that he had an alcohol problem. Julian might have felt like Duncan was manipulating him, which was probably true, but Kiara was certain that it was motivated by love for his son. Hopefully, Julian could come to understand that.

"I'll let you know," she said with a gentle smile.

"Thank you."

As she climbed the stairs, she heard Duncan's steps heading down the hallway to where his office was located. Clutching the envelope in her hand, she hurried to her room.

Once inside, she went to the loveseat by the window and sank down on its soft cushions. Smoothing the envelope on her lap, she stared at her name.

Kiara Burke...

Duncan had helped her submit the paperwork for a name change after confirming it was what she wanted, so it was official now. It wasn't that she wanted the Burke name necessarily, but she wanted to have the same last name as her child. And since she was entitled to it by marriage, she'd taken Duncan up on his offer.

Kiara had no idea why Julian would choose to write to her instead of Duncan or someone else in the family, so she opened the envelope with some trepidation.

Taking a deep breath, she turned the envelope over and slid her finger under the flap, carefully unsealing it. Once it was open, she pulled out the contents, hoping she'd get a glimpse of how Julian's time in treatment had gone so far.

She unfolded the letter to find two pieces of premium thick paper filled with the same black scrawl that was on the envelope.

Dear Kiara,

I hope this letter finds you well. I wanted to reach out and let you know how things are going here. The therapist suggested that I "open lines of communication" with people who are important in my life. Right now, I'd have to say that you are the most important.

Kiara wanted to hold those words close to her heart, but she let them slip by. She knew that the only reason she was the most important person to Julian was because she was pregnant with his child. And considering the relationships he had with other members of his family, being the most important didn't exactly elevate her all that much.

The first week here was terrible. I didn't think it would be that bad—I've had hangovers before, obviously—but this was different. The shaking started the day after I arrived. My hands first, then my whole body. I couldn't sleep, couldn't eat. The doctors kept checking on me, monitoring my vitals. They said withdrawal can be dangerous, even fatal.

Kiara's breath caught as she read those words. He'd been through withdrawal? The casual way he'd mentioned it could be fatal made her stomach clench. She pressed one hand to her chest, feeling her heart rate quicken.

She continued reading, her eyes scanning the handwriting that was becoming easier to decipher.

I really didn't think I was that reliant on alcohol. Or that my body had become so dependent on it. In my mind, it was just to help me mentally. Clearly, I was wrong... but don't tell Duncan that.

This second week has been better physically, but worse mentally. They have us in group therapy sessions where we're supposed to "share our stories" and "identify our triggers." I sit there listening to people talk about losing their families or their careers because of drinking, and I feel like a fraud.

My problem isn't that severe. I still have my job waiting for me. I have money. I have a roof over my head. Even though everyone here is from a wealthy background, many have suffered more than I have. Many have had people cut them out of their lives completely because of their drug or alcohol use. I, at least, still have all of you.

Kiara was glad that he understood that. His support system was strong, and despite the lack of closeness with his parents and siblings, they did care about him.

I'm not sure why I'm writing this all down. I guess I just need to get it out. Sorry for choosing you as my confidante.

How are you doing? How is the baby doing? Do you know yet if it's a boy or a girl?

If you want to vent about anything to me, you're welcome to write back and lay it on me. It would be a nice distraction from life here.

I'm still not sure how long I'm going to be here. Hopefully not too much longer.

Guess I'd better end this so I can get it into the mail. Take care of yourself and the little one.

He just signed it, *Julian*, without any *love* or even *sincerely*, but that didn't really matter. He'd written to her. Of all the people he could have chosen to confide in, he'd picked her. And while she wasn't going to place any importance on that, she was grateful that he wasn't shutting her out.

Shifting, Kiara stared out the window, but her mind wasn't on the scenery. She mulled over everything Julian had shared with her.

Her romantic side really wanted to grab hold of the fact he'd written to her. It wanted her to believe that she was important to him beyond being the carrier of his child.

Realistically, however, she knew it was because she was the safe one. The convenient one. She knew nothing about what other relationships Julian might have in his life. He could have a best friend he'd never introduced her to. Maybe a circle of close friends that he hadn't told her about. And he probably hadn't told them about her either.

Why would he share about a temporary marriage?

Looking down at the letter, Kiara spread her hand out over the words. Regardless of the reasoning behind Julian choosing her, it was a moment she wouldn't take for granted.

As she sat there, Kiara remembered Duncan's request for an update on his son. She wouldn't divulge the details of what Julian had told her, but she could offer some reassurance to Duncan.

Kiara carefully folded the letter and slipped it back into the envelope. She would write to Julian later, but first she needed to let Duncan know that his son was okay.

Not that she'd share the details about withdrawal symptoms or Julian's reluctant acceptance that he had a problem. Those confessions belonged to Julian alone.

She pushed herself up from the loveseat, fatigue making her movements slower than usual. The walk had taken more out of her than she'd expected. Still, she made her way downstairs to Duncan's office, pausing outside the heavy wooden door to collect her thoughts before knocking.

"Come in," Duncan called.

Kiara stepped inside, the familiar scent of leather-bound books and Duncan's subtle cologne greeting her. He looked up from his computer, his expression softening slightly when he saw her.

"Did you read the letter?" he asked, gesturing for her to take a seat in one of the leather chairs across from his desk.

"Yes," Kiara said, settling into the chair. She rested her hands on her lap, the envelope containing Julian's letter safely upstairs in her room. "He seems to be doing okay. The physical adjustment at the start was a bit of a challenge for him, but he's doing better now."

Duncan studied her face for a moment, and Kiara wondered if he could tell she was holding back details. "That's good to hear. Has he mentioned how much longer he expects to be there?"

"He's not sure yet," she replied honestly. "I think they evaluate his progress as they go."

Duncan nodded, seeming satisfied with her answer. "I appreciate you letting me know. I've been concerned. I know he probably thinks I sent him to the treatment center as a punishment, but it really wasn't."

Kiara didn't know how to respond, so she didn't. She suspected that Duncan just needed to talk.

"I was worried about him," he said, his gaze going distant. "No parent likes to see their child destroying themselves, especially when they don't know why it's happening."

Kiara found herself nodding, even though she couldn't fully understand Duncan's perspective as a parent. The closest she'd come to that kind of protective love was what she felt for Angie, and now, increasingly, for the tiny life growing inside her.

"I'm sure he knows you care about him," she said softly, though she wasn't entirely certain that was true. Julian's letter had carried undertones of resentment, even if he'd tried to mask them with humor.

Duncan's expression grew thoughtful. "I hope so. Sometimes as a parent, you have to make decisions that your children won't understand or appreciate, at least not right away."

The weight of his words settled over her. Soon, she'd be making those kinds of decisions for her own child.

"Was there anything else in the letter that concerned you?" Duncan asked, pulling her from her thoughts.

Kiara shook her head, pushing aside the memory of Julian's description of his withdrawal symptoms. Those details felt too personal to share, even with his father. "No, nothing that concerned me. He was just updating me on how he's adjusting."

Duncan's shoulders relaxed slightly. "Good. Thank you for sharing that with me. I know Julian values his privacy, so I appreciate you giving me what you could. I know this whole situation has been overwhelming for both of you. An arranged marriage isn't likely what either of you had planned for your lives."

The understatement almost made Kiara laugh, but she managed to keep her expression neutral. "No, it wasn't."

"I hope you know that my decision wasn't made lightly," Duncan continued, his voice taking on a more formal tone. "I believe it's what's best for the child, and ultimately for both of you as well."

Kiara nodded, though privately she wondered if Duncan truly believed that or if he was simply trying to convince himself that his ultimatum was justified.

“Do you plan to write Julian back?” Duncan asked.

Kiara hesitated, then nodded. “I think it’s important to keep the lines of communication open while he’s there. And since he chose to reach out to me, I figured I should write back.”

“You’re right,” Duncan said. “Thank you for doing that. It’s good he’s communicating with someone, and I’m glad it’s you.”

Kiara wasn’t sure what to make of that statement, but she didn’t press for an explanation. Pushing up from the chair, she said, “I’ll let you get back to work. I just wanted to give you an update.”

Duncan also got to his feet. “Thank you for that.”

As Kiara made her way back upstairs, her mind was already composing the letter she wanted to write to Julian. Back in her room, she settled at the small desk and pulled out a sheet of the cream-colored stationery that had been in the drawer when she'd moved into the room.

Propping her chin on her hand, she stared at the paper, her mind suddenly blank as she considered what to share with Julian.

There was so much she wanted to tell him. Things like how she’d felt hearing the baby’s heartbeat for the first time. Or how she worried about becoming a mom. They were things soon-to-be parents might normally share with each other in the course of a pregnancy, but she didn’t think they were at a place in their relationship for her to do that.

And they might never be.

Regardless, she felt she owed him something, so she picked up her pen and began to write a letter to her husband.

CHAPTER SEVEN

Julian got up after a restless night. *Another* restless night. He'd known that he was using alcohol to help him fall asleep, but it had apparently also helped to keep him knocked out for the night.

He hadn't had a restful night since arriving at the treatment center. Each morning, when his alarm went off to get him up for the day, he had to drag himself out of bed.

Would it ever get better?

After a shower, he made his way to the dining room. The smell of food and the sound of muted conversation mixing with the clink of silverware on dishes greeted him well before he reached the door.

As Julian stepped into the doorway, his gaze swept the room, taking in the now familiar faces, along with a couple of new ones.

Though he'd moved in the same circle as a couple of the people currently at the center, he hadn't had extensive contact with them. He'd been surprised at some of the people there, ones he'd recognized but never met. It was likely that they were surprised to see him there as well.

Hearing the stories from some of them in the group therapy had been revealing. So many of them had been like him, hiding personal problems, relationship issues, and family stresses behind smiles, all while downing drink after drink or indulging in their drug of choice.

Of everyone there, he'd found himself spending the most time with a man named Elijah Sutcliffe. He was the son of a wealthy, well-known televangelist, and was yet another person who had seemed out of place in an alcohol and drug treatment center.

Julian spotted Elijah sitting at a table alone, so he made his way over to him and took one of the empty seats.

Elijah looked up from his plate and gave him a nod. “Morning.”

"Morning," Julian said, reaching for the coffee carafe that sat at the center of the table.

He poured himself a cup of coffee, which was a far better brew than he would have expected in a place like that. Julian had assumed rehab would mean terrible food and bitter coffee, but the Crystal Haven Wellness Center obviously catered to a clientele accustomed to luxury.

"Sleep any better?" Julian asked, reaching for a croissant from the basket in front of them.

Elijah shook his head. "Not really. You?"

"Same." Julian buttered his croissant methodically. "Two weeks in and I still feel like I've been hit by a truck every morning."

“The biggest truck in the world,” Elijah agreed.

One of the servers approached the table with a plate, which he set in front of Elijah. The server then turned to Julian.

“Breakfast today is Eggs Benedict with roasted asparagus, sourdough toast, and an assortment of fresh fruit.”

His stomach was still not happy with the torture it had gone through the previous week, but he needed to eat something. “Sounds good.”

Just like the coffee, he couldn’t really complain about the food they were served at the center either. It was as good as anything Mrs. Stevens made.

He savored his coffee while he waited for his meal to arrive. When the server put the plate down on the table in front of him, Julian thanked him, then focused on his food.

The eggs were perfectly poached, and Julian wondered if he could manage them without his stomach revolting. He'd lost weight since arriving at the center—his clothes hung a bit looser now, though he suspected that that wasn't entirely a bad thing.

"Looks like we're getting some mail today," Elijah commented, gesturing with his fork toward the staff member approaching their table.

Julian looked up to see Marcus walking toward them with some envelopes in hand. His heart quickened slightly. Had Kiara written back?

"Mr. Burke," Marcus said, extending two envelopes to him. "These came for you this morning."

He held out the third one to Elijah. "And there's one for you too, Mr. Sutcliffe."

Julian looked down at his envelopes, noting the return address of the estate on both. One was written in Duncan's familiar handwriting. The other was addressed in a feminine script. The name on the return address was *K. Burke,* which could only be from Kiara.

Julian wanted to rip hers open and read it right away, but he set it aside to read in his room. He wasn't sure if he wanted to read Duncan's at all.

Elijah had opened his envelope and pulled out the contents. Smiling, he said, "It's from my sister and my mom. They must have had a letter-writing party."

After a brief hesitation, Julian decided to go ahead and open the one from Duncan. It was several sheets of paper, but only one had his dad's writing on it.

Dear Julian,

I hope you are doing well. Though Kiara didn't share the contents of the letter you sent her, she did assure me that you were okay. Thank you for writing to her.

I know you might view your time at rehab as a punishment, but I need you to know that I arranged it out of love. It pained me greatly to see you so unhappy and drowning your emotions in alcohol. I was scared I was going to lose you completely.

My hope is that you will find some peace, and maybe even some joy once alcohol is no longer dominating your life. But don't do rehab just for me. Do it for yourself and for your baby.

I'm including some emails I've received from Sean about Fem-Pulse that I thought you'd like to read.

Take care of yourself, son.

Julian stared at the words, finding they blurred slightly before he blinked rapidly to clear his vision. His emotions since he'd stopped drinking were so much nearer the surface. Or maybe he was just feeling them more deeply now that he didn't have work and alcohol to numb them.

"Everything okay?" Elijah asked, concern in his voice.

Julian cleared his throat as he looked up at the man. "Yeah. It's a letter from my dad. We're not close.

Elijah gave a nod. "Yeah. I'm not close to my dad either."

"I've been so mad at him for essentially forcing me to come here," Julian said, then lifted the letter. "But he told me that he did it because he didn't want to lose me."

"You're fortunate," Elijah said. "My dad probably wishes I'd kicked the bucket."

"What?" Julian didn't know a lot about Christians, but he was pretty sure they weren't supposed to wish their children dead.

"I've lived behind the curtain," Elijah said. "I've seen what the world hasn't, and it's not pretty. The man people see behind the pulpit is not the man we saw in our home. I struggled with the disparity and often questioned my dad about it. Usually to my detriment."

Julian wasn't sure how to respond, but he could only imagine how that might impact someone. "Did someone in your family encourage you to come here?"

"My sister and my mom. My mom is wealthy in her own right because of her family, and she's paying for me to detox."

"So she cares about you," Julian stated.

Elijah nodded. "She and Miriam both do. My other brothers, however, are very much like my dad."

It was more than Elijah had shared previously, at least in Julian's presence.

"Who's your other letter from?" Elijah asked, gesturing to the cream-colored envelope that lay next to his plate.

"My... wife," Julian said.

Elijah's brows rose. "You're married?"

"Yes." He paused before adding, "And she's pregnant."

"Congratulations," Elijah said, though his tone held a note of caution. "Recent marriage?"

Julian nodded, running his thumb along the sealed edge of the envelope. "Very. Right before I came here, actually."

He'd written to Kiara on impulse, not really expecting a response. Now that he had one, he wasn't sure he was ready to read it.

"You don't seem thrilled," Elijah observed, pushing his half-eaten breakfast away.

Julian sighed. "It's complicated." That was the understatement of the century.

"It seems like relationships usually are."

"Do you have a significant other?"

Sadness filled Elijah's face. "Yes. Well, I *had* a significant other. She broke up with me not long before I came here."

"What was she like?" Julian asked, sensing the man's heartache went deep. He'd never loved any woman so much that ending things had hurt him the way Elijah appeared to be hurting.

Some of the sadness on his face faded into contemplation and affection. "She is... incredible. Smart, caring, passionate about her faith. She works at a nonprofit that helps kids in trouble find stability." Elijah's voice grew softer, more distant. "Her name is Grace. She has a laugh that could light up a room, you know? And she saw through all the pretense, all the family name stuff. She saw *me*."

Julian felt a pang in his chest, something he couldn't quite identify. He'd never spoken about a woman the way Elijah spoke about Grace. The closest he'd come to that kind of devotion was to his work.

"What happened?" Julian asked, though he suspected he already knew the answer.

"I happened." Elijah's jaw tightened. "I was drinking too much, disappearing for days at a time. She tried to help, tried to get me to see that I had value, despite what my dad might say. I wanted her type of faith, but I just couldn't get past the twisted beliefs I grew up with."

"She sounds like a wonderful woman."

"She is," Elijah said. "And stupid me took her for granted, believing her love for me would be enough that she'd still stick around, even with me acting the way I did. But since I've been here, I've realized that it was *my* love that wasn't strong enough. I loved the numbness alcohol gave me more than I loved her. Because if I had loved her like I should have, I would have gotten help when she begged me to."

"You're here now," Julian said. "That has to count for something."

"Maybe," Elijah said with a shrug. "But I don't expect her to wait. She deserves better than me."

"Maybe better than you in your previous state," Julian said, though he wasn't sure that was the right thing to say. "But you're trying now. You're getting help, right?"

"Yes. I've even requested a Christian counselor," Elijah said. "I need someone who understands why faith plays such a big role in my struggles."

"Both of my sisters are Christians," Julian said.

Elijah angled a look at him. "You have sisters?"

"Yeah. It's a long story. I also have a half-brother."

"Do you get along with them?"

Julian considered his relationship with his siblings. Honestly, they'd been no better than the one he had with his dad.

"I'm not close to them," Julian said. "Annie gets after me about my drinking, and we argue at times. Benji's a lot younger than me. He's still in high school."

"I'm sure that they care about you," Elijah said. "Your sisters are probably praying for you."

Julian nodded, because each of them had told him that in the days leading up to his departure for the center. He'd even gotten a text from Cole, Annie's boyfriend, letting him know he'd be praying for him.

He hadn't known how to respond to that, so he'd just thanked the man.

"Have they ever talked to you about their faith?"

"Annie's tried," Julian said. "But I haven't really been interested."

"Do you mind if I talk about it?" Elijah asked. "It's such an integral part of my life."

"Despite your experience with your father, you still want to claim the same faith as him?"

"There is a genuine faith," Elijah said, gazing down into his coffee. "But my father only wore his faith as a cloak, to be taken off as soon as he was behind closed doors."

Though Duncan wasn't necessarily the same in public as he was in private, the changes weren't negative. He was stern and forceful when dealing with business matters, but when he was with the family, he was generally more laid-back.

Julian had often chafed at the restrictions Duncan wanted to implement for the family, especially regarding safety, but he'd known it was because he was worried about something horrible happening to them. Duncan had never gotten past the kidnapping of Annie and Angela.

Hearing about Elijah's experience with his father made Julian a bit more grateful for what he had with Duncan.

"Is your wife a Christian?"

Julian actually had no idea, but given she was so close with Angela, it was possible. "I'm not sure. She's best friends with one of my sisters, so it's possible she is."

Elijah gave him a curious look, the earlier sadness gone from his expression. "It really is complicated, isn't it?"

"What?"

"Your marriage. You don't seem to know her very well."

Julian sighed. "I don't. After a night of drinking, we made a decision that resulted in her getting pregnant."

"And you got married because of that?"

Julian nodded. "My father told me that if I wanted to keep my position in the company, I had to marry her and go to rehab. So here I am." He lifted his left hand and wiggled his fingers. "Married and getting sober."

"Wow... that's a lot."

Julian nodded and reached for his coffee again, needing something to occupy his hands. The conversation had veered into territory that made him uncomfortable–not because of Elijah's openness, but because it forced him to confront how little he actually knew about the woman he'd married.

"What's her name?" Elijah asked, settling back in his chair.

"Kiara." It felt strange to name her as his wife. It was still an unfamiliar connection, despite everything that had happened between them. "She grew up on the same property where Angela–that's one of my sisters–was held after she was kidnapped."

Elijah's eyebrows rose. "That sounds like quite a story."

"It is." Julian found himself explaining more than he'd intended, telling Elijah about the kidnapping, about Kiara and Angela coming to live at the estate, about the late-night conversations in the library that had led to their current situation.

Julian was sure that Duncan wouldn't have been pleased with him revealing all of that to someone, but something told him he could trust Elijah. He hadn't come to rehab thinking he'd meet someone who could become a friend. And yet, it felt like Elijah was becoming just that.

After they'd talked for a few more minutes, Julian glanced at his watch. "I think I'm going to go to my room for a few minutes before the group session. I need to read the rest of my letter."

The two of them left the dining room together and walked toward the section of the large building where the rooms were located. Their rooms were on the same side of the hallway, but a couple of doors apart.

"See you in a bit," Elijah said as he continued down the hallway.

Julian let himself into his room, which looked more like a hotel room than the hospital room he'd expected. It was decorated in shades of blue and gray with white trim. There were heavy dark blue curtains framing a large window that gave him a view of the distant mountains, and the bedspread on the surprisingly comfortable bed matched the curtains.

They were all responsible for keeping their rooms tidy, and he'd had to get used to making his own bed. Their laundry was still done for them, which was good because he wasn't sure he'd know how to do it.

Julian settled on the one comfortable chair in the room, a recliner, and turned Kiara's letter over in his hands. The cream-colored envelope felt heavy with possibility. What had she written? Was she angry? Indifferent? The uncertainty made his stomach clench.

He slid his thumb under the flap and carefully opened it, pulling out several sheets of matching stationery. Her handwriting was neater than his, with gentle curves that somehow suited her.

Dear Julian,

Thank you for your letter. I was surprised but happy to hear from you. I've been hoping things were going okay, so it was good to hear that after a rough start, you're feeling better.

After I read your letter, I told your dad that you were doing alright. He was concerned, so I hope that was okay. I didn't share any of the details of what you wrote.

I'm doing better than I was. The morning sickness is still there, but the medication Doctor Misha prescribed helps... sometimes. I still get tired easily, but I've been trying to walk every day. The doctor says it's good for me, and I think she's right.

I'm starting to notice a small bump now. Nothing obvious when I'm dressed, but definitely there. I haven't had my first ultrasound yet, but it's scheduled for next week. I'm both excited and nervous to see our little bean for the first time.

Julian was struck by the words "our little bean." She saw the baby as something that connected them, not just as her child. He tried to imagine what she might look like, with the first signs of pregnancy showing. The image was fuzzy in his mind. He knew her face, of course, but he hadn't paid close attention to her figure before, and he had no memory of it from their time together.

I still don't know if it's a boy or a girl, but they might be able to tell me at the ultrasound. I'm not sure whether I want to find out or be surprised at the birth. What do you think?

Julian paused in his reading, surprised she'd asked for his opinion. What did he think? He hadn't considered whether he wanted to know the gender ahead of time.

It felt like such a normal question. The kind of thing expectant parents might discuss over dinner or while preparing the nursery. Not something spouses who were essentially strangers would debate via letters sent back and forth while one was in rehab.

Duncan has been checking on me daily, which is both sweet and a little overwhelming. Elizabeth has been wonderful too, giving me ginger tea and ginger candy to help with the nausea.

Angie's been a constant support through all of this, just like she always has been. She's excited about being an aunt, though I can tell she worries about me even though she doesn't need to. I'm doing fine.

I've been spending time at the construction site for the house. It's coming along quickly. Duncan insisted they work longer hours to finish sooner. I think he wants Angie and me to have our own space ASAP, which we appreciate.

I've been thinking a lot about what you wrote regarding feeling like a fraud in group therapy. I don't think you should feel that way. Just because your problems look different from others doesn't make them less real. You were hurting enough to need help, and that's what matters.

The words hit something in Julian's chest, a tightness he hadn't known was there. He appreciated her validating what he was going through without comparing it to people whose struggles might be more impactful than his.

Take care of yourself, Julian. I'd love to hear more from you if you have the time to write. Let me know what you think about finding out the baby's gender.

As ever... Kiara

Something settled inside Julian as he folded the letter and slid it back into the envelope. He hadn't expected to want to have a connection with Kiara, but receiving this letter from her made him feel hopeful for the future.

It would be important for them to have open lines of communication and the ability to deal with each other if they were going to positively parent this child. He appreciated that Kiara was already asking his opinion about the baby, and it made him think things would go better for them as parents than he'd originally thought they might.

CHAPTER EIGHT

Kiara was curled up in bed again, reading another of her books before calling it a night. It was how she always ended her day, and she was glad to no longer have to restrict her reading to "one more chapter" if the story was compelling her to keep reading. She had no job that required her to get up early in the morning. And with the money Duncan had given her, she had an unlimited book budget, which meant she was never short of books to read.

There was a soft knock on her door, then it cracked open. "Kiki? Are you awake?"

"Yep." She pushed herself up to sit against the headboard, then leaned over to snap on the lamp on the nightstand.

Angie skipped around to the other side of the bed and plopped down next to Kiara, a big smile on her face.

Kiara lifted her eyebrows. "What's up?"

"He asked me!" Angie held out her left hand, her fingers splayed. On her ring finger was a diamond that sparkled in the lamplight.

Kiara gasped, her heart leaping in her chest. "Jude proposed?"

"Yes!" Angie bounced on the bed, her blue-green eyes shining with excitement. "He took me to the same spot where Jim found us."

"Really?" Kiara frowned. "That's not very romantic."

"It was though," Angie insisted. "He said he wanted to reclaim that beautiful spot with good memories, not the horrible ones from that day. He prayed with me about it, then he got down on one knee and proposed. It was amazing. So amazing."

When she'd first realized that Angie's feelings for Jude were more than just a crush, Kiara hadn't been sure about them as a couple. Jude was so serious and reserved, and he was over a decade older than Angie. But it had quickly become clear that Jude would give his life for Angie, and Kiara knew it wasn't just because of his job.

There was a yearning in her heart for the kind of love that Angie and Jude shared. Even though they were so different, it seemed that sharing a faith and love for each other had given them a solid foundation for something more serious and, hopefully, long-lasting.

Kiara reached for her sister's hand, examining the ring more closely. It was elegant without being ostentatious—exactly Angie's style.

"It's beautiful," Kiara whispered, emotion tightening her throat. "I'm so happy for you, Angie."

And she was. Love might be something she wanted for herself, but that didn't mean she wasn't happy that her sister had found it.

"I still can't believe it," Angie said, her voice softening as she gazed at the ring.

After everything they'd been through, seeing her sister this happy felt like a miracle. Kiara squeezed Angie's hand, blinking back tears that suddenly pricked at her eyes.

"Have you told Duncan and Elizabeth yet?" Kiara asked, trying to keep her voice steady despite the emotion swelling inside her.

"Not yet," Angie said. "I wanted you to be the first to know, so we'll tell them tomorrow. It won't be a surprise to them, though. Jude said he asked for Duncan's blessing, so he knows it's happening."

"That's so old-fashioned, but it sounds exactly like something Jude would do," Kiara said with a laugh. "When are you thinking of having the wedding?"

"Soon," Angie said. "With Jude having been shot, we've realized that life is too short to put off something we both want, just so we can plan a fancy wedding. Plus, we only have a few people we want there, and most live here on the estate."

"What do you mean by soon?"

"Probably a month or two."

"Well, I suppose Duncan will be able to fund pulling a wedding together in a short time."

Angie laughed. "I suppose. He did it for you and Julian."

"I hope you're planning something a little more meaningful than what we had, given that you're actually marrying a man you love."

Angie stared at her for a moment before she nodded. "I suppose it will be a bit more elaborate, but not much, I don't think."

Kiara wished she hadn't brought up her wedding and tried to move on from the subject. "I'm surprised you've gotten engaged before Annie, since she and Cole have been dating longer."

"They might get engaged at the end of the basketball season. I think right now he's focused on the playoffs."

Kiara agreed that it was probably going to happen sooner rather than later, given how the couple acted when they were together.

It was hard not to feel a little jealous of Angie and Annie. They were both with men they loved and who loved them deeply in return.

As a romantic at heart, Kiara had wanted that for herself. Instead, she was married to a man she barely knew. And he definitely held no love in his heart for her, and probably not even affection.

She tried to suppress the pain in her heart as she leaned against her sister. "I'm happy for you, Angie. Truly."

"Thanks, Kiki." Angie rested her head on Kiara's. "I want you to be my maid of honor."

"Matron of honor," Kiara corrected her.

There was a moment of silence before Angie said, "Yes. My matron of honor."

"I'd be honored."

"Thanks, sis."

"Who is going to be Jude's best man?"

"I think it's going to be Cooper."

They chatted for a few more minutes, then Angie left to go to her own room. After turning off the lamp, Kiara slid back down under the covers. Her tablet lay abandoned on the bed beside her.

In the darkness, she stared up at the ceiling. Warm tears slid from the corners of her eyes, soaking into her hair. Crying had never been part of who she was. Jim saw tears as a weakness and would often punish them for crying. But without that threat, her emotions came to the surface more easily. Although it was possible that the pregnancy had something to do with them too.

She didn't bother to wipe the tears away. There was no one there to see them. No one there to question her complicated feelings at the news of Angie's engagement to Jude.

Her heart ached with a complex mix of joy and sorrow that she couldn't untangle. She was genuinely happy for Angie. Her sister deserved all the love and happiness in the world. But watching her sister's radiant joy only highlighted the emptiness of her own situation.

Kiara pressed her hand to her stomach, feeling the slight firmness there. In a few months, she'd have a baby to love and care for. That should be enough. It had to be enough. Because once Julian divorced her, she'd have to navigate life as a single mom.

But the romantic part of her heart—the part that had devoured love stories since the first time she'd gotten her hands on one—mourned for what she'd never have. She'd only ever hoped to get married once, and that that one marriage would be filled with love and would last a lifetime.

Instead, she'd married a stranger out of necessity, not love. There would be no tender moments of discovery, no growing intimacy, no shared dreams for their future.

The baby would arrive in a few months, and she still had no idea what her marriage would look like by then. Would they divorce as soon as the baby was born? Or would Julian wait a couple of months?

His letter had been kind, even thoughtful, but it had reflected the correspondence of two strangers navigating an impossible situation. Not the words of a husband to his wife.

She needed to keep her focus on what she had—a baby. And not what she didn't have—a loving husband.

Picking up her tablet, she touched the screen to bring it to life and settled in to read at least one more chapter. Hopefully, it would pull her out of her head enough that she could sleep.

For some reason, reading about fictional characters falling in love gave her hope for herself, while hearing about it happening to the people around her didn't.

The next morning, Kiara was late going downstairs, so all the hot breakfast food had already been put away. However, there were still some pastries and fruit sitting on the buffet in the breakfast room.

She poured herself a glass of water, then put a chocolate croissant on a plate and filled a small cup with assorted berries and carried them to the table.

She hadn't been there long when Angie appeared with Annie behind her. They also grabbed some drinks and pastries before joining her at the table.

"How are you feeling today, Kiara?" Annie asked as she lifted her mug of coffee.

"At the moment, I'm feeling okay," she said. "But check back in five minutes."

Annie chuckled. "That doesn't sound fun."

"It's not really," Kiara agreed. "But to be honest, the nausea is getting a little better."

"I hear we're having another wedding," Annie said.

"Exciting, huh?"

"I hope that Cole gets the idea," Annie said. "Maybe you could toss me your bouquet."

"Well, considering you'll probably be the only single woman there, that shouldn't be too hard."

"Good morning, ladies," Duncan said as he walked into the breakfast room. "Are you all well?"

"Yep," Annie responded. "Although maybe *well* isn't how Angie's feeling. I think *extremely well* might be more accurate."

Duncan chuckled. "I never thought I'd be happy that my daughter was marrying my head of security, but here we are. And Elizabeth and I are very happy with the news."

"I'm glad," Angie said. "Jude means the world to me."

Turning from Angie, Duncan held out an envelope to Kiara. "This came for you."

She hesitated for a second before she took it. She'd been hoping to receive another letter but hadn't known if Julian would feel inclined to write again.

As she took it, Duncan said, "I received one as well, and it seems he's doing okay."

"I'm glad," she said.

Duncan looked at her for a long moment, then nodded. "I'll talk to you ladies later."

After he'd left, both Annie and Angie turned their attention to Kiara.

"Are you going to read your letter?" Angie asked.

"Is this the first letter you've received from him?" Annie tacked on before Kiara had a chance to respond.

"No."

"No?" the twins asked in unison.

"No, I'm not going to read the letter yet," Kiara said, her attention on Angie before she looked at Annie. "And no, it's not the first letter I've received."

"Really?" Annie sounded surprised. "That's amazing. I'm so glad he's communicating with you. How's he doing?"

Kiara chose her words carefully, wanting to protect Julian's privacy like she had with Duncan. "As you might imagine, it hasn't been a walk in the park, but he's pushing through."

"That's good," Annie said.

Angie gestured to the envelope she held. "So you're not going to read your letter?"

"Not here."

Annie and Angie exchanged a glance, then Angie said, "Why not?"

"Because you'll both want to know what it says, and I've told Julian that I wouldn't betray his confidence."

Annie's brows rose as her eyes widened. "Are you falling for my brother?"

Kiara stared at Annie. "No. That would be foolish."

She'd come to that conclusion early on. Like when she'd seen Julian the day after they'd been intimate, and he'd clearly not remembered what had happened. And on top of that, he hadn't seemed remotely interested in her romantically when he was sober. It was only after he'd had several drinks that he'd viewed her as something more.

Kiara had seen enough pictures of him with women online to know that he had a 'type', and she was not it. She didn't think she was unattractive, but she definitely wasn't blonde, and she had curves even when she wasn't pregnant.

"Why would that be foolish?" Annie asked. "All things considered, he's not a horrible man. I know he has some issues, but he's working on them."

"I just don't think it would be a good idea."

"You know, when Cole first started showing an interest in me, I was sure he was just bored or something because I wasn't anything like the women he usually dated," Annie said, relaxing back in her chair, her cup of coffee in her hands. "I'm glad I got past that because he's been nothing but wonderful to me. So don't assume, just because of who Julian might have dated before, that things can't develop between you."

"Well, Julian hasn't expressed any interest in me, so it's a good thing I'm not falling for him." Any more than she already had... "It would just complicate things."

"You're pregnant with his baby," Annie pointed out, as if Kiara had forgotten. "So you must have interested him at some point."

"All that proves is that I interested blackout drunk Julian. Not sober Julian. And I don't think any of us want Julian to be drunk anymore."

Annie sighed. "No, we don't."

"So just accept—like Julian and I have—that this marriage is for now, not forever."

Angie's expression saddened, which wasn't what Kiara wanted. She was supposed to be excited and happy about her wedding.

"My focus is on the baby," Kiara said. "And how excited I am to meet him or her."

"It will be nice to have a baby around again," Annie said. "I remember when Benji was born and how much I loved helping Elizabeth with him."

"I've never taken care of a baby, so I'm going to need all the help I can get."

"No worries there," Annie assured her. "I have a feeling there will be at least three of us ready to help you whenever you need it."

"I'll hold you to that." Kiara finished the last bit of her croissant, then said, "I'm going to head back up to my room for a bit to read my letter."

"Are you going walking later?" Angie asked.

"Probably. It looks nice out."

"I want to go with you," she said. "So come get me before you go."

"Okay. I will."

Leaving the twins in the breakfast room, Kiara clutched her letter tightly as she climbed the stairs. Her stomach was once again a bit nauseous, but she didn't know if it was because of the baby or nerves over the letter from Julian.

Once in the privacy of her room, she sat in her favorite chair and pulled the fluffy blanket she kept there over her lap.

Taking a deep breath and exhaling heavily, she slid a finger under the flap and carefully broke the seal.

Once again, the pages were filled with his bold scrawl in black ink. Hunching over the letter, she began to read.

Dear Kiara,

I hope that you and the baby are doing well and that the nausea has eased up. I'm sorry I can't ask informed questions about your pregnancy as I know nothing and currently don't have the ability to search for information on the internet.

You asked about my thoughts on finding out the gender of the baby. I think it would kind of be nice to know. It would give us a connection to him or her.

Kiara smiled at his words. She was going for the scan in two days, and she'd planned to ask for the gender to be put in a sealed envelope until she heard from him. But now that she had, she could go ahead and find out and let him know when she replied to his letter.

However, if you'd rather not know, I'm okay with that. I don't have much of an opinion on things pertaining to the baby, to be honest. Do you have a preference for a girl or boy? I never really thought I'd have kids, so I have no idea which I'd rather have.

Kiara hadn't really thought too much about it either. Healthy was the first thing she hoped for the baby. Part of her thought that maybe it would be better if the baby was a girl if she was going to be a single mom. But given this was the first Burke grandchild, it was likely Duncan would want a boy.

She was glad that Julian wasn't dropping subtle hints about the baby possibly not being his. She didn't doubt that there would still be DNA testing done once the baby arrived. If that was what happened, she wouldn't object or take offense because she knew the truth. And she wanted them to be assured of the truth too.

Things here are going better physically. The wicked withdrawal from the constant alcohol use has lessened. I'm still struggling to fall asleep at night. My mind seems to think that bedtime is the perfect time to think about everything.

I've been talking to a guy here who's a Christian, and it's been rather interesting. I know that Annie and Angela are Christians. Are you? Do you go to church with Angela?

The questions gave Kiara pause. When Angie had first started going to church in Briar Hollow, Kiara had assumed it was just because Angie didn't want to disappoint Miss Ida. But then she'd continued to go. Kiara had accompanied her on occasion, but at the time, it hadn't resonated with her.

Angie had started to attend church with Jude once she'd gotten settled at the estate. She asked Kiara periodically if she wanted to join her, but Kiara had yet to accept.

This guy has a kind of messed up past with Christianity, and yet he's passionate about it in a way I wouldn't have thought someone with that history would be. We've had some discussions about his faith, and they've been interesting. Our conversations have given me a lot to think about. Plus, they've been a good way to pass the time. I didn't think I'd actually like spending time with anyone while I was here, and that's kind of been true, except for Elijah.

Kiara didn't think the conversations Julian had had with her had given him anything to think about. In fact, she was fairly certain that he didn't recall much of what they'd talked about.

Their discussions had centered mainly on surface stuff like movies and TV shows they liked to watch. Julian had talked about some of the many places he had traveled to, which was a subject Kiara hadn't been able to contribute to.

Still, she'd enjoyed their evenings together and had wondered if he would say the same. Perhaps he preferred conversations that gave him something to mull over.

Regardless, it didn't matter. She no longer thought she had a chance with Julian the way she had had during those evenings they'd spent together. While he appeared to be a good man, he wasn't the man for her.

She just had to keep reminding herself of that so she wouldn't make the mistake of falling more in love with the man than she already was.

With that thought in mind, she returned her attention to the letter.

Duncan sent me some printed emails from Sean, the head of the FemPulse research in Singapore, so I've had a chance to get caught up on that, which I really appreciate. Not having instant access to that information is something I really miss being here.

Well, I think I need to end this. My hand is starting to cramp. I haven't ever written so much by hand before in my life, I don't think.

Take care of yourself and the little one.

-Julian

Kiara folded the letter and slipped it back into the envelope as she considered its contents. Julian's tone had seemed more relaxed in this one, and she hoped that meant that he was fully accepting the treatment at the center. For his sake and the sake of their child, Kiara wanted Julian's time at the center to be successful.

She placed the letter on the end table beside her chair, deciding she'd write back after her appointment. That way she could tell him whether they were having a boy or a girl. The thought sent a flutter of excitement through her belly.

Her hand drifted to the slight swell of her stomach. "What are you, little one? A boy or a girl?" she whispered. "Your daddy wants to know."

The word "daddy" caught in her throat. Would Julian ever truly be a father to this baby beyond biology and financial support? The question lingered in her mind as she stood up, realizing immediately that she'd done it too quickly.

A wave of dizziness hit her, forcing her to grip the armrest until it passed. The morning sickness medication helped, but it didn't eliminate every symptom. She pressed her other hand to her forehead, waiting for the room to stop tilting.

When the dizziness subsided, she made her way to the bathroom since the frequent need to pee was also a new part of her life. Once she was done, she sent a message to Angie to see if she wanted to go for a walk.

As she waited for Angie to respond, her mind went back to the questions Julian had asked about her faith. Angie had never pressured her to get involved in the church the way she had, but Kiara had seen how her sister's faith sustained her through difficult times. It had given Angie a peace that Kiara sometimes envied.

Peace was something she could really use in her current situation, so maybe she should talk to Angie about her faith and the peace she seemed to have, regardless of what was going on.

Kiara found herself wanting to be the best person she could be for the sake of the baby, and if part of that was finding out more about God, she would gladly do it.

CHAPTER NINE

Julian was tempted to ignore the knock on his door, but he dragged himself out of his chair to answer it. He wasn't having a good day, and he didn't want to see or talk to anyone, even though that wasn't really an option at the center.

"Mail for you, Mr. Burke," the man in the hallway said when Julian opened the door.

Taking the envelope from him, Julian said, "Thanks."

Closing the door, his spirits lifted a bit when he saw Kiara's familiar handwriting on the front of the envelope.

He returned to his chair and sank down with a sigh. Staring out the window at the glorious view, he tapped the envelope on his leg. He wanted to get into the right mindset before reading her letter.

The therapist in their session the previous day had decided it was time to press harder to get to the source of Julian's excessive drinking. They'd touched on it in past sessions, but the man hadn't pressed when Julian had brushed it off as just something that he'd enjoyed that had gotten out of hand.

Unfortunately, the therapist hadn't believed him.

So far, the sessions he'd attended had been focused on the other parts of his life. His job. His family. His friendships. His relationships—past and present. They'd even delved into the kidnapping and the impact it had had on him.

They'd talked about a lot of things. More than Julian had talked about to anyone ever before. He'd told him about pretty much everything of significance in his life, and even some non-significant things. All in an effort to avoid having to discuss *that* incident.

But Julian had known it was only a matter of time. He was pretty sure that if he didn't deal with it, he would end up drinking again. All it had taken to bring the urge to the forefront in an overwhelming way was the thought of talking about what he'd done.

So he knew he had to face it head-on. And once he told the therapist, he was pretty sure he'd have to tell Duncan.

His stomach lurched as he imagined that conversation. And boy, did he want a drink to dull the anxiety that caused.

He'd shoved the memory of that day down deep and covered it with a river of alcohol. But now the river had dried up, and the memory was laid bare.

Maybe it was time to lance the boil and let all the poison out. Accept the consequences as a man, even though he'd only been a child when it had happened.

He might lose his job, but he had plenty of money of his own. He wouldn't be destitute. He might be alone, but he wouldn't be without a roof over his head or food on his table.

And he'd have a child. Provided Kiara would let him see the baby after his revelation.

He stared down at the envelope in his hands. Would the letter tell him if the baby was a boy or a girl?

It was possible that Kiara had chosen to wait until the birth, but he found that he really didn't want that. He wanted to know now.

Focused on that, Julian opened the envelope and pulled out the thick sheets of cream paper. Unfolding them, he focused on the gently curved letters.

Dear Julian,

I hope you continue to do well. We are fine here. My morning sickness is much better. Instead of feeling sick all day, it's usually just first thing in the morning... like it's supposed to be.

And the baby is doing really well too. I decided I wanted to know the gender as well, so at my ultrasound today, I asked them to tell me. And after a little coaxing to get the baby in the right position, they told me we're having a BOY!

Julian inhaled sharply, and he was surprised by the press of tears in his eyes. He was going to have a son.

Sudden dread filled him as he imagined a relationship with his son that was similar to what he had with his dad. Could he be a good father to a son?

He'd already failed miserably in his father-son relationship with Duncan. And he hadn't been a much better brother to his siblings, especially Benjamin.

Had he ever had a successful relationship? One that was balanced and uplifting?

His best relationships were probably with people he worked with, like Sean. It was easier to meet work relationship expectations than personal ones.

But a child... a son... could he somehow figure out how to be a good father to him?

I didn't really care whether it was a boy or a girl, but I figured it might be easier to have a girl as a single mom.

Julian's stomach clenched as he read the words. *Single mom.* He'd essentially told her that they'd be getting a divorce at some point in the future, so it wasn't a surprise that she was thinking that way.

So why was he reacting like it wasn't something he wanted? They didn't love each other, so there was no reason for them to stay married.

Most of the relationships I've had with men (my adoptive father and brother) haven't been great. I just want to give this little boy the childhood I never had, with lots of love and security. A place where he's safe.

Julian wanted that too, but he wasn't sure what that looked like.

So, I guess we need to discuss names. I don't have any ideas yet, but if you have a name that is important to you or your family, let me know.

I have included a picture from the ultrasound so that you can see what the baby looks like... sort of! Angie was with me. I had her take a video in case you wanted to see it someday.

He should have been with her. He should have been there to hear that they were having a son. Already he was missing out on things with him, all because he had a drinking problem.

Something that felt like resolve settled within him. He might not want to deal with his past, but he had to do it for the sake of his son. The little boy deserved to have a father who was present and whole.

There was nothing he could do to change what had happened in the past, but he had to tell Duncan and deal with the consequences. It was time to try to free himself from the guilt he'd carried for so many years.

With that settled in his mind, Julian continued to read the letter.

More good news! Jude proposed to Angie the other day, and no surprise, she said yes. They're planning a wedding really soon, like in a month or so. I'm Angie's matron of honor. Do you think you'll be able to be here for it?

Julian wasn't sure how much longer he'd be there, and he wasn't sure he wanted to attend a wedding, especially Angela's, when he was dealing with the mess his life was in.

You asked me in your letter if I was a Christian and if I went to church. The answer is no, I'm not. I have gone to church sporadically with Angie over the years. I haven't thought much about it, but as I've watched Angie deal with everything recently, I've wondered about God and her faith in Him more than usual.

Angie is not a brave person by nature, but over the past few years, she's pushed herself to do things. Since she started going to church, she's memorized a Bible verse she recites to herself when faced with something difficult. It says something about being able to do everything with God's help.

As I look at what lies ahead for me—and now our son—I think perhaps I'm going to need God's help to be the mom I should be to him.

Angie also seems so content and at peace with what's happened to her and even what happened to Jude. I envy her that because I've been anything but content lately. I think I might ask her about going to church with her and Jude.

Before Julian could dwell too much on what she'd shared, there was a soft chime from the intercom panel installed in every room. It was followed by the announcement that lunch was being served.

He skimmed the last bit of the letter, which was only a couple more lines letting him know she appreciated his letters and hoped that he continued to do well.

As he put the letter back into the envelope, he found the picture she'd included of the ultrasound. He stared at it for a minute, barely able to make out the features in the baby's profile.

There was a knock on his door, and from its rhythm, Julian knew it was Elijah. He got up and went to open the door.

"Ready to grab some lunch?" the man asked.

"Yep," Julian said. "But first, here."

Elijah took the picture and bent his head to look at it. When he lifted his head a moment later, he was smiling.

"Amazing. Did she find out what the gender is?"

"A boy."

Elijah handed the picture back to him, then clapped him on the shoulder. "Congratulations, Dad."

"Thanks." He took the picture back to the table, then left the room with Elijah.

They walked in silence to the dining room, Julian's mind still processing the news.

A son. The word felt weighty... significant in a way he hadn't anticipated.

As they entered the spacious room with its panoramic views of the mountains, Julian noticed his steps felt lighter despite the heaviness in his chest.

The room hummed with subdued conversation and the clink of silverware against china. Julian filled his plate from the buffet, barely registering what he was selecting. His thoughts kept returning to the grainy ultrasound image, his first glimpse of his son.

"You look like you're in shock," Elijah commented as they settled at their usual table. "Good news should make you happier."

Julian stabbed at a piece of grilled chicken on his plate. "I am happy. Just... processing."

"Having second thoughts about fatherhood?"

"No." Julian surprised himself with his certainty. "I'm not having second thoughts about fatherhood. I'm having second thoughts about myself as a father."

Elijah set down his fork, studying Julian's face. "What do you mean?"

Julian pushed his food around his plate, appetite gone despite having skipped breakfast that morning. The dining room suddenly felt too crowded, too public for the weight of his thoughts.

"Like I mentioned before, my relationship with my own father is... complicated. Always has been." Julian lowered his voice. "And there's something I've never told anyone. Something that happened when I was a kid that's been eating at me for years."

"Is that why you started drinking?" Elijah asked, his voice equally quiet.

Julian nodded, throat tight. "That was easier than facing it. Than dealing with the guilt."

"Guilt's a heavy burden to carry alone," Elijah said.

Julian met Elijah's steady gaze across the table, recognizing something familiar in the other man's eyes—understanding born of personal experience. The weight of carrying secrets, of letting shame dictate choices.

"Twenty-four years," Julian said, his voice barely above a whisper. "I've been carrying this for twenty-four years."

Elijah leaned forward slightly, his expression encouraging but patient. Julian appreciated that he didn't push, didn't demand details. Just waited.

Julian's fingers found the edge of his napkin, twisting the fabric as memories he'd spent decades drowning threatened to surface. The dining room noise faded to a distant hum as he forced himself back to that day—the day that had changed everything.

“I told you already about my twin sisters being kidnapped when they were three," Julian began, his throat dry. "They were kidnapped by our nanny and one of the security guards. I heard them talking about it, and when Sandra realized that, she tried to just brush it aside. She promised me my favorite candy and a new toy if I didn’t say anything. I agreed to keep quiet about it. The day they abducted the twins, I found a small box under my pillow with several chocolate bars and a new Lego set that I’d been wanting."

“And you never told anyone?”

He shook his head. “At that point, it was too late. But if I’d still told someone even after they were taken... it maybe could have made a difference. My family had all the money in the world, but I cared more about candy and a new toy.”

Julian’s voice cracked on the last sentence, and he felt overwhelmed by the urge to cry. To break down and let out all the sorrow and guilt he’d carried for most of his life.

It had been bad enough when they hadn’t known where Angela was. But her eventual return had revealed the rough life she’d had with Jim and Sandra.

And he was responsible for that.

Julian knew that even though he didn't want to walk through what was to come, he did it with the hope that once he was through it, he'd find freedom from the guilt and peace.

"I guess it's time to give Dr. Carlisle what he wants," Julian murmured.

"I'll pray for you," Elijah said. "God cares about you, and He would want you to be free from the chains of your past."

Julian wished that he understood more about what Elijah was saying. However, right then, his focus was on revealing his long-held secret to people who might come to hate him for what he'd done.

His father. His sister. His... wife.

Later that night, he wrote a letter to Kiara. But rather than reveal the turmoil he was currently experiencing, Julian tried to keep the tone of the letter lighthearted as he wrote about their little boy and gave another general overview of what was happening at the center.

He told her about the activities that were available to them there. The hiking trails. The tennis courts. The swimming pool. The weight room. The hot tub and sauna. All of it was more suitable for a spa. He'd availed himself of some of it, like the hiking trails and the weight room, all in an effort to distract himself from his inner turmoil.

The next morning, he woke after a restless night and found the resolve to admit to what had happened when he was a child was still with him. The confession would start with his therapist.

Over the next couple of days, he had intensive sessions with Dr. Carlisle, which eventually ended with the decision that they would request that Duncan come to the center to meet with Julian and the therapist.

Julian was glad that there would be a third party there to help him share what he'd done.

A few days after his decision to tackle his past, Julian sat in Dr. Carlisle's office, his palms sweating as he waited for his father to arrive. The familiar leather chair that had become his confessional seat over the past weeks now felt like an electric chair. Every muscle in his body was coiled tight, ready to spring him from the room if his courage failed him.

The murmur of voices in the hallway made his stomach lurch. Dr. Carlisle glanced toward the door, then back at Julian with the calm, encouraging expression that had become familiar.

"Remember what we discussed," the therapist said quietly. "This isn't about punishment. It's about healing."

Julian nodded, though his throat felt like sandpaper. The knock came soft but firm, and Dr. Carlisle rose to answer it.

"Mr. Burke, thank you for coming," the therapist said, stepping aside to allow Duncan entry.

Duncan stepped into the room, and Julian's chest tightened as their eyes met. Duncan looked older somehow, lines of worry etched deeper around his eyes than Julian remembered. The expensive suit couldn't hide the tension in his shoulders or the way his jaw was set in that familiar hard line.

"Julian." Duncan's voice carried its usual authority, but there was something else there. Concern, or maybe even fear.

"Dad." The word came out rougher than Julian had intended. It was a term he rarely used. He gestured to the chair Dr. Carlisle had positioned across from his own. "Thanks for coming."

Duncan settled into the chair, his movements careful and controlled. Julian could smell his father's cologne, the same scent he'd worn for as long as Julian could remember. It brought back a flood of memories—being small enough to sit on Duncan's lap, before everything became complicated.

"Dr. Carlisle said you needed to discuss something important," Duncan said, his gaze moving between Julian and the therapist. "He was rather insistent that I come immediately."

Julian's hands clenched into fists on the arms of his chair. The words he'd rehearsed with Dr. Carlisle over the past two days seemed to evaporate from his mind. His father sat less than six feet away, waiting for an explanation that would shatter everything between them.

"There's something I need to tell you," Julian began, his voice barely audible. "Something I should have told you twenty-four years ago."

Duncan's posture shifted slightly, becoming more tense as his steely gaze sharpened.

"It's about the time when Angela and Annie were kidnapped," Julian continued, forcing himself to meet his father's gaze. "I knew it was going to happen."

The silence in the room became suffocating. His dad's expression hardened.

"What do you mean?" Each word was enunciated in a cold, hard voice.

Julian knew that tone. It was one he'd heard Duncan use in the past. However, it had always been used in business settings.

For all their issues, Duncan had never turned that cold, hard voice on him. The fact that he did then wasn't surprising. What *was* surprising was how much it hurt.

"What do you mean, Julian?"

Taking a deep breath, Julian pulled his shoulders back and looked his father in the eye. "The day before the girls disappeared, I heard Sandra and Jim talking about how they were going to take them."

"You *heard* them?" Duncan demanded. "Why didn't you say anything?"

Julian wished he could say that they'd threatened him. That would have been better than the truth.

"Sandra promised me candy and a toy if I didn't say anything," Julian said, hating the tremor in his voice. "So I didn't."

"You had plenty of toys and candy." Anger flared in Duncan's eyes. "You sold your sisters out for candy and a toy."

The words pierced Julian deep in his heart. "I know. I'm sorry."

"You're *sorry?"*

Julian flinched as if he'd been struck. His father's words echoed in his mind–*you sold your sisters out*–and the truth of them made bile rise in his throat.

He'd known this was coming, had prepared for it during endless sleepless nights, but hearing the accusation spoken aloud by Duncan felt like a physical blow.

"Please," Dr. Carlisle interjected, his voice calm but firm. "Let Julian finish."

Duncan's jaw worked, muscles tensing beneath his skin. His gaze never wavered from Julian's face.

The cold fury there made Julian want to shrink into his chair and disappear. He'd seen his father angry before, but never like this. Never directed at him with such intensity.

Julian could see the effort it took his father to remain seated. He could practically feel the rage radiating across the small space between them.

"There's nothing more to say," Julian said, his voice hollow. "I was a stupid child, and I chose candy over my sisters' safety. I've lived with that choice every day since."

"I understand you're angry, Mr. Burke, but Julian was just a child when this happened. A child making a poor decision shouldn't carry the same weight as an adult making that same choice."

"Even a child should know the difference between right and wrong," Duncan said, his voice still carrying that terrible coldness. "Especially when it comes to his sisters' safety."

Julian felt tears burning behind his eyes, but he refused to let them fall. Not now. Not when he'd already shown himself to be weak and selfish.

"You're right," Julian said, his voice cracking. "I should have known better. I should have told you immediately."

"Do you have any idea what your sister went through because of your silence?" Duncan demanded, leaning forward in his chair. "Do you understand what you cost this family?"

Julian's throat tightened. Each accusation landed like a physical blow. The weight of his father's disappointment crushed him more thoroughly than any punch could have.

"I do," Julian managed to say. "I've imagined it every day since they disappeared."

"Imagined it?" Duncan's voice rose. "Angelica lived it! While you were enjoying your privileged life, your sister was being abused by those people. And for twenty-four years we thought—" His voice broke slightly. "We thought she was dead."

Julian couldn't meet his father's gaze anymore. The fury and pain there were too much to bear. He stared at his hands instead, noticing how they trembled despite his efforts to keep them still.

He said nothing because he realized, in that moment, there was nothing more to say. There were no words that would ease the weight of disappointment and anger his father had towards him.

Was this the end of his time in the family? Was this going to be the rejection he'd always feared?

“I need to go,” Duncan said, getting to his feet.

Julian didn’t move. He didn’t look up. He couldn’t bear to watch his father walk away from him, filled with anger and disappointment.

Dr. Carlisle followed Duncan out of the room, but he returned a minute later and took his seat behind his desk.

“I don’t think that could have gone much worse,” Julian murmured.

“It was a shock for your father,” Dr. Carlisle said. “With time, I’m sure he’ll calm down.”

Julian nodded, just because he didn't want to talk about it anymore.

What he wanted more than anything was a drink. And then another one. And another one. Until he was drunk enough to numb the pain and wipe away the memory of this meeting so he could slip into the oblivion of sleep.

"How are you feeling?" Dr. Carlisle asked.

Julian mulled over his answer, mindful of their previous sessions. The man had an uncanny ability to sniff out untruths when it came to how a person said they were feeling.

"A little shocked," he said. "I guess I was hoping for the best, which I should have realized was not the greatest approach."

"I don't think you were wrong to hope for the best," Dr. Carlisle said.

Julian talked to him for a few minutes longer, then managed to end their session without revealing too much of how shattered he felt inside.

Hurrying back to his room, he was glad no one stopped him. He wasn't in the mood to talk to anyone right then, his thoughts too weighed down by his imagining how angry Angela was going to be when she learned the truth. And if Angela was angry and hurting because of him, as her sister's protector, Kiara was sure to be furious with him.

The ache in his heart intensified, and all he wanted to do was walk out of the treatment center and find the nearest bar. The only thing that kept him from doing that was his son. If Kiara didn't decide to keep him out of their son's life because of all this, Julian knew he needed to have dealt with his past so he could be a good dad to him.

That had become extremely important to him.

CHAPTER TEN

Kiara smiled as she read her latest letter from Julian. He'd seemed happy about learning the gender of the baby. He'd even sent some name suggestions.

I'm partial to names like Tom or Jerry. Or even Fred or Barney.

If she hadn't watched cartoons before being taken by Jim and Sandra, she might have thought he was a little nuts. But since she'd seen both cartoons while still with her birth parents, his suggestions made her laugh. She wasn't sure she liked any of them for their baby, but she appreciated getting a glimpse of Julian's sense of humor.

The letter hadn't been as long as previous ones, and after she was done reading it, she felt a bit let down. He hadn't talked about how he'd been doing personally, except for sharing that he'd been making use of the hiking trails around the center and the weight room.

Kiara was concerned for him, so she'd hoped that he would update her on how he was feeling physically and mentally, and maybe share his thoughts on God. But instead, it had been a more lighthearted letter.

Maybe that was good. Maybe it meant that he was beginning to have a more upbeat approach to life now that the alcohol was out of his system, and he was feeling better physically.

She left the letter on her desk to reply to later that day and made her way downstairs. When she reached the main floor, she spotted Duncan walking with Elizabeth toward the wing where his office was located.

He'd left the previous day on the helicopter, though she hadn't known where he was going. It must have been close however, since he was back already.

"Good morning, Kiara," Elizabeth said. She gave Kiara a smile, but it was a mere shadow of the woman's normal smiles.

"Good morning," Kiara replied, then looked at Duncan. What she saw made her frown. The man looked like he'd aged a decade in the past twenty-four hours. "Is everything okay?"

"Would you mind finding Angela and meeting us in my office, please?"

Kiara's stomach clenched in a way that had nothing to do with her pregnancy. She wanted to demand an answer to her question, but she just nodded and hurried back upstairs as quickly as she could.

"What's up?" Angie said when she opened her door.

"I think something's happened, but I'm not sure what. Duncan wants to see us in his office." She paused. "He doesn't look good."

"What?" Angie went to her bed and grabbed her phone. "He wanted to see us both?"

Kiara nodded. "But he didn't say why. And when I asked him if everything was okay, he didn't answer me."

Together, they went back downstairs, then turned in the direction Duncan and Elizabeth had been headed.

"Come in," Elizabeth said when they arrived in the open doorway to Duncan's office.

Duncan was seated behind his desk, but he didn't look at them as they walked in. Elizabeth ushered them over to the cluster of furniture they usually sat in when meeting with Duncan.

"We're just waiting for Jude," she said as they sat down together on the couch.

Angie reached out and took Kiara's hand as they exchanged a worried look. Duncan had never looked so... not himself. He'd always appeared in control and polished.

When Jude stepped into the room, he took in the scene with a frown. "Is everything okay?"

"Come in, Jude," Duncan said as he got up from behind his desk. "Have a seat."

Kiara and Angie shifted over so that Jude could sit beside Angie. She kept hold of Kiara's hand while also reaching out for Jude's.

Elizabeth sank down on the loveseat, then took Duncan's hand, forcing him to sit beside her. The concern on the woman's face was as alarming as Duncan's demeanor.

"What's going on?" Jude asked.

"I got a call from the treatment center yesterday letting me know that Julian wanted to speak to me."

"Is he okay?" Kiara asked before she could stop herself.

Duncan looked at her for a long moment, which only served to ramp up her anxiety. "He's... okay."

That was hardly reassuring, but Kiara had learned enough about Duncan to know he would say what he wanted to say in his own time and in his own way.

Biting her lip, Kiara tried to keep from pressing for more information.

"Why did he want to speak to you?" Angie asked, clearly not having the same reservations. "And why do you need to speak to us?"

"I actually need to speak to you," Duncan said, keeping his gaze on Angie. "I wanted you to have Kiara and Jude here for support. And also, this impacts Kiara since she's married to Julian now."

"Okay," Angela said. "So why do you need to speak to me?"

"Julian has been working with a therapist to get to the root of his drinking," Duncan began. He looked down at his hands, which were clasped around one of Elizabeth's. "He wanted me to come to the center so that he could tell me what has been causing him to drink so excessively."

"And it has to do with me?" Angie asked.

Duncan looked up and nodded. "He told me that the day before you and Annalisa were kidnapped, he heard Sandra and Jim talking about taking you two. When Sandra realized he'd heard their plans, she promised to give him... to give him candy and a toy if he didn't tell anyone. So he didn't."

Angie's hand tightened on Kiara's. "He knew what was going to happen?"

"I'm not sure he knew the details, but he knew enough that he should have told someone."

Jude put his arm around Angie, and she shifted closer to him.

Kiara wasn't sure how she felt about the revelation. Selfishly, she was glad it hadn't worked out any other way, because if Angie hadn't ended up with Sandra and Jim, they never would have met. And Kiara couldn't imagine her life without Angie.

It would also have meant she wouldn't have ended up pregnant, and she didn't want to think about not ever knowing the baby she carried.

But for Angie's sake, Kiara knew that it would have been for the best if she'd never been kidnapped. She would have had a much better life, and she would have met Jude sooner.

A heavy silence filled the room as Kiara's thoughts turned to Julian. This revelation explained so much, and she wished she could see him and talk to him about the situation.

Feeling Angie move beside her, Kiara looked over to see her leaning against Jude's chest. They were all waiting for her reaction.

"I want to see Julian," she finally said, her words soft.

"What?" Duncan's face creased with a frown.

"I would like to see Julian and speak with him."

"I don't know if that's a good idea."

"It's what I want," she said. "It's what I need to do."

Duncan stared at Angie, then sighed. "When do you want to go?"

"As soon as possible."

"Jude?" Duncan turned his attention to his head of security.

"I'm ready to go whenever she is."

If Duncan had hoped that Jude would protest, that wasn't going to happen. It was proof that Jude would defer to what Angela wanted, especially when it concerned her specifically.

"Fine." Duncan slapped his thighs and got to his feet. "I'll have them prepare the helicopter."

"I want Kiara to come with us, too," Angie said.

Duncan glanced at her. "Do you wish to go with us?"

"Yes," Kiara said without hesitation. She and Julian might not have a genuine marriage, but this affected the father of her child. She wanted to see him and see for herself that he was okay.

"Be ready to go within the hour," Duncan said. "We'll stay one night at a hotel near the rehab center. I'll have my assistant make the arrangements."

When Angie got to her feet, Kiara and Jude also stood. The three of them left the office together.

"Are you really okay going with us?" Angie asked as they walked down the hallway to the stairs.

"I am. I'll just have to take some throw-up bags with me."

"I'll make sure you have them," Jude said. "I'll see you back here in forty-five minutes, okay?"

Nodding, they hurried up the stairs to their rooms. Kiara grabbed a small, quilted bag she'd bought online on a whim when she'd seen it on her social media and began to pack.

Her clothes didn't fit very well anymore, but she still hadn't purchased any maternity items. That should probably be something she did soon.

She already wore a pair of thick leggings, but she swapped out her sweatshirt for an oversized sweater. She put a pair of pants that had a bit more stretch to them into her bag, along with a blouse that was loose fitting.

Next came her toiletries, though she took a few minutes to apply a bit of makeup before adding them to her bag. She put her pills and her ginger candies in her purse so she'd have easy access to them.

After she'd put everything in the bag, she took a moment just to make sure she hadn't forgotten anything. At the last minute, she went to her desk and picked up a couple of pieces of the stationery and slid them into a folder to keep them from getting crumpled.

If she had the time, she might write Jude a letter while on the plane, just in case she didn't get to see him or he didn't want to see her.

With everything packed, Kiara still had a few minutes before she had to meet Angie and Jude. She sank down onto the edge of her bed and took a deep breath.

Her thoughts went to Julian again, and she wondered how he was doing. Duncan had seemed upset—even angry—over what Julian had told him, which Kiara could understand. But if he'd reacted in anger to what Julian had revealed, it was possible that Julian was struggling.

Would Julian want to see her? Would he accept her support?

Only time would tell, but Kiara felt strongly that she should be there. And if he rejected her presence, she wouldn't take it personally. Or at least she'd try not to. After all, the situation didn't really involve her. She was going because Angie wanted her there.

Her phone chimed with a text message from Angie. *Ready when you are.*

Kiara slowly pushed herself up from the bed, her hand instinctively moving to steady herself, but thankfully, there was no dizziness this time.

She grabbed her bag and purse, then made her way downstairs to where Angie and Jude waited near the back entrance. Angie's face was pale, but her expression was determined, while Jude stood close beside her, his protective stance more pronounced than usual.

"You sure you're up for this?" Angie asked, studying Kiara's face with concern.

"I'm fine," Kiara assured her, though her stomach was starting to churn with a combination of nausea and nerves. "How are you holding up?"

Angie's smile was shaky. "I'm doing okay, actually. Though I'm not thrilled at the idea of riding in the helicopter or the plane again."

That was the least of Kiara's concerns. She actually really enjoyed flying, though it might be an interesting mix now considering her pregnancy.

When Duncan and Elizabeth showed up with their bags, they all left the house to climb into the waiting SUV. The three of them climbed into the rear row, while Duncan and Elizabeth were in the middle. Two members of the security team were in the front.

It was a short drive to the helipad, where a couple more security team members waited.

"We're going to be a full flight today," Jude commented as they walked to the waiting helicopter.

It took a few minutes to get all the bags loaded and for them to board. Kiara ended up in the row with three seats alongside Angie and Jude. Duncan and Elizabeth were seated facing them in the two-seat section. The security personnel were in the section closest to the pilot.

They all put their headsets on as the doors were closed, and the blades began to spin. Kiara opened her purse and took out a ginger candy and popped it into her mouth, then turned her attention to the window.

She loved to fly, and as the helicopter lifted off the helipad, she watched the trees and the big house gradually grow smaller.

"Does Julian know we're coming?"

Kiara was startled at the sound of Angie's voice in her ears. She always forgot that they could hold conversations when they had the headsets on.

"I called the center and let them know we were coming," Duncan said.

That meant that Julian might not know that they were on their way. Kiara wasn't sure that was a good thing. Hopefully, someone—preferably his therapist—would let him know and help him prepare. Especially if things had already gone badly with Duncan.

Within twenty minutes, they were landing at the airport in Coeur d'Alene. It didn't take too long to transfer to the airplane waiting for them. Kiara chose to sit in one of the single seats.

"We have sandwiches prepared for you," the flight attendant said as they were getting settled. She told them what was available, then took their orders for the sandwiches and drinks. "Once we are in the air, I'll bring your selections."

Kiara glanced over to see that Angie had a firm grip on Jude's hand, and her expression was tense. It said a lot about her determination to speak to Julian that she was willing to fly to do so, when it was something she really hated to do.

Once again, she stared out the window when they were finally moving down the runway. She loved the way her stomach swooped as the plane broke free from gravity and began its ascent. Strangely enough, the feeling didn't bring on the need to throw up.

Watching out the window, she could see that the snow was gone, and though there was still a sparseness to the landscape, leaves were beginning to reappear on the shade trees. Soon, spring would be in full bloom, and Kiara was looking forward to it.

Once the plane leveled off, the attendant brought their food and drinks. When the flight attendant had said sandwiches, Kiara had figured they'd be simple like the ones she always made.

But no. These were made on specialty bread with fresh ingredients and actual slices of turkey. Not the deli meat she'd been expecting.

There were sides of potato chips and raw veggies with a small cup of dip. It was perfect for her.

Once she'd eaten, Kiara pulled the paper out of the folder she'd retrieved from her bag before they'd stored it on the plane.

Staring out the window, she watched the clouds stream by as she mulled over what to write to Julian. She didn't know whether she should broach what he'd revealed to Duncan or just stick to what they'd been discussing in their letters already.

In the end, she decided to respond to what he'd written in his last letter, and maybe add a bit at the end about his recent confession.

Following his light-hearted approach to names earlier, she decided to respond in kind.

I didn't watch a lot of television as a kid, so I have no inspiration for baby names from that direction. However, I read a lot of books. So, I'd like to put forth Charles (as in Ingalls), Aslan (from Narnia), or Gilbert (Anne of Green Gables).

She had no idea if he'd read any of those books, but it was really all she had to offer. When it came right down to it, though, she didn't have a strong preference for a name.

She did, however, have a few names she would vehemently oppose. Jim or James. Craig. Andy or Andrew, which had been her biological dad's name.

After writing a bit more about that, she paused and stared out the window again. She tried to figure out the best way to broach the subject of what he'd revealed to Duncan.

"Ladies and gentlemen, we will be preparing for descent soon."

Kiara shifted her attention to listen to the instructions. Since she wouldn't be able to write much more, she just finished the letter off with *I hope to see you in a little while.*

She signed it, then folded the papers and put them in the envelope and addressed it. After putting it into her purse, she slid the purse under her seat.

The two-hour flight had gone by quickly, and soon they descended. She took in the view as they broke free from the clouds, eager to see yet another part of the country.

As soon as they landed at the airport, they loaded into the waiting SUV and drove to the hotel where Duncan's assistant had made reservations for them. She, Jude, and Angie were in a suite. While she and Angie shared a room, Jude had the room on the other side of the suite.

"Are we going to the center right away?" Kiara asked as she set her bag on one of the queen-size beds in the room.

"I think so," Angie said. "Duncan seemed eager to get the purpose of this trip over with."

Kiara sat down on one of the chairs in the room. "What are you going to say to Julian?"

Angie sank down on the end of her bed and sighed. "I'm not sure. I think I'll know when I see him."

There was a knock on the door of their room, and Kiara looked over to see Jude standing in the open doorway.

"Duncan wants to leave in thirty minutes," Jude said. "Can you be ready?"

"Yes." Angie got up and went to her fiancé. Jude gathered her into his arms and held her close.

Not wanting to intrude, Kiara grabbed her bag and went into the attached bathroom. She switched out of her leggings and sweater into the slightly more formal pants and blouse.

The blouse was loose, but when she turned in profile to the mirror and stretched it taut over her abdomen, she could see her growing bump. She hadn't felt any movement yet, but the doctor said it could happen at any time now.

Releasing her blouse, Kiara used her comb to smooth her hair, then pulled it up into a ponytail.

There were butterflies in her stomach at the thought of seeing Julian. The letters they'd shared back and forth had forged a deeper connection than what they'd previously had. That wasn't saying much, perhaps, since prior to her getting pregnant, they hadn't really been all that close.

Even so, it felt like she knew Julian better than she had before. It was a connection she hadn't thought they'd be able to develop. But at least on her end, they had.

Leaving the bathroom, she didn't see Jude and Angie in the bedroom, so she went out into the main part of the suite. Angie was on the couch, while Jude stood near the window, on his phone.

When he ended the call, he turned to them. "Ready to go?"

Was she? Kiara wasn't sure, but she followed them out of the room without hesitation.

CHAPTER ELEVEN

Julian lay flat on his back on his bed, his arm thrown over his eyes. After making an appearance for lunch, to stave off any worried reactions from the staff, he'd retreated to his room once again.

Dr. Carlisle had given him some slack and hadn't forced him to attend the group sessions since his father's visit. The tradeoff was that he had had additional one-on-one appointments with the therapist.

He was fighting a huge battle against the desire to drink, and had he had access to some alcohol, it was a battle he would have lost. He'd wondered more than once what the staff would do if he called for a ride and left the center to go to the nearest bar.

Elijah had tried to get him to talk, but Julian had shut him down.

After the confrontation with his dad, he'd had to get a tight hold on the storm of emotions inside him. However, he knew that if he loosened that grip even a little, things would spin out of control, and he would abandon all the progress he'd made so far.

The worst part of what was happening was that he couldn't blame Duncan for his reaction. It was what he deserved. If he hadn't thought he'd deserved that sort of reaction, he wouldn't have been driven to drink, and he would have revealed the truth much sooner.

But where did he go now?

Duncan likely wouldn't want him back on the estate, especially if he took his job from him. Would Kiara be willing to move? Or would he never get a chance to see his son?

Suddenly, it seemed like he had a lot more to lose than he ever had before.

A knock on the door startled him. Moving his arm, Julian lifted his head to stare at the door. He didn't want to answer it, but he had a feeling that if he ignored the knock, whoever it was would assume something was wrong and enter, anyway.

Shifting to sit up, he swung his legs over the edge of the bed. "Come in."

He ran his hands through his hair as the door swung inward to reveal Dr. Carlisle. The man stepped into the room and shut the door behind him, a worried expression on his face.

"What's up, doc?" He couldn't help himself, even though joking or laughing was the last thing he felt like doing right then.

Apparently, it was the last thing the doctor felt like doing too because he didn't even crack a smile.

"Your father has returned," Dr. Carlisle said.

Julian lifted his brows. "Duncan's here?"

"Yes, he's back, and he's brought your sister with him."

"Angela?"

Dr. Carlisle nodded. "She wants to speak with you."

Julian felt cold wash over him. He was barely handling his father's rejection. He wasn't sure how he'd be able to deal with whatever Angela had to say to him.

In some ways, he was surprised that it was Angela who had come. She hadn't shown herself to be confrontational. Annie was more likely to confront him on his behavior, so it would have made sense if she'd returned with Duncan.

"Can I refuse to see them?" Julian asked, leaning forward to rest his head in his hands.

"You could... but I think you need to talk to your sister to know exactly where you stand with the person who was most impacted by your actions."

"Oh, I know where I stand with her," Julian muttered. "We didn't get very close after she returned, so it's no skin off her nose if she rejects me in her life."

"Let's not make assumptions."

Julian sighed and got to his feet. "Okay. Let's get this over with."

The doctor ran his gaze over Julian but made no comment on his appearance. It was just as well because Julian didn't have the energy, nor the inclination, to change into something more appropriate to meet his father and Angela.

He was wearing his favorite pair of worn jeans and a long-sleeved white T-shirt. It would have to do.

Slipping his feet into his Doc Martens, he left the room with the doctor.

"Are we meeting in your office?"

"Yes, I'll instruct Marcus to have them join us once we're there."

Julian assumed Jude was with them, and probably another bodyguard or two. He hoped it would just be Duncan and Angela for this meeting because he didn't need even more people to witness what was to come.

When they reached his office, Dr. Carlisle said, "Did you want to talk at all before I have Marcus bring them here?"

Julian shook his head. He just wanted to get it over with so he could return to his room.

The doctor hesitated for a moment, then picked up his phone and instructed Marcus to bring Duncan and Angela to his office. He didn't hang up right away, listening to something Marcus said.

"Just the two of them," he told him.

Julian was relieved to hear that. Though he supposed that Jude would want to be there for Angela as her fiancé, not necessarily as her bodyguard, he still didn't want him there.

When there was a knock on the door, Julian got up from the chair he'd been sitting in and moved to stand beside the desk, shoving his hands into his pockets so no one could see how they trembled.

Bracing himself for what was to come, Julian tried to school his expression to not show even an iota of what he was feeling inside.

Once this was over, he'd return to his room and the solace it offered.

His gut tightened as the office door opened, and Angela walked in, followed by Duncan.

Angela's gaze swept the room, and when it landed on him, she came to a stop. Julian wanted to avoid her gaze, to look anywhere but at her. However, he met her gaze head-on.

When she finally moved, there was no hesitation as her strides brought her to him. She lifted her hands, and he braced himself for a slap. Instead, she reached out and cupped his cheeks.

"Oh, Julian," she said gently. "It's okay. I understand."

Was this a dream? Was this his hope that things would be okay manifesting itself in a dream?

Wrapping her arms around him, she held him tight. Julian froze, then pulled his hands from his pockets and hugged her back.

A sob escaped him, shocked out of him by her actions. "I'm... sorry."

"I forgive you," she said. "I forgive you."

He could hardly believe the words, and he was afraid to let go of her in case it wasn't real.

Angela held him for several minutes, neither of them speaking. Julian felt the tension that had coiled in his shoulders and chest slowly begin to ease. The storm of emotions he'd been holding back threatened to break free, but for the first time in days, it didn't feel catastrophic.

When Angela finally stepped back, her eyes were bright with unshed tears, but her smile was genuine. "You were just a boy," she said softly. "So young. You made a mistake that any child might have made."

"You truly forgive me?" Julian asked.

"It's what God would want me to do," she said, her expression soft... loving. "But beyond that, I *want* to forgive you. You're my brother, and I love you."

She loved him? When was the last time someone had told him that they loved him? He couldn't even remember.

Julian's throat constricted. He'd imagined this conversation a thousand times over the years, but never like this. Never with forgiveness offered so freely.

"But if I had told someone—" he started.

"Maybe things would have been different," Angela interrupted gently. "Or maybe they wouldn't have. We'll never know, and that's okay. Plus, if things had worked out differently, I wouldn't have Kiara in my life, and I can't imagine that. I might not even have Jude."

"Or you might have had Jude sooner."

"But I'm the person I am now because of the life I've lived and the experiences I've had," she said. "If I hadn't had that, I might be a different person who wasn't drawn to Jude, or he might not have loved that version of me. Everything worked out as it should have. I believe that."

"Really?"

Angela nodded. "What I do know is that you've been carrying this guilt for twenty-four years, and that's twenty-four years too long." She reached out and took his hands in hers. "I want you to let it go, Julian. For your sake, and for your son's sake."

Julian felt something crack open inside his chest at her words. The weight he'd carried for so long—the crushing guilt that had driven him to drink himself into oblivion night after night—began to shift. Not disappearing entirely, but loosening its stranglehold on his heart.

"I don't know how," he whispered, his voice raw.

"One day at a time," Angela said, squeezing his hands. "The same way you're learning to live without alcohol."

Julian became aware that Duncan had moved closer during their exchange. When he looked at his father, he saw something different in the older man's expression. Something softer had replaced the cold fury from their last meeting.

"Son," Duncan said, his voice rough. "I owe you an apology. I should never have reacted the way I did. I was out of line. I'm sorry."

Julian wanted to accept his apology, but there was a part of him that wondered if Duncan would have had that response had Angela railed at him for what he'd done. Had he apologized because Angela had?

He couldn't dwell on that right then. The miracle of Angela's forgiveness was uppermost in his mind. She'd given him something more than just forgiveness, which in and of itself was amazing. She'd also touched his heart with her love.

He'd wrecked her life, and yet she'd still accepted him as her brother, offering forgiveness and love.

Reaching out, he pulled her close again, and she came willingly with a soft laugh.

"Thank you," he murmured against her hair. "Thank you for everything."

"You don't have to thank me," Angela said. "I want to help ease the burden of guilt that you carry. You can put it down now. You no longer need to feel its weight on your soul."

Julian closed his eyes, hoping it would be as easy as that.

When they stepped apart again, he smiled down at her. "I hear that congratulations are in order."

Angela's face lit up in response to that, and she held out her hand so that he could see the ring on her finger. "I'm over the moon."

Julian was happy for her. After all she'd been through in her life, she deserved to find love and happiness, even if it was with Jude.

Not that he wasn't a good man. In fact, he was probably a better man than Julian. It was just that they'd had some tense exchanges over the years.

"Do you think you might be able to come to the wedding?" she asked.

"It depends on when it is, and how things are going here."

"We haven't settled on the exact date yet, but probably within the next month," Angela said. "And I'd love to have you there with us. It's just going to be small. Family and a few friends."

Though Julian hadn't enjoyed attending weddings over the years—and sadly, that included his own—he found he wanted to be there for Angela's. Maybe it was something he could work towards.

"I'll see how it goes," Julian said, not wanting to make a promise, though he really did hope to be there.

"Did you want to see Kiara?"

"See her?" Julian asked. "Is she here?"

Angela nodded. "She's with Jude and the other security team members in the waiting area."

"Yes, I'd like to see her." He glanced over at Dr. Carlisle. "Would that be okay?"

The doctor hesitated, then gave a nod. "I think that would be fine."

"I can go get her," Angela offered.

"We'll have Marcus bring her," the doctor said. "And we'll give them a bit of privacy."

Angela gave Julian another hug. "I hope to see you again soon."

"Julian," his dad said, holding out his hand. "We'll talk again."

Though he took Duncan's hand and gave it a firm shake, Julian still had mixed feelings about the man. Even more mixed than he'd already had. He didn't know if that would ever not be the case.

Once they'd left the office, Julian pressed his palms against his jeans. He wasn't sure why he was nervous about seeing Kiara, but he was.

Would she be as understanding and forgiving as Angela had been? Though what he'd done hadn't impacted Kiara, it had impacted someone she loved very much. She might have a different outlook on things than Angela.

When the door swung open again, Kiara came into the room, and the man with her shut the door behind her, leaving just the two of them in the quiet of the office.

"Hey!" She gave him a smile as she walked toward him. The smile faded as she got closer. "You look terrible."

Julian lifted his brows at her and gave a huff of laughter. "Thanks."

"I didn't mean anything bad by it," she said, lifting her hand to cup his cheek briefly. "Just that you look really tired."

"I am," he admitted. "Between getting sober and now all of this, I haven't been sleeping well."

"How did things go with Angie?"

"She didn't tell you?"

"I figured she wanted to come here to tell you she forgave you."

"Yes, she did. Does that surprise you?"

"Not at all," Kiara said. "That's the sort of person Angie is."

Julian put his hands into his pockets. "How do you feel about what I did?"

"I'm not angry with you," Kiara said as she crossed her arms loosely. "It's not really my place to forgive you. Plus, I'm kind of selfish in this situation."

"What do you mean?"

Kiara lowered her gaze to the floor. "If you hadn't done what you did, Angie never would have come into my life." She looked back up at him. "And I needed her in order to survive the way my life was growing up. In a harsh and unloving world, she brought a gentleness and love that I desperately needed."

"And you protected her in exchange," Julian observed.

Kiara nodded. "Yes. She gave me something I needed, so the least I could do was give her what she needed. And I'll always give her that. I love her, and I'm grateful that she's in my life."

"She's stronger than I thought she was," Julian observed, as he gestured to the chairs by Dr. Carlisle's desk.

After they were seated, Kiara said, "I would say a lot of that strength has come from her becoming a Christian."

"Really?"

Kiara nodded. "She gained some sort of confidence after she made that decision. Not that she takes on everything without fear or apprehension. It was just that she somehow finds the strength somewhere to tackle those difficult situations head-on."

"I'm grateful she offered forgiveness when she didn't have to."

"I think the only people she might struggle to forgive are Jim and maybe Sandra. But even then, she'd try."

Julian was fine talking about Angela. But given their limited time, he wanted to know how Kiara was doing. How the baby was doing.

"How are you feeling these days?" he asked.

Her hand went to her stomach. "I have good and bad moments, but the good are gradually becoming more than the bad."

"I'm glad to hear that. Have you felt him move yet?"

"No, not yet," she said. "Or at least not that I've recognized as movement. Given I'm dealing with nausea, I might be missing his early kicks."

"I'm sure there will come a time when you'll know for certain."

"Definitely." Grinning, she got to her feet and turned sideways. She smoothed her blouse against her stomach. "The growing belly is a pretty good indication that he's getting bigger."

Julian stared at the slight swelling of her stomach. Though she hadn't been thin prior to getting pregnant, it was still clear that the bump was from the pregnancy.

Leaning forward, he reached out but then stopped himself. They didn't have the type of marriage where he could touch her growing belly without permission.

But then Kiara moved closer to him, took his hand, and placed it on her belly. "You won't feel any movements, but feel how firm it is. It's kind of weird."

It was, but in a good way. In an amazing way. That was his son growing inside her. Julian might never have planned to have children. But now that he knew he was going to become a parent someday soon, he was glad, in a way, that the choice had been taken from him.

As he stared at his hand, splayed across Kiara's belly, Julian knew that he owed his son a sober father. Kiara would probably have their son most of the time, but Julian resolved to be a good dad and to be there as often as he could be. Maybe it was time to take Duncan up on the offer to build a place for himself on the estate.

There was a light knock on the door, then the doctor poked his head in. "You need to finish up soon, Julian."

Julian nodded as he moved his hand from Kiara's stomach. "Just give us a couple more minutes." As the door shut again, Julian got to his feet. "Thank you so much for coming. I really appreciate it."

Kiara smiled. "I'm glad I could be here. When Angie said she wanted me to come with her, I had no problem agreeing."

He was glad for everything that had transpired over the past hour. It helped him focus on what was important.

Together, they walked to the door and left the office. Dr Carlisle was waiting in the hallway. "We can go to the waiting area so you can say goodbye to your family."

When they reached the room, Julian saw his dad sitting with Elizabeth, while Jude had his arm around Angela where they sat. All of them stood up as he and Kiara walked into the room.

"Thank you again for coming," Julian said, addressing his comments mainly to Angela. "I really appreciate it."

Angela came over to Julian and gave him another hug. "I'm glad I could come. I'll be praying for you, and I hope to see you at the wedding."

"I'll try my best to be there." Julian gave her a light squeeze, then let her go.

Next, he took the hand Jude held out to him and gave it a firm shake.

"I'll be praying for you as well," Jude said, his expression serious.

"Thank you."

"Take care of yourself, son," Duncan said as he approached him with Elizabeth at his side. "I apologize again for my reaction yesterday. I understand it might take you time to forgive me, but I hope we can have a conversation again in the near future."

Julian took the hand he offered and nodded. He still had mixed feelings about his interaction with Duncan the previous day, but hopefully Dr. Carlisle would be able to help him work through it before they had that conversation.

As the others walked toward the exit, Julian turned to Kiara. When she moved closer to him with her arms open, he didn't hesitate to gather her close. He held her for a long moment, then released her.

"Here," she said as she stepped back. He looked down to see that she was holding out an envelope. "I wrote it not knowing if I'd see you, but you might as well read it."

"Thanks." Julian took it with a smile. "I'll write you back. I promise."

"I look forward to it."

As he watched them walk through the door, Julian felt a sense of... calm. The despair that had been filling him had receded, but it wasn't completely gone. He knew he still had a lot of work to do, but after the visit from Angela and Kiara, he felt like he had the motivation to do the hard work.

CHAPTER TWELVE

Once back at the estate, things kicked into high gear as Kiara pitched in to help Angie plan the wedding. Even though it was going to be a small one, Duncan had insisted that she get the best of everything.

Kiara found she was almost more excited about the planning than Angie was. Her sister just wanted to get married and didn't care about all the details. Same with Jude.

So Kiara phoned florists, photographers, caterers, bakers, while Elizabeth worked her connections to find someone who could make Angie's wedding dress in a month. It was amazing the doors an unlimited budget opened.

In amongst the appointments and phone calls, Kiara wrote letters to Julian in response to the ones he sent. He seemed to be doing much better, and it seemed likely that he'd be home for the wedding.

The most interesting thing to her in the letters was Julian's comments about the conversations he was having with his friend, Elijah. From what he said, Kiara felt like his interest in spiritual things had grown.

Because of what he'd shared, Kiara had started asking questions of her own, sometimes going to Angie with Julian's letter in hand to get her thoughts. And she'd actually ended up going to church with Angie and Jude.

She still wasn't sure how Christianity fit into her life, but Angie was a great encouragement, willing to answer any question she might have. And if she didn't have the answer, they'd gone to Jude.

On that day, they were having a final fitting of their dresses. The designers and their seamstresses had flown in for the event. In addition to Angie's gown, they had also made dresses for Kiara, Elizabeth, and Annie.

Duncan's assistant had found a short-term rental near the estate for the team, which was where they'd stayed each time they'd come to Serenity for the initial consultation and then subsequent fittings.

"Are you ready to go?" Angie asked as she came into Kiara's room.

"Yep." Kiara got up from her desk, where she'd been working on a letter for Julian.

"You're not going to have time to mail that letter," Angie said.

"What do you mean?" Kiara asked as she picked up her phone and purse.

"Didn't Duncan tell you?"

Kiara froze. "Tell me what?"

"Julian is coming home this week."

"Really?" Her stomach fluttered with nerves, and she wasn't even sure why. "That's great news."

"I thought you might like that."

"I'm happy for him because it means they must have decided he was in a good enough place in his sobriety to be able to leave the center."

"I think all alcohol has been taken out of the house, and we won't be having any at the wedding, so there won't be temptation for him here."

"I'm sure Julian will appreciate that."

They left the room and walked down the hallway to the staircase. "Also, Julian talked to Jude and Duncan about bringing his friend Elijah here."

Kiara wondered how the man's presence would impact things at the estate. She'd kind of hoped that she and Julian would be able to spend time together, but now with Elijah there, it seemed less likely.

It dawned on her then that perhaps she'd read a bit too much into the exchange of letters they'd had since he hadn't mentioned anything to her about Elijah coming home with him. The thought dampened her excitement about Julian returning to the estate, but it was probably the reminder she needed that what she and Julian had wasn't real.

When they reached the mudroom, Jude was waiting for them. He gave Angie a kiss.

"Anthony and Lucy will go with you today," he said. "Since you're insisting I can't even be in the vicinity when you're trying on your wedding dress."

"It's bad luck if you see me in it before the wedding."

Jude chuckled. "As if you believe in luck."

"I know." She gazed up at him with a smile. "I just want you to be surprised."

"You'll look beautiful no matter what you wear," he said.

She leaned into him, wrapping her arms around his waist. "I love you."

Kiara looked away, trying to ignore the ache that flared to life whenever she witnessed the deep love between Angie and Jude. She was happy for Angie, so happy, and that was what she was trying to focus on as the wedding drew closer.

She followed the pair out to the waiting SUV, where Anthony was behind the wheel with Lucy waiting by the open rear door. Elizabeth came out shortly after them, while Annie was going to drive herself with Dawn.

Once the three of them were seated inside the SUV, Lucy shut the door. It was a fairly quick drive from the estate to the rental.

The designer and her seamstresses were all set up with sewing machines and dress forms. They'd been flown to Idaho in Duncan's plane, so they had been able to bring everything they needed.

"Welcome." Alex of Alexandria Designs greeted them with a wide smile. "Are you ready to try on your dresses?"

They all nodded, and then they were sent off, one at a time, to change into their dresses. Annie went first, and even though she wasn't an official bridesmaid, she was still getting a new dress made.

While they worked with Annie, Kiara and Angie looked at the other dresses. It was amazing the work the design team had been able to do in such a short period of time.

Her dress was a soft lavender and had an empire waist to accommodate her growing belly. It was the perfect color for a late spring/early summer wedding.

Kiara tried not to compare everything to her own wedding, but it was hard not to. Her wedding had been rushed, and she hadn't even considered that she could have anything but an off-the-rack dress.

Maybe she'd known in her heart that this wasn't the wedding to spend much money on. It hadn't meant anything to Julian, so it hadn't meant anything to her. Or at least she'd told herself it shouldn't.

Soon, it was her turn, and the designer went into the room with her to help her into the dress.

"This looks so lovely on you," the woman said as she circled around Kiara, gently tugging at the material in spots. "How does it feel?"

"Like a dream," Kiara said, smoothing her hand over her stomach. "With plenty of room for the belly."

The woman chuckled softly. "You are glowing, and this color looks perfect on you."

She followed Alex out to the circular stand and stepped up on it with the woman's help. They'd been told to wear the underwear they planned to wear on the wedding day, as well as the shoes.

Kiara had chosen a lower heel, but it was still higher than she usually wore.

"You look amazing, Kiki," Angie said from where she sat on the couch. "So beautiful."

"I agree," Elizabeth said. "You look very lovely."

Alex and one of the seamstresses checked the length of the dress and how it fit around her bust and stomach. In the end, they decided it just needed to be hemmed a little.

Once her turn was done, Kiara sat down and waited as Elizabeth tried on her dress. The woman moved with an elegance and grace that Kiara could only dream of having one day.

As she sat there, she wondered when Julian was actually going to arrive. And was he just coming for the wedding? Was he going to head for New York once it was over?

Things were going to change, and the realization made Kiara nervous. The only things that would stay the same were the baby growing inside her and her desire to stay at the estate. Her home.

"We'll have all the alterations done in the next two days," Alex said after they'd all tried on their dresses.

When they got back to the house, Kiara sat down with Angie and Annie to go over all the plans and make sure they hadn't missed anything. With the wedding on Saturday, there wasn't much time left.

They joined Duncan and Elizabeth for lunch, which was when Kiara got the information she'd been wanting.

"So it appears Julian and Elijah will be arriving on Thursday," Duncan said. "I'll be sending the plane for them."

"Isn't it weird that Julian is bringing a stranger here?" Annie asked. "You don't usually let someone we don't know come here to the estate."

"This was a request from Julian," Duncan said. "And I had Jude do a background check on Elijah. He seems like a genuine guy."

"I've actually met his mother," Elizabeth said. "We've served on a charity board together in the past. She was a lovely woman."

"Though his father has made significant money through his... church, Elijah's mother has her own wealth," Duncan said. "I get the feeling that her husband wouldn't be where he is today without her. Thankfully, it appears Elijah is closer to his mother than his father."

"His father is definitely... questionable in his beliefs," Annie said. "So hopefully Elijah holds different ones."

"I don't know anything about him," Angie said.

"I'll tell you about him later," Annie offered. "It's a bit of a crazy situation with delusions, power, and, I believe, brainwashing."

Kiara's brows rose at that, wondering how much Julian knew about Elijah's father. Not that she was going to hold who his father was against Elijah. She knew better than most that who a person was didn't always reflect who their parents were.

"Kiara, you should be able to move into your house within the next month," Duncan said, shifting the conversation in the way he usually did when he wanted to change the subject. "You and Julian need to discuss how you want to work out your living arrangements."

"Our living arrangements?" Kiara asked.

"Well, your house was designed with two master suites because Angie was initially going to live there with you. Now that she's going to be moving in with Jude, there would be room for Julian."

Kiara had always assumed that Julian would split his time between New York and the estate, and that when he was at the estate, he'd stay in the main house.

Would he even want to stay with her?

She had actually tried not to think too much about the fact that when she moved into the house, she would be living alone for the first time in her life. It wasn't something she was eager to experience.

"I'll talk to him," Kiara said. "And we'll figure it out."

"Good. I know he'll still have to travel for work, but I'd rather this be his home base than New York. At least in these early days of his being sober."

Kiara nodded. She understood what Duncan meant, but at the same time, Julian was the one who would have to face the temptation of alcohol. Eventually, he'd have to do it alone, when no one else would be around to see him make the choice to indulge or stay sober.

"I hope the baby will keep him coming back," Elizabeth said. "A boy needs his father around, as well as his mother."

"Have you decided on a name yet?" Duncan asked.

Kiara shook her head. "Not yet. We have a few options, but we haven't settled on anything yet. Julian's initial suggestions were Tom and Jerry. Or maybe Fred or Barney."

Elizabeth laughed, while Duncan frowned at her. "I'm afraid I don't like any of those names."

"Not to worry," Kiara said with a grin. "I don't either. We've moved on."

"They are cartoon characters, darling," Elizabeth said as she rested her hand on Duncan's arm. "He was joking, I believe."

"He was," Kiara agreed.

"Oh. Well, I'm quite relieved to hear that," Duncan said. "I realize I don't have a say, but I might have argued a bit about those suggestions."

The conversation veered into name choices as Elizabeth told them why they'd chosen Benjamin, and Duncan shared what he remembered of the decisions he'd made with Jill for the twins and Julian.

Kiara had no idea where her name had come from. She assumed that some thought had gone into it since her middle name was Noelle, and she was born in December.

Looking down at her bump, Kiara ran a hand over it, wondering how her mom had felt when she'd been pregnant with her. Had she been excited? Had her dad looked forward to feeling her move in her mom's belly?

Given how they'd treated her, and how easily they'd given her up to Jim and Sandra, she doubted that they had cared about her in or out of the womb.

"Kiara?"

She looked up to find concerned gazes on her.

"Are you okay?" Angie asked, reaching out to cover Kiara's hand where it rested on her belly.

"I'm fine," she assured her. "Sometimes I just get lost in wondering what life might be like with this little one."

Angie smiled. "Well, I can tell you one thing that's in your son's future, and that is love. Lots and lots of love."

That made Kiara smile. "Yes. Lots of love."

Kiara knew that she had Angie to thank for knowing what love was. Until she'd met Angie, there had been no love in her life. And if it hadn't been for Angie, there wouldn't have been any even after Kiara had been taken from her family by Jim and Sandra.

Once the meal was over, Kiara decided to take a walk. She needed some fresh air and some time to gather her thoughts about the days ahead. Though she was usually glad for Angie's company on some of her walks, Kiara was glad that on that day, her sister had other things demanding her attention.

The day was warm, and the sun was shining brightly. They were officially well past the snowy days of winter and even the cool ones of early spring. She no longer needed to wear a jacket when she went for her walks.

As usual, she came to a stop near the house. It had an interesting design with two wings, joined by a combined living space with Angie's dream kitchen. It would have been perfect for them.

She'd assumed that Angie's suite would sit empty. But now, it sounded like Duncan wanted Julian to take over those rooms.

Did she want to share space with him like that?

She and Angie had been excited about once again having a place of their own. Of being able to cook meals together. Of being able to do their own chores.

If someone even a year ago had said that she'd look forward to doing her own laundry, cleaning the house, or cooking her own meals, she would have told them they were crazy.

But did she want to do those things in a space that Julian also occupied?

She'd been trying not to think of Julian as *husband.* He was *father of her baby* or *Angie's brother.* Never her *husband.*

She certainly didn't think of herself as his wife, and she really doubted that Julian viewed her as such. Their marriage was a means to an end, nothing more.

Tipping her head back, Kiara stared up at the clear blue expanse of sky. She rested her hands on her stomach as she drank in the beauty.

It was the same sky she'd looked up at in Briar Hollow, wondering about the world beyond the small town. Now she had experienced it, and it was more than she had ever imagined it would be.

"Mrs. Burke?"

Lowering her head, Kiara saw the foreman standing a few feet away from her. She gave him a smile as she greeted him.

"Would you like to come inside?" he asked. "We've gotten quite a bit more done since the last time you checked it out."

"Sure." Falling into step beside him, Kiara walked across the bare earth that she'd been assured would one day be covered with a beautiful landscape.

When she stepped into the house this time, she viewed it in a different light. Instead of imagining her and Angie living there, she tried to see herself living there with Julian. And one day, their son.

It still amazed her how quickly the work on the house had progressed. Duncan had certainly lit a fire under them, fueled, no doubt, by copious amounts of money.

For the first time, it was more than just bare bones. There were painted walls, the stone fireplace, and cabinets and counters had been installed in the kitchen. All things chosen by her and Angie. It was looking more and more like a home.

"We'll be done with the painting and flooring by the end of the week. The decorators will be in after that."

"You guys have worked so hard on this," Kiara said. "It's amazing."

"Having our budget expanded made it possible to hire more workers and to work longer hours."

"Well, thank you for all your hard work."

After she'd finished speaking to the man, Kiara left and finished her walk. She had a couple of days to prepare for Julian's arrival, and then it was the wedding.

Once the weekend was over, life would be different. Again. Only this time, she and Angie would be moving in different directions. Not completely apart, but definitely separate for the first time in their lives as sisters.

For a moment, her pregnancy hormones grabbed hold of her emotions, and tears sprang to her eyes.

She brushed them aside as they fell, but rather than try to stop her tears, she allowed them to flow as she walked. Maybe she needed this time of sadness. Then, once it was over, she would put it behind her and focus forward, instead of continuing to grieve the loss of the way things had been for her and Angie for so long.

When her emotions were under control once again, Kiara returned to the house.

On Thursday, as they once again sat around the lunch table, Duncan announced that the plane was on its way to pick up Julian and Elijah. Kiara tried to ignore the flutter in her stomach at the news.

It had been a few weeks since she'd last seen Julian, and even though they'd continued to write letters, she didn't feel like she was prepared for the reality of him being around more.

"Guess we'll have a full table for dinner tonight," Angie said.

"I wish Cole could make it," Annie said with a sigh. "But since they have a game this weekend, he couldn't get away."

"Are you planning to go to any of the playoff games?" Duncan asked. "Since we already know they're going to be playing."

"Yes. I do hope to make it to a few of them. I'll take Benji with me." She narrowed her gaze at her dad. "And yes, I'll pick the games that don't interfere with school."

"Thank you," Duncan said. "I will be leaving next week for New York."

"For just a visit?" Annie asked.

Duncan shook his head. "I need to stay there for an extended period of time. It's been okay to work from here for the past few months, but there are some major meetings coming up that I need to attend in person."

"I'm going with him," Elizabeth said. "But if you need me here for anything, you just have to let me know."

"Will Julian be returning to New York as well?" Angie asked, giving voice to the question that Kiara had but was uncertain about asking.

"He will have to join us for a week or two," Duncan said. "And he might want to fly to Singapore to check on the projects there since he's been out of touch for awhile. There are also other projects in Europe he needs to follow up on, so he might be traveling for a bit."

Kiara listened as they discussed Julian's schedule as if he didn't have a wife or a baby on the way. It was a stark reminder—one she needed—that things really weren't any different than they'd been before the wedding.

The vows she'd said and the piece of paper she'd signed were insignificant in the grand scheme of things. She couldn't help but wonder if Julian had the same view of their marriage.

The letters they'd exchanged had drawn them closer as friends but hadn't changed the parameters of their marriage.

She needed to remember that.

CHAPTER THIRTEEN

Elijah reached out and cupped Julian's shoulder. "Ready to go home?"

His voice came through the headset Julian wore as they prepared for takeoff in the helicopter for the final stretch of the trip to the estate.

"I have mixed feelings," Julian admitted.

He could have just agreed that he was ready to go home and left it at that, but he and Elijah had forged a friendship over the weeks they'd been together in the treatment center. And they'd pledged to always be honest as they held each other accountable.

Honesty was an odd concept for Julian. Not that he'd been dishonest in his dealings with people, but he'd spent most of his life hiding how he truly felt. How he was dealing with things. He'd never known someone he could be open with, while also being confident that they wouldn't betray him.

"I don't have a lot of happy memories at the estate," he said. "I spent a lot of my time there drunk."

"Well, maybe it's time to make some new—happy—memories there."

Julian hoped that was possible, but there were a lot of bad memories to overcome.

"How do you plan to deal with Kiara?"

Julian glanced over at him as the helicopter lifted off the ground. "What do you mean?"

"You're married," Elijah stated, as if Julian could forget that. "Do you plan to try to build a relationship with her?"

Julian frowned. That hadn't been his plan. His and Kiara's marriage was the one thing they hadn't discussed at length, but he thought he'd been pretty clear on where they stood with regards to their marriage.

"I plan to build a friendship with her," he said. "That's why I've been writing to her. I know that it's best for our son if he has two parents who get along while they co-parent."

Elijah didn't push the topic, but his question had put the thought in Julian's mind that people might have some expectations about him and Kiara now that they were both going to be at the estate. It could make things really awkward if people started hinting that they needed to make something more of their marriage than they'd intended.

He didn't think Kiara had those expectations as their letters have never held a hint of wanting things to be different than they were. He felt like she understood that he was trying to help them establish a foundation on which to build their parenting relationship.

"This is a really beautiful part of the country," Elijah said as he looked out the window next to him.

"Yes, and the estate has some beautiful views of the mountains."

"While Texas has some mountains, we don't live near them."

"Have you ever skied?" Julian asked.

"Nope."

"Well, come winter, we'll have to go skiing."

"I think I'd rather water ski than ski down a mountain."

"We can do that too," Julian said. "We have a boat that we can take to a nearby lake to go skiing."

"Do you plan to stick around here for awhile?"

"For a bit," he said. "But I want to go to Singapore soon. Do you want to come with me?"

"I'm not sure what I'd do."

"You could be one of my bodyguards."

Elijah chuckled. "Just because I look like I could beat someone up, I'm not sure I actually could."

"Jude could teach you." Julian hesitated, then said, "Actually, I wouldn't mind having you along as an accountability partner. Especially when I first start going into environments where I previously used to drink a lot."

"I don't have a problem traveling with you," Elijah said. "But at some point, I have to figure out what I'm going to do with my life, separate and apart from my dad. I don't have any real skills beyond my ability to write songs, sing, and play a few musical instruments. I don't *have* to work thanks to an inheritance from my grandparents, but I want to do something productive in my life. Something honoring to God."

Focusing on work was about the only thing that had kept Julian from going completely off the rails. He understood why Elijah would want something like that to focus on.

For the next week at least, they'd be at the estate. Julian really wanted to go to Singapore, and he did want Elijah to travel with him. Anthony would, of course, go with him as his bodyguard, but Julian kind of looked at Elijah as a guard for his sobriety. Just as he was capable of protecting himself if he had to, he was also capable of remaining sober by himself. However, both would be easier with nearby help.

Tipping his head toward the window, Julian stared out at the familiar landscape. It was a short trip from Coeur d'Alene to the estate, and all too soon, the estate came into view.

Was he ready for this?

It didn't really matter whether he was or not. It was happening. Thankfully, with Angela's wedding that weekend, he wouldn't be the sole focus of people's attention.

The helicopter slowly lowered, then settled on the helipad. They removed the headsets and unbuckled their harnesses.

When the door swung open, Julian spotted Anthony waiting for them with an SUV. Elijah followed him off the helicopter, then they walked to where Anthony stood.

"Good to see you again, Anthony," Julian said as he held out his hand to the man.

Anthony greeted him with a smile as he took his hand, then he reached out to clap Julian on his shoulder. "It's good to have you back. You look good."

"This is Elijah," Julian said, gesturing to him. As the men shook hands, he added, "This is Anthony, the man responsible for keeping me safe and mostly out of trouble."

While a couple of guys were taking care of their luggage, they climbed into the SUV and headed for the house.

When they reached it, his dad and Elizabeth were waiting there to greet them. Julian tried to ignore the knot in his stomach as he greeted them, then introduced them to Elijah.

"It's lovely to have you here," Elizabeth said with the graciousness she always showed. "And Julian, welcome home."

She approached him and took his upper arms in her hands as she smiled up at him, then offered her cheek for his kiss. They'd never been super close, but she had always been kind to him.

"The girls have gone to pick up the dresses for Saturday," Elizabeth said. "But they should be back soon. In the meantime, let me show you to your room, Elijah."

Before they could move, Duncan said, "Julian, you might need to contact your mother sooner rather than later. She's been hounding me about you for the last few days."

Julian winced. "I'll give her a call later."

He had no idea what she would say to him, but he suspected it would be something along the lines of him not having a drinking problem. Prior to going to the treatment center, he would have appreciated hearing that. But now, having addressed his drinking, he knew he certainly had had a problem with alcohol.

Elizabeth led them upstairs to the wing opposite Kiara and Angela's rooms. Julian always stayed in the same room, and Benji's was just down the hall.

"Here you go," Elizabeth said, stepping through the open doorway opposite Julian's. "If you need anything, you just let us know."

"Thank you," Elijah said. "This is very nice. I'm sure it will be fine."

"Wonderful." Elizabeth gave him a smile. "I'll leave it to Julian to give you a tour, but I hope you'll make yourself at home. You're very welcome here."

After she'd left them, Elijah turned to Julian. "She seems very nice."

"She is," Julian agreed. "She was our nanny after my parents divorced following the kidnapping, but she's always been closer to Annie than to me. My mom was still very active in my life, so Elizabeth never took on the role of mother for me the way she did for Annie."

"She reminds me of my mom," Elijah said. "I've always wondered how she ended up with my dad. At least your dad seems to be a decent enough guy, unlike mine."

"He is."

Though Julian still had mixed feelings about his father, if Duncan was one thing, it was respectable. He might be a hard nose in the business world, but he was fair.

"Speaking of parents, I need to call my mom and let her know we've arrived safe and sound."

"I'm sure Elizabeth and Duncan would be fine with her visiting you here, if you'd rather have her come here instead of you going to where she is."

Elijah stared at the phone in his hand. "I might do that. I'll see how eager she is to see me."

They were interrupted by the arrival of one of the security team with their bags and Elijah's guitar case. He'd had the instrument at the treatment center, but Julian hadn't heard him play it yet.

"When you're done talking to your mom, do you want a tour?" Julian asked. "We should have time before dinner."

"Sure. This shouldn't take me too long."

Julian had barely finished unpacking his bag when Elijah reappeared.

"Ready to go?" Julian asked.

At his nod, they left Julian's room and headed down the hallway.

As they walked, Elijah said, "Were you surprised that Kiara wasn't here to greet you?"

"A little," Julian admitted, trying to stick with his desire to be open and honest with Elijah. "But I understand that they are in the midst of wedding prep, and Kiara is matron of honor, so it makes sense that she has things to do with Angela."

Before heading down the stairs, Julian pointed out the other wing as well as the rarely used sitting area on the landing between the two wings.

He'd never brought someone to the estate before, and he was kind of surprised that Duncan had agreed when he'd asked if Elijah could come back with him. It probably helped that Elijah was wealthy in his own right—though not as wealthy as the Burkes—and wasn't after their money.

As they descended the grand staircase, Julian couldn't help scanning the entry hall for any sign of Kiara. The space remained empty except for one of the housekeepers dusting a side table.

"This place is even more impressive inside," Elijah commented, his voice echoing slightly in the high-ceilinged foyer.

Julian nodded. "I'm not sure why Duncan wanted such a large house with so many bedrooms. This is the closest we've been to filling them all, and even then, there's still two or three that are empty."

He showed Elijah the main living areas—the formal living room with a wall of windows overlooking the mountains, the dining room with its massive table that could seat twenty, and the less formal family room where they gathered sometimes.

"And this is my dad's office," Julian said, gesturing to the closed double doors. "And his and Elizabeth's suite is further down there."

He led him toward the kitchen, planning to take him to the rec center, but he heard voices in the mudroom.

Julian felt his pulse quicken as he led Elijah toward the voices. He hesitated for a moment, suddenly uncertain if he was ready to see Kiara face to face again after weeks of letters and just that one brief meeting at the treatment center.

"Everything okay?" Elijah asked quietly from beside him.

Julian nodded, took a breath, and stepped into the mudroom. Angela was there with Annie, both of them hanging garment bags on hooks along the wall. However, there was no sign of Kiara. The disappointment that washed through him was unexpected and unsettling.

"Julian!" Angela spotted him first, her face lighting up with a smile. She crossed the room and hugged him tightly. "I'm so glad you made it."

"Wouldn't miss your big day," he said, returning her embrace.

"Welcome home, brother," Annie said, then surprised Julian by giving him a hug. "I'm glad you're home. You look so much better."

"Thanks," he said, feeling oddly touched by her comment.

The treatment center had been good for him physically—healthy food, regular sleep, exercise. But it was more than that. Something inside him felt different, freer but also more grounded.

"And you must be Elijah." Angela extended her hand to his friend. "I'm Angela, one of Julian's sisters."

"It's nice to meet you," Elijah said, shaking her hand. "Thank you for welcoming me into your home."

Annie also greeted the man and introduced herself.

"Where's Kiara?" Julian asked, trying to keep his tone casual. "Elizabeth said she was with you."

"She went right upstairs," Angela said. "She wasn't feeling so good. The nausea and exhaustion come and go. This pregnancy has put her through the ringer, especially when we've been running around all day. But she'll probably be down for dinner."

Julian nodded, still not sure how he felt about seeing her again.

For the duration of his time in the treatment center, he'd shared things with her in letters that he might not have if they'd been speaking face to face. It had been easy to just imagine she was a friend because there had been no romantic interactions in their letters. They hadn't even closed their letters with *Love.*

Being there in person was going to be different. Everyone there knew they were married, but they weren't living as if they were. It was going to be awkward, and Julian didn't do well with awkwardness when it involved him.

He didn't want people asking him if they were going to try to make a go of it. And he didn't want to have to constantly watch his interactions with Kiara, so people didn't get the wrong idea. He counted Kiara as one of his friends now, and he wanted to keep their interactions a reflection of that.

While in treatment, he hadn't thought a lot about the fact that he was married. His focus had been on getting through the withdrawal and then learning how to live with what he'd done as a child. But now he was back, and there was no avoiding that one of the people at the estate was his wife.

"Well, I'm going to give Elijah a tour," Julian said. "We'll be back in a bit."

Leaving the girls to their wedding prep, Julian led the way out of the house. Over the next half hour, he showed Elijah the security building and then the rec center.

"Do you play basketball?" Elijah asked as they stood on the basketball court in the rec center.

"Not really. Benji is the one who uses it the most, and also Annie's boyfriend when he's here." When Elijah jumped and pretended to shoot an invisible ball at the hoop, Julian said, "Do you play?"

"It was that or football," Elijah said. "But my mom put her foot down and said no football. My dad tried to fight her on it, but she stood firm."

"I wasn't into team sports much. I played tennis and did some track, but I wasn't very good at either of them."

"Maybe I can shoot some hoops with Benji," Elijah said.

"I'm sure he'd enjoy that."

After they left the rec center, they continued walking on the road that circled around by Jude and Annie's homes.

"What's going up here?" Elijah asked as they approached the building site.

"This is Angela and Kiara's house."

"Is Kiara going to stay here alone?" Elijah asked.

"What do you mean?"

"Would Jude move in with Angela here? Or would Angela move in with Jude?"

Julian thought of the large log cabin style home that Jude lived in and figured there was little chance they'd choose to share space with Kiara.

"I'm not sure," he said. "But I assume they've figured something out."

Julian knew a bit about the layout of the house that was being built, since he'd been around for some of the discussions about it.

Kiara and Angela had decided on two separate wings, each with a master suite connected by a common kitchen. It made sense at the time, but somehow, Julian doubted that they would have decided on that design had they known that Angela would never live there.

"It looks like it's almost done," Elijah said.

"Yeah, it does. I think Duncan was hoping to have it finished before the baby arrived."

Julian was a bit curious about what it was like inside, so he headed in that direction with Elijah trailing behind him.

He climbed the steps to the front door and checked to see if it was locked. The door swung open, and immediately he could hear the sounds of workers inside.

"Let's have a look around," Julian said. "I'm curious."

"Hello," a middle-aged man called out to them. As he got closer, he said, "Oh, hello, Mr. Burke."

After introductions were made, the foreman gave them a tour of the house. As he walked through the rooms, Julian could see how the house would have been perfect for Angela and Kiara. He wondered if Kiara was disappointed that she wouldn't be living with her sister.

"That's a really nice place," Elijah said as they left several minutes later.

"It is," Julian agreed.

"Why don't you have a place here?" Elijah asked. "It seems like all your siblings do."

"I do have a plot of land that Duncan has set aside for me, but I've had no desire to put down roots here."

"Do you think that will change now that you have a baby on the way?"

"I don't know." That was the most honest answer he had at the moment. "I'm pretty sure that Kiara won't be interested in moving to New York. She's too close to Angela to want to move that far away. So if I want to see my son, I'll need to come here."

They circled back to the main house, then went inside. It was nearing dinnertime, so they went back upstairs to their rooms.

"Does your family dress for dinner?" Elijah asked.

"Sort of. Duncan prefers no jeans or T-shirts. I usually wear slacks and a button-down."

"Sounds good," Elijah said. "My dad always insisted on a tie, which was pretty ridiculous."

"Here at the estate, we only dress more formally at special dinners like Thanksgiving and Christmas."

"And for the wedding on Saturday, I imagine."

"Yes, we'll be dressed up for that. Do you have a suit with you?"

"I certainly do," Elijah said. "My mom insisted I pack one when I went to the treatment center. Maybe she assumed there would be a graduation program. I doubt she thought I'd need one to attend a wedding, however."

"You'll have to take a picture to show her."

"You're sure it's okay for me to attend?"

"Yes. I checked with Duncan already."

"Okay. Well, let me go get freshened up."

"You've got twenty minutes," Julian said as he opened the door to his room.

"Yes, sir."

In his room, Julian went through the motions of preparing for dinner. At the treatment center, things had been a bit more relaxed, and he found that he had enjoyed that.

Buttoning his shirt, he felt like he was putting on a costume. For the longest time, he'd chosen to wear suits, even when he didn't need to. It was like he hoped that people would see his professionalism and not look beyond it to his internal struggles.

He went to his bathroom to brush his hair, but he didn't apply the product that he usually used to keep it in place. He'd gotten used to not styling his hair while in the treatment center. It was a small thing, but it made him feel more comfortable.

With five minutes until dinner, Julian left his room. Elijah's door stood open, and he appeared as soon as Julian rapped on his door jamb.

As they approached the stairs, Julian spotted Kiara coming toward them with Angela. Julian's steps slowed as he took in the sight of her.

Her curly hair was pulled back in a ponytail, and she wore a loose-fitting floral top that skimmed over her bump. She looked tired, and her face a touch paler than he remembered, but her eyes—those warm hazel eyes—brightened when she saw him.

"Julian," she said, with a smile. "Welcome home."

Something unexpected shifted in his chest at her words. *Home.* Was this place home to him now? He wasn't sure, but hearing her say it felt right somehow.

"Thanks," he managed.

When he reached her, he hesitated, uncertain how to greet her. A handshake seemed too formal, a kiss too intimate. He settled for a brief, gentle hug, careful not to press too close to her growing belly.

"How are you feeling?" he asked, his voice softer than he'd intended.

"Better after a nap," she said. "I read somewhere that a lot of women feel great during the second trimester. I am not one of those women. I just hope I feel good for the wedding."

"This is Elijah," Julian said, stepping back to include his friend in the conversation.

"It's wonderful to meet you." Kiara's face lit up with genuine warmth as she extended her hand to Elijah. "Julian's told me about you in his letters."

Julian watched as Elijah shook her hand, noting how his friend's expression softened at her friendly demeanor.

"All good things, I hope," Elijah said with a smile.

"Very good things," Kiara assured him. "I'm glad you could come for the wedding."

Angela cleared her throat. "We should probably head down. You know how Duncan gets when we're late."

As they made their way down the stairs, Julian walked beside Kiara while Angela and Elijah chatted behind them. The delicious aroma of dinner drifted up from the kitchen, and Julian realized he was starving.

It had been a rare feeling when he'd been at the estate in the past. Alcohol had played a big role in his meals. He'd washed every dinner down with it, and his hangovers had often robbed him of his appetite for breakfast.

Glancing over at Kiara as they walked into the dining room, his gaze went to her belly. That little boy was the reason he needed to get his act together.

No more using alcohol to dull his feelings. His thoughts went to the alcohol that was still hidden in his closet, and he knew he needed to get rid of it. Soon.

CHAPTER FOURTEEN

Kiara was uncertain if Julian expected her to sit next to him at the dinner table that night, but she felt a strong need to reinforce—especially to herself—that they were married in name only. Which meant they didn't need to sit next to each other.

Instead, she chose a seat between Angie and Elizabeth. Julian was seated across the table from her, with Elijah and Benji on either side of him.

Since they had exchanged letters, Kiara had been prepared for the mental changes in Julian. What she hadn't been prepared for were the physical ones.

He no longer had the gaunt look that had been present before heading to the treatment center. Even when she'd gone there to see him a few weeks ago, he'd still looked hollow-cheeked with a haunted gaze.

But as she looked at him across the table, she thought he'd never looked more handsome. His eyes had a light in them that had been lacking before, and he just looked healthier. Even happy.

Kiara struggled with the knowledge that he probably didn't see an improvement when he looked at her. Despite the nausea she battled off and on, she'd still gained weight, and it wasn't all just in her belly. She was also aware that she looked tired a lot, especially if she didn't put on makeup.

She knew it shouldn't make a difference what Julian thought. They weren't in a relationship, and their marriage was just temporary. Despite that, she didn't like the idea that he would only see negative changes in her.

Her emotions were a mess most days, and that was even when Julian wasn't there. Now that he was, and the reality of their situation was in her face every day, she could only imagine where her emotions were going to end up.

There were just so many ups and downs in the days ahead.

Kiara was genuinely happy that Julian's treatment had been successful, but it was going to be hard to have him around, especially for the wedding. She was also happy for Angie and Jude, but she was going to miss having Angie live under the same roof as her.

"Is everything ready for the wedding?" Duncan asked.

"Yes," Elizabeth responded. "The floral delivery and decorating will be done Saturday morning, and the caterers will be here early in the afternoon. The ceremony starts at five, and we should be ready to eat by seven."

"Is a photographer coming?" he asked.

"Yes, I'm bringing one in from New York that I've worked with before. Same with the hair and makeup people."

"NDAs?"

"All signed," Elizabeth assured him. "I had our lawyer take care of it, and he said they've all been signed."

"So are you experiencing wedding jitters, Jude?" Duncan asked, turning to the man seated to his right.

Everyone laughed at the question. It was hard to imagine Jude having any sort of nerves, let alone jitters.

"No jitters here," Jude said.

"None here either," Angie added. "Just excited."

"The plans for the honeymoon are all in place," Duncan said.

"Where are you going?" Julian asked. "Or is it a secret?"

"Not a secret," Jude replied. "Duncan has generously offered the use of his island."

Just when Kiara thought she understood how rich Duncan was, something else would come up. Like finding out he owned a whole island in the Caribbean. It was unfathomable.

"We're leaving Sunday morning," Angie said. "And we'll be gone for two weeks."

Two weeks sounded like an eternity. When Kiara had first heard how long Angie planned to be gone with Jude, she'd felt a moment of panic at being left alone on the estate.

Kiara got along with Annie okay, but even though the woman looked like Angie, she wasn't her. Because of that, Kiara wasn't sure how she was going to get through the two weeks without contact with Angie.

Under the table, Kiara wrapped her arm around her belly. She had to remember that everything she was doing now was for him. And if she could survive those years with Jim and Sandra at the homestead, she could survive two weeks without Angie, while living in the lap of luxury.

"Stop being such a baby," she murmured to herself.

Angie leaned over to her. "Are you okay?"

Kiara gave her a quick smile. "I'm fine."

Her sister didn't seem to buy her response, but she didn't press her. Kiara might have been worried that Angie would delve into it later, if not for the fact that there were too many other things she needed to focus on.

Friday was spent doing last-minute prep for the wedding, including settling the photographer, hair, and makeup people into the same short-term rental that the designer and seamstresses had used.

The pastor from Angela and Jude's church, who would be marrying them, as well as Jude's best friend and best man, Cooper, and his wife, Melanie, came to the estate for a brief rehearsal on Friday afternoon. The ceremony was pretty simple, so it didn't require much rehearsal.

Since Angie and Jude only had one person each standing up with them, Annie wasn't part of the wedding party, but she'd taken over the organization of the event, along with Elizabeth.

Kiara was glad that on the day of the wedding, her only responsibility was being a witness for Angie and Jude. She wasn't sure she had the emotional or physical fortitude to do much more than that.

"You look beautiful," Kiara said, emotion swelling within her as she stood in front of Angie in her wedding dress on Saturday afternoon.

The dress Angie had chosen was an A-line style with a halter neck. The bodice was covered in lace, but the rest of the dress was white satin.

Angie had decided to wear her hair up, with loose tendrils framing her face. Her diamond drop earrings were a gift from Duncan and Elizabeth.

"So do you," Angie said. "How are you feeling?"

"Really good." Kiara was very grateful that it wasn't a lie. It was her hope that any nausea would stay away until after the ceremony at least.

Once everything was done, it could come on with a vengeance, and she wouldn't complain.

"I'm so glad," Angie said with a smile. "I've been praying that you'd feel good for the day."

"Are you ready for the pictures?" Elizabeth asked as she approached where they stood.

"Yep," Angie said, taking the bouquet of orchids and roses that Elizabeth held out to her.

They went outside to the garden, where Jude and Angie were going to have their first look. Kiara stood back with Annie and Elizabeth, watching as Angie approached Jude, who stood with his back to them.

When Angie reached Jude, she didn't touch him right away. She appeared to be saying something to him, but the others were too far away to hear. Jude's head was bent, and when Angie laid her hand on his back, he hesitated for a moment before turning to face her.

His usually stoic expression was nowhere to be found as he gazed down at Angie. Reaching out, he touched her cheek gently before gathering her into his arms.

The photographer unobtrusively captured everything from a short distance away from the couple. She waited for Jude and Angie to end their moment, then waved everyone else in the wedding party over.

Once the wedding party was done with their pictures, it was time for the family ones.

Kiara wasn't sure she would have originally been included in the family pictures. However, now that she was married to Julian, she was instructed to join them.

When the photographer requested just the immediate family plus Jude, Kiara stepped away. Angie started to protest, but Kiara gave her what she hoped was a reassuring smile.

This would likely be the photograph Duncan had on his desk after Julian divorced her. Though she'd always be Angie's sister in her heart, her legal connection to the family would be severed at some point in the future.

"Julian and Kiara?" the photographer called out. "Your turn."

Kiara frowned as she glanced at Angie. "I'm not sure that's a good idea."

"Why not?" Angie asked. "You're married, plus it would be nice for the baby to have a picture of his parents together."

Obviously, Angie wasn't going to accept Kiara's protest, so Kiara turned to Julian. But he wasn't any help. He just shrugged and stepped toward where the photographer waited.

Kiara's heart was pounding as she joined Julian. The photographer approached them and showed them how she wanted them to pose. Kiara tried to relax as Julian stood behind her, his arm around her waist. She didn't the pictures to reveal how awkward she felt, but she wasn't sure how to accomplish that.

After the photographer had taken a couple of shots of that pose, she moved them to stand facing each other. Kiara was convinced that these were going to be the worst pictures ever taken.

The photographer was obviously unaware that they weren't a happily married couple, and she kept wanting them to gaze at one another and hold each other in ways that didn't come naturally to them.

The woman was a pro, however, and she was able to get them to relax and mostly let go of their awkwardness.

"This feels like we're taking pictures at prom," Julian murmured.

"I never went to prom," Kiara said.

"You didn't miss much. Just imagine this with pimples and braces."

Kiara laughed. "I can't imagine you with either."

"Pimples weren't an issue, but I did have braces."

Imagining Julian as a teen helped take Kiara out of the awkwardness of the moment, and after a couple more poses, the photographer declared them done.

Next up were Duncan and Elizabeth, who posed together with ease. Kiara didn't know if it was normal to take pictures of everyone separately at a wedding, but she thought perhaps Elizabeth wanted to take advantage of them all being together and nicely dressed.

Once all the pictures were done, she and Angie returned to the solarium, while the others went to the white tent that had been set up for the ceremony and then the reception.

Angie slipped her arm through Kiara's and leaned her head against her shoulder. "Thank you for everything, Kiki. I know this hasn't been easy."

"It's been fine. I'm just so glad to see you happy."

"I want you to be happy too," Angie said.

"I *am* happy," Kiara said, hoping she wouldn't push. "If the nausea would just disappear completely, I'd be thrilled."

Angie laughed softly. "You can text me while I'm away. Let me know how you're doing."

Kiara shook her head. "Nope. That's your special time with Jude. You need to focus just on him."

"I want you to at least check in every two or three days. We don't have to video chat. I just want to be reassured that you and the baby are doing okay."

Kiara was grateful for her sister's thoughtfulness, but she was still determined not to intrude on their honeymoon. "Okay. I'll send a quick text every couple of days. Just so you don't worry."

"Thank you." Angie squeezed her arm. "I know you've got Julian here now, but..."

"But he's not you," Kiara finished for her. The truth of those words settled heavily in her chest. Julian might be her husband on paper, might be the father of her baby, but he wasn't her person the way Angie had always been.

And she had always been Angie's person. That had changed a bit already, but after today, Jude would fully take on that role in her sister's life. It was hard not to feel like she was losing a huge part of her identity. Of her usefulness.

A knock on the door interrupted them, then Annie poked her head in. "It's almost time. Are you ready?"

Angie straightened, a radiant smile transforming her face. "More than ready."

Kiara felt a flutter of emotion as she watched her sister's happiness. This was what love looked like. This was what Kiara had always hoped for her sister—to be cherished by someone worthy of her gentle heart.

"You're going to make me cry," Kiara said, blinking rapidly to hold back tears. "And then my makeup will be ruined."

Angie laughed softly. "Can't have that." She took a deep breath. "Let's go. I can't wait to be Mrs. Jude Kessler."

They followed Annie to the entrance of the tent. Duncan was already waiting there, looking handsome in his dark suit, his expression a mixture of pride and wistfulness.

"You look beautiful," he said to Angie, his voice gruff with emotion.

"Thank you," Angie replied, taking his arm.

The music shifted, signaling Kiara's cue to enter. She squared her shoulders, forced her lips into a smile and made her way down the aisle.

The tent had been transformed into something magical. White fabric draped the interior, and flowers created arcs and arrangements that made the space feel like an elegant garden. Warm light filtered through the white canvas, casting everything in a soft, romantic glow.

Kiara walked slowly, aware of the guests turning to watch her progress.

Elizabeth sat in the front row with Benji beside her, both of them beaming. Annie had taken her seat as well, and Julian sat next to her with Elijah on his other side.

He looked handsome in his dark gray suit, his hair styled but not overly formal like it used to be. Their eyes met briefly, and he gave her a quick wink and a smile. Kiara's stomach flipped, and she had to keep herself from staring at him.

With some difficulty, she looked away from Julian to Jude, who stood at the altar with the pastor and Cooper. Jude had his hands clasped in front of him, and his gaze was on the back of the tent. He had a small smile on his face, which told Kiara just how happy he was, since smiles weren't something that seemed to come easily to the man.

In fact, Angie was the only one who seemed to be worthy of his most genuine and affectionate ones.

Jude's mom, her husband, and their kids had come for the wedding, and it had been kind of funny to watch her try to fuss over Jude, who was really not having it.

Once she reached the front, Kiara took her place and turned to watch as Angie waited for her turn to come down the aisle.

As the string quartet that Elizabeth had hired began to play the song Angie had chosen to walk to, Kiara focused on her sister. Angie's attention was completely on Jude, and the slow pace Annie had told her would work well with the music she'd picked out, was nowhere to be seen. It almost looked like Angie was pulling Duncan down the aisle.

Kiara couldn't help but smile at the conflict between Angie's eagerness to get to Jude and Duncan's reluctance to give away the daughter he'd so recently found.

When Angie reached Jude, she handed Kiara her bouquet so she could take Jude's hands. As the pastor spoke, Kiara turned toward the couple but let her gaze go distant. She knew she couldn't let herself listen too much to the vows Jude and Angie shared because she didn't want to cry.

Thankfully, the ceremony didn't take too long, and soon the pastor was pronouncing them husband and wife. Jude had a smile that matched Angie's as he took her in his arms for their first kiss as a married couple.

As people clapped, Angie turned to Kiara to take her bouquet back. She gave Kiara a hug, then she and Jude walked back up the aisle. Everyone followed them out of the tent and moved to the area of the garden where a small selection of bar-height tables had been set up along with a table of hor d'oeuvres.

While they were sampling the hor d'oeuvres, the catering crew went to work setting up the tent for the dinner that was to follow. When it was time to return to the tent, they found that all the chairs had been moved to circle large round tables. The tables, covered with crisp white tablecloths, had lovely spring floral centerpieces arranged around white pillar candles.

The food was amazing, and Kiara was glad that her stomach cooperated and allowed her to enjoy it. Part of her responsibilities as matron of honor was to give a speech. It was something she'd struggled to prepare because she hadn't wanted to share too much about their past. Instead, she'd focused on what Angie meant to her, which had inevitably brought her emotions to the surface, but she'd managed to get through it.

But by the time all the festivities were done, Kiara was exhausted. Saying goodbye to Angie, knowing she wouldn't see her for two weeks, had been a challenge to accomplish without crying again. However, she'd been determined to send her off with a smile so that Angie wasn't distracted by worrying about her.

When she finally reached her room, Kiara was relieved to get out of her dress, remove her makeup, and take the pins out of her hair and let it down. She worked her fingers against her scalp, then changed into the loose shorts and T-shirt she usually slept in. The shorts were stretchy enough she could pull them over her growing stomach.

Finally comfortable, she sat down on her bed. Her feet were sore from spending most of the day in a pair of uncomfortable shoes. With no one to rub her feet, she spent some time rubbing them for herself.

She frowned when she heard a soft knock on her door. Sliding off the bed, she slowly made her way to the door, then cracked it open, not really wanting anyone to see her in her pajamas.

"Hey," Annie said with a smile. "Just wanted to check and see how you were doing after everything today."

"I'm tired," Kiara admitted as she opened the door more fully. "And my feet are a little sore, but other than that, I'm fine."

"Did you need anything?" she asked.

Kiara tilted her head to lean it against the edge of the door. "Nope. I'm good. My water bottle is full, and I have a little stash of my favorite granola bars if I get hungry."

Annie smiled. "I told Julian you were probably fine, but he wanted me to make sure."

Kiara wasn't sure what to make of that revelation. "Yep. I'm fine."

"Good. And if you need anything while Angie's gone, just let me know."

"Thanks. I appreciate that."

"I can't believe that I've been the one dating the longest, and yet, Julian and Angie have both gotten married before me."

"Are you hoping Cole proposes soon?"

"Definitely," Annie said. "If he'd been here for this, I would have made sure Angie and Jude did a bouquet and garter toss. Given we would have been the only single adults present, the odds of us catching them would have been pretty good."

Kiara wondered how long it would be before she'd have to attend another wedding.

"Anyway, I'm going to head home," Annie said. "I'm whipped too."

"Thanks for checking on me."

"You're welcome." Annie gave her a quick wave, then headed down the hallway toward the stairs.

Kiara shut the door behind her and went back to her bed, still uncertain what to make of the fact that Julian had sent Annie to check on her. It would be easy to read more into it than had likely been his intent. However, she could only assume he wanted to make sure the day hadn't been too physically taxing for her, since she was pregnant with his son.

It hadn't been, but as she sat back down on her bed, Kiara wondered if she could go to a massage therapist and just have them rub her feet and legs.

She rubbed her feet a bit more, then washed her hands before crawling into bed. The room was lit only by the lamp on her nightstand, giving it a cozy feel, which she loved. It helped to settle her a bit more.

However, as she let her thoughts wander back over the day, she had to deal with the deep sadness that settled into her soul.

A tear slipped down her cheek before she could stop it. She'd managed to hold it together through the entire day, but now, alone in her room, the emotions she'd been tamping down surged forward.

Kiara wiped at her face, annoyed with herself. She should be happy, not crying in her bed like a child.

But the contrast between Angie's beautiful wedding and her own hasty ceremony was just too stark to ignore. And the way Jude looked at Angie... and the way he protected her... took care of her. It was clear that she was the most important person in the world to him. It was how Kiara had always dreamed the man she married would feel about her.

She'd had to be strong for so long. She'd taken care of Angie, protecting her when she could from Jim and Craig's abuse. It had meant that she'd had to shoulder that abuse on her own. But it had been okay because she loved Angie.

She'd always hoped that one day there would be a man out there who would cherish and protect her. Who would look at her and see her as worth loving.

But she felt like she'd thrown away that chance by giving in when she shouldn't have. Now she was married to a man who viewed her simply as the mother of his child and possibly a friend.

"Stop it," she whispered to herself. "This isn't helping anything."

She reached for her tablet on the nightstand, hoping to distract herself with a book. But as she touched the screen and it came to life, the picture she'd chosen for her lock screen appeared. It was of her and Angie, both smiling broadly at the camera.

The picture was a good reminder that no matter who came into their lives, they would always be sisters. She hadn't lost her sister with her marriage to Jude, she had gained a brother-in-law who hardly smiled.

Kiara chuckled at the thought, glad for the break from her heavier emotions.

She had to focus on the positive things in her life. The baby growing within her. The safety and security she now had that she could also offer her son, sparing him the uncertainty and challenges that she'd faced as a child. And soon, she'd have a home of her own. A beautiful home that she would make sure was filled with love for her little one.

Now, if her pregnancy hormones would just chill out and not drag her down into emotional outbursts that she'd rarely, if ever, had before getting pregnant, things would be fine.

CHAPTER FIFTEEN

As Julian sat down at the table for lunch the next day, he noticed that Kiara wasn't there. He hadn't seen her since the wedding, and he hoped she was doing okay with Angela not being there.

He'd heard the helicopter lift off around eleven that morning and knew it was taking Angela and Jude to Coeur d'Alene, where they'd use the family jet to fly to where they'd be honeymooning.

It was hard for Julian to imagine Jude married, especially to his sister. But there was no doubt that Jude was devoted to Angela, and she to him.

Their love wasn't shown through over-the-top displays of affection, but in the way Jude made sure that Angela was taken care of before he took care of himself. Whether that was holding her chair at the table, or bringing her coffee when they came to breakfast.

Julian couldn't say that was how he'd ever treated the women he'd been with. Well, he might have held a chair or opened doors, but other than that, he hadn't gone out of his way to take care of the women he dated.

He never would have thought he'd consider that he needed to look to Jude's example for anything in his life. And yet, here he was, appreciating how the man cared for Angela.

"Is Kiara joining us for lunch?" Julian asked when she hadn't shown up by the time everyone else was there.

"It appears that she won't be," Elizabeth said as she passed Duncan the bowl of salad they were beginning their meal with. "The nausea she deals with can rob her of her appetite. She'll eat when she feels well enough to. If she doesn't show up, it usually means that she doesn't feel like she can eat anything."

"Does she get enough to eat?" Julian asked.

"Mrs. Stevens makes sure that there is food available for her, and she knows she can eat anything she wants in the kitchen. Sometimes different foods appeal to her."

Julian was glad that she was eating, even if it wasn't when everyone else did.

As the meal progressed, conversation ranged from the wedding to Annie's plans to go to LA with Benji for the potential championship-winning basketball game. Duncan had certainly changed his tune on Cole, and Julian thought perhaps another wedding was in the offing.

"Julian, could I see you in my office after lunch?" Duncan asked.

The request for a meeting wasn't a surprise, so Julian nodded.

"Want to go shoot some hoops, Elijah?" Benji asked.

"Sure thing," Elijah said with a nod. "It's been awhile since I've played though, so you'll have to take pity on this old man."

When the meal ended, Elijah and Benji headed off to the rec center. Annie left to go to her house, while Elizabeth went to her office, which was essentially another small solarium next to their suite.

That left Julian to walk with Duncan to his office. He didn't know exactly what this conversation might be about, but he was trying not to let their past interactions color his approach to this one.

He knew that he needed to improve his relationship with Duncan, despite the harsh words he'd had for him when Julian had revealed the secret he'd held for so long. If Angela could forgive him for what he'd done as a child, he could try to forgive Duncan for his harsh words.

When they walked into the office, Duncan directed him to the sitting area instead of the chairs at the desk. That was unusual for their meetings, which just added to Julian's uncertainty about this one.

Duncan sat down in one of the armchairs, so Julian took the loveseat that faced him.

"First of all," Duncan began, "I want to apologize again. I shouldn't have gotten as upset as I did. You were a child, and I hadn't been the father I should have been to you. If I had been, perhaps you would have felt confident in coming to me and sharing what you'd heard. I'm sorry for that."

Julian was at a loss for words. He'd expected that there might be another apology offered, but Duncan's acknowledgement that he'd been a rather distant father at that time was surprising.

Would it have made a difference? Julian wasn't sure. Either way, there was nothing they could do to change what had happened. Duncan had changed as a father after the kidnapping, and in some ways, had swung completely in the opposite direction.

"I understand that it came as a shock to you, and I'm sorry it took so long for me to tell you what had happened."

"I hope we can move beyond this," Duncan said. "I'm proud of you for sticking with the treatment, and I hope that now that you've been able to deal with what happened in the past, you won't find the need to drink so overwhelming."

It was true he didn't feel overwhelmed by the need to drink all the time like he had before going to the treatment center. Unfortunately, his resolve hadn't truly been tested as of yet.

His thoughts went to the alcohol that was still in the closet in his room. He needed to get rid of it before something came up that would tempt him to drink.

"I wanted to talk to you about Kiara," Duncan said.

Julian straightened in his seat. "Is there something wrong?"

"No, continuing bouts of nausea aside, she seems to be doing well. And we were thrilled to hear that she's having a healthy baby boy. Though of course we would have been thrilled with a girl too."

"I hope that I'll be a good father," Julian said, but then wished he could take the words back as soon as he'd uttered them.

"I think the best thing you can do is know your child," Duncan said. "I've come to realize how different each of you are. Even Annalisa and Angelica. As twins, you'd think they would be more alike, but that's not really the case. Elizabeth has shown me how important it is to look at each of you as individuals. Admittedly, I haven't been the best father, so maybe you should just do the opposite of whatever I've done."

"The thing I struggled with the most has been your overprotectiveness," Julian admitted. "But now that I consider my responsibility to my son, I think I understand it a bit more. Especially in light of what happened with the twins."

Duncan's head bobbed. "I know I go overboard with some of the security protocols, but I barely survived my failure to protect the girls. I couldn't imagine going through that again."

"Let's hope it never happens again," Julian said. "We have a good security team now."

"We do," Duncan agreed. He glanced out the window for a moment before looking back at Julian. "Are you planning to return to New York full-time?"

"I haven't decided yet," Julian said. "I know I need to go at some point to see Mom, and I want to go to Singapore again soon."

"At the risk of interfering in your life again, might I suggest you consider making the estate your home base? At least for a little while."

"I've been thinking about that," Julian told him.

"With Kiara being pregnant, I think it might be good for you to be here."

Julian nodded. "I do want to be close by when the baby is born."

"The thing is, I worry a bit about Kiara being all alone in her new house. If something should happen, there wouldn't be anyone there with her."

Julian stared at his dad. He knew as well as Duncan did that there were ways to monitor Kiara, even if she was alone. And even if he did live in the house with her, he would still be away for stretches of time.

"As you know, the house is designed with two separate suites, each with three rooms, and a shared living space between them. So you'd still have your own space, and she'd have hers."

Julian hadn't considered that they wouldn't continue to live separate lives. He didn't think it would be fair to Kiara to live as a married couple when they'd agreed that a divorce was in their future.

"Have you talked to Kiara about this?" he asked.

"Just in passing."

"When will the house be ready?"

"The report I got last Thursday was that they were just working on the finishing touches, so over the next week, the designer will be here to set up the interior. We would still have time to repaint Angela's side and order furniture for you."

Julian leaned back in his chair, staring at the empty fireplace. What would it cost him to live in the house with Kiara? Nothing, really.

It might be better than having to stay at the main house when he was at the estate. And it would mean he'd be aware of how Kiara was doing and offer help where he could.

"Okay. If she's willing, I'll move into Angela's wing of the house."

Duncan smiled. "Wonderful! I really think it would be best for the two of you."

Julian wasn't sure if it was the best solution on every level, but when it came to the baby, it likely was.

"I'll talk to her about it," Julian said, not wanting Kiara to feel under obligation to Duncan to agree to something she didn't want.

"Elizabeth and I will be going to New York on Wednesday, then on to Basel and Dublin. If you want to come with us to New York on the plane, then continue on to Singapore from there, you're more than welcome to join us."

"I'll check my schedule and see if it works for me to go now, given I have a lot to get caught up on."

"Sounds good. I know that Sean will be glad to show you what's been happening."

"And I'm looking forward to seeing it."

"Hopefully, the suite at the house will be ready by the time you get back." Duncan paused, then said, "That was all I needed to discuss with you. Was there anything you wanted to talk about?"

Julian shook his head. "I think I'm going to go watch Elijah and Benji shoot some hoops."

Together they left the office, but Duncan turned in the direction of his and Elizabeth's suite, while Julian headed upstairs to change from the clothes he'd worn for Sunday dinner into something more comfortable.

Wearing jeans and a T-shirt, he left his room to go downstairs. When he reached the top of the stairs, he saw that Kiara was already partway down them.

He waited at the top until she reached the bottom, then called out to her as he jogged down to join her. "Hey, Kiara. Wait up."

Kiara turned to look at him, her hand resting on her stomach. She wore a pair of shorts and a loose-flowing top. Her curls were gathered in a high ponytail with a few tendrils escaping to frame her face.

"How are you feeling?" he asked as he reached her.

"Better than this morning," she said.

"What are you up to now?"

"I'm going for a walk. I try to get out at least once a day for some fresh air and exercise."

"Mind if I come with you?"

He'd planned to join Elijah and Benji, but perhaps his time was better spent with Kiara. Especially considering the conversation he'd had earlier with Duncan.

"Not at all," she said. "Just be forewarned that I move at a snail's pace these days."

"That's fine."

They left the house, stepping into the warmth and sunshine of the afternoon. Kiara gestured in the direction she planned to go.

"Have you eaten today?" he asked.

Kiara nodded. "I have some granola bars that I keep in my room. Some days that's all my stomach will tolerate until later in the day."

As they walked, Julian decided to broach the subject of the house. "Are you happy with how the house is coming together?"

"Very happy. It has everything that we asked the architect for, and the interior designer has done a great job taking our ideas for the inside and fleshing them out."

"Am I right in assuming that Angela is moving into Jude's place?"

There was a slight pause before Kiara responded. "Yes. It's the best thing for her and Jude, being newlyweds and all."

"Will it bother you to be on your own in the house?"

"I'm not sure," she said. "I've never lived alone before." She hesitated. "Maybe I'll love it."

The tone of her voice led Julian to think that she didn't believe that. "Would you be open to having a housemate?"

Her steps slowed, and she turned to look at him. "A housemate?"

Julian folded his arms as he faced her, suddenly uncertain how he wanted her to respond. "I'll be spending more time here at the estate while we wait for the baby, and thought maybe, if you were agreeable, I could take the other suite in the house. That way, you wouldn't always be alone, in case you need help."

Kiara stared at him for a long moment. So long, he wondered if she was just not going to respond to him. Her expression was unreadable, so he didn't get any help there.

Finally, she turned to continue walking, and Julian took two long steps to catch up with her, then shortened his stride again.

"Is your dad forcing you to do this?" Kiara said.

Julian was glad to be able to say that he wasn't. "He mentioned that it might be an option for me if I plan to spend more time here. However, he's not forcing me to move in with you. He just offered it as a suggestion. If you say no, that's fine. No one will make you agree to this."

"I suppose it makes sense," Kiara said. "There's no use in half the house sitting empty."

"If you need to think about it, you're welcome to take some time before giving me an answer."

They were nearing the house, and Kiara headed in the direction of the front door. Julian followed her up the steps, then waited as she punched in a code on the door lock.

"This is the one day of the week there are no workers here," Kiara said as she pushed the door open.

It was definitely quieter than it had been the last time he'd been there. The smell of paint and other building materials hung in the air.

"Angie designed the kitchen," Kiara said as she headed in that direction. It was at the back of the house, with large windows that looked out over a currently muddy yard and the forest beyond. "It was her dream kitchen, but she seems happy with the one at Jude's too."

There was a solarium at the back, and though there was a separate dining area, it wasn't a formal room like at the main house. It wasn't a home set up for a household staff the way the main house was.

"This is my suite," Kiara said, gesturing to a door that stood open.

Leading him through it, she explained in more detail than the foreman had, what each of the rooms were for.

He found the small library interesting. She'd mentioned in letters that she liked to read, but perhaps *liked* was too mild of a term, given she'd devoted an entire room to books. She also pointed out the room that had originally been set aside for a guest room, which would now be a nursery.

Once they were done on her side, she led him to the side Angela had designed. It had a sitting room in addition to two bedrooms, as well as a luxurious bathroom.

He noticed that in the bathrooms of both suites, there was a double sink and a large walk-in closet that would be plenty of space for two people.

Had they planned to live there together with their spouses?

"Angela had worked on the decor for this side with the interior designer, so it might not be to your preferences."

"I'll give the designer a call and see if it's too late to make some changes," Julian said, then turned to look at her. "As long as you don't mind."

Kiara shrugged. "I don't. You might as well make it to your liking."

Julian was still unsure how Kiara really felt about him moving in, but she didn't seem strongly opposed to it.

"Would having a trial period make this easier for you?"

She squinted at him. "Trial period?"

"Yes. Let's give it a month of us both living here, and if it doesn't work for you, then you can tell me and I'll move out."

"Just like that?"

"Just like that," Julian agreed. "I want you to be comfortable. Having someone you don't know well in your space might be more than you like. I won't get mad if you tell me that you don't think it's working out."

"And if it's not working out for you?"

Julian took a moment to mull over the question. For some reason, he hadn't really considered that he might not be happy living in the same space as the woman carrying his child.

"I guess then I'll let you know too."

They left the suite, and Kiara went to the glass garden doors that led off the dining room. There was a large deck at the back of the house beyond the solarium.

"We're going to have a greenhouse and a garden back here. Angie wants to be able to plant herbs and vegetables."

"Are you still going to do that?"

"We might not get a garden in this year, but we'll probably plant some herbs."

It was an interesting combination of their previous life on Jim's homestead and their new one at the estate. Julian tried to imagine his mom or Elizabeth working in a garden, but the picture just wouldn't gel.

When they left the house, Kiara locked the door, and then they walked down the steps side by side. He glanced back at the house as they walked away, and for a moment, he had an image of the windows glowing warmly. Welcomingly. Like a home.

He'd never had a place that had made him feel like it was truly home. His apartment in New York was expensive and well-furnished, but walking through its door didn't make him feel a sense of homecoming. And the main house on the estate was definitely not a place he would call home.

"I'm probably going to be flying out to New York with Duncan and Elizabeth on Wednesday," he told her. "And then possibly on to Singapore to check in with the company there."

"How long are you going to be gone?" she asked.

"A week and a half to two weeks." He grimaced. "I also need to check in with my mom and let her know what's been going on."

"Are you going to tell her about the baby?"

Julian nodded. "As much as I'd rather she not know, I think I'd better."

"Is she going to think I got pregnant to trap you?"

Julian gave a huff of laughter. "You've only met her once, but you already have her number. It's highly likely she will, but that's irrelevant."

"Will she want to meet the baby?" Kiara asked.

"Probably," Julian said. "But you don't have to worry about dealing with her. I'll make sure she doesn't try to exert any pressure on you in regards to the baby. It will help that you and the baby will be here, and she lives in New York. She doesn't like visiting Idaho."

"Is it because your dad and Elizabeth live here?"

"Yes," Julian said. "Even though she was the one to initiate their divorce, she hates that Duncan married the nanny. Early on, she tried to blackball Elizabeth in New York elite circles, but Duncan threatened to cut back on the money he gave her if she kept it up."

"Has your mom always been like this?"

Julian thought back to his childhood, something he rarely did. "Mom wasn't really a hand's on parent. Neither was Duncan, for that matter. It wasn't until after the kidnapping that he became more so. She never changed. I've had to accept how she is if I wanted a relationship with her."

"I guess being rich doesn't always make a family immune to difficulties."

Julian shoved his hands into the pockets of his jeans as they walked. "No. In some ways, having excessive amounts of money makes close relationships more difficult. It was too easy for my parents to hire people to take care of us. They'd say goodnight to us, but they weren't the ones reading us stories and tucking us into bed."

"I'm not planning to hire a nanny," Kiara said. "That's not negotiable."

"I'll support whatever you want to do," Julian said. "I know you'll have people around to help you out."

Kiara nodded. "Angie has already said she's going to help me. She plans to be the best aunt ever. And Annie has said she's excited to have a baby around again."

"I'll help however I can," Julian said. "But honestly, I have zero experience with babies. I've never even held one. Maybe I held the twins when they were little, but I certainly don't remember it."

"I don't remember holding a baby either," Kiara admitted, then gave a soft laugh. "This poor little guy. He's getting two inexperienced parents."

"Hey, if teenagers can figure it out, I'm sure we can."

They exchanged a smile and a laugh, and Julian was relieved he wasn't the only one feeling a bit out of his depth with the parenting thing.

He was also glad that Kiara had agreed to share the house with him because he really did want to be a part of their son's life as much as possible. And he wanted to support Kiara too.

Change was coming in his life, and, surprisingly, he was okay with it. And he thought the main reason for that was Kiara's approach to everything. She was taking it all in stride and accepting what he could offer without demanding more of him.

She'd been supportive of him, and he wanted a chance to be that for her, even though he wasn't as confident in his ability to be what she needed as a pregnant woman. Hopefully, she'd tell him if there was something she needed that he could help her with.

CHAPTER SIXTEEN

Kiara took a long shower, then dressed in a pair of white shorts and a loose-fitting floral blouse with small cap sleeves. Both items were maternity. She'd finally caved and bought several outfits that would hopefully get her through the last part of the pregnancy.

She applied a light layer of makeup, then scrunched her curls, leaving her hair loose for a change, held back only by a headband.

That afternoon, Angie and Jude were due back. And on the same private flight, coming in from New York, would be Julian. Kiara was excited about Angie coming home, but her feelings about Julian's return were a bit more mixed.

He'd stayed in contact with her while he'd been away, though they'd mainly just exchanged brief text messages. This time when he came to the estate, he'd be moving into the house with her, and the trial month would begin. She was nervous about it. Mainly because she was worried about how she would feel with him in such close proximity.

If she'd found the previous version of Julian attractive, this new version of him was even more appealing. He treated her with a care and concern now that hadn't been as apparent when they'd first hung out together.

She knew it had more to do with her pregnancy than with her personally, but it would be hard not to want to read more into it.

The past couple of weeks had flown by. Most of it had been tied up with the house, as the designer had been there to complete the interior, moving in all the furniture and décor they'd agreed on.

She'd apparently been more than happy to rework her plans to make the design for Angie's rooms more suitable for Julian. Kiara was sure that money had once again greased the wheels of that particular situation.

Once she was ready, she grabbed her phone and water bottle and left her room. She'd been in the house for two nights, and it was still hard for her to believe that it was hers. Finally, a forever home.

She might not be sharing it with Angie the way she'd thought she would, but it was still her home. It might take some time to get used to sharing a space with Julian, but thankfully, it was large enough that they shouldn't be in each other's way.

Having her own space to retreat to was the only reason she'd agreed to him living in the other suite in the house. Time would tell if it was a good decision.

She stepped out onto the porch, taking a deep breath of the fresh summer air. The sky was clear, and everything looked vibrant and green after the rain they'd had a couple of days earlier.

Excited to see Angie again, Kiara walked down the steps and along the interlocking stone sidewalk to the road. They were working on the landscape surrounding the house now, but it still looked a little rough.

She didn't have a car yet, since she had no license, but Duncan had suggested she start learning to drive one of the UTVs so she didn't have to walk everywhere. For the moment, however, she was fine with walking.

As she walked, she could hear the distant sound of the helicopter approaching. When she reached the helipad, she spotted a couple of members of the security team standing next to two UTVs.

They greeted her with nods and smiles, then they all turned their attention to the approaching helicopter. As it slowly lowered to the helipad, Kiara waved, even though she couldn't clearly see anyone. She doubted that Angie was seated by the window, though, since she really didn't enjoy flying.

The rotors slowed, and soon, the door opened. Appearing first was Angie, who waved to Kiara, then ran toward her.

As they wrapped their arms around each other, Kiara felt relief fill her to have Angie back. "I missed you so much."

"I missed you too," Angie murmured. As they separated, Angie gripped Kiara's arms and looked closely at her. "How are you? How's the baby?"

They'd kept in contact via text, but Kiara hadn't pushed for long conversations. The texts had been more for just quick check-ins to assure each other they were okay.

"I'm fine. The baby's fine. How are you?"

"I'm great," she said with a beaming smile.

Kiara was glad to see her so happy. She deserved it.

"I'm glad you're home," Kiara said.

"Me too. We had a wonderful time. The island... the beaches... the water... it was all so beautiful, but I'm ready to get back to life here."

Hooking her arm through Kiara's, Angie turned to watch the men as they unloaded the bags from the helicopter. Kiara spotted Julian standing with Jude, the two of them talking.

"I hear Julian is taking my suite in the house," Angie said. "Are you okay with that?"

"Yes. We talked about it and agreed to a one-month trial."

Angie's brow furrowed in concern. "Are you sure about this?"

"About as sure as I am about anything these days," Kiara said with a laugh. "It's fine. Don't worry about it."

"I am a bit worried," Angie told her. "It seems like Julian has changed since he went to the treatment center, but only time will tell."

Kiara understood where Angie was coming from, but unlike everyone else, she'd maintained contact with Julian throughout his treatment. She thought she had a better handle on how he was doing than most of the others.

"Are you ready to head home, love?" Jude asked as he approached them.

"Yep."

"We can catch up tomorrow," Kiara told her. "You need some time to get settled at Jude's."

"Well, I want to see the house now that it's all finished."

"I think you'll like it," Kiara said. "It looks amazing."

"I'll be over first thing in the morning," Angie promised as she hugged Kiara. "Love you."

"Love you, too."

When Jude and Angie headed toward one of the waiting UTVs, Kiara spotted Julian standing next to the other one, watching her. He wore sunglasses, so she couldn't see his eyes, but he smiled as she walked to where he waited.

"Do you want a ride back to the house?" he asked, gesturing at the UTV.

"Which house?" she asked.

"Uh... our house?"

"Yep. I'll take that ride."

Julian waited as she climbed into the second row of seats, then settled in beside her. Anthony and another security team member drove them to the house.

"Wow," Julian said a few minutes later, coming to a stop just inside the front door. He set his suitcase down and looked around. "This looks great. Are you happy with it?"

"I am. The designer did a great job with everything."

"I'll need to get the rest of my stuff from the big house," Julian said, picking up his suitcase again. "I'm curious to see how my suite came together on such short notice."

Kiara followed him through the door that led into his set of rooms, hoping he'd be happy with what he'd ended up with.

"Oh, very nice," Julian said as he walked into his bedroom. "I ended up giving the designer a fair amount of leeway with decisions, and she didn't disappoint."

The designer had changed the paint color from the soft mauve Angie had wanted to a warm taupe that mixed well with the navy-blue accents of the room. It definitely had a masculine vibe when compared to what Angie had planned for the room.

Julian set his suitcase down by the dresser, then turned to face her. "Are you happy with your rooms?"

"I am," Kiara said. "The nursery turned out really well too."

"Would you mind showing it to me?" Julian asked.

"Not at all," she said, then led him across the house to her suite.

Kiara was pleased that he was interested in seeing their son's room. She didn't know how involved he'd end up being once he was born, but she hoped Julian would be there for him as much as possible.

"I like the bears," Julian said as he looked around the room. "Very cute."

"I thought so. I had the option of zoo animals, but I liked the bears better."

She made her way across the room and settled into the rocker next to the crib. Julian leaned against the doorjamb, his arms crossed.

"Did you pick out everything in here?" he asked.

"Essentially," she said. "Megan would present me with two or three options, and I'd choose from them. And for this chair, she actually had three delivered and told me to pick the one that I found most comfortable. That ended up being this one. We ordered two of them. One for in here, and one for my bedroom."

"Did you enjoy the process?"

"I did. Megan made it very easy. Maybe if she'd given me a ton of options, I would have gotten overwhelmed. Thankfully, I didn't find it too difficult to select between two or three styles."

"She didn't really present me with any options."

"Did she ask you if you wanted that?" Kiara asked as she set the chair into motion.

"Yes, but I told her to just go with what looked best."

"I guess that explains why she asked me what I thought you might prefer for a few things."

"And what did you tell her?"

Kiara shrugged. "Once again, I asked her for a couple of options based on what you'd told her, then I chose from those what I thought you might like."

"Well, you did a good job," Julian said. "It all looks great."

Kiara was glad he was happy with the outcome. She'd tried to choose things that she thought created a homey and comfortable environment for him.

She had no idea how living together would go for them. It would be different than when they'd both lived in the main house together. In a way, that had kind of felt like living in a hotel. Even though it was still more elaborate than any place she'd ever lived, moving to the house had felt like coming home.

She wondered if Julian had felt the same way. He probably wasn't in the mindset of thinking of it as home just yet. Not when they still had the trial period to go.

The house was going to be her home, regardless. But at some point, he'd probably move out. Whether it was in a month or when they got divorced, it wasn't his forever home like it was hers.

"Are you still eating at the main house?" he asked, straightening from the doorjamb.

"Yes. I usually join Benji and Annie since Duncan and Elizabeth are still gone," she said.

"Do you just walk over?" he asked. "Or do you call for a ride?"

"I've just been walking. They did say I could have a UTV, but I haven't taken them up on the offer yet."

"Maybe when we walk over for dinner, I'll grab a UTV."

"You know how to drive one?"

"Yep. I was driving a small one when I was around ten. You'll be safe."

Kiara laughed. "I'm not worried."

"Good." He glanced at his watch. "Should we head there now?"

"Sure." She managed to get to her feet without looking too cumbersome, then they made their way through the house to the front door.

Julian kept pace with her as they walked, though she was sure he probably could have made the walk in half the time.

"Is Elijah coming back?" Kiara asked.

"At some point. He went to visit his mom's family, and his mom and sister were going to join them."

"How did your visit with your mom go?"

"About how I thought it would," he said with a humorless laugh. "She was unimpressed with my having gone for help to get sober. She didn't think my drinking was a problem."

"Did *you* think you had a problem?" Kiara asked.

Julian was silent for a moment, then said, "I don't think anyone with a drinking problem initially thinks they have one. I was sure that I could handle it. I was still able to do my job. It wasn't until I didn't have access to alcohol anymore that I realized it was a physical problem. And once I was past the worst of the physical withdrawal, I realized it was also a mental problem."

"And your mom didn't understand that?"

"No."

"Did you tell her about what happened when you were a kid?"

"Not yet," he said. "I know I need to, but I kind of felt like I was dropping a lot on her already."

"Like the baby and us getting married?"

"Yes. She was angry and convinced that you were trapping me."

Kiara wasn't surprised to hear that. Jill didn't have a very good impression of her to start with. Her ending up pregnant probably just reinforced what she already thought about Kiara.

There was a part of her that wondered if Julian had thought that as well. He'd never acted like he was suspicious of what had happened, even though he had no memory of the time they'd had together.

"She'll come around eventually," Julian said. "But I'm not going to let her around the baby if she doesn't accept you as his mother."

Kiara appreciated Julian's willingness to stand up for her, and she hoped that would be the case when it actually happened.

"I don't want to come between you and your mother," she said.

"If she chooses to have that attitude toward you, she's the one coming between me and her."

As they approached the security building, Julian said, "Let's pop in there for a minute and let them know we need a UTV."

It didn't take long, and Anthony promised to have a UTV waiting for them at the house after dinner.

When they walked into the house a few minutes later, Kiara told him they'd been eating dinner in the breakfast room. Without Duncan and Elizabeth there, mealtimes had been a little more relaxed, which Kiara really appreciated.

Annie and Benji were already in the room and greeted Julian with smiles. Once they'd all taken their seats at the table, Annie said a prayer for the meal.

Conversation flowed differently than it had when she and Angie had first arrived. Julian was no longer sitting there, sullenly nursing a drink while everyone else had chatted. This time he was an active participant in the conversation.

"I hear congratulations are in order," Julian said to Annie.

Annie beamed. "Yes! Cole and his team won the championship, and then I won when he asked me to marry him."

"How soon are you getting married?" he asked.

"Well, so far, no one has had a long engagement, so we're not going to buck the trend."

Julian chuckled. "So next week?"

"More like three weeks now. Elizabeth has been organizing some of it from New York, and I've already had a meeting with the dress designer."

"These quick weddings would not be possible for the average person, I don't think," Kiara said. "Unless they were eloping."

Annie nodded. "That's true. We're very fortunate."

"Do you think Duncan would have guessed at the beginning of the year that within seven months, all three of his adult children would be married?"

Annie laughed. "I have a feeling that would have been his definition of a nightmare, and yet, he's survived."

"I would have thought Angie and Jude would join us for dinner," Benji said. "Since they just got back today."

"I think they're still in their honeymoon phase," Kiara said. "And Angie enjoys cooking, so I wouldn't be surprised if she wanted to cook a meal for Jude in their own home."

"Do you enjoy cooking?" Benji asked.

"Probably not as much as Angie," Kiara admitted. "But I can cook well enough. Once I get some groceries, I'll probably do some cooking as well. I appreciate being able to come here for meals, but since there's a lovely kitchen in the new house, I should probably use it."

"I like to cook sometimes," Annie said. "But I'm glad for the option of coming here when I don't want to."

"I'll go wherever the food is," Julian said with a laugh.

"Now that you're not drinking most of your meals, you look a lot better," Annie remarked. "Was the food at the treatment center good?"

"It was excellent," Julian said. "Almost as good as Mrs. Stevens' cooking."

Though Kiara had no issues with Duncan and Elizabeth, she had to admit that she really appreciated the more relaxed atmosphere within the family with them gone. And seeing Julian relaxed and interacting in a positive way with his siblings also made her feel good.

Her life was intrinsically linked to his now, so the happier and healthier he was, the better it was for her, but most especially for their son.

Following the meal, Annie left to go back to her place, and Benji went to the rec center to shoot some hoops.

"I want to grab a few things from my room," Julian said, then hesitated, lifting a hand to rub his chin. "Would you mind coming upstairs with me?"

"Uh, sure," Kiara said, wondering why he'd need her help if he was just getting a few things.

She got to her feet, then walked with Julian out of the breakfast room. The stairs were getting more challenging as her pregnancy progressed, and she was sure there would come a time when she outright refused to climb them.

When they reached his room, Kiara looked around curiously. She'd never been inside it, but from what she could see, she hadn't missed anything. The room was basically the same setup as the rooms she and Angie had used.

"Why don't you sit over here?" Julian said, gesturing to the perfectly made bed.

Since he had a sitting area, just like she and Angie had in their rooms, Kiara wasn't sure why he wanted her to sit on the bed. However, she didn't question him, curious about what was to come.

She moved over to the bed and sat down, wiggling a bit to move back from the edge, since it was a little higher than the bed she was used to.

Julian came to stand in front of her, his expression serious. "I need to show you something. Just wait a minute."

Kiara watched as he walked to what she assumed was the walk-in closet. He disappeared inside, leaving her to wait in uneasy anticipation.

CHAPTER SEVENTEEN

Julian pressed his sweaty palms against his jeans. Maybe he shouldn't have asked Kiara to come to his room to watch him do what he needed to do. However, he wanted the accountability that came with having someone there to witness it.

With trembling hands, he reached for the large chest that sat at the back of the walk-in closet. Going down on one knee, he punched in the code on the lock of the chest. He lifted the lid, then stared at the bottles of alcohol that sat lined up on the bottom of the chest.

Nine of them. There had been twelve there at one point, but he hadn't had a chance to restock before leaving for the treatment center.

He'd been determined never to run out. If Duncan had removed all alcohol from the house, he'd planned to still be able to drink from his own stash.

Reaching inside, he picked up one bottle and tucked it into his elbow. Then he picked up two more, one in each hand. Straightening, he left the closet.

Kiara was watching the closet, so as he walked out, she saw him right away, her eyes widening when she spotted what he carried.

"It isn't my intention to put the weight of my sobriety on you," Julian said, "but I want to be accountable to you, starting with this."

"What is that?" she asked.

"This is my stash. The one I kept in case Duncan removed all the alcohol from the house. And sometimes, it was what I drank when I decided that I still needed more alcohol after coming upstairs to my room."

"That's a lot of alcohol."

"It is," he agreed. "And this isn't all of it."

Kiara's brows rose. "How much do you have?"

"Six more bottles. Nine in total."

"What are you going to do with it?"

"I'm going to get rid of it," he said. "I'm going to pour it all down the drain."

Turning, he moved in the direction of the open bathroom door. Stepping up to the sink, he set the three bottles on the sink counter, then cracked the seal of one of them.

He exhaled heavily before he tipped the bottle over. The golden liquid glugged out of the bottle, into the sink, and down the drain.

As the bottle emptied, he felt a rising panic. These bottles were his lifeline. They were his ability to deal with the difficult parts of his life. What if something came up and he couldn't cope with it without the alcohol? Maybe he should keep just one bottle.

When he felt a soft touch on his arm, Julian set the empty bottle down, then glanced at Kiara. She was gazing at him with an understanding expression.

"You can do this," she said. "I know you can."

The tightness in his chest eased a little, and he gave a single nod before reaching for another bottle.

"Can you go get the others?" he asked.

He wasn't sure that he'd retrieve all of them if he was responsible for bringing them to the bathroom to empty.

"Of course."

Kiara disappeared, and by the time she reappeared, he'd emptied the second bottle. She set the three bottles she carried down on the counter, then went to get the rest.

After she'd brought him all six, instead of leaving the bathroom and returning to her seat on the bed, she remained at his side, her hand on his back. She didn't say anything more. Just stood there, steady and quiet, her presence giving him the strength to pick up another bottle.

He cracked the third one open. The familiar aroma of the alcohol escaped the bottle, and he thought for a twisted second of tipping it back. Not to swallow, just to let it hit his lips. But the knowledge that Kiara was watching made something hot and embarrassed settle inside him.

Turning the bottle over, he watched its contents spiral down the drain. The sound was both satisfying and sickening.

He emptied the fourth bottle and set it beside the others. The four glass bottles lined up before him were almost accusatory in their presence. A pointed reminder of his weakness.

Kiara's hand didn't leave his back. Instead, she applied a light, encouraging pressure. It felt strange—comforting and foreign all at once. No one touched him like that, with care and support.

Kiara was seeing him at a vulnerable moment, and usually he would have hated that. He would have hated anyone seeing him like that. But he didn't sense judgment in her. Just support and concern.

"Halfway there," he muttered.

He twisted the cap off the next bottle, hesitating a second. He just couldn't seem to get past the temptation. The scent again drifted up and filled the air, reminding him of how much he wanted to take a drink. To take a swig and slam the bottle down, revealing to Kiara how hopelessly flawed he really was.
But he didn't want her to see that. It wasn't why he'd asked her to come to his room while he'd purged his stash.

Instead, he poured it into the sink. The splash of the liquor hitting the porcelain reminded him of all those nights he'd stood in the library, pouring the alcohol into a glass, and then drinking it, the burn intense in his throat as he tried to block out the world.

He didn't speak again as he settled into the rhythm of emptying bottle after bottle. Open, pour, set down. Repeat.

The last bottle was the hardest. Maybe because it was the end, or maybe because it was the rare one he'd brought back from Europe and saved for... what? A celebration? A disaster? It had been expensive and was probably irreplaceable.

The urge to close the bottle and return it to the chest in his closet, one final backup, flashed through him. But the silent pressure of Kiara's hand and the heavy expectation in the room swept the thought away.

He tipped the bottle over and watched as the amber liquid flowed into the sink and down the drain. Once it was empty, that final bottle joined the others on the counter.

The air in the bathroom reeked like a dive bar, and he had flashbacks to waking up reeking of the same smell. The idea shamed him.

With the task done, Julian braced his fists on the counter on either side of the sink and let his head hang forward, his head throbbing, the acidic tang of spilled booze lingering in his nose and throat.

Kiara still hadn't said anything, but she was closer now, her weight shifting beside him. He couldn't think of what to say, but he felt a need to fill the silence.

"Thanks," he said, voice unsteady. "That sucked."

"But you did it," was all she said.

He didn't know what response he'd expected—some speech, maybe. But the simplicity of her words cut through the shame and revealed a weird kernel of pride. He almost laughed, but it caught in his chest, coming out as a strangled exhale.

He lifted his head and saw his reflection in the medicine cabinet mirror—raw and red-eyed, jaw tense. But though there was emotion and strain on his face now, he still looked healthier than he had on the mornings when he'd woken up hungover.

Straightening, he rubbed a hand along his cheek, feeling the grit of a day's growth. His mind was settling, and his body was surprisingly steady.

Julian realized in that moment that he'd expected himself to fail. The worry that had driven him to hide the bottles of alcohol so he'd always have something to drink wasn't completely gone, but not having the backups didn't make his skin crawl with anxiety the way it once had. He'd done it.

He looked sideways at Kiara. She had leaned her hip against the counter, arms crossed, her expression still free of judgment or condemnation. She had suffered because of his drinking. He hadn't taken care of her like he had other lovers he'd had over the years. And yet here she was, offering her support.

"I wasn't sure I'd do it, you know," he said.

Kiara shrugged, but there was something bright in her eyes. "I knew you would."

"You did?"

She nodded and picked at the peeling label of the closest bottle on the counter. "You seem like someone who, when he decides something, follows through."

"I'm not sure that's true," he said.

"Well, at least it was in this case. You were brave," Kiara said, as if this was unarguable. She peeled the label with methodical patience, stripping it bit by bit, rolling the torn paper between thumb and finger. "It's not nothing, what you just did. I'm glad you let me witness it."

He felt a strange tightness in his stomach. Something he couldn't put his finger on. On some level, he had felt it was necessary to prove to Kiara that he could do what needed doing when it came to alcohol. Why that had been important, he didn't know.

"Let's get these cleaned up," Kiara said, gesturing to the empty bottles. "Then you can put this behind you."

Physically, maybe. Mentally? It might take a little more time before he could be truly grateful that he didn't have those backups anymore.

They gathered up the bottles, then Julian led her from the room. Down in the kitchen, they dumped the bottles into the recycling bin.

"Are you ready to go back to the house?" Julian asked.

Kiara nodded. "Are you?"

"I'm just going to grab a few things from my room, then we can go."

"I'll wait down here."

Julian jogged back up the stairs and grabbed a duffel bag from his closet. He added some things from the bathroom and his dresser, figuring he could get the rest of his things the next day. Including the now-empty chest that had contained his stash.

The following Saturday, Angela had invited them all to dinner at her and Jude's. He and Kiara walked over from their house, enjoying the warm late afternoon air.

He'd been at the house for a couple of days so far, and it had gone well. Kiara was an easy person to share space with, and he found that he liked living there better than at the main house. He hoped that the living arrangement continued to go well, and that Kiara also agreed so that he wouldn't have to move out.

"I wonder what we're having for dinner," Julian said as they made their way along the road. "Does she have a meal that she enjoys making?"

"Not really," Kiara replied. "Back in Briar Hollow, we kind of just made whatever we found on sale at the store."

"So it's a surprise for you too?"

"Yep, I'm sure it will be good though," Kiara said. "Angie has always loved to cook, so I have a feeling she'll have found something interesting to make for us."

"You don't like to cook like she does?"

"Though I know how to cook pretty well," Kiara said, "I never really enjoyed it the way Angie did. I think that was partly because I *had* to cook. Jim insisted that Angie and I do all the cooking. And if he didn't like it... well, there were consequences."

"You can always eat at the main house if you don't want to cook," Julian said. "I'm pretty useless in the kitchen myself, so I'll be relying on Mrs. Stevens."

"I actually want to start cooking again," Kiara said. "I have a home with a beautiful kitchen, and with a child on the way, I feel like I shouldn't be relying on other people to cook my meals."

They reached Jude and Angela's before they could continue the conversation, and Jude answered the door when they knocked.

"C'mon in," Jude said as he stepped back, opening the door wider.

Julian laid a hand on Kiara's back, urging her to precede him into the house. As he followed her in, he glanced around. He'd never been in the house before, but he'd always assumed that it would be a rather stark environment.

However, the place had a homey vibe going on, with pictures on the wall and bits of decor on a small table in the hallway. As they moved further into the house, he saw colorful throw cushions on the overstuffed furniture in the living room. There were candles and framed pictures sitting on the end tables.

Everywhere he could see touches of Angela. Or at least he assumed it was Angela's touch because he didn't think Jude cared about that sort of thing.

As they headed for the kitchen, there was another knock on the door, and Jude turned to answer it, welcoming Annie and Benji into the house.

"Hey, you two," Annie said, greeting them with a smile. "How are you doing?"

"I'm good," Julian said, then turned to Kiara.

"I'm doing good too, and so is baby boy."

"No name yet?" Annie asked.

"Not yet," Kiara replied. "We honestly haven't really talked it over, but I have some ideas."

Julian didn't have much of a preference about the name. Considering Kiara was doing all the work of growing the baby, he kind of thought maybe she had more of a right to choose the name. Plus, he didn't even remember their time together that had led to the pregnancy. This whole thing felt more like her show, and he was just along for the ride.

"Are you taking any suggestions?" Annie asked.

"People are welcome to offer suggestions, but I can't guarantee we'll take them," Kiara said.

"Hey!" Angela came from the kitchen, approaching them with her arms open wide. She first hugged Kiara, then Annie. "I'm so glad you could make it."

"It smells delicious," Kiara said. "And I'm hungry."

Angela laid a hand on Kiara's belly, then bent over, her head close to the bump. "Hey there, little guy. Are you making Mommy hungry?"

Kiara chuckled, and for a moment, Julian was stuck on the word *Mommy*. Kiara was Mommy, and he was going to be Daddy. It was a stunning thought.

"Let's go sit down," Angela said, gesturing to the large table that was set with enough places for all of them.

"Can I help you with anything?" Kiara asked.

"Nope. Jude's going to help me," Angela said, reaching out to take her husband's hand. "He's been my assistant all day, and he's done a great job."

She beamed up at him, and a small smile crossed Jude's face before he leaned over and pressed a kiss on her forehead. "She's been a pretty good boss."

Julian had a hard time believing Jude would let anyone boss him around, but there was something between the married couple that brought out a softness in the man. A side of Jude that Julian wasn't sure he'd ever seen.

As Jude and Angela went to the kitchen, the rest of them made their way to the table. Julian pulled out a chair for Kiara. She gave him a curious look as she sat down and allowed him to help her scoot the chair closer to the table.

Julian had been taught how to treat a woman, but he realized that Kiara hadn't been exposed to that type of treatment, especially from him. However, as the mother of his child, she deserved the best treatment he could offer her.

"It smells good," Benji said as he sat down on the chair across the table from Julian. "And I'm hungry too."

Jude came to the table with a large casserole dish, steam rising from its surface. After he'd set it on the table, he returned to the kitchen. Over the next few minutes, the couple carried in the rest of the meal.

After pouring them drinks—the options being water and juice—Jude and Angela sat down, each of them taking a seat at opposite ends of the table.

"Let's pray," Jude said, surprising Julian for a moment. He'd known Jude and Angela were both Christians, but sometimes he forgot that.

As he listened to his brother-in-law pray, Julian was reminded of Elijah and the many conversations they'd had about Elijah's faith and what it meant to him.

Once the prayer was over, Angela said, "I made baked chicken with spinach dip and mozzarella cheese, roasted parmesan potatoes, honey-glazed carrots, and a Caesar salad."

Also on the table were buns, which Julian suspected Angela had made herself.

Unlike the multi-course meals they often got at the main house, all the food was served at once. Julian found that he liked the more casual meal, and everything was delicious.

"This tastes great, Angie," Kiara said. "Did you make the spinach dip yourself?"

Angela nodded. "I found a recipe for it. We had something similar when we were on our honeymoon, and I loved it so much that I decided I wanted to recreate it once we got home."

As Angela spoke, Julian saw a radiance in her. A happiness that eased some of the pain he carried for his actions all those years ago.

Conversation flowed easily as they ate, more easily than Julian might have thought it would with Jude being part of it. It gave him a glimpse into his siblings' lives—as well as his wife's—that he hadn't had before. Or maybe he hadn't wanted to have before.

Now, with his mind and his emotions free from the hold of alcohol, his interest in life had been renewed. Where previously his only interest had been in his work, now, he wanted to have these connections with the people in his life.

After they finished the meal, they all got up to help clear the table before Angela brought dessert to the table. It was a brownie cheesecake, which was the best Julian had ever eaten. When he told Angela as much, she beamed at him.

"I'm glad you like it," she said. "I'm having fun learning new recipes and trying them out on Jude."

"My kitchen has never gotten as much use as it has recently," he said with a chuckle. "And I've had to work out twice as hard to offset all the great food I've eaten."

"If you're going to have a dad bod soon, you'd better have a kid to go with it," Benji said with a smirk.

Jude scowled at the teen. "I'm not going to have a dad bod."

"But I'm not opposed to having a baby soon," Angela said as she grinned at her husband. "There's no reason to wait."

"It would be nice for baby boy to have a cousin close in age," Kiara said, running her hand over her bump. "So don't wait too long."

"Well, that's two votes for getting pregnant ASAP, love," Angela said.

Annie's hand went into the air. "Three!"

"Four!" Benji called out.

"Let's make it five," Julian said, enjoying seeing Jude's expression turn incredulous.

"We're not making a decision about having a child by group vote," Jude growled.

"I think it's the perfect way to make this decision," Annie said. "We're family, after all."

Laughter filled the room as everyone seemed to enjoy having fun at Jude's expense. It was something Julian had never experienced before, especially with his family. He'd kept his distance from Annie and Benji over the years, using alcohol to cope with the secret he couldn't share.

But now, the family bonds were tightening. However, for once, they didn't feel like a noose.

CHAPTER EIGHTEEN

Kiara tugged her dress into place over her bump. She'd rarely worn dresses over the years, since they'd never been practical. But now that it was summer, dresses were more comfortable for her.

Stranger than her wearing a dress was *why* she was wearing one. As she scrunched product into her curls, she wondered if she still had time to back out.

When Angie had asked her the previous night if she wanted to go to church with her and Jude, for some reason, Kiara had said yes. Her sister had seemed so excited at the prospect, and Kiara hadn't wanted to disappoint her.

For their whole life together, Kiara had tried her best to protect Angela and to make her happy, if possible. So, not wanting to see Angela's happiness dimmed by declining the invitation, she'd said yes.

Surely, she could survive an hour in church. She'd done it before, so there was no reason why she couldn't do it again.

It wasn't that she didn't want to go to church. It had more to do with not knowing what to expect, or what expectations Angie might have because Kiara agreed to go with her.

Once she was ready, Kiara left her room and went to the kitchen to grab some breakfast before Jude and Angie picked her up. She needed to make sure she had something in her stomach.

As the kitchen came into view, Kiara's steps faltered. Julian was standing in front of the coffee pot, dressed like he was headed out somewhere.

Usually, he wore jeans and a T-shirt around the estate. Right then, he had on a pair of black slacks and a light blue button-up shirt, tucked into his pants. His hair also looked like it was styled, rather than lying in loose waves the way he'd been wearing it lately.

Was he headed somewhere on business? He hadn't mentioned anything about a trip, but that didn't mean much. After all, he didn't owe her any details about his schedule.

He glanced up as she approached, a smile growing on his face as he greeted her. "Good morning."

"Good morning." She went around the opposite side of the large island and headed for the fridge to pull out a container of yogurt and then grabbed some granola from the pantry.

"Do you want a cup of coffee?" he asked as he turned to lean back against the counter next to the coffee maker. He lifted his mug to take a sip.

She was tempted but shook her head. "I try not to drink any unless I really need the caffeine. I slept well enough last night that I think I'll be okay."

"You won't fall asleep during the service?" Julian asked.

"I certainly hope not," she said. "That would be extremely embarrassing. Especially if I started snoring."

"I'll poke you in the ribs if you do," he offered.

Kiara stopped stirring the granola into her yogurt and focused on Julian. "Are you going to church too?"

Julian nodded. "I decided that I'd like to give it a try. Elijah has talked about his faith a lot, so I thought I'd see what someone else has to say about it."

"Well, I'm going because I didn't want to disappoint Angie. She seemed so happy, I didn't want to turn her down."

"This will be a new experience for me," Julian said. "I've only attended church on special occasions like Christmas, and that was mainly back when I was a teen, and Duncan and Elizabeth could force me to go."

"I've gone a few times with Angie in the past." Kiara returned to preparing her yogurt. "But church never really clicked with me the way it did with her."

"Maybe it will be different this time," Julian said.

"Maybe." Kiara got herself a glass of water, then went to sit on one of the bar stools at the island counter. "Do Jude and Angie know you're coming?"

"Yes. I had to let Jude know for security purposes. Two bodyguards will be coming with us, so we'll be taking one of the estate's SUVs."

"I wonder how the bodyguards feel about attending church this morning?"

"Oh, they get used to going to all sorts of places," Jude said. "Church is probably one of the least stressful locations they've had to go."

"Did you have breakfast?" Kiara asked as Jude sat down on a bar stool.

"I had a piece of toast. I'm not a big breakfast eater, to be honest."

"I don't mind breakfast," Kiara said. "We always had to eat it because Jim didn't want us to have any excuse not to have energy to do all the work he had for us during the day."

"So he thought breakfast was the most important meal of the day?"

"Something like that." Kiara swallowed a spoonful of yogurt. "At least I'm able to eat breakfast most days now. Ever since morning sickness hit, it has been a difficult meal to tolerate."

"How are you feeling this morning?" he asked.

"Not too bad," she said. "I find that eating small amounts every couple of hours helps to keep the nausea at bay."

"Are you bringing food with you?"

Kiara laughed. “Oh, these days, I always have a stash of food, candy, and a bottle of water in my bag. I had to change my usual purse for a bigger one to accommodate all my necessities.”

“Candy?”

“Ginger candy,” she said. “It helps to control the nausea. I wouldn’t be able to drag out a granola bar and start munching on it in the middle of the service if the nausea kicks in.”

“We can sit near the back, so if you have to slip out, you don’t have to walk past everyone.”

“I think that might be a good idea, though I’m sure Jude and Angie sit near the front.”

“We’ll hang out at the back with Anthony and whoever else comes with us.”

When Kiara’s phone beeped, she pulled it out of her purse and checked the message. “Jude and Angie are on their way.”

Julian got to his feet and went to the sink to rinse out his mug. Kiara finished the last of her yogurt, then put her bowl into the dishwasher.

“Got everything?” Julian asked as she picked up her purse.

“Yes. I think so.”

They walked out onto the large porch to wait for the SUV. It was a beautiful, sunny and warm morning, and Kiara enjoyed it in a way she never would have during their life on the homestead. Sunny and warm in Kentucky usually ended up being hot and humid in the afternoon, which meant they were sweaty and gross.

When the SUV pulled up, she saw Anthony and Lucy in the front seats, while Jude and Angie were in the second row. Jude climbed out and stood by the open door.

“Would you like to sit next to Angela?” he asked when Kiara reached him.

“No. I’m fine sitting in the back with Julian.”

Jude looked over at Julian, who gave him a nod. “I’m good in the back.”

Kiara sometimes forgot that Jude was technically Julian's employee. She probably shouldn't have said he'd be sitting in the back with her.

However, Julian apparently had no problem with the plan. Once Jude folded part of the middle seat forward, Julian climbed in and sat down, then leaned forward to offer Kiara his hand.

She took it and allowed him to help steady her as she stepped up into the SUV. As soon as she was seated, she let go of his hand so she could put her seatbelt on. "Thanks."

"Anytime."

Jude lowered the seat back into place, then climbed in and took his place next to Angie. From her seat behind them, Kiara saw Jude reach over and take Angie's hand. She turned to smile at him, then leaned her head on his shoulder.

Emotion pricked at Kiara's eyes, and she turned her gaze to the window beside her. She was so glad to see Jude offering Angie affection. He'd always been so reserved that Kiara had been concerned that he wouldn't be affectionate with Angie the way she wanted without her being the one to initiate it.

Seeing the interaction between the two was bittersweet. She was happy that her worst fears hadn't been realized, and that Jude had seen value in Angie. That he'd found her worth loving.

Something told Kiara that she wasn't going to experience the same thing.

When she'd first been taken from her family, her eight-year-old self had been so excited. Finally, she'd be with people who wanted her. Who would *love* her.

Only that hadn't been the case. No matter how good she had tried to be, they never loved her the way she'd hoped they would. Sandra had always favored Angie, and though Kiara had initially resented Angie because of that, she'd soon realized that the sweet little girl with blonde hair and blue-green eyes actually loved her.

She'd followed Kiara around, trying to help her. When she fell or got hurt, she'd wanted Kiara to help her feel better. And when Kiara would get hurt or cried, Angie had been right there, hugging her and stroking her hair.

Angie had been the one person who had been there for her, regardless of what else was going on in their lives. She'd even stood up for Kiara when Sandra would get frustrated with her.

And now Angie had someone who loved and protected her. She'd been able to offer Jude a pure and beautiful love.

Kiara had made a bad decision and ended up in a loveless marriage that had an end date.

She moved her hand to rest it on her stomach. At least she would be left with someone to love. Someone who needed her, and who would hopefully, one day, come to love her. It wouldn't be the type of love she'd dreamed of, but it would be enough.

But the first thing she had to do was pack away the bitter in moments like these, and just focus on the sweet. Overall, she was in a much better situation than she'd been in in Briar Hollow.

And for now, she needed to focus on preparing for her baby and figuring out how to be the best mom she could be for him, despite having had two very poor examples of motherhood so far in her life.

She couldn't keep letting those thoughts and feelings drag her down. If Angie sensed that she was feeling even a little depressed, it would make her worry. And the last thing she wanted was to put a dent in her sister's happiness.

While Angie might be currently distracted by her new marriage to Jude, it wouldn't last forever. Sooner or later, she would focus on Kiara again, and as Angie's big sister, it was Kiara's responsibility to keep her from worrying.

No more feeling sorry for yourself, Kiara. You have so much to be thankful for. Focus on that. Your life is great.

"You feeling okay?"

Julian's voice drew Kiara out of her thoughts. She blinked rapidly a few times, making sure there was no lingering emotion threatening to spill out in tears before she turned to look at him.

"Yep."

"Riding in a car doesn't make you feel sick?"

She shifted around to face him more fully, grateful for the distraction. "I've never had motion sickness, and it seems my morning sickness isn't triggered by motion. I even had no problem flying in the helicopter."

Angie turned her head to look at them. "She *loves* being on the plane and in the helicopter. Unlike me."

Julian smiled. "I rather enjoy flying myself."

"Maybe we should have flown to Coeur d'Alene for church," Kiara said with a grin at Angie.

Angie shook her head. "Hah. No."

"I would have kept you safe," Jude said.

"I know you would." Angie smiled at him as she clasped her hand around the back of his neck. "But I'd rather you not be put in that position to begin with. At least not more than you have to."

For the remainder of the drive, the conversation was light, and Kiara was grateful for the distraction. When they reached the church, Anthony parked the SUV.

Jude opened the door and got out, then helped Angie from the vehicle. He flipped the seats forward so that Julian and Kiara could climb out of the back seat.

The six of them walked to the doors of the church, following other people heading inside the large building.

Lucy went in first, while Anthony held the door for the rest of them. It was odd to think there might be a security concern at the church, but Kiara didn't question the need for the bodyguards. Duncan's word was law when it came to the protection of his children.

"We're going to sit at the back," Julian told Jude. "Just in case Kiara needs to step out."

"That's fine," Jude said, then turned to Angie. "Do you want to sit at the back with them?"

Angie nodded. "If it's not too much trouble."

"No trouble at all, love," Jude assured her.

After a brief conversation with the bodyguards, Jude led them to a row near the back. Angie followed him into the row, then Kiara went next. Julian sat on Kiara's other side, while the two bodyguards took seats in the row immediately behind them.

Julian shifted on the pew beside her, and Kiara wondered if he regretted his decision to join them at church.

As she looked around, Kiara realized they were garnering some attention from others in the sanctuary. She glanced sideways at Julian to see how he was taking it. He was looking straight forward, and Kiara thought maybe he was reading the information that was being shown on the screens at the front of the sanctuary. It seemed like he was totally oblivious to the attention he was receiving.

This was the first time she'd been out in public with Julian, so she had no idea if he was usually oblivious to the attention he got from people. Jude, on the other hand, seemed to be on alert, his gaze roaming the sanctuary.

There was movement in the row beyond Jude, and a couple sat down next to him. Kiara recognized them as Cooper and Melanie, who had been at Jude and Angie's wedding. Angie leaned past Jude to hold out her hand to Melanie, who smiled warmly at her, then gave Kiara a little wave.

There was no time for conversation, though, as the music that had been playing faded away when a man moved to the podium. Soon, they were invited to stand for some singing. Julian smoothly got to his feet, while Kiara was a bit more cumbersome, and she had to use the pew in front of her to leverage herself up.

"You okay?" Julian murmured, turning toward her.

"I'm good."

Rather than face fully forward, Julian kept part of his body angled toward her, as if he was concerned that she was going to keel over and he'd have to catch her. Kiara doubted there was much likelihood of that. She hadn't fainted yet.

She didn't know the songs that the congregation sang, and she assumed Julian didn't either because he wasn't singing. Angie, however, knew them all and sang with confidence.

As she read the words on the screens at the front, Kiara found them to be both worshipful and full of hope. They were different from the songs she heard on the music streaming services or social media.

As they sang a song called *How Great Is Our God,* Angie lifted her hands, her head tilted back as her eyes closed. The words washed over Kiara as she took in the people around her. They were worshipping God, singing about how wonderful He was and how He was deserving of their praise.

God had always been such a distant entity in Kiara's mind. But in that moment, He felt real and present. These people believed He was there with them. That He was accepting of their praises. They weren't just praying and asking Him for things. They were praising Him. Worshipping Him.

She'd never experienced anything like it before in her life. Even when she'd attended church with Angie in Briar Hollow, she hadn't felt like this.

The music quieted as one of the musicians prayed, thanking God for His presence in their lives. For the work of His hands in the world. For the hope they had because of what He'd done.

As the prayer ended, another song began, its words filling the screens on either side of the stage. The song had an almost Celtic sound to it as a woman began to sing. *In Christ Alone My Hope is Found.*

Kiara was once again drawn in by the words. There was so much hope and promise in them. Glancing over at Angie, she saw that Jude had his arm around her as they both sang, their eyes lifted heavenward. Their worship seemed to not be constrained by those around them. In fact, it was a shared worship.

Since she didn't know the songs, she felt like she was on the outside looking in. However, Kiara also knew that she didn't have to stay on the outside. Angie had spoken about her faith enough that Kiara knew that, just like her sister had decided to become a Christian, Kiara could as well.

But was she ready to do that?

As she stood there, the music swelling around her, Kiara felt movement in her belly. She'd been feeling fluttering for a little while already, but this felt more substantial. As if her little boy wanted to remind her that she wasn't alone.

Swaying in time with the music, Kiara pressed her hand against the spot where she'd felt the movement. As they continued to sing, she wondered if she could have hope in Christ for her future. For her little boy's future.

When her marriage to Julian eventually ended, would God be there for her if she had faith like Angie did?

Though the thought was comforting, there was a kernel of fear inside her that she wouldn't be worthy of God's presence in her life. So many had deemed her unworthy... unwanted.

Even now, she was only where she was because of Angie. Because *Angie* was wanted. Because Angie had wanted Kiara there.

If she lost everything, could she still have God? Would He still be there for her?

Kiara didn't know the answer to that, and she was scared to get to the point where she might discover what that answer was.

CHAPTER NINETEEN

Given that he'd never been in a regular church service before, Julian wasn't as uncomfortable as he'd thought he might be. He knew that was due in large part to the many conversations he'd had with Elijah.

Because Elijah had been the worship leader for his dad's services before he'd left the ministry, he'd talked at length about how he viewed worship through song.

"Our hope is in Christ alone," the pastor declared as he took his place behind the pulpit and they all took their seats again. "Praise the Lord!"

People around them echoed the pastor's words as he opened his Bible on the pulpit.

Julian shifted in his seat, trying to get comfortable for the duration of the sermon. He ended up putting his arm along the back of the pew behind Kiara. It allowed him to stretch out a bit, and Kiara didn't seem to be bothered by it.

"What does it mean to have our hope in Christ?" the pastor asked. "It means that we don't put our trust in the things of this world. Not in money, not in relationships, not in our jobs or our health. All of those things can fail us. But Christ? He never fails."

Julian found himself leaning forward slightly, drawn in by the pastor's words despite himself. He'd spent his entire life trusting in things that had ultimately failed him—alcohol most prominently. He'd trusted it to numb his pain, to help him forget. But where had that gotten him?

The pastor moved from behind the pulpit, walking across the stage with a confidence that reminded Julian of his father addressing a board meeting. "The world promises security but delivers chaos. It promises fulfillment but delivers emptiness. It promises freedom but delivers bondage."

Julian felt a strange tightening in his chest. Those words hit uncomfortably close to home. He glanced at Kiara, wondering if she felt the same strange resonance. Her face was tilted up toward the pastor, her expression thoughtful, one hand resting on her rounded belly.

"But in Christ," the pastor continued, his voice rising with conviction, "we find true security. A promise of everlasting life. True fulfillment. Not because our circumstances change, but because He changes us from within. And we are given true freedom since we are no longer bound by the shackles of our sin."

Julian shifted in his seat again. He'd been to countless business presentations, motivational speeches, even a couple of political rallies. All of them had had captivating speakers, but this felt different... more personal somehow, as if the pastor were speaking directly to him rather than addressing a room full of people.

"When we place our hope in Christ alone," the pastor said, "we're no longer at the mercy of our circumstances. We're no longer defined by our mistakes, our sin, or our failures."

The word "failures" seemed to hang in the air. Julian's mind flashed back to his childhood—the secret he'd kept, his role in the twins' kidnapping. The treatment center had helped him begin to address that guilt, but it still lingered, a shadow over his heart.

"We all have a past," the pastor said, as if reading Julian's thoughts. "Every single one of us has things we're not proud of. Things we wish we could undo. But here's the good news—Christ already paid the price for those things on the cross. Your past doesn't have to define your future. In First John chapter one, verse nine, it says *If we confess our sins, He is faithful and just to forgive us our sins and to cleanse us from all unrighteousness.*"

Julian felt something catch in his throat. He hadn't expected to be so affected by a sermon. He'd come to church out of curiosity, maybe to understand Elijah better, but now he found himself genuinely moved.

The pastor continued, speaking of forgiveness and redemption, of how Christ could transform a life and make it new. Julian listened, his mind racing with memories of his own broken life. The secret he'd kept. The flippant way he'd treated women. The alcohol and sex he'd turned to in order to find a way to feel something other than the guilt he carried.

But lately, he'd been working hard to get sober, to fix his relationships with his family, to be the kind of man who could be a good father to his son. Was it enough? Could he truly overcome his past?

As the pastor continued speaking about grace and second chances, Julian felt Kiara shift beside him. She'd placed both hands on her belly now, a small smile playing on her lips. He wondered if the baby was moving. The thought that his son was right there... growing, developing, becoming a person, filled him with equal parts wonder and terror.

"When we place our hope in Christ," the pastor said, "we're not just hoping things will get better. We're standing on the solid foundation of God's promises. And His promises never fail."

Julian thought about the promises he'd made to himself over the years. The promise not to drink as much. The promise to be a better son. To be a better brother. But he'd failed, over and over, undermined by the memory of what he'd done. He'd eventually given up even trying to be a better person.

Could he make new promises—ones that wouldn't fail? He needed to think about it. Maybe have another conversation with Elijah.

It just seemed too easy. Too simple. When everything else in his adult life had resulted from hard work, it just seemed impossible for something so good to be available so easily.

The service continued with another song and a final prayer. As everyone stood around them, Julian removed his arm from the pew behind Kiara, flexing his fingers to restore circulation.

"What did you think?" Kiara asked, turning toward him as they stood up.

"It was... thought-provoking," Julian said honestly. "Different from what I expected."

"Me too," she admitted. "I've been to church before, but this felt different somehow."

As they filed out of the pew, Julian noticed several people glancing their way with curious expressions. He was used to being recognized—the Burke name was well known in the business world, and his face had been plastered across the internet for years. Still, it felt different to be recognized in a church.

"Julian, Kiara," Angela said, turning to them as they reached the aisle. "You remember Melanie and Cooper, right? They were at our wedding."

The woman—Melanie—smiled warmly. "It's wonderful to see you both again. Angela's told us so much about you."

Julian shook their hands, feeling slightly uncomfortable. What exactly had Angela told them about? His drinking? Their unplanned pregnancy? The hasty marriage that had followed?

"We're glad you're here," Cooper said with a smile, and when he offered his hand, Julian took it in a firm shake. "I hope you'll come back again."

Julian wasn't sure if he would or not. Right then, he had questions that he didn't feel comfortable asking Jude or Cooper. Maybe once he'd had a chance to speak with Elijah, he'd have a better idea of whether he'd come back again.

"Well, we'd better go grab our kids before they page us to come get them," Melanie said with a laugh. "It was good to see you both again. Hope we see you again soon."

Once they'd left, the four of them moved from the sanctuary out to the foyer with Lucy leading them and Anthony following behind.

"Do you want to go for lunch?" Angie asked.

"I wouldn't mind that," Kiara said. "I'm hungry."

Angie chuckled. "Lately, you're always hungry."

In the end, they decided to go to a family-style restaurant. Julian had never been there before, but it smelled appetizing when they walked into the building.

Anthony and Lucy stood by the door as they walked in, their eyes scanning the restaurant. Julian had grown up with security, and he was usually in places where having a bodyguard wasn't strange. But now that they were in a more relaxed environment with... normal people... he was more aware of how his presence—and that of the security guards—drew attention in a way he wasn't as accustomed to.

The hostess greeted them, her eyes widening slightly when she saw him. A flirty smile crossed her face, which made Julian uncomfortable. He stepped closer to Kiara, hoping to make it clear that he was not available for the type of interaction she might be looking for.

Previously, it had never bothered him when women had flirted with him, even when he was out on a date with another woman. None of the women had meant anything to him. He wasn't proud of the attitude he'd had, and he definitely had a different one when it came to Kiara.

She was the mother of his child and, for the time being, his wife. As such, she deserved the respect that he had never given those other women.

As the hostess led the way deeper into the restaurant, Julian followed the group, with Anthony and Lucy bringing up the rear. Jude had made sure the hostess knew that they needed two separate tables, though still close together.

They were shown to a booth, where Julian slid in next to Kiara, letting her take the inside seat while he positioned himself on the outer edge. It felt protective somehow, though he couldn't have explained why. Protecting wasn't his job. That was why they had bodyguards.

"What do you recommend?" Kiara asked, opening her menu.

"Everything here is good," Angela said. "But I especially love their fried chicken."

Julian scanned the offerings, surprised by the home-style options. He'd rarely eaten at places like this, usually opting for high-end restaurants where the meal was served in courses, and the food was artfully arranged.

"I think I'll get the pot roast," Kiara said, closing her menu decisively. "With extra mashed potatoes."

"Is that the best thing here?" Julian asked, looking over his own menu.

The home-style options were so different from his usual fare. Something about a place like this, with its high-back booths and laminated menus, made him feel both out of place and strangely comfortable.

"I think so," Kiara replied, patting her belly. "And Baby Boy approves."

"Then I'll trust your judgment." Julian closed his menu and set it on the table. "I'll have the same."

"So what did you think of the service?" Angela asked, leaning forward with an eager expression after the waitress had taken their orders.

Julian shifted in his seat, unsure how to answer Angela's question. The sermon had touched on things he was still processing—his guilt, his failures, the possibility of redemption.

"It was interesting," he said finally. "Different from what I expected. Less... judgmental, maybe."

"Pastor Mark is really good at making the gospel relatable," Angela said. "That's what I love about this church. It's a place where broken people can find healing."

Broken people. The phrase resonated with Julian. He certainly qualified.

"What about you, Kiara?" Angela asked. "What did you think?"

Kiara took a sip of her water before answering. "I liked the music. And the message about hope... it was nice to hear that our past doesn't have to define our future."

Julian glanced at her, wondering if the sermon had touched her in the same way it had affected him. He'd been so caught up in his own thoughts during the service that he hadn't considered what might be going through her mind.

"I liked that part too," Julian said. "About not being defined by our past."

He noticed Kiara's expression soften as she glanced at him, and he wondered if she had a past that she didn't want to be defined by. She rarely went into detail about the years she'd spent growing up with Angela on the homestead.

"That's what I love about Christianity," Angela said. "It's all about grace and second chances. Finding a new life in Christ."

Second chances. The concept was both appealing and terrifying. Did he deserve a second chance after what he'd done? After the years he'd wasted drinking himself into oblivion?

Their food arrived, steam rising from the generous portions of pot roast and mashed potatoes. Julian was surprised by how appetizing it looked, even though it wasn't beautifully plated like at the high-end restaurants he frequented.

Before they began to eat, Jude said a brief prayer of thanks for the food.

Kiara closed her eyes as she took her first bite of pot roast, letting out a small hum of appreciation. "This is exactly what I needed."

Julian sampled his own meal, surprised by the rich flavor and the way the meat fell apart under his fork. It wasn't the refined cuisine he was accustomed to, but there was something deeply satisfying about it.

"Good choice," he told Kiara, who smiled at him before digging into the mashed potatoes with enthusiasm.

As they ate, the conversation shifted to more casual topics. Angela's decorating plans for her and Jude's home. Kiara's ideas for the garden at their house.

Julian found himself relaxing into the normalcy of it all. No business deals to negotiate, no social climbing to navigate. Just a simple meal with family.

"So, Julian," Jude said during a lull in the conversation, "are you planning to stay at the estate for a while, or are you going to head back to New York soon?"

Julian finished chewing a bite of pot roast before answering. "I'm planning to be here unless there are things that I need to take care of elsewhere. Like the upcoming fundraising gala and the board meetings."

He glanced at Kiara, who seemed focused on her mashed potatoes. He couldn't read her expression, but he hoped his decision to stay wasn't unwelcome. So far, living in the house together had gone smoothly. Better than he'd expected, actually. They'd fallen into an easy rhythm, respecting each other's space while sharing meals occasionally.

"That makes sense," Jude said. "And how's the house working out for both of you?"

"I think it's been good so far," Julian said. "Kiara's been very gracious about sharing her space."

"Our space," Kiara corrected him softly. “For now, it’s our space.”

Julian caught the slight hesitation in Kiara's voice, the way her eyes flicked to him before returning to her food. *For now.* The unspoken implication hung between them. This arrangement had an expiration date. The trial period they'd agreed to, yes, but beyond that, their entire marriage was temporary.

"Well, I'm glad it's working out," Angela said, breaking the momentary tension. "I was worried it might be awkward."

"It's been fine," Kiara assured her. "The house is big enough that we don't have to be in each other's space if we don't want to be."

Julian nodded, though a strange twinge of disappointment fluttered in his chest. Was that how she saw their arrangement? Two people sharing a house but avoiding each other?

It wasn't like that at all for him. Despite having separate spaces, Julian enjoyed the moments they spent together. Whether it was sharing breakfast in the kitchen or sitting in the living room in the evening, Kiara reading while he worked on his laptop.

"We're figuring it out," Julian said, keeping his tone casual. "Day by day."

Kiara glanced at him, a flicker of surprise crossing her features before she nodded. "Yes, we are."

The conversation shifted again, and Julian listened as Jude and Angela discussed some upcoming renovations they were planning for their home. As they talked, Julian noticed the way Jude's hand rested on the table, palm up, and how Angela's fingers interlaced with his without either of them seeming to think about it. The casual intimacy of the gesture struck him.

He and Kiara had nothing like that. Their relationship was built on necessity, not affection. They shared a house, would share a child, but there was no handholding, no casual touches, no wordless communication that came from genuine intimacy.

He wasn't sure how to have that type of relationship. Or if he even wanted to.

Though Duncan and Elizabeth had, by all accounts, formed a good marriage, they weren't super affectionate in public. Sometimes when it was just the family, he'd see more affection between them. But it was Annie and Cole and now Jude and Angela who had shown him how a relationship could really be.

He wasn't sure how to share casual affection with someone the way his siblings did with their significant others. Julian had a feeling that even Benji, with his high school girlfriend, knew more about that than he did.

Did Kiara want that sort of relationship?

It didn't make sense to pursue a more physical relationship when they'd both agreed that their marriage wasn't a permanent arrangement. He hadn't gotten the feeling that she wanted something different from what they had.

There were times when he wondered how they'd ended up sleeping together. He wished he could remember that night so that he understood better how they'd ended up where they now were.

It added a weirdness to the situation that Julian didn't dwell on, but it was always present in the back of his mind.

That things had unfolded the way they had felt like another failure on his part. He should have known better than to fool around with someone so close to the family. Her ties to the family meant that if he did something to upset her, it would upset Angela. And if Angela was upset with him, Duncan would be upset with him too.

It left him feeling like at any given time, he was balancing on a precipice, and that failure was just waiting for him to put a foot wrong. Unfortunately, he couldn't see a future in which he wouldn't put that foot wrong.

The sermon that morning was still in his mind, but Julian struggled to believe that all he had to do was trust in God to help him overcome his failures. It felt like he had to prove to himself and to God that he had the ability to face temptations and struggles on his own and not falter.

CHAPTER TWENTY

Kiara could hardly believe that she was in New York City. It was the biggest city she'd ever been to, but she'd quickly discovered that she wasn't a big-city girl. She much preferred the open spaces of the estate, or even the smaller places like Briar Hollow or Serenity Point.

But she was there now, preparing to attend the fundraising gala for Burke Pharmaceuticals, so she'd just have to make the best of it.

Once the hair and makeup people left, Kiara took a few minutes to gather herself together. It had been a bit of a whirlwind since arriving in New York the previous afternoon. Earlier that morning, she'd had a fitting for her dress, and thankfully, it hadn't needed any alterations.

Elizabeth had had the dress made for her by the same team that had made the dresses for both Angie's and Annie's wedding. It was beautiful. More beautiful than any dress she'd ever worn. And that included her wedding dress.

The dress was made of chiffon and lace in a deep shade of burgundy. It had a sweetheart neckline and an empire waist to accommodate her bump. The most stunning part of the dress was the chiffon cape that flowed from her shoulders, which were covered in lace. Her arms were bare, but the cape offered a bit of coverage.

The dress was very comfortable. More comfortable than she would have expected a formal dress to be. The shoes, on the other hand, didn't look like they were going to be comfortable at all.

As she looked in the mirror, Kiara marveled at how beautifully the hairstylist had styled her hair. She'd made the most of Kiara's natural curls in the updo she'd created. And the woman who had done her makeup had done a great job of enhancing without overpowering her features.

Kiara hadn't worn makeup much in her life, so she was glad someone had come in to do it. If she thought she could replicate what the woman had done, she might try to wear makeup more frequently.

"Anthony just texted to see if you were ready to go," Lucy said as she came into the bedroom where Kiara had been getting ready.

"Yes. I think so," she said, sitting down on one of the chairs in order to put her heels on without falling over.

She had thought she'd stay at Julian's apartment when she came, but she'd ended up in a suite at the same hotel where the fundraising gala was being held. Lucy had the other room in her suite, while Julian and Anthony had their own suite. Cole, Annie, Duncan, and Elizabeth were also staying at the hotel.

Benji, Angie, and Jude had stayed behind at the estate, and for a moment, Kiara wished that she had too. This event was way out of her comfort zone, but she'd allowed the seed of hope in her heart to propel her to accept Julian's invitation.

She carefully got to her feet and took a few steps in the shoes to make sure she was okay. She'd tried them on earlier and had been able to walk in them, but with the dress on now, she wanted to make sure she didn't trip on the hem.

"You look beautiful," Lucy said.

"Thank you." Kiara looked over at her bodyguard. "Is that the uniform for the security people?"

"Yep." Lucy glanced down at the black pantsuit she wore. "And honestly, I'm happy to be wearing this instead of that."

Kiara laughed. "You are probably more comfortable, but I think I should be able to deal with this for a few hours. I doubt I'll be closing down the event."

They left her room and went into the living room area of the suite to wait for Julian and Anthony. The baby kicked her as she sat down in one of the armchairs, and she gently rubbed the spot. His kicks had become much more pronounced as she entered her third trimester.

So far, Julian hadn't asked to feel the kicks, but Angie and Annie had both gotten excited the first time they'd each felt the baby kick.

When there was a light rap at the door, Lucy went to open it. Julian walked in first, followed by Anthony, who was dressed similarly to Lucy.

Julian looked like he'd just stepped off the cover of a luxury menswear catalog. His charcoal gray tuxedo was impeccably well-fitted. The jacket was open, revealing the vest he wore beneath it. His shirt was stark white, and his bowtie was dark gray. The only color in his outfit was the crisp pocket square peeking from the breast pocket, which was the same shade as her dress. His black shoes were shined to a high gloss, and his hair was styled precisely.

Julian looked perfectly at ease in the formalwear, like he wore it every day, not just for special occasions.

When he spotted her, he gave her a small smile. "You look nice."

Nice. An ache pulsed in her heart momentarily. She supposed it was too much to hope that he thought she looked beautiful.

However, rather than let him see her hurt, she smiled back and said, "Thank you. You look very dashing yourself."

"Thanks." He smoothed a hand down his vest. "We should probably get going so I don't get any more texts from Duncan asking where we are."

Kiara got to her feet, then picked up the small clutch she'd been given to match her dress. She hadn't been sure what to put in it, so all it held was her phone, her room key, and some tissues.

Lucy led the way out of the suite, followed by Kiara and Julian, and Anthony brought up the rear. As they headed down the hallway, Julian's phone chimed, and he pulled it out of his pocket.

"Duncan," he murmured, then tapped out a message as they headed for the elevator. "I hope he's hassling Cole and Annie as much."

They were the only ones in the elevator, and it rapidly descended with no stops. As the doors slid open, Julian returned his phone to the pocket inside his suit coat, then offered her his arm. After a brief hesitation, Kiara slid her hand around his elbow, glad that she'd gotten her nails done before she'd left Serenity.

The four of them made their way down a long hallway before coming to large doors leading into the ballroom where the dinner was taking place.

Inside, the ballroom was overwhelming by every measure. The soaring ceilings had lengths of gauzy fabric draped throughout the room in shades of autumn to reflect the changing season. The floor to ceiling windows gave a stunning view of the New York skyline since the ballroom was on the thirty-fourth floor. Her suite was on the fiftieth, and it too had amazing views of the city.

The decor was a mix of orange, yellow, brown, burgundy, and gold. So much gold. Even the silverware on the tables was gold. There were floral centerpieces that contained flowers that were unknown to Kiara. Everywhere, there were sparkles and warm lights.

Kiara was well and truly out of her league, and it took all of her strength to stay relaxed when all she wanted to do was clutch Julian's arm more tightly so he wouldn't leave her side.

Unfortunately, Julian was carrying a tension of his own. He seemed distracted, and they'd barely spoken at all since she arrived. It was another thing that had her questioning if she should have come.

"Hello, you two," Elizabeth said as she and Duncan approached them, a vision of elegance.

The dress she wore was a deep emerald green and looked stunning with her coloring. Duncan was at her side wearing a black tuxedo with a pocket square that matched his wife's dress.

"You look beautiful, Kiara," Duncan said with a warm smile.

"That color looks stunning on you," Elizabeth added. "Just gorgeous."

"Thank you." Their words were a balm to the ache of Julian's less than enthusiastic reaction to her appearance. "You both look very lovely."

Cole and Annie entered the ballroom, and as she caught a glimpse of them, Kiara was reminded of the first time she'd seen Annie. It had been the picture that had changed everything for her and Angie.

And just like there had been photographers present at that event, there were some there that evening, already snapping shots of them.

Compliments were passed around, then Elizabeth and Duncan led the way to the table where they'd be sitting. Along the way, they greeted people, some of whom Kiara recognized from having seen them on television. Some were movie stars. Others were singers. All of them left her a little starstruck.

She worked hard to keep her expression calm, hiding the nerves that were steadily increasing. Hopefully, Julian couldn't feel her trembling. She didn't want him to think she was scared... even though she was.

"David and Celeste, I'd like to introduce you to my daughter-in-law, Kiara," Duncan said to an elegantly dressed couple who were around his age.

The woman was dripping with jewels, but her smile was warm as she turned to Kiara. "Oh, my dear, it's lovely to meet you."

Her handshake was firm, and Kiara got the feeling that this was a woman who was confident in her role in life.

"It's nice to meet you too," Kiara said.

The woman's gaze dipped to the bump that could no longer be hidden, even if she'd wanted to. "And I see it's double congratulations for you and darling Julian."

"She and Julian are expecting our first grandchild," Elizabeth said with a beaming smile. "And we are so excited."

"Grandchildren are a blessing," David said. "All we have to do is love them, while their parents have to make the tough decisions."

"And get up with them through the night," Celeste added with a light laugh.

"Also with us tonight is Cole Halverson," Duncan said as he motioned for Annie and Cole to step forward. "And this is Annie, his wife."

They'd decided not to reveal who Annie was just yet, but Duncan had also wanted to include them in the evening, given that Cole was one of the donors and a spokesperson for the Burke Foundation.

Kiara breathed a sigh of relief as the attention moved off her. When Julian turned to say something to Anthony, Kiara moved her hand from his arm. She gripped her clutch with both hands as she looked around the room.

When her gaze landed back on Annie, Kiara wasn't surprised to see how at ease she appeared to be. She might have been raised away from the limelight, but she'd clearly been taught how to exist within it.

Julian's mother had been right. She did need lessons to know how to fit in. If Kiara had realized just how far out of her comfort zone she'd have to go that night, she might have stayed at the estate.

At the time, she'd been swayed by the fact that Julian had asked her to accompany him. She'd thought he'd *wanted* her there with him. Now she wasn't so sure. He was distracted and clearly on edge, and it seemed like maybe it hadn't been his idea for her to be there.

Her goal had been to make it through the evening without embarrassing the Burkes. And now she needed to make it through the evening without embarrassing herself, since the realization had come to her that Julian wasn't as excited to have her as his date as she had been to be there with him. She couldn't count on his support.

Annie came to stand next to Kiara. "Looks like loads of fun, huh?"

"It's beautiful," Kiara said, not sure she should admit she no longer wanted to be there. "Elizabeth has certainly put a lot of effort into it."

"She has," Annie agreed. "I just hope my dad doesn't expect me to ever do something similar."

Annie and Cole stayed close to her, even as Julian moved away to talk to someone else.

"Dad, can we sit down soon?" Annie asked. "My feet are dying in these shoes."

Duncan lifted his eyebrows at her comment. "Elizabeth manages just fine, and she's older than you."

"Yes, but she's used to it," Annie said. "I'm not. Plus, Kiara isn't either, and she's pregnant to boot."

Duncan gave Kiara a sympathetic look. "Just a few more minutes, and we can be seated."

"Maybe I should have told him my feet hurt too," Cole said as Duncan moved away from them to where Elizabeth was speaking with another couple.

"Do they?" Kiara asked the tall man.

Cole grinned. "Actually, they kind of do. I much prefer my basketball shoes. These types of shoes pinch my toes. And this bowtie is choking me."

"We didn't have to come," Annie told him with a little nudge in his ribs.

"It was important that we did," Cole said as he slipped his arm around her. "But I think we should all vote to stay home the next time an event like this comes up."

"I can agree to that," Annie said with a nod. "What about you, Kiara?"

"I doubt I'll be invited to any similar events in the future."

"Why?"

"I'll have a baby to take care of." Plus, she'd be Julian's *ex*-wife by then, and he wouldn't be inviting her to anything.

"I suppose that's a good enough reason," Cole said.

"Maybe we need that reason," Annie told him as she gave her husband a coy smile.

Kiara felt a pang of longing as she watched their interaction. It was more lighthearted than Angie and Jude's relationship, but no less affectionate and loving.

She looked away from the couple, and her gaze landed on Julian. He stood talking to a couple of men about his age, all dressed similarly to him, but to Kiara's eyes, he was the most handsome. As she watched, a beautiful Asian woman joined the group and greeted Julian with a friendly smile.

When Julian kissed the woman's cheek, Kiara turned her back to them, not wanting to watch any more of their interactions. She tucked away the hurt she felt, knowing she couldn't deal with it right then.

"Ladies and gentlemen, thank you all for coming to this special evening," Elizabeth said from behind a podium on a small stage. "I would ask that you find your seats."

There was a low murmur of conversation as people moved toward the tables and sat down. Annie pulled Kiara along to the table Elizabeth had said was theirs. Cole held a chair for Kiara and then the one next to her for Annie. He sat down on his wife's other side.

Julian approached the table with the woman and one of the men he'd been talking to. They also took seats at the table, with Julian between Kiara and the man, while the woman sat on the man's other side.

"Sean and Ava, this is Kiara, Annie, and her husband Cole," Julian said. "Sean and Ava are from our Singapore division of Burke Neurotech. They're here for meetings this coming week."

Kiara had heard the names before when Julian had spoken about the work in Singapore. It was clear that Julian considered the two more than just employees. And it made her wonder if Ava was part of the draw Julian felt to Singapore.

The table was large enough for ten people, and soon Duncan and Elizabeth joined them, as did a couple Duncan introduced as the chairman of the board for Burke Pharmaceuticals.

As the meal was being served, Annie leaned close to her and spoke in a soft voice. "If you get confused about which fork to use, just poke my leg, and I'll help you out."

Kiara appreciated Annie's sensitivity to her situation. It helped to calm some of her nerves. Some... but definitely not all.

While they ate a delicious meal, a string orchestra played in the background. After the dessert was served, they were treated to stories about the people who had benefited from the fundraising efforts in years past.

Kiara found it all fascinating because she hadn't had a clear understanding of what the Burke Foundation actually did. The stories definitely helped clarify that for her.

Through it all, Kiara sensed that Julian remained on edge. Though he continued to speak with the people at their table, he shifted frequently and didn't eat all the food they'd been served. Which, to her mind, hadn't been a lot to begin with.

"Cole is going to make us order room service after this," Annie muttered.

Annie's words made Kiara give a soft huff of laughter. "I'm eating for two. I might need room service as well."

Once the meal was over, two women went up on the stage with Elizabeth. One gave a personal report of what the foundation had done for her, and then the other shared what they hoped to accomplish in the coming year.

When they were done speaking, Elizabeth announced that the dance floor was open. Kiara knew she wouldn't be dancing, and she was actually fine with that. Dancing was something she'd never learned how to do, so she didn't want to embarrass herself by pretending she could.

Julian, Sean, and Ava had gotten up and gone to speak with someone at another table. Duncan and Elizabeth were circulating throughout the room, and the other couple at the table had gone to the bar.

"Would you like to dance, babe?" Cole asked Annie.

"I don't want to leave Kiara on her own," Annie said.

"Oh, don't worry about me," Kiara told her. "Baby boy and I will just hang out here together."

"Are you sure?" Annie asked, her brow furrowed. "Julian should be here with you."

"No, seriously, I'm fine." She didn't want to sit there by herself, but she also didn't want them to think she wasn't able to do it. "Go enjoy yourselves."

After a moment, Annie nodded, then took Cole's hand when he offered it. Kiara watched as the couple took to the floor. Their height difference was even more noticeable, but that didn't stop them from moving together smoothly as they performed an elegant dance.

Kiara glanced over at the wall nearest to their table, taking comfort when her gaze met Lucy's. The woman gave her a small nod.

"Hello." The soft greeting had Kiara turning her attention back to the table in time to see a dainty woman with highlighted blonde hair sit down in the chair Cole had recently vacated, leaving one empty seat between them. The woman held out her hand. "I'm Emilia."

"I'm Kiara."

"You must be Julian's wife."

Kiara hesitated for a moment, her gaze going to where Julian stood with a glass in his hand, still talking to Sean and Ava. "I am."

"Oh, you're very lucky. He's a great catch," the woman said. "He's a very handsome man. All the ladies have had their eyes on him. Well, except for me." She lifted her left hand to reveal a large diamond ring. "I've already got my Prince Charming."

"Actually, the things that make Julian a great catch have very little to do with his looks."

A finely plucked brow lifted. "Oh really? Why would you say that?"

"He has many other qualities that make him a great man. The fact that he's handsome isn't even near the top of that list."

"Do tell," Emilia said with a small smile. "I'd love to hear what you think makes him so special."

Once again, Kiara hesitated. It felt a bit like a trap, but she couldn't figure out the woman's angle. "He's smart and passionate about his work. He is determined when he sets his mind to something. He's also kind and caring."

"You definitely sound like a woman in love," Emilia said, giving her a wink. "I wonder what good qualities Julian would say you have. And if he also feels that he is lucky to have you for a wife."

And there it was.

Kiara felt the trap closing in and struggled to know how to respond.

"No worries, my dear." Emilia reached out to pat her hand. "Everyone already knows why he married you. It was well known among the women that if they managed to get pregnant by Julian Burke, he'd probably marry them. And even if it had nothing to do with love, the payoff would be worth it. I assume you thought the same thing, because I doubt he would have married someone like you otherwise."

Someone like you.

The woman's words reinforced what Jill had said to her. She would never fit into the Burkes' world, and there was nothing she could ever do to be good enough for that social circle.

"So, congratulations on being the one who finally captured the man," Emilia said. "I just hope that it's really his. But either way, I doubt you'll have him for long."

Kiara had no idea what this woman wanted from her. Was a friend of hers one of the women who had wanted to land Julian?

Keeping her expression calm, Kiara gave her a small smile. "I appreciate your... concern, but I assure you, everything is fine."

The woman stared at her for a long moment, then got to her feet. "For your sake, I hope that's true."

Kiara didn't bother watching Emilia walk away. She stood up, mindful of her heels, then picked up her clutch and made her way to Lucy.

"I'd like to go up to the room now," she said. "I'm beat."

"I heard what that woman said to you," Lucy told her with a frown. "Don't pay any attention to her."

"I don't plan to," Kiara said. "I just think I'm ready for this evening to be over. I don't think I really fit into this world."

"Well, don't look at that as a failure," Lucy muttered. "I've stood on the fringes of this world for several years, and for every perfectly lovely person, there are at least three snarky and spiteful ones."

"Since I've run into one of each tonight, I think I'll call it a day," Kiara said.

"Did you want to let Julian know you're going up?"

Kiara glanced over to see he'd moved further into the room, circulating much like his father was doing. Only Duncan had his wife at his side.

"No, he already knew that I'd probably call it an early night. Let's just go."

Now that she'd made up her mind, Kiara was in a hurry to leave. With a nod, Lucy walked beside her to the exit of the ballroom. They made their way to the elevator and then up to their suite.

"Could you unzip me, please?" Kiara asked as she stepped out of her shoes. "I don't think I can reach the zipper on my own."

"Of course."

Holding the gown in place across her chest, Kiara thanked her. "I'll see you in the morning."

"And if Julian contacts me to find out where you are?"

"Just tell him my feet hurt, and I was tired. I'll talk to him tomorrow."

It wasn't until she was behind the closed door of her room that Kiara let go of the tight control she'd kept over her emotions.

With a deep exhale, she dropped her arms, allowing the dress to puddle at her feet. She closed her eyes and tipped her head back against the door.

The evening was supposed to have been nothing more than a social event. An opportunity to support the work Elizabeth had done. And yet, it had opened old wounds, which left her feeling vulnerable and alone.

Stepping over the dress, Kiara bent and picked it up. After she'd returned it to the hanger it had been delivered on, she decided to take a shower to wash away the evening. To wash away the things that weren't *her*. And if there were some tears shed as she stood beneath the water, they were washed away as quickly as they fell.

When she felt more in control of herself again, Kiara got out of the shower and dried off. Pulling on a thick robe, she went to the counter where her skincare products waited.

She stared at herself in the mirror for a long moment, no longer seeing the polished version of herself. Instead, her hair lay in damp waves across her shoulders, and her face was bare of all makeup.

This was who she was. Someone who hadn't belonged in the world she'd struggled to inhabit earlier that evening.

She might not have liked it, but this was a reminder she needed. Over the past few weeks, she'd gotten too used to playing house with Julian. Too settled into their life together. She had to remember that it was an illusion. None of it was real. None of it.

This was not where she belonged, and after seeing Julian and the others in their element at the gala, Kiara wasn't sure she belonged in the Burke family in any capacity.

As she took in her reflection, Kiara saw heartbreak in her eyes. How was she supposed to move forward with the knowledge that she didn't belong anywhere?

When you give your heart and your life to God, you belong to Him. The words of a sermon the pastor had preached came to her in the stillness of the bathroom. *You become His child. He will love and care for you. Even in the direst of circumstances, you will not be alone.*

He'd spoken of redemption, of belonging to the family of God, and of living a life of hope and purpose in God. But so far in her life, she'd not fit in. Never had she felt like she truly belonged anywhere, and it was a stressful and lonely feeling.

How was it possible that becoming a Christian could change that? God wasn't someone who could hug her or sit down for a conversation with her. But even so, there was a longing in her heart to belong to someone.

Over the past few weeks, she'd continued to attend church, even when Julian hadn't been there to go with her. Each sermon had offered her more to think about, and she knew what she needed to do to become a child of God. But she hadn't taken that step yet.

Staring at herself in the mirror, Kiara faced her fear of being rejected once again. It was the one thing that had, so far, kept her from committing fully to God.

But maybe it was time to face that fear head-on and put her trust in Him. To commit to living her life to glorify Him, and to hope that God would help her with the feelings she had.

She didn't know what she needed to do exactly, but the pastor had mentioned it several times. She just needed to find it in the videos of his sermons online.

Under the covers of her bed a few minutes later, Kiara pulled up his list of sermons on the website and began to search for the information that she hoped would change her life.

CHAPTER TWENTY-ONE

Julian hated every minute of the fundraiser. He'd never been thrilled to attend events like the one that evening, but alcohol and seeking out the company of a beautiful woman had usually been enough to make them tolerable, if not enjoyable.

When he'd agreed to come, he hadn't thought about how being in that environment again would shake him. Quite literally. He'd been offered alcohol several times throughout the evening, and it had taken everything within him to turn it down.

He'd had to clench his hands into fists to keep from reaching out to take a flute of the champagne. And the temptation to go to the bar where he could order something stronger was nearly overwhelming.

From the moment he'd put the tuxedo on, Julian had been fighting an internal battle. If he'd realized how bad it was going to be for him, he would never have asked Kiara to come.

He'd never brought a date to any previous fundraisers, especially the ones that the Burke Foundation was involved with. Duncan expected him to mingle and connect with the people who were present, and he hadn't ever wanted to do that with a date on his arm. He'd usually waited to connect with a woman until after he'd satisfied Duncan with his circulating.

That evening, he could have taken Kiara around with him, but he didn't want to force her to spend even more time on her feet. She'd mentioned her shoes not being comfortable, and it seemed best to let her stay at the table with Cole and Annie.

He'd glanced over periodically to keep an eye on her, and she seemed to be doing okay.

"Julian, my boy!"

Turning away from his view of the table, he greeted the older man approaching him. Clarence Livingston had been in his life for as long as he could remember. The family story was that he had once been Julian's grandma's boyfriend.

His grandma had always been coy about it, and his grandpa had only scowled when asked. With both of them now gone, Marcus was the only one who knew the truth.

Regardless, Julian liked the old man and considered him an uncle. He gave him a hug, then stood chatting with him for several minutes.

Even though he was well into his eighties, Clarence lived a full and adventurous life. Most recently, he'd taken his yacht for an extended cruise around the Caribbean and had apparently found a girlfriend.

"You live the most interesting life of anyone I know," Julian told him.

"That's really sad," Clarence replied with a shake of his head. "You're too young to be living a boring life. Though I hear that congratulations are in order."

Julian still wasn't sure how to respond to that because he didn't know if they were referring to the wedding or the baby on the way. "Thanks."

"Is your wife here with you tonight?" Clarence asked.

"Yes." He turned in the direction of the table again and noticed that it was empty. "I left her at the table since she's pregnant and wearing uncomfortable shoes. She must have gone to the bathroom."

"I'll wander by there in a bit," Clarence said. "I need to go chat up Mrs. Dante."

Julian lifted his brows. "I thought you had a girlfriend."

"Oh, I do, but it's my duty to make Mrs. Dante smile."

"Well, then you must take care of that."

Clarence gave him a jaunty tip of the hat he wore, then sauntered away, twirling the fancy cane he carried everywhere.

Julian watched him go, then glanced around. He spotted Cole and Annie on the dance floor, but the table was still empty.

"Hello, Julian."

He recognized the voice, even before he turned to see Emilia Levine. They'd known each other for years, and her husband was one of the friends he'd had since college. She was one of the few women who hadn't tried to capture his attention because her sights had always been firmly set on Jarrod Levine.

Bending, he brushed a kiss to one cheek and then the other. "Where's your husband?"

"He's circulating. His dad made him promise to make contact with certain people."

That wasn't too unusual. "You aren't helping him?"

"Oh, I'm going to, but I wanted to say hi," she told him. "And to let you know, I had a quick chat with your wife. She seems... lovely."

Julian frowned. "I hope you were nice to her."

"Of course." Emilia gave him a smile that didn't put him at ease. "I just wanted her to know that she didn't have to fake anything around us."

Julian put his hands on his hips. "What do you mean by that?"

"Oh, just that we all know that you only married her because she was pregnant. And I congratulated her on being able to accomplish what so many women had failed to do."

"Emilia, why would you do something like that?" he demanded. "Kiara's done nothing to you. She doesn't deserve to be the target of your pettiness."

"Maybe you should have just kept her out of sight," Emilia said with a shrug. "You brought her into our world. She has a right to know that people are aware of the circumstances."

Julian was furious, but not just at Emilia. He was angry with himself for not realizing that this would happen.

"Oh, and I don't know if you're aware, but I think your... wife... might have fallen in love with you," Emilia said with a smirk. "She had some lovely things to say about you. I didn't tell her that she was wasting her time. She'll figure that out soon enough."

"Why are you so hateful?" Julian demanded. "It's not like I rejected you for her."

"She isn't a part of our world, Julian," Emilia said as she crossed her arms, her expression sobering. "You need someone who knows how to support you. Who knows how to protect the Burke name."

"Are you assuming that my father is opposed to Kiara?" Julian asked. "Because I can assure you that he is not."

Her eyebrows lifted at that. "I think you're just saying that."

"Let's go find him, and you can ask him yourself."

"If he truly does feel that way, then you both need help protecting the Burke name from people who might take advantage of you."

Julian laughed. "You know nothing about my family. Nothing at all. And from this point on, you need to stay away from me and every member of my family."

Emilia looked like she was going to argue, but then she spun around and walked away.

This wasn't the first time he'd dealt with stuff like this. And it wasn't even the first time Emilia or one of her friends had tried to warn him away from a woman.

But this time around, there was more at stake. There was a baby on the way, and Julian needed to make sure that the world he came into was filled with people who loved and cared for him.

Sometimes it felt like some rich people had nothing better to do with their time than to meddle in other people's lives. Or they felt like they had to gatekeep the wealthy world from anyone they deemed as less worthy than them. Just like his mother had done to Elizabeth.

Julian had to be honest that it hadn't really bothered him in the past. In fact, he really hadn't cared. His world had revolved around his job and drinking, and the women he'd dated had all been from his social circle.

He stared down at the glass he held, hating that it was ginger ale and not something stronger. The evening had gone horribly, and he was to blame.

He'd been so focused on his own struggles that he'd been oblivious to what was going on around him. That had been a mistake. Yet another one.

With a glance at the bar, Julian felt a strong urge to go swap out the glass he held for something with more substance.

But as he moved in that direction, Anthony appeared at his elbow.

"What is it?" Julian muttered.

"Everything okay?"

Julian gave him a sideways glance. "Why shouldn't it be?"

Anthony didn't say anything, just remained in step with him as Julian headed back to the table. The man's role was to protect him from outward security threats, but apparently, he'd decided he needed to protect Julian from himself as well. And he wasn't wrong.

"Did you see where Kiara and Lucy went?" Julian asked when they reached the still empty table.

"They went up to their suite."

Julian turned to frown at the man, more concerned now that he was aware of what had transpired between Emilia and Kiara.

"Did Lucy say why they were leaving?"

"She said that Kiara was tired and that her feet were hurting."

It made sense, but after his conversation with Emilia, Julian wondered if that was the real reason. "Maybe I should go check in on her."

"Let me call Lucy to see if Kiara is up for a visit."

Julian wanted to protest that he should be able to see his wife if he wanted to, but he held his tongue. He was a husband in name only, so he had no right to make a demand on Kiara's time.

As Anthony stepped away with his phone, Julian sank down on a chair at the table. His gaze settled on Annie and Cole, still out on the dance floor. The two of them gazed at each other as if they were the only two people in the world.

They were still technically in the honeymoon stage, since they'd only been married a month and a half. It was reminiscent of Angela and Jude.

He supposed it was only fair that the twins, who had been so negatively impacted by his actions, had found happiness with the people they'd married. And perhaps the struggles he was facing were his payment for what he'd done.

The unfortunate thing was that Kiara had gotten caught in the middle of his mess. She deserved better than that.

"Lucy said she's gone to bed," Anthony told Julian when he reappeared.

Julian gave a nod that he heard, though he didn't look at the man.

He was still sitting there when Cole and Annie returned.

"Hey, bro," Annie said as she sat down in the chair Cole held for her. "Where's Kiara?"

Julian wanted to ask her why she'd left Kiara all by herself at the table, but he knew the blame lay with him, not Annie. "She was tired and her feet hurt, so she went upstairs with Lucy."

"I'm about ready to call it a night too," Annie said. "They need to let us wear sneakers to these events."

"You do realize that you can do what you want, right?" Julian asked. "You're a Burke. We're not restrained by the fashion rules."

Annie laughed. "Yeah. Two problems with that. First, Dad. Second, Elizabeth. Also, I'm not keen on drawing attention, and being a fashion rebel would do just that."

"Do we need to talk to Duncan and Elizabeth before we leave?" Cole asked.

"I'll tell them you've gone," Julian said with a wave of his hand.

"Are you sticking it out to the very end?" Annie asked.

"I'm usually expected to."

Annie stared at him for a long moment. "You don't look happy about it."

"I'm not," Julian said. "But I've survived hundreds of these types of events over the years."

"I feel like I owe you," Annie told him. "Since you've always had to come to these things, while I never did."

"Even if you'd had to come to them, it wouldn't have meant that I didn't. Duncan would have insisted I be here, regardless."

"Maybe you need to just say no," she said. "If what you say is true about being a Burke, then it shouldn't matter if you're here or not."

Julian wondered if maybe it was time to have a conversation with Duncan. Being in this environment so soon after going to rehab was a challenge he hadn't expected. Unfortunately, it had taken being put in the situation for him to realize that maybe he wasn't strong enough to handle it just yet.

"How long are you guys hanging around New York?" Julian asked.

"I think we're going to head home tomorrow afternoon. Dad said we could use the plane. Are you coming back to the estate soon?"

"No," he said. "I've got meetings here all week."

Normally, he would have been excited about them, but right then, he just felt drained. Still, he was sure that once the week got underway, his excitement would return. Sean and Ava were there to present information about FemPulse and the steps they were taking for FDA approval, so it was an exciting time.

"Well, hopefully you'll be back soon," Annie said. "Not long until your baby boy is born."

Yet something else that was weighing on him and making him question himself. Would he be a good father? Right then, he didn't feel like he would.

He wished that Elijah had been able to come to the fundraiser, because he would have been a good support... an understanding support. But he'd had to go to Texas with his mom and sister to deal with some family matters.

"Hey, Dad."

Julian looked over his shoulder to see Duncan and Elizabeth approaching them, hand-in-hand. They came to stand next to Julian and Annie.

Duncan rested his hand on Julian's shoulder. "Where's Kiara?"

"She was tired and went upstairs."

"That's understandable," Elizabeth said. "I'm just glad she was able to join us for a little while."

"I doubt she feels the same way," Julian told her. "Emilia cornered her for a conversation."

"Jarrod Levine's wife?" Duncan asked.

"Yes."

"Did she upset Kiara?"

"I haven't had a chance to talk to her about it yet. I was talking with Clarence when she and Lucy went upstairs."

"I hope that she's okay," Elizabeth said. "I wanted this to be a special evening for her."

When Duncan moved his hand from Julian's shoulder, Julian got to his feet. "I hope you don't mind, but I think I'm going to have an early night tonight."

"Are you okay, Son?" Duncan asked.

"I'm fine, but we're moving into the part of the evening at these events where alcohol is... tempting for me."

"I see," Duncan said. "Then by all means, feel free to leave."

Julian appreciated that his dad seemed to understand his struggle. He hated that it was still a struggle. He wanted the time in rehab to have equipped him to the extent that he wouldn't be tempted by alcohol anymore. But that wasn't the case. And he wasn't sure it ever would be.

"I'll probably see you tomorrow," he said as he held out his hand to his dad and then to Cole. He gave Elizabeth and Annie quick hugs, then looked around for Sean and Ava. When he spotted them, he walked to where they were chatting with several other people Julian recognized as Burke board members.

They'd all be meeting that week, so it was good that Sean and Ava were socializing with some of them. It would make the meetings later on a bit easier since the introductions were already taken care of for some of them.

"We can meet for dinner tomorrow," Julian said after he'd let them know he was leaving the event. "I'll give you a call."

He shook hands with Sean, Ava, and the other board members, then made his way out of the ballroom with Anthony by his side. As they neared the door, he spotted Emilia with her husband. He met her gaze for a long moment, then looked away, dismissing her.

When they reached their floor, instead of going to his suite, he headed for Kiara's. He rapped lightly on the door, anticipating that no one would answer, but instead, the door swung open to reveal Lucy.

"I know you told Anthony that Kiara went to bed, but I just wanted to check on her."

Lucy stepped back to let them into the suite. "I haven't seen her since she went into the bedroom."

"How was she?"

Lucy didn't answer right away. Since she technically worked for his family, Julian could force her to answer him. However, he didn't want to put her in that position. If Kiara confided in Lucy, Julian didn't want to take that away from her.

"She felt a bit out of her comfort zone."

"Did you hear her conversation with Emilia Levine?"

"The tiny blonde?" Julian nodded. "I heard a bit of it."

"Did Kiara seem upset by it?"

Lucy hesitated. "I'm not sure if she was upset, but she definitely didn't seem happy to have made a new friend."

Julian looked toward the closed door, wishing he had the right to go in and check on her. He wanted to speak with Kiara and make sure she was okay.

He felt like he'd failed her that evening by being so focused on his own struggles. Could he ever make it up to her?

"Can you let her know I'll come by tomorrow morning?" Julian said.

Lucy nodded. "Will do."

When he got back to his suite, Julian paused in the shared living space, staring across the room at the bar. He had no idea if there was alcohol in the cupboards or fridge. Something told him that Anthony had made sure there wasn't.

Turning away, he headed toward the door to his room. In the bedroom, he took off his jacket, vest, and bowtie, and laid them on the bench at the foot of the bed, then sat down at the desk in the corner of the room.

He had to try to make things right with Kiara. Remembering how they'd communicated through letters when he was at the treatment center, Julian felt compelled to open the drawer and pull out the stationery provided by the hotel.

With pen in hand, he stared out the window at the twinkling New York skyline. Away from all the distractions of the evening, and with silence surrounding him, Julian realized just how much of a mess his emotions were.

Anger. Resentment. Concern. Self-recrimination. And more that he wasn't really prepared to dwell too much on just yet.

Dear Kiara ~ I want to apologize for how this evening turned out. I hadn't even considered how this event might unfold for me, given it was my first one since becoming sober. But the closer the gala got, the more anxious I felt about it. And today, the worry I had about it eventually overshadowed everything else. Even your experience attending something like this for the first time.

I am sorry for that. I should have been more aware of what you were facing tonight. I wouldn't blame you if you were angry with me for what happened.

Emilia told me about her conversation with you. Just know that she is wrong for what she said to you, and no one in our family feels the way she does.

Julian stared at the words he'd scrawled on the parchment. They seemed so... simple when the situation was so complex.

He was tempted to crumple the paper up and start over, but he wasn't sure a second attempt would be any better.

With an exasperated sigh, Julian pushed away from the desk and got to his feet. He removed his cufflinks and then took off his shirt.

He wanted to divest himself of the clothing he'd had to wear that night. Clothing that felt like a costume because he'd had to play the role of dutiful son and heir apparent to Burke Pharmaceuticals. It was a public role that had always been easier when alcohol was available.

After he'd changed into a pair of sweats and a T-shirt, he sat back down at the desk, determined to finish the letter. He wasn't sure he'd actually give it to Kiara, but he needed to get it out.

CHAPTER TWENTY-TWO

Kiara was slow to get moving the next morning because that was just how it was most days anymore. Physically, she might have found starting the day challenging, but emotionally, she felt much more settled than she had the night before.

She'd ended up watching three of the pastor's sermons. Two were ones she'd heard already, but in browsing through the available videos on the church's website, she'd found another one that had a title that had piqued her interest.

That had been the one that had given her the clearest understanding of how to become a Christian and what it meant to become a child of God. At the end of that sermon, several people had walked to the front of the sanctuary to commit their lives to God.

While she watched the response to that sermon, Kiara had also prayed, confessing her sins, and asking God to take control of her life. She hadn't suddenly felt less alone, but there was a part of her that now felt like she had somewhere to turn when those emotions got the best of her.

She'd called Angie to let her know what she'd done, and her sister had become super emotional. Though Kiara hadn't called her with the plan of distracting her, Angie had been so happy with the news that she hadn't asked detailed questions about how the evening had gone.

At some point, she figured that Angie would want more details about the gala, but hopefully by then, the sting of the evening's events would have eased.

Hunger finally drove her from the bed, and she got up and changed out of her comfy pajamas into a pair of maternity jeans and a loose-fitting shirt. She pulled her curls up into a ponytail, then went through the steps of her morning skincare routine.

When she left her room, Kiara found Lucy was already up and dressed in her usual uniform of a black T-shirt and black cargo pants. She didn't have her guns on, but Kiara had no doubt they were nearby.

"What would you like for breakfast?" Lucy asked.

Kiara sat down at the table and rested her hand on her bump, considering the question. One day something would appeal to her that wouldn't interest her at all the next.

"I'd like some waffles with whipped cream and berries."

Lucy chuckled. "Sounds good."

Kiara stared out the large windows at the skyline of New York City. It was a cloudy day, and unlike the sparkling lights of the night before, everything was a blah shade of gray.

"Julian stopped by last night," Lucy said once she'd placed their breakfast order with room service.

Kiara schooled her expression before turning her attention to Lucy. "What did he want?"

"He wanted to check on you. I told him that you were tired. He did ask if I'd heard the conversation between you and that woman."

How had he known about that? "What did you tell him?"

"That I'd heard a bit, but he didn't press for more information."

Kiara was glad to hear that. "It wasn't anything noteworthy."

Lucy gave her a look. "Oh, I think it was, and clearly Julian seemed to think it was, too. Otherwise, I'm not sure why he would have asked about it."

The last thing Kiara wanted to do was relive that conversation. "It really wasn't anything."

"She didn't look like she was being particularly friendly."

"She wasn't," Kiara admitted. "But she isn't the first person who's told me that I don't belong in this world."

Lucy scowled but didn't say anything more. She set a cup of coffee on the table in front of Kiara, correctly deducing that she'd want one that morning.

"Thanks." She added some cream and sugar, then picked it up and took a small sip. Coffee wasn't something she completely denied herself, but she never had more than one cup a day, if that.

It wasn't long before there was a knock on the door, and Lucy opened it to admit a person from room service. The man rolled the cart over to the table and unloaded several plates.

"Are you super hungry this morning?" Kiara asked, eyeing the plates on the table.

"I figured you might decide you wanted something else besides the waffles."

Kiara chuckled. "Baby changes his mind frequently."

"I know how it goes," Lucy said as she sat down across from Kiara.

"Really? Do you have kids?" The two of them had gotten to know each other more since she'd been assigned as Kiara's permanent bodyguard, but Lucy had never mentioned kids.

"No. I don't have kids, but I'm the eldest of seven. I have clear memories of my mom's last four pregnancies and how her appetite fluctuated, even within the span of a meal."

Kiara had just taken a bite of her waffle, so she just nodded her understanding. Already, the bacon on one of the plates was calling her name.

When there was another knock on the door, Lucy glanced toward it, then got to her feet. It wasn't a huge surprise to see Julian in the doorway.

"Why don't you join Anthony in my suite?" Julian said as Lucy stepped back to let him in.

Though Lucy glanced at Kiara, she didn't hesitate to return to the table to pick up her plate and mug of coffee. Without a word, she left the suite, closing the door behind her.

"Did you want some coffee?" Kiara asked. "I think there's still some left in the carafe."

Julian turned to the buffet against the wall, where there were several drink options. As he poured himself some coffee, Kiara took in his appearance.

He looked different from the previous night. More relaxed in a white cotton button-down shirt with the sleeves rolled up, tucked into a pair of blue jeans. As handsome as he'd looked the night before, she preferred this look.

She was most comfortable with that version of him because it brought him closer to her level.

She'd always been most comfortable in leggings or jeans and a T-shirt, though recently, she'd begun wearing dresses more frequently. The looser, the better. Her growing bump didn't like anything too restrictive around it.

As Julian sat down across from her in the chair Lucy had vacated, he stared at the plates of food before looking at her. "Hungry this morning?"

"A little," she said. "Lucy ordered more than I actually asked for because she thought I might decide I wanted something more."

"She certainly got you some options."

"Help yourself," Kiara told him. "I'm not going to eat it all."

He seemed content with just his coffee, but Kiara was still hungry, so she returned her attention to her plate of waffles... after she'd picked up a couple of pieces of bacon.

"How did you sleep?" Julian asked. "Lucy said you were tired."

"I was. It's been a busy couple of days." She contemplated sharing what she'd done the night before, but for some reason, she just couldn't find the words.

"It has been, and it's not over yet for me, with meetings all this week." Julian took a sip of his coffee. "Were you planning to stick around and do some sightseeing?"

Kiara didn't even have to think about her response. She shook her head. "I miss home."

"Is it because of what happened last night?"

"Last night just showed me that I don't really know how to move in your world."

"That's not a bad thing," Julian said. "And just because someone says you don't belong, that doesn't mean they're right."

"What do you mean?"

"How well do you think Elizabeth fit in when my dad first married her? She was a nanny. I'm pretty sure if you asked her, she'd tell you that she wasn't welcomed with open arms either. My mom still had friends in this world who likely made Elizabeth's life miserable."

"But she seems so at ease now," Kiara said, remembering how elegant and graceful Elizabeth had been the previous evening. "A natural."

"She's paid her dues," Julian said. "But also, my dad's wealth helped. And that will be the case for you as well. Emilia will pay a price for what she said to you."

Kiara lowered the forkful of waffle she'd been about to eat. "What?"

"She had no right to say the things she did to you. For some dumb reason, she thought she was doing us a favor or something, acting like she knew things that she didn't."

"She seemed very confident."

Julian gave a shake of his head. "Only because she really knows nothing about our family. And even if she knows me, she doesn't know my dad at all. Attacking a member of his family will never lead to anything good."

Kiara wanted to say she wasn't part of the family, but technically, she was. For now.

"She wasn't completely off the mark though," Kiara said. "She correctly determined why we'd gotten married."

"Yes, but she also claimed that you were in love with me, so she doesn't know everything. Though I'm not sure why she thought that."

"I'm pretty sure I know," Kiara said, figuring she might as well be upfront about it rather than pretend like she had no clue. Denying knowledge might make Julian think it was true... and she couldn't have that.

He leaned back in his chair and crossed his arms. "So why did she think that?"

Kiara took a sip of her coffee before responding. "She told me that I was so lucky that you'd married me, because of how handsome you are."

"Okay?"

"I told her there was more to you than your looks, like how you're hardworking and determined. Stuff like that." She gave a shrug. "I guess she thought that because I appreciated those qualities in you, I must be in love with you."

Julian didn't seem to know how to respond to that. He stared at the table as he lifted his mug for another sip.

"The thing is, I could say the same for Cole, Jude, and even your dad. All three of you are attractive, but it's your character traits that make you good men."

"I guess I can see how Emilia might have come to her conclusion," Julian said. "For some people, how a person looks or their wealth is what makes them most attractive."

"I don't happen to believe that," Kiara said.

Kiara watched him carefully as she took another bite of her waffle. She needed him to believe that her words had come from a place of friendship, and nothing more.

"You are a bit of a rarity with that viewpoint in this world."

"I think Elizabeth, Annie, and Angie all feel the way I do."

Julian nodded. "And none of you were raised in this world, so it didn't shape how you view things like this."

But Julian had been, so it was likely that he would put more weight on how a person looked. He'd want a woman who looked stunning on his arm. Someone who looked like Emilia. Or Ava, who had both looks and smarts.

"Regardless of what Emilia said, I want to apologize for my part in how things went last night," Julian said. "I shouldn't have left you alone."

"You didn't need to babysit me," Kiara told him. She didn't want him to feel like she was a burden, even though she undoubtedly was.

"It wasn't about babysitting you." He shifted forward to rest his arms on the table. "I should have done a better job of making sure you were surrounded by good people. So, people like Emilia wouldn't have had the opportunity to talk to you alone."

"I survived," Kiara said. "And it's unlikely I'll see her again."

Julian nodded. "You won't."

Kiara had figured it would be the only event she'd be invited to, but it kind of hurt for Julian to agree so easily. It shouldn't have hurt because she really didn't want to attend another one anyway. However, she hadn't guarded her emotions or her heart as well as she should have, so it did bring an ache to her heart.

"Would it be okay if we talked about the baby for a minute?" Kiara asked, wanting to steer the conversation away from a memory she'd rather not dwell on.

"Sure," Julian said, seeming to be relieved to move on as well. "What's on your mind?"

"Well, first, his name," she said. "Do you have any ideas? Any names you'd like to be considered?"

He thought for a minute and then said, "Honestly, I don't have any strong preferences. If you want to come up with suggestions, we can discuss them."

His response wasn't too surprising, but she had hoped that he'd want to give more input into naming their son.

"Okay. I'll see what I can come up with." She hesitated, a bit reluctant to broach the next subject, but she knew she needed to. Now that she was in her final trimester, she found herself wanting to nail down as many of the details as she could. "Second, I was wondering if you planned to be in the delivery room when I'm in labor."

Kiara could see right away what his answer was going to be. She had hoped that he'd want to be present for the birth of their son, but it wasn't a surprise that he didn't feel the same way.

"I'm not sure how I'd do in the delivery room," Julian said with a grimace. "I think maybe you'd be better off with Angie. I wouldn't be of much help."

"That's fine," Kiara told him, though from the ache in her chest, it was anything but. She felt like she was walking through a minefield of hurt. Every subject she brought up inflicted pain upon herself. "I just wanted to make sure you knew you were welcome to be there if you wanted."

Kiara's biggest fear was that Julian wouldn't interact with their son the way she wanted him to. Perhaps he still had some doubts about the baby being his. Or maybe he had never planned to be a hands-on father.

"Is everything going okay with the baby?" he asked.

"Yep. The doctor said he's growing as he should, and the ultrasound didn't show anything of concern."

"That's good," he said. "And everything is ready at the house?"

She nodded. "I've been buying clothes for him, and so have Elizabeth, Annie, and Angie. Annie has also made several things for him. She's so talented. I think he's going to be one well-dressed baby boy."

Julian smiled at that. "I'm sure he'll be one of the most photographed babies, too."

Kiara had thought about doing a maternity shoot because she'd seen so many of them on social media. However, those had all involved the father, and she was pretty sure that Julian wouldn't want to participate in something like that.

She had been taking pictures and videos of herself each week, just to have. This might be the only pregnancy she ever experienced, and she wanted a record of it.

"Since you don't plan to stay for sightseeing, are you going back this afternoon with Cole and Annie?"

"I wasn't sure when they were going back," she said. "But I figured I'd either go with them or just book a ticket."

"No need to fly commercial if you want to leave this afternoon."

"Do you know what time they're leaving?" Kiara asked.

"I don't know their actual departure time. Let me see what Annie says." He pulled out his phone and sent off a quick message. "Last night she said they were flying out in the afternoon, but I don't know if it was early or late afternoon."

Kiara felt a sudden longing to go home. She looked out of the window at the view. She'd always been a small-town or country girl. The big city didn't appeal to her, and after the experiences she'd had there in the past twenty-four hours, she was ready to leave it behind.

"Annie said the plane is scheduled to depart at one, so they plan to leave here at noon."

"And they're okay if I go with them?"

"Definitely," Julian said with a nod as he tapped out a response. "Just make sure you and Lucy are ready to go by noon."

"We will be."

"I'll probably be back at the estate next weekend or the week after, depending on how the meetings go this week."

"Are you going back to Singapore soon?"

"I'm not sure yet. Since Sean and Ava came here for the meetings, I don't need to travel to them. Which is probably just as well because Duncan has some other trips scheduled for me."

Kiara wondered if he'd always traveled that much. It seemed like he was on the go an awful lot. It had made sharing a house with him pretty easy, since their time together had been fairly limited so far, and it sounded like maybe it was going to continue that way.

"I'm going to be leaving the hotel today too," Julian said. "I'll be going to my apartment now that the event here is over."

Kiara wondered what his apartment was like, but he hadn't offered to show it to her. And she wasn't about to ask to see it.

Unfortunately, it was becoming very clear to her that even though she *knew* there was an end date to her marriage to Julian, she still wanted to know more about him.

She wanted to have a place in his life, the way he had a place in hers. The communication they'd had while he was in the treatment center had given her hope that they were moving toward a closer relationship, but that didn't seem to be the case.

It seemed that no matter how much they shared with each other, there was still a wall between them. Julian was definitely keeping his distance from her in a lot of ways. She'd thought his moving into Angie's part of the house would bring them together, but that hadn't really been the result.

In the evenings, which was when they'd spent time together, Julian usually pulled out his laptop and continued to work, after having worked all day. She would end up reading, which wasn't bad, but it didn't foster much communication between them.

She wasn't sure that they would even have a close friendship once everything was done. They would be two acquaintances parenting their child.

It felt like a rejection of who she was, even though he hadn't really rejected her. It just felt like she wasn't worthy of having a place in his life.

"I should probably let you and Lucy get your stuff together if you're going to be able to leave at noon," Jude said, looking at the expensive watch on his wrist. Kiara noticed that the ring she'd placed on his finger was still there, so that was something.

Kiara glanced at the screen on her phone and saw that it was almost eleven, so they wouldn't have much time. When Julian got to his feet, she did as well, turning toward the door at the sound of a knock.

"That'll be Lucy," Julian said, then went to let her and Anthony in.

"We're catching a ride back to Serenity with Cole and Annie," Kiara said to Lucy. "We need to be ready to leave by noon."

Lucy glanced at her watch, then nodded. "That's doable for me. Does that work for you?"

"Yes, I'll be ready to go."

"We'll be checking out as well, Anthony," Julian said. "Let's meet down in the lobby at noon."

Kiara sat back down at the table after the men had left. "I'm going to eat a little more."

"Go for it," Lucy said as she headed for her room.

After finishing her waffle, she grabbed one more piece of bacon, then got up from the table.

The nice thing about traveling private was that she didn't have to worry about what she was wearing. Comfort was uppermost in her mind when she chose her clothes in general, but especially when traveling.

Kiara gathered up her things and quickly packed her suitcase. She returned the dress from the night before to the garment bag it had been delivered in.

By the time eleven forty-five rolled around, Kiara was ready to go. She took one last look around the large suite, then headed for the door.

Lucy instructed the person who had come to get their bags where to deliver them, then they walked toward the elevator.

"Have Julian and Anthony gone down already?" Kiara asked.

"I'm not sure," Lucy said.

Kiara wondered if Julian had said they'd be down there just so he wouldn't have to say goodbye.

When they reached the hotel lobby, Cole and Annie were already there, sitting together on an elegant loveseat. Dawn, Annie's bodyguard, was also there, standing close to them.

"You ready to go home, Kiara?" Annie asked as Kiara sank down into an armchair across from her.

"Definitely."

"Me too," Annie said. "I don't think I've been missing anything by not attending events like the gala over the years."

"You won't be able to avoid them for the rest of your life, love," Cole said.

"I know, and I'll be fine with that as long as we can go home right afterwards."

"I don't know how Elizabeth does it," Kiara said. "I found last night to be exhausting. I realize that part of that is pregnancy, but still... I'm ready to go back to the estate."

"So, are we ready to go?" Cole asked.

"Julian said he was going to meet us here," Kiara said. "But perhaps something came up."

"They're on their way down," Dawn said as she looked up from her phone.

Kiara tried to ignore the relief that statement brought her. And her heart beat faster when she spotted Julian and Anthony heading toward them. Julian was talking on his phone, but he lowered it as they reached their group.

"Morning, sis," Julian said. "And Cole."

"Morning, bro." Annie got to her feet, then offered her hand to Cole to help him up. "We were just about to head out."

"Sorry. Got hung up on a call with Duncan."

Kiara maneuvered her way to her feet with some effort. Sitting in the comfy chair probably hadn't been her smartest idea.

"The SUVs are here," Dawn said.

Their group migrated out to the curb, where two SUVs waited. One was for their luggage, while the other was for the passengers. Cole and Annie climbed into the third row, while Lucy went to the front passenger seat.

Dawn rounded the SUV to get into the middle row on the other side. Before climbing into her seat, Kiara turned toward Julian.

"Have a good week," she said.

"Thanks. You too."

He stepped closer to Kiara and offered her a hug. Kiara welcomed it, wanting that brief connection with him before they went their separate ways again.

As they moved apart, he bent forward a little and rested his hand lightly on her bump. "You be good for your mama, little guy." Julian straightened, removing his hand from her stomach. He pulled something from his back pocket and held it out to her. "Here."

Kiara glanced down to see a folded envelope. She took it from him, but she didn't have a chance to say anything before Julian stepped back. She turned to the open door and climbed into the SUV.

Julian moved to the door as she settled into her seat. Their gazes met for a moment before he closed the door and stepped back. The SUVs rolled into motion, and the hotel—and Julian—were left behind.

Kiara looked down at the envelope and unfolded it. Her name was scrawled across the front of it in a familiar penmanship.

Why had Julian written her a letter? They'd just had a conversation where it was only the two of them present. Surely, he could have said whatever he needed to then.

Did this mean it was something bad?

With that thought in her mind, Kiara slipped the envelope into her purse. She'd read it later when she didn't have an audience, just in case it was something that might provoke an emotional response.

CHAPTER TWENTY-THREE

All the way to his apartment, Julian questioned his decision to give the letter to Kiara. He'd considered tossing it after he'd written the first couple of paragraphs, but then he'd felt compelled to get everything out.

In the end, he'd told her about his struggles at the gala and then apologized for the role they'd played in his distraction the previous night. He could have just told her while they were having breakfast, but he'd gotten used to sharing more vulnerable things through letters, not face to face.

So he'd taken the easy way out and written it out rather than say it to her in person.

He wanted to be able to communicate better with her, but while he had no problem with business conversations, personal ones were more challenging. Over the years, he could count on one hand the number of deeply personal and vulnerable conversations he'd had with people other than his therapist at the treatment center.

The ridiculous thing was that he knew that Kiara would have been supportive. After all, she'd stood at his side as he'd poured his stash of alcohol down the drain. But doing that had made him look strong. Like he wasn't weakened by temptation.

The gala had been the opposite. There had been too many times when he'd been so close to taking the offered alcoholic drinks. If Anthony hadn't come alongside him, he wasn't confident that he wouldn't have found a way to get a drink.

He wasn't sure if Kiara would respond, but he spent the day waiting for a text from her. It wasn't until nearly eight o'clock that night that he got a notification that he'd received an email from her in his personal email inbox.

He tapped to open it, bracing himself for her response to what he'd told her

Dear Julian ~ Thank you for your letter. I'm sorry that I didn't understand the stress you were under last night. I just assumed that events like that would be easy for you. I wish I'd realized you were struggling.

Julian wasn't sure what she could have done. But perhaps if he had been focused on her instead of himself, he could have done something for her. His regret over how he'd abandoned her was huge.

I hope that the week ahead isn't too stressful for you. I have no idea what board meetings are like, but I imagine they aren't all fun and games.

I'm glad to be back home. I don't know if it's my nesting instinct or what, but being here soothes something inside me. It's great to be able to walk into the nursery and sit in the rocking chair.

Unbidden, the image of Kiara in the nursery came to his mind, the chair slowly rocking as she rested her hands on her belly, a serene look on her face.

That was home.

He realized that then. It wasn't his perfectly decorated apartment. Nor the main house on the estate. No, home was the place where Kiara and his son were. Somehow, they had become his home, and Julian wasn't sure what to do about that revelation.

It's also beautiful here. Coming to the estate on the helicopter was just gorgeous. All the lovely colors of autumn. I can't wait to go for a walk and take some pictures.

I'm ready to call it an early night, and I'm looking forward to sleeping in my own bed. Hope you're enjoying being in your own bed too. Have a good night!

Take care ~ Kiara

Julian relaxed back in his chair and stared out the dark window, taking in the lights of the city around his apartment. He was glad that Kiara had replied, and that she had been so understanding. More understanding than he deserved, if he was honest with himself.

He took a few minutes to send a message back to Kiara, but he didn't tell her everything that was on his mind. He needed the time to sort through his emotions, something he wasn't used to doing.

In the past, he'd used alcohol to help him deal with any emotional upheaval. Although maybe "deal" was too strong of a word because what he did was more like ignore the emotions until he'd drunk enough to bury them deep in the recesses of his mind.

Since his sessions with the therapist, he was more aware of the right way to work through difficult emotions. However, his default was still to push them aside, and he was doing that again by not writing about them in his letter to Kiara.

He promised himself that he *would* talk in depth to her about everything at some point. Just not yet. And not through an email.

The next two weeks were crazy busy, and when Julian climbed aboard the family jet to fly back to Idaho, he was desperate for a few days of downtime.

He followed Duncan and Elizabeth onto the jet, then waited for them to choose their seats before taking one himself. They had been with him for the past two weeks, first in New York City, and then they'd flown to Dubai to their office there for five days before coming back to New York. They were all ready for a chance to get over jetlag and unwind.

It wasn't long before they were in the air, and Tracy, their flight attendant, brought them beverages and offered food. Julian just asked for a cup of coffee, though in the past, he'd usually have had a drink or two on the flight.

Not drinking was still a struggle, especially when he was in situations where he had previously had several drinks. But so far, he'd managed to resist the temptation.

After he finished his cup of coffee, he leaned his seat back, hoping he might be able to sleep. As he closed his eyes, though, his thoughts went to Kiara.

They'd kept in contact over the past two weeks. It hadn't been quite daily since he'd been tied up a lot. First with the board meetings and then with the trip to Dubai. Her emails to him had been a welcome distraction in his busy days.

Her messages had made it sound like she was doing well, and her latest appointment had confirmed that the baby boy was growing like he should be.

Julian had been a bit surprised when she'd asked him if he wanted to be in the delivery room. It hadn't even entered his mind that he could be there when the baby was born. It seemed like a very... personal thing.

Of course, he and Kiara had already had a moment that was extremely personal, but he had no memory of that time.

He didn't feel strongly enough about being in the delivery room to press for something that might be uncomfortable for her. Plus, he was pretty sure that Angie would want to be there with her.

It was hard to believe that in less than a month and a half, he would be a father. He had no idea what that would look like. There probably wasn't much he could do for the first several months.

The Burkes always had nannies, though Elizabeth had only had one part-time for Benji. She was definitely a more hands-on parent than he remembered his mom being. And maybe there was something to be said for that, since Benji had a better relationship with Elizabeth than Julian and the twins had with their mom.

Even though his mind was busy, he eventually drifted off. But it seemed like it was no time at all before Tracy was waking him with a gentle shake.

Blinking, he sat forward and straightened his seat. He ran a hand through his hair, then turned to look out the window. Now that it was well into October, the fall colors were abundant and beautiful.

Once they were on the ground, they transferred to the helicopter. Julian had brought more of his stuff from New York, so he had three large suitcases for them to switch from the jet to the helicopter.

"Ready to go home, Son?" Duncan asked, resting his hand on his shoulder.

Home... Was that what the estate had become? Or was it Kiara and the baby?

"Yep. It'll be nice to have a break."

Julian climbed onto the helicopter first, then turned to offer his hand to Elizabeth. Once Duncan and the security team were on board, the pilot started the engine.

The trip to the estate passed quickly, and soon the helicopter was descending toward the helipad. Once they had landed, it was a quick unloading of the helicopter onto the UTVs.

"Will you be at dinner tonight?" Duncan asked as they walked to the edge of the helipad.

"I'm not sure," Julian said. "I'll see what Kiara is doing."

"If not tonight, maybe we can all have dinner together tomorrow."

"Sounds good."

Anthony was waiting with one of the UTVs and had his bags all loaded in the back. Julian swung himself into the front seat beside Anthony.

"To Kiara's?" Anthony asked.

"Yep."

The drive from the helipad to the house was short. Once there, Julian grabbed one of his suitcases while Anthony took care of the other two.

"Do you want me to carry them to your room?" Anthony asked when they set them down on the porch by the front door.

"I'll take care of them," Julian said. "Thanks for the help."

Anthony gave him a two-fingered salute, then jogged back down to the UTV. After he'd driven away, Julian approached the door. He hesitated for a moment, wondering if he should knock.

In the end, he turned the handle, figuring if it was locked, then he'd knock. The knob turned easily, and the door swung open.

Immediately, he was greeted by the aroma of food. Warmth and spice, and the smell of fresh bread wrapped around him. A tightness he hadn't even been aware of in his chest loosened.

And when he spotted Kiara in the kitchen, he had a feeling of coming home. Of being home.

"Hi there," he said as he stepped through the door into the open living space.

"Hey." Kiara smiled at him as she wiped her hands on a dish towel and came toward him. "How was your trip?"

"Long," he said. "Even though we had an overnight after our trip from Dubai to New York, it kind of felt like one long journey."

As she neared him, Julian could see that her belly had grown even more since he'd last seen her. Since he'd given her a hug goodbye in New York, it only seemed natural to give her another hug as a greeting.

Having her in his arms felt right, but the hug was brief. Too brief. Julian wished he could have held her longer. However, he wouldn't make things awkward by prolonging the contact when she was clearly done with it.

"It smells delicious," Julian said. "Is there enough for me?"

"Of course," Kiara said. "I made plenty in case you were hungry."

"I'm starving, actually." He hadn't felt like eating on the flight, but now, with the tempting aromas in the air, his stomach rumbled.

"I made some beef stew, and Annie helped me with some sourdough bread."

He followed her as she walked back toward the kitchen, noting that the dining table had been set for two.

"Don't you have any luggage?" Kiara asked as she stirred the contents of a large pot.

"My suitcases are on the porch."

"The food isn't quite ready, so you have time to bring them in if you want."

With a nod, Julian turned and headed for the door. After he'd taken his suitcases to his suite, he made the snap decision to change into something more comfortable.

He settled on a pair of flannel pajama pants and a faded sweatshirt from his college alma mater. Even though he hadn't been wearing a suit while they traveled, it still felt like he'd changed out of his work persona.

Back in the kitchen, he found that Kiara had put the food on the table and divested herself of her apron. She had on leggings and an oversized sweater that had plenty of room for her bump.

"Water okay?" she asked as she stood next to the table with a pitcher in her hands.

"Perfect." He wasn't sure what the other option might be for him since he no longer drank alcohol. Milk maybe?

In addition to the tureen of stew, there was a bowl of salad and a basket containing thick slices of bread. It was the perfect meal for a chilly fall evening.

Remembering his manners, Julian helped Kiara with her chair, then sat down across from her. When she didn't immediately serve herself, Julian said, "Don't wait on me."

"Oh. Okay." Kiara hesitated, then reached for the large spoon in the stew. She ladled some into the wide bowl in front of her, then returned the spoon to the tureen and moved it so it was in front of him.

Julian's stomach rumbled again in anticipation of what was to come. And his first bite of the stew was an explosion of flavor.

"You were right that you can cook," he said. "This is delicious."

"This is something I've made a lot of," she said. "Beef stew was a favorite throughout the fall and winter months for Jim. I wouldn't have thought I'd enjoy making it if I didn't have to, but it seemed perfect for today."

"Well, let me be sure to tell you how much I appreciate you making this. It's wonderful."

"I've been cooking more now that I have my own kitchen, even though it was designed by Angie."

"Duncan wants us all to eat at the house tomorrow for dinner," Julian said. "Do you feel up for that?"

"Sure. I think I have something that fits and will be appropriate for dinner."

"It would be nice if Duncan would relax his standards for dressing when it's just us family."

"I'm just glad he doesn't expect us to wear clothes like we had on the night of the fundraising gala."

"I don't think I'd join them for dinner if that was the case," Julian said as he dipped a chunk of bread in his stew.

They ate in silence for a few minutes, then Julian remembered something he needed to tell her. "Elijah is arriving tomorrow to stay for a bit."

"Oh, that will be nice."

For a moment, Julian wondered what Kiara thought about Elijah. They'd never really talked about him, but she'd hung around him when he'd been there previously. Was Elijah the type of guy she would have gone for, had an evening of alcohol not led to some questionable decisions?

Julian frowned. The thought had come out of left field, but he realized he really didn't like that idea.

"Is he flying in?" she asked.

"No, he's driving from Texas."

"Is he staying here in the house? We didn't really plan a space for visitors, but the rec room in the basement has a pull-out couch, and there's a bathroom down there as well."

Julian considered it, then said, "I think it will work better if he's at the main house. Especially since it's not that far away."

As he ladled another helping of the stew into his bowl, he asked, "What have you been up to this week? I'm sorry my emails kind of fell off. Duncan was trying to make the most of our time in Dubai."

"Well, I've spent quite a bit of time practicing driving a UTV. Jude decided it was time I learned. He's having one delivered that is modified to accommodate an infant seat."

"How did your driving go?"

"I think I did pretty well."

"Maybe we'll have to go for a drive," he suggested, surprised that it actually sounded appealing.

They talked a bit more about driving around the estate as they finished their meal.

"Do you want some dessert?" Kiara asked.

"I don't want you to go to any trouble," he replied.

"It's no trouble. Just cookies and brownies that I baked with Angie yesterday."

"Sounds good. Do you want to have it in front of the fireplace?" Jude asked. "I can start a fire."

"Oh, I'd like that. Thanks to Jim, I know how to start one, but it's not my favorite thing to do."

Julian went into the living room while Kiara cleared off the table. By the time she joined him, he had a good fire going, and warmth spilled out into the living room.

Julian stood staring down into the flickering flames. He welcomed the warmth and the coziness and acknowledged just how much he needed it after the hecticness of the past two weeks.

He heard movement behind him and turned to see Kiara approaching with a plate of cookies. She set it down on the coffee table, then straightened, resting her hand on her stomach.

"Do you want coffee?" she asked.

"Are you making some for yourself?"

She shook her head. "I'm going to have some hot chocolate. Would you rather have that?"

"It's been forever since I last had hot chocolate."

"The way I make it is amazing," she told him. "You should have a cup."

Julian couldn't help but smile. "Okay. You've convinced me."

He trailed her back to the kitchen, then stood at the island counter, watching as she prepared two large mugs of hot chocolate. When she was finished, she slid one to him, and they carried their mugs to the living room.

They settled on the couch, with Julian taking one end while Kiara took the other, tucking her feet beneath her. The flickering fire cast a warm glow across the room, creating dancing shadows on the walls. Julian took a careful sip of the hot chocolate, letting the rich, sweet liquid coat his tongue.

"You weren't kidding," he said, surprised by how good it was. "This is amazing."

Kiara smiled, her face brightening at the compliment. "It's a secret recipe. Well, not really. When I made up a batch of the mix, I added some cinnamon and a little bit of cayenne pepper."

Julian took another sip, detecting the subtle spices that gave the hot chocolate depth and complexity. "The spice really makes a difference."

"That's what I think too." She reached for a cookie and took a small bite. "So how was Dubai? Did you get to see anything outside of the office?"

"Not really," Julian admitted, settling more comfortably against the cushions. "I was pretty much confined to meetings the whole time. I did get to eat at a few good restaurants though."

"That's something at least."

Julian watched the fire for a moment, feeling the tension of travel gradually releasing from his shoulders. There was something soothing about being here, in this house, with Kiara's quiet company and the crackling fire.

"How about you? What else have you been up to besides learning to drive UTVs?"

Kiara's fingers traced the edge of her mug. "I've been reading a lot about childbirth. I found some great books, and there's a class at the hospital next week that I'll be going to."

Julian felt a flicker of guilt. He should probably be learning about childbirth too, even if he wasn't going to be in the delivery room. "The class sounds good. When is it?"

"Tuesday evening at seven. It's a two-hour class."

Julian nodded, considering his schedule. "Would it be okay if I came with you? I mean, I know I said I wasn't going to be in the delivery room, but I should probably at least understand what you'll be going through."

Surprise flickered across Kiara's face, followed by something that looked like hope. "Really? You'd want to come?"

"Yeah, I would. Even if I'm not in the delivery room, I should know what's happening."

"I'd like that," she said softly, her fingers curling more tightly around her mug. "It would be nice to have someone with me."

Julian felt a twinge of concern. Had she been planning to go alone?

"Angie wasn't going to attend with you?" Julian asked, reaching for a cookie.

Kiara sipped her hot chocolate before answering. "I haven't asked her. I think I was hoping..." She trailed off, then shook her head slightly. "Anyway, I'd really like it if you came."

Julian nodded, feeling a strange mixture of relief and anticipation. "Then I'll be there."

The fire popped and crackled, sending a shower of sparks against the screen. Julian watched the flames dance, feeling more at peace than he had in weeks. There was something about being here, in this space, with Kiara, that felt right. It felt like... home.

Kiara put her mug on the end table, then burrowed into the cushions on the couch. The silence that settled between them was comfortable, and Julian didn't feel the need to break it.

When he glanced over to check on Kiara a few minutes later, he saw that she'd fallen asleep. If she hadn't looked so comfortable, he might have woken her so she could go to bed. Instead, he pulled a large blanket from the back of the couch and spread it over her.

Rather than going to his room, he shifted closer to Kiara and pulled the end of the blanket over himself too, then leaned back against the cushion behind him. He didn't know if he'd be able to fall asleep, but he'd stay there until Kiara woke up.

As Julian stared at the crackling fire, contentment swirled through him. It was a foreign feeling, and he wasn't sure what to make of it.

He turned his head to look at Kiara. She was curled on her side, her head resting on a cushion, with her hands tucked under her chin. Her dark eyelashes fanned out across her cheeks.

When he'd first met her, she'd already had some curves, but the pregnancy had softened her features a bit more, and it looked good on her. He wondered if the baby would have her dark curls and hazel eyes, or if he'd have lighter brown hair and green eyes like him.

He hoped that regardless of who the baby looked like, he inherited Kiara's easygoing personality and the determination that had helped her through the years of growing up in an environment that was anything but easy.

He had never thought about having children, but as he considered the situation he found himself in, he was glad that Kiara was the mother of his child. She was devoted to those she loved, and he knew that she would love their child in a way he'd never been loved by his mom.

Julian just hoped that he'd be a good father. With Kiara's help, he thought he had a better chance than he would have had without her.

CHAPTER TWENTY-FOUR

Kiara woke with a start, the urge to use the bathroom coming on suddenly, as it often did. She straightened her legs, then froze when she heard someone groan.

Struggling to sit up, she looked over and saw that she'd kicked Julian. He blinked blearily at her.

"I'm sorry," she said. "I didn't mean to kick you."

His hand landed on her foot. "It's okay. No harm done."

"I need to use the bathroom," she whispered.

Kiara wasn't sure why she felt the need to speak so softly, since it was just the two of them in the house. She carefully extracted her foot from his gentle grasp.

The fire had died down to embers, casting just enough light for her to see Julian's rumpled hair and creased face. He looked younger somehow, softer around the edges without his usual guardedness.

Kiara pushed the blanket aside and maneuvered herself off the couch, one hand automatically going to support her lower back. The baby shifted, pressing against her bladder with renewed urgency.

When she returned a few minutes later, Julian was on his feet, running his hands through his hair. He'd folded the blanket and placed it on the arm of the couch.

"What time is it?" Kiara asked, glancing toward the windows where darkness still pressed against the glass.

Julian checked his watch. "Just after three."

"I didn't mean to fall asleep on you," she said, attempting to calm her own wayward curls that had escaped her ponytail while she'd slept.

"Well, as you can see, I also couldn't resist the lure of sleep." He stretched his arms above his head, arching his back a bit. "But I think I need to spend the remainder of the night in an actual bed. I'm too old to be sleeping on the couch."

Kiara rubbed her lower back. "And I'm too pregnant."

Julian walked over to the fireplace and stirred the embers with the poker. "Want me to turn off the lights?"

"Sure, thanks." Kiara smoothed her hands over her belly. "I'll see you in the morning."

Without looking back, she walked toward the door that led to her suite of rooms. She closed the door behind her, then continued into her bedroom.

As she swapped her clothes for the oversize T-shirt that she felt most comfortable sleeping in, she tried not to dwell on the evening with Julian. Or to put any importance on what had transpired.

Friendship...

That's what she had set her mind on after everything that had happened at the gala.

She had accepted that, because they were married, she had to share space with him, and if she wanted peace in her home, they needed to get along. So friendship was the best way to achieve it.

To that end, she'd responded to his emails. She'd prepared dinner for them. She'd conversed with him, answering any questions he had.

But in all of that, she had kept at the forefront of her mind that no matter what her feelings might be, Julian wouldn't feel the same way about her. It had been relatively easy to stay focused on friendship until she'd fallen asleep and woken up to find that Julian had covered her with a blanket and stayed with her in front of the fire.

Now, her heart clamored for all kinds of foolish things that she knew she couldn't have.

After brushing her teeth and going through her nighttime routine—even though it was three o'clock in the morning—she crawled into her bed and tugged the thick comforter up to her chin.

As she lay in the darkness, she prayed, as she so often did throughout each day, that God would give her strength and wisdom. That He would be with her and help her and Julian to be the best parents possible to their son.

What she didn't pray for was that Julian would come to love her. That felt selfish. If God only answered one of her prayers, she wanted it to benefit her son, and that would be her and Julian being good parents.

The next morning, Kiara was slow to get out of bed. She spent some time scanning through social media. She wasn't very active on her accounts, but she loved looking through other people's posts. Especially now that the majority of her timeline was pregnancy and baby focused. She'd purchased more baby things at the promptings of posts on social media than she probably should have, but some of the stuff was just *so* cute.

When hunger began to make her feel a bit queasy, Kiara slid out of bed. She flipped the comforter back into place, then began to prepare for the day.

The only thing on her schedule that day was dinner at the main house. It had been awhile since they'd all been together for a meal, so she was actually looking forward to it.

The house was quiet as she came out of her suite, but the aroma of coffee was in the air, so she assumed that Julian was already up.

In the kitchen, she walked to the sink and stared out at the backyard, checking on the weather like she did every morning.

It looked like it was another cloudy and rainy day. A day that spoke of the transition that was to come as they moved through fall into winter. Their second winter in Idaho.

Turning away, Kiara began to prepare her breakfast. She heated a pan, then put a couple of slices of bacon in it. While they cooked, she mashed up some avocado and seasoned it. After the bacon had cooked for a bit, she moved it to the side of the pan and added an egg, scrambling it with a fork.

Once everything was almost done, she cut a couple of pieces of the sourdough bread and stuck them in the toaster. She stared at the small appliance, remembering her horror at how much it had cost. For that price, it should have done more than just toast the bread.

When the toast was done, she carefully arranged everything on the plate. She'd just made herself a cup of tea when the front door opened.

Kiara looked up to see Julian walk in, dressed as if he'd been working out. He wore a pair of sweats and a zippered hoodie that was open over a T-shirt. His hair was disheveled.

"Good morning," she said.

He gave her a quick smile as he walked toward the kitchen. "Sleep well?"

"Not too bad," she said. "How about you?"

"My body clock is still dealing with jetlag, so I didn't sleep much after we woke up."

"You're going to be tired," she said. "Do you want some breakfast?"

"What are you having?" he asked as he sat down at the counter.

"I made some avocado toast," she said, gesturing to her plate. "Do you want some?"

"I don't want to inconvenience you."

"It's no problem. You can have one of those, and I'll make a couple more pieces."

She transferred one of the pieces of toast to another plate, then put more bacon in the pan. For as much as she'd hated making food for Jim and Craig, she didn't mind doing it for Julian.

Julian didn't start to eat until she had prepared the second batch and sat down beside him.

"Thank you," Julian said, taking a bite of the toast. "This is really good."

Kiara smiled at the compliment, though she tried not to read too much into it. Friends complimented each other's cooking. It didn't mean anything more.

"So what were you up to this morning?" she asked, noticing how his workout clothes clung to him slightly, as if he'd been sweating or had gotten caught in some rain.

"I went for a run. The estate has some nice trails, and I figured I'd better try to get a run in before it started to rain."

"From the look of the sky, we won't be getting too many breaks today, so I hope you enjoyed it."

Julian chuckled. "Not sure I enjoyed it, but I was glad it didn't start to sprinkle until I was nearly home."

Home. Was that just a slip of the tongue? Or did he really think of the house as home?

Kiara couldn't deny that she hoped it was the latter. Because if he thought of it as home, he might be more inclined to spend time there with their son.

They ate in companionable silence for a few minutes. The baby shifted, and Kiara adjusted her position on the stool, trying to get comfortable.

"Are you okay?" Julian asked.

"I'm fine," she said, adjusting herself again. "He's just really active this morning. I swear he's going to be a soccer player considering all the kicking he does."

Julian's expression softened as his gaze dropped to her belly. "May I?" he asked, his hand hovering uncertainly in the space between them.

Kiara's heart skipped a beat. Julian had touched her bump briefly in New York, but this felt different somehow. More intentional. "Of course."

She guided his hand to the spot where the baby was most active. For a moment, nothing happened, and she worried her son would choose this moment to settle down. Then came a firm kick right against Julian's palm.

Julian's eyes widened. "Wow. That was... strong."

"Tell me about it," Kiara said with a laugh. "Sometimes he wakes me up with his gymnastics routines."

Julian kept his hand there for a moment longer, his expression one of wonder. Another kick came, and he laughed softly, the sound warming something deep inside her.

"He's definitely strong," Julian said, slowly withdrawing his hand. "Must be all that good food you've been feeding him."

Kiara smiled, trying to ignore the lingering warmth where his hand had been. "I try to eat healthy, but sometimes all he wants is ice cream."

"I can't blame him for that," Julian said, returning to his breakfast. "Ice cream is a solid choice."

After they finished eating, Kiara cleared their plates while Julian made himself a cup of coffee. The domesticity of the moment felt both natural and dangerous. Natural because it flowed so easily between them, dangerous because it made her heart yearn for things she couldn't have.

"I should probably shower and change," Julian said. "But I was thinking–if you're up for it–maybe we could go for a drive around the estate later? You could show me your UTV skills."

"I'd like that," Kiara said, surprised by how much she meant it. "Jude says I should practice as much as possible."

"Great. I'll be back in a bit, then."

Kiara watched him disappear into his suite, trying not to dwell on how comfortable everything felt between them that morning. The way he'd touched her belly, the genuine wonder in his eyes when he felt their son kick. It was so easy to imagine that it was real. That they were a normal couple expecting their first child.

But they weren't. And pretending otherwise would only lead to heartache.

She busied herself cleaning up the kitchen, then went to change into something suitable for an outdoor drive. She opted for jeans and a warm sweater, knowing that even with the UTV's enclosed cab, the October chill would seep in. After fixing her hair, she gathered a few snacks and filled a thermos with hot chocolate, packing everything into a small bag.

Julian emerged from his suite looking refreshed, his hair still slightly damp from the shower. He'd changed into jeans and a burgundy Henley that made his green eyes seem more vivid somehow.

"Ready?" he asked, grabbing a jacket from the coat rack by the door.

"Almost." Kiara retrieved her jacket—a new one she'd bought when her regular one no longer fit comfortably over her growing belly. "There's a UTV in the garage. Jude wanted me to have one here, though it's not the one he ordered. That one hasn't been delivered yet."

"Hopefully, it has good heat so you can drive it through the winter months."

"Jude assured me it had a good enclosure and heater, which I had told him was necessary for the baby."

"And for you," he said. "You need to be warm as well."

Kiara smiled at him, appreciating that he was thinking of her comfort too.

"Well, I packed some hot chocolate, so we'll both be warm," she told him, holding up her small bag. "And some snacks, just in case we get hungry while we're out."

Julian smiled, and something about that simple expression made her heart flutter. "Always prepared. I like that."

“I've learned,” she said. “Hunger comes on me at the oddest moments since I've been pregnant, so I've learned to have a small stash of snacks with me at all times.”

As they stepped into the garage that was attached to the back of the house, he pressed the button to open the door. Crisp air flooded into the space, carrying the earthy scent of wet pine and earth.

The UTV sitting in the spacious garage was smaller than some she'd seen around the estate, but it was still sturdy-looking with an enclosed cab that would keep them protected from the elements.

"This one's pretty straightforward," Julian said as he walked to the driver's side and opened the door. "You drive, I'll navigate."

Kiara hesitated. "Are you sure? You probably know the trails better than I do."

"I'm happy to let you take the wheel.”

She still wasn't very confident driving it yet, so she hoped that Julian wasn't in the mood for speed. He stood close as she pulled herself up into the UTV, then he shut the door once she had settled into the driver's seat.

Julian slid into the passenger seat and closed his door. The click of the latch seemed to seal them into their own little world, separate from everything else.

The interior of the UTV was smaller than a car, so they sat more closely together. Close enough that Kiara got a whiff of his cologne. Or maybe it was his shampoo or soap. Whatever it was, it was a warm, spicy scent that made her want to cuddle close to him and just inhale it.

Instead, she focused on the task at hand.

"Jude gave me a few lessons," Kiara said, settling her hands on the wheel. "But I'm still learning, so don't expect any fancy driving."

"I'm not worried," Julian said, his voice calm and reassuring.

She turned the key in the ignition, and the engine rumbled to life. The vibration traveled through the seat and up her spine, not unpleasant but noticeable. The seat was already set for her since she was the last person to drive the UTV.

Taking a deep breath, she put the vehicle in drive and eased out of the garage. The UTV responded smoothly to her touch, rolling down the short driveway and onto one of the estate's well-maintained paths.

"Which way should we head?" Kiara asked.

So far, she'd stuck to the main roads on the estate, though she was aware there were trails and dirt roads that led through the trees to different parts of the vast property.

"Right will take us down toward a small lake," Julian said. "The view there is pretty spectacular, especially with the fall colors."

Kiara turned the wheel, carefully navigating the UTV along the winding trail. The vehicle bumped a bit over the uneven surface, but the suspension absorbed most of the impact. She kept her speed low, concentrating on the path ahead.

Julian seemed relaxed beside her, one arm resting on the door as he gazed out at the passing scenery. The forest around them was a tapestry of gold, orange, and crimson, the leaves still clinging to branches despite the recent rain.

"You're doing great," Julian said after they'd traveled for several minutes in comfortable silence.

"Thanks." Warmth spread through her at the compliment.

She hadn't anticipated spending time with him the way she was, and she knew she had to be careful to just live in the moment. Julian had just gotten home from a long and, by all accounts, busy trip, and she had a feeling that he was looking for ways to unwind.

If that was the case, and if he wanted to spend some of that time with her, she certainly wasn't going to turn him down.

As they drove deeper into the property, the trees grew more dense, creating a canopy of autumn colors overhead. Occasionally, sunlight broke through the clouds and filtered through the leaves, casting dappled patterns on the path before them.

"There should be a clearing just ahead," Julian said, pointing through the windshield. "The lake is right beyond it."

Kiara slowed the UTV as they approached the opening in the trees. The trail widened, and she carefully navigated around a fallen branch.

"You really are good at this," Julian said. "Jude must be a decent teacher."

"He was patient," Kiara replied, unable to suppress a small smile at the praise. "I was pretty nervous at first, but he kept telling me I couldn't possibly be worse than Benji was on his first time driving one of these."

Julian laughed. "I heard about that. Apparently, he nearly drove straight into the garage door. Though that was a few years ago, so I assume he's improved since then."

The UTV emerged from the tree line, and Kiara gasped. Before them stretched a small lake, its surface rippling gently in the rain. The water reflected the surrounding trees in smudges of autumn colors—fiery oranges, deep reds, and golden yellows. Mountains rose in the distance, their peaks partially obscured by low-hanging clouds.

"It's beautiful," she breathed, easing the UTV to a stop in a flat clearing near the shore. She put the vehicle in park and turned off the engine, letting silence settle around them.

"This is one of my favorite spots on the property," Julian said, his voice softer now that the engine's rumble had ceased. "Not many people come out here."

Kiara unbuckled her seatbelt, but she didn't open the door. Unfortunately, the rain was falling a little more steadily, though it still wasn't torrential.

"It's nicer when it's not raining," Julian said. "But it's still a nice spot."

The interior was heated, so it was comfortable to sit there and talk. Their conversation was light, not delving into any subjects too deeply.

It reminded her of the nights they'd spent talking in the library, only without the alcohol. She was glad to know that they could still have those conversations and communicate face to face because it would hopefully build a solid foundation for them in the future when they had to co-parent their son.

There would be some big decisions that lay ahead, and Kiara wanted to know that, despite them not being a family, Julian would continue to have their son's best interests at heart.

Having moments like these with him grew her confidence that despite the rocky start to their relationship... their friendship... they would be able to raise their son to know that he was loved and wanted.

That desire had become almost an obsession. Because of how she'd been raised, she wanted to do everything in her power to give her son the opposite of that. And if it meant she had to put aside her own hopes for love, she could do that.

CHAPTER TWENTY-FIVE

Julian felt refreshed after spending time at the small lake with Kiara, even though it had been raining. After a hectic couple of weeks, the outing had been a welcome slowing down.

When they left the lake, Julian asked Kiara to drop him off at the main house since Elijah would be arriving shortly. Kiara had opted to head back to her house, so Julian stood and watched as she slowly pulled away in the UTV. Once she disappeared from view, he turned and went into the house.

"Good afternoon, Son," Duncan said as Julian walked into the living room. Also present were Elizabeth, Annie, and Cole.

Julian greeted each of them, then said, "Elijah is arriving in a few minutes."

"His room is ready," Elizabeth assured him.

"No room for him to stay at your place?" Annie asked.

Julian hesitated to respond because he didn't know why he hadn't taken Kiara up on her offer of the basement space for Elijah. "We don't really have an actual spare room. Just a pull-out couch in the basement."

"I guess the girls didn't figure they'd need to have space for guests when they designed the house."

"Each suite has two bedrooms," Julian said, "but I've got my second room set up as an office, and Kiara's extra room is now a nursery."

They chatted for a bit more before Julian received a text on his phone letting him know Elijah had just passed through the front gate. Julian excused himself and went to the mudroom door to wait for him since that's where he'd park his car.

It was great to see his friend again, and after he took his stuff up to the room where he'd be staying, they set off for the rec center. Elijah was eager for some physical activity after being in his Jeep for the past three days.

Benji ended up joining them at one point, and when he did, Julian took a seat on one of the benches that lined the wall. The competitiveness of the play amped up considerably with Benji's arrival, and Julian couldn't keep pace with it.

They kept playing until it got close to dinner. Julian headed to his house while the other two returned to the main house to shower and change.

It was quiet when Julian let himself into the house. He looked toward the door to Kiara's suite, but it was closed.

Though he wanted to check on her, he went to his suite instead. She knew what time they needed to be there for dinner, so presumably she'd be ready on time.

In his suite, he changed out of his casual clothes into a pair of black slacks and a long-sleeved dark green button-down. He brushed his hair into its usual style, adding a bit of product to hold it in place.

When he left his suite, Julian saw that Kiara's door was still closed, and he felt a bit of concern. He walked toward the door, planning to knock on it.

He'd just about reached it when the door swung open. Kiara's eyes widened when she spotted him.

"Is everything okay?" she asked, her hand still on the doorknob.

"Yep. I was just coming to see if you were ready to go for dinner."

"I am," she said with a nod. She stepped through the doorway, then closed the door behind her. "I just forget that everything takes a bit longer these days. Not to mention trying to find something to wear. "

"Well, you look very nice," he said, taking in the long-sleeved light pink blouse that flowed over a long fitted black skirt. Her hair was loose, with the curls hanging down past her shoulders.

She gazed at him for a moment before she said, "Thank you. You look very handsome as well."

Julian gave her a quick smile, then gestured toward the garage. "Shall we go?"

Nodding, she fell into step beside him as they walked to the door of the garage.

"Do you want to drive?" he asked as he pressed the button to open the overhead door.

"No, you can have that honor this time."

Julian walked around the UTV and opened the door for her. Offering her his hand, he helped her up onto her seat, then closed the door.

It was dark out already, but the road was well lit with streetlamps all along the way. Once November hit, which wasn't that far away, the estate would be decorated for Christmas. Elizabeth insisted that their celebration of Thanksgiving wouldn't be lessened by the presence of some Christmas decorations.

For the first time in over seventeen years, there would be a baby celebrating its first Christmas. His baby. His son. It was crazy to think about.

He wondered if Kiara was going to decorate their house, or if she'd want to hire someone to do it for her like Elizabeth usually did. Given the baby would only be a month or so old, he didn't know if she'd feel up to doing it on her own.

When they got to the house, they found that the others were there already. Angie greeted Kiara with a hug, then they were all ushered into the dining room.

Julian took his seat beside Kiara and went on to enjoy one of the most relaxing family dinners he'd ever experienced at the estate. It was exactly the opposite of how things had been at the gala.

Later, as he and Kiara prepared to go home, they made arrangements to go to church in Coeur d'Alene the next day. They decided to take two vehicles, with Jude and Angela going in Jude's truck, while Julian, Elijah, and Kiara would go with their bodyguards in an SUV.

After saying goodnight to everyone, Julian once again drove the UTV back to the house. Kiara let out a sigh as she walked into the kitchen.

"Tired?" Julian asked, becoming more aware of how physically taxing the pregnancy was on Kiara.

"A little."

"Want a fire?" he offered.

She glanced over at him. "If you want to light one, sure."

"I'm happy to do that."

"I'm going to get into something a bit more comfy," she said as she headed to her room.

Julian decided to also change before starting the fire and quickly went to his room to pull on a pair of pajama pants and a T-shirt.

Kiara still wasn't out when he went to the fireplace to start the fire, but he'd just gotten it going when she joined him.

She lowered herself slowly onto the same end of the couch she'd taken the last time. As the flames grew, Julian got to his feet and joined her on the couch. He settled in, keeping a comfortable distance between them.

In the past, he'd brought his laptop out to work on while they'd sat together in the living room. Now, he left it in his suite and just enjoyed being in the moment.

The warmth from the fire radiated across the room, casting dancing shadows on the walls. Julian watched the flames for a moment, feeling more at peace than he had in weeks.

"This is nice," he said softly. "I didn't realize how much I needed this quiet time until now."

Kiara nodded, tucking her feet beneath her. "It's good to have you home. I mean—" She glanced away. "Back at the estate."

Julian smiled at her correction. Home. The word resonated in a way he hadn't expected. "It's good to be back. Traveling is part of the job, but it's wearing on me more than it used to."

"Is that why you seemed so tired when you got back yesterday?" she asked.

"Partly that. Partly the jetlag. Partly that I was just thinking about some things." He leaned back, letting the cushion take his weight. "It's been a crazy few months, you know?"

"I do know," Kiara said, her hand moving to rest on the curve of her belly.

Julian watched the gentle rise and fall of her hand with each breath. Something about the quiet intimacy of the moment, just the two of them bathed in firelight, made him want to be honest in a way he rarely was.

"I've been thinking a lot about becoming a father," he admitted. "About the kind of father I want to be."

Kiara's expression softened. "And what have you decided?"

"That I want to be better than my dad was." The words came out before he could filter them. "Don't get me wrong. Duncan provided everything we could ever need materially, but he wasn't... present, really. At least not until after the kidnapping. Then, he became obsessed with protecting us."

"That's kind of understandable, though."

Julian nodded. "But I want to find a balance so our son doesn't feel smothered."

"I'll help you with that."

That was actually reassuring to Julian. They came from such different backgrounds that it might have caused problems. But since they both wanted something different from how they'd been raised, he had hopes that they could find some middle ground and figure out what was best for their son.

They talked for about an hour, each sharing things about their childhoods that they'd struggled with, and what they hoped to be able to do differently for their son.

It was enlightening for Julian, and in some ways, distressing as he learned more about the life Kiara had lived on the homestead. What made it even more difficult to hear was coming to understand in more detail what Angela also went through as a result of his actions as a kid.

"I'd better go to bed," Kiara said after giving a big yawn. "Falling asleep out here isn't an option since I have to be up for church tomorrow."

Julian wished their time together didn't have to end, but he could see she needed to rest.

He got to his feet, then held out his hand to Kiara. "Need a hand?"

"I'd like to say no," she said as she reached out to take it. "But a lift would be nice."

As he helped her to her feet, her belly bumped into his hip. He reached down and rested his hand on her stomach. "Hey, little guy, be good and let your mama sleep tonight."

When he looked up, his gaze met and held Kiara's. There was a sudden rush of emotions inside him that he didn't know what to do with. He didn't even recognize what all of them were.

But there was a longing to be able to go to bed with her. Not for anything more than to just hold her in the darkness and talk. To feel his son move beneath his hand as he listened to Kiara's breaths deepen as she fell asleep.

Given that he'd never wanted to actually sleep with any of the women he'd been with, it was a new, confusing feeling.

"Thanks for the help," Kiara said as she stepped back from him. A small smile crossed her face, but it didn't quite reach her eyes. "I'll see you in the morning."

Julian stood watching her as she walked away, and he didn't know what to do. He didn't understand what was happening inside of him, and as with so much lately, he didn't know how to deal with it.

He slept fitfully that night, thoughts of the situation weighing heavily on his mind. When he got up the next morning, he still had no answers, but he had come to a certain realization.

Something had changed inside him over the past few months. It had started with getting sober and finally revealing the secret that had weighed him down for so long. But it hadn't stopped there.

The fact that he was feeling more at home on the estate was also a major change. But probably the strangest change was his willingness to attend church and to really hear about a faith that he'd previously had absolutely no interest in.

His feelings for Kiara were undergoing a shift as well. From not feeling one way or the other about her, to now feeling a great deal for her, he was experiencing emotions he'd never dealt with before.

Out in the kitchen after he'd gotten ready for church, he started the coffee, then looked in the fridge to see what he could make for them for breakfast. Unfortunately, he wasn't a cook.

He knew she liked avocado toast, but it was unlikely that she'd like *his* version, which would most likely be burned or undercooked.

"What are you looking for?"

Turning, Julian closed the fridge door. Kiara was walking toward him, dressed in a matching burgundy sweater and skirt that hugged her belly. She looked more rested, so he hoped she'd had a good night's sleep.

"I was trying to decide if I should inflict my cooking on you."

"You know how to cook?"

Julian chuckled as he leaned back against the counter, giving her space to move around the kitchen. "No. But unless you want to hire a chef, I'm beginning to think I should learn."

"That's not in my plan," Kiara said as she opened a bag of bagels. "I don't mind cooking the meals we don't eat at the main house."

Julian frowned. "I don't want to make work for you."

"You're not," she said as she put the bagel halves into the toaster. "If I don't feel up to cooking something, we have the main house as an option. Elizabeth told me I'm always welcome, so I assume that applies to you too."

"But do you *really* enjoy doing the cooking?" he asked.

"Strangely enough," she began as she opened the fridge. She appeared a moment later with a tub of cream cheese and a container of strawberries. "I'm finding that I do enjoy it. I'm not as passionate about it as Angie, who is apparently having great fun trying all sorts of recipes. But since I don't really have anything else to do with my time, cooking has become something I enjoy."

"Do you want to grab me a couple of plates?" Kiara said, gesturing to the cabinet he stood next to.

He turned and opened the door to retrieve two plates. Moving close, he set the plates on the counter in front of her.

For the next couple of minutes, they worked together to get the simple breakfast on the plates, then Julian carried them over to the table. Kiara filled mugs with coffee, then joined him.

"I hope this is enough for you," she said.

"It's great," he assured her. "I appreciate you making it."

She gave him a smile that brightened her face. "I hope baby boy appreciates it too."

Julian really did appreciate the things she did for him, but he didn't want it to be a one-way street. He wanted to be able to help her out too, but he wasn't quite sure how. Something told him that she was a very self-sufficient person and would decline help if offered.

Once they were done with breakfast, they cleaned up the few dishes they'd dirtied, then got ready to leave for church. They took the UTV to the main house, where they met up with Elijah and the bodyguards.

Elijah took the back seat while Julian sat in the middle row with Kiara. The trip to Coeur d'Alene passed quickly, and soon they were walking into the church.

When he noticed Elijah keeping his head ducked down as they walked through the foyer, Julian realized that his friend was aware that he might be recognized. He hoped that it didn't happen, especially since Elijah appeared to want to avoid any attention.

As with the last service he'd attended, the music was uplifting, and the pastor's sermon was thought provoking.

He and Elijah had talked a lot about what being a Christian meant. For every question he'd had, Elijah had been able to direct him to a passage in the Bible that answered it.

When Elijah had asked him what was holding him back from taking that final step, Julian hadn't had an answer for him. Part of it, he knew, had to do with feeling like he'd be taking on another set of expectations that he wouldn't be able to meet.

He was afraid to take on the responsibilities of being a Christian, only to fail in front of his family and Elijah.

But for the first time in his life, he had a strong desire to be a better man. He wanted to be a good father, and someone his son would look up to and admire. And in a moment of shocking revelation, he wanted to be a better man for Kiara. He wanted her to know that he would always be someone she could count on.

He wanted to leave the person he'd been behind.

If Julian knew one thing, he knew that he wasn't going to be able to do any of that on his own. Was God the answer to his becoming a better man?

Everything he'd heard from Elijah and through the pastor's sermons said He was, so maybe it was time he took that final step and trusted that God would give him what he needed in order to be better.

Unfortunately, it only took a day for Julian to be faced with a situation where he had to let Kiara down.

"I'm not going to be able to go with you to the class at the hospital," Julian said after he got off a phone call with Sean. "I need to go to Singapore."

Kiara frowned. "Has something happened?"

"Yes." Julian sat back down on the couch.

He'd started the fire after they'd returned from dinner at the main house. Unfortunately, he'd received a call from Singapore just minutes later. "Sean called to let me know he's concerned about a possible theft of research material for the FemPulse."

Kiara's brows rose. "Someone has stolen information from your company?"

"Yes. And Sean was concerned that they were bugging his electronics to monitor, so they'd know if he suspected anything. He actually bought a burner phone, then went to a hotel where he removed everything he wore and left it in the bathroom with the shower running so he could call me."

"That is... crazy. He must be really worried."

"He is," Julian agreed. "But we need to deal with this as soon as possible. We can't let it slide."

"You're not going by yourself, are you?" Kiara asked.

"No. I'll have Anthony and Elijah with me, but I'll also be taking a larger security force, including our cybersecurity team."

Kiara's face creased with worry. "Is it safe for you to go there with something like this happening? It sounds like corporate espionage."

"That's exactly what it is," Julian said, running a hand through his hair. "But we need to handle this quickly before more damage is done."

The warmth from the fire couldn't touch the chill that had settled in his chest. He'd been looking forward to attending the class with Kiara. It had felt like an important step—one that would show he was committed to being involved, even if he hadn't planned to be in the delivery room.

"I understand," Kiara said softly, her hand moving to her belly in that protective gesture he'd noticed she often made. "How long will you be gone?"

"I'm not sure. A week at minimum, but it could be longer depending on what we find." Julian watched as disappointment flickered across her face. "I'm sorry about the class."

"It's okay. I understand that this is important."

Julian nodded, but the guilt still gnawed at him. After wanting to be there for her, to help her, he was already letting her down. "I'll make it up to you."

"You don't need to do that," Kiara said, shifting on the couch to face him more directly. "Your work is important."

"So is this," Julian insisted, gesturing toward her belly. He meant it too.

Kiara's expression softened. "When do you have to leave?"

"Soon. I'll be taking the jet to New York to pick up the IT security team members, then we'll fly to Singapore." Julian leaned forward, resting his elbows on his knees. "Elijah has already agreed to go along with us, but I still need to speak with Duncan."

Elijah had responded to his text almost immediately, stating he'd be happy to join him on the trip. Julian was glad he'd have his friend with him, especially with how uncertain the situation was.

Kiara nodded, a small smile touching her lips. "That's good. I'm glad you won't be alone."

"I hate leaving so soon after just getting back," Julian admitted. The fire crackled, sending up a shower of sparks. "It feels like I'm running out on you."

"You're not running out on me," Kiara said, her voice soft but firm. She reached out to rest her hand on his arm. "This is your job, and it's important. There are a lot of people depending on you, and from what you've told me, this research could be life-changing for people."

Julian covered her hand with his as he studied her face, searching for any sign that she was just saying what she thought he wanted to hear. But her expression seemed genuine, even if there was disappointment in her eyes.

"I'll keep in touch," he promised. "Daily updates."

"I'd like that."

A log shifted in the fireplace, sending up a shower of sparks. Julian kept his hand over hers as he watched the flames dance, his mind already racing through everything he needed to do before departure. Meet with Duncan, pack, brief the security team, review the data that Sean had sent him that had first roused his suspicions.

"I should probably start getting things ready," he said. "First, I need to meet with Duncan, then I need to get packed. My plan is to leave for Coeur d'Alene by three a.m."

"So early?"

"We need to get going, and with the time difference, we probably won't get to New York until around noon. I hope that we can leave for Singapore not long after. This time, we're taking a private jet rather than flying commercial. Duncan's assistant will arrange for us to take a larger plane since we have further to fly, plus we'll be having meetings during the flight over to review everything."

"How long will the flight take?"

"From New York? Around twenty-two hours. We'll have to make at least one refueling stop."

"Will you be able to sleep?"

"Yes. The seats are pretty comfortable on those types of jets, plus there might be a bed, depending on which plane we end up with." He let out a sigh. "I need to head back to the house to talk with Duncan. Do you need anything before I go?"

She shook her head and gave him a soft smile. "I'm good. I might be in bed before you get back."

Julian took her hand fully in his, turning to face her as he shifted closer on the couch. The reluctance to leave her was strong, and he knew walking out that door was going to be the hardest thing he'd done in awhile.

"Take care of yourself," Julian said, then reached out to gently lay his other hand on her stomach. "And I hope Baby Boy doesn't give you too much trouble."

"We'll be fine." She smiled at him, her expression gentle. "You take care of yourself too."

"Don't worry about me." He could see the concern on her face. "I will have good people with me to make sure I'm safe."

"Don't take any unnecessary risks," she said. "Our son needs his daddy."

"I'll be careful. I promise."

Julian leaned forward to press a kiss on her forehead. He didn't know why he did it, but it felt right.

"I'll see you when I get back." He got to his feet. "But don't hesitate to message me if you need to. Just keep in mind the time difference if I don't answer right away."

She gazed up at him with wide eyes and nodded. "See you soon."

Julian was loath to leave her, because suddenly it felt like there was so much unsaid between them. But he had to go. With a final look, he turned and walked to the door leading into the garage. In deference to the cold, he'd take the UTV to the main house to see Duncan before returning to get his things ready to go.

The timing of this was the worst, but hopefully he'd be home well before the baby arrived.

CHAPTER TWENTY-SIX

Rubbing her bump, Kiara slowly walked toward the kitchen. It was tightening again. It had been doing that off and on for the past couple of days, but over the last few hours, it had been happening more regularly.

At her appointment earlier in the week, Doctor Misha had said everything was looking good. She had two and a half weeks until her official due date, but the doctor had cautioned her about pinning all her hopes on that date because she could go beyond it.

But now Kiara was wondering if she could also deliver the baby early. According to what she'd read, it was possible she was just experiencing Braxton Hicks contractions.

Standing in the kitchen, she stared out the window but didn't really see the scenery as she rubbed her stomach.

She wasn't sure she was ready to have the baby yet, especially if this was something more than just Braxton Hicks. Angie was in New York with Jude, who had flown there to help deal with the security issues that had come up because of what had happened in Singapore. Annie and Cole had traveled to LA to finish cleaning out his house there, which had just recently sold.

And Julian was still in Singapore. The security issue had taken longer to resolve than he had anticipated because the situation had turned out to be a real mess. She felt for him because in the messages they'd exchanged and the brief calls they'd had, she'd sensed how stressed he was.

Unable to focus on anything, Kiara left the kitchen and walked to the nursery, settling into the rocker. Laying her hands on her stomach, she set the rocker into motion with her foot.

After another brief period of abdominal tightening, she pulled her phone out and opened the app she'd downloaded to prepare for tracking her contractions. She just hadn't anticipated needing it so soon.

They were coming fairly regularly but weren't very close together. And thankfully, they weren't painful. Just a bit uncomfortable.

Her thoughts wandered as she rocked, going as they often had over the past ten days to those moments before Julian had left. The way he'd held her hand, then kissed her forehead...

She couldn't put it out of her mind, but she also didn't know how to interpret it.

It was hard not to hope that there was something more behind his actions. As much as she'd tried to keep her feelings for him buried, they had only grown as he'd become more caring. And he'd also seemed to become more invested in the pregnancy and their son.

But the more she allowed those thoughts to surface, the more she had to remind herself of their arrangement. He had made it clear from the beginning that this was temporary. That after the baby was born, they would get a divorce and move on with their lives, only connecting because of their son.

The thought left her with mixed feelings. As anxious as she was to meet her son, she wasn't looking forward to the end of her marriage. She'd come to enjoy Julian's presence in the house... in her life.

Another tightening gripped her abdomen, making her pause in her rocking. This one felt a bit stronger than the others. She checked the time and entered it into the app, worrying a bit as a pattern began to form.

"Not yet, little guy," she murmured, smoothing her hand over her belly. "You need to stay in there for a couple more weeks."

When she heard a soft knock, Kiara looked up and saw Lucy standing in the open doorway. The bodyguard had taken to coming to check on her several times throughout the day now that pretty much everyone in the family was away from the estate.

Kiara hadn't thought she'd come to appreciate Lucy the way she had. Early on, Annie had mentioned she'd clashed with Lucy whenever she'd guarded her, but Kiara had been so thankful for the woman, especially during the pregnancy. She'd offered information and encouragement that had helped put Kiara at ease.

"Everything okay?" Lucy asked, leaning against the doorjamb.

"I'm just having some Braxton Hicks," Kiara said, no longer entirely convinced that's what they were. "They're not painful, but they're pretty regular."

Lucy's brow furrowed a bit as she pushed away from the door jamb and came further into the nursery. She hovered her hand over Kiara's stomach. "May I?"

"Sure."

Lucy moved her hand around, pausing when her stomach tightened again. Kiara picked up her phone and added it to the app.

"Have you had contractions like this before today?" Lucy asked.

"Not like this," Kiara admitted. "They weren't this regular."

"I'll probably stick around for a bit, just to see what happens." Lucy walked toward the door, then turned back. "Do you want something to eat or drink?"

"I wouldn't mind some berries and lemon water," she said. "Everything is in the fridge."

When Lucy left her, Kiara leaned her head back, wishing that Julian and Angie were there. If she was in labor, she was going to be facing it alone.

She'd prepared herself for that, though. Angie had insisted that it was Julian's responsibility to be in the delivery room. Kiara hadn't told her yet that Julian had declined to be there with her.

For some reason, Angie seemed to think that Julian would want to be there for the labor, and in her mind, it wasn't just because he wanted to meet his son. Angie had been dropping hints that she thought Julian might have developed feelings for her. Kiara wasn't sure what had led to that assumption, but it was wrong.

When her belly began to tighten again, Kiara frowned. What if this was for real?

She wasn't ready.

The contraction had ended by the time Lucy returned with a bowl and glass. "Here you go."

"Could you make a hotel reservation for tonight in Coeur d'Alene?"

Lucy froze. "Do you think it might be time?"

"I'm not sure, but I'd like to be closer to the hospital in case it is."

"Okay. I'll get it sorted out," Lucy said. "How soon do you want to leave?"

"Half an hour?"

Lucy nodded, then left the room. Kiara ate the berries and drank some water, all the while thinking of what she needed to add to the bag she'd packed just a few days earlier.

When Lucy came back, Kiara took her offered help to get out of the chair. "I know that you probably have to tell someone where we're going, but can you make sure that whoever you tell doesn't pass that info on? I don't want anyone to get worried in case it's a false alarm."

"I can do that," Lucy assured her. "Now, where's your bag?"

"In my bedroom," Kiara said as she headed toward it after leaving the nursery. "I just need to add a couple of things."

"I'm going to run to my place and pack a bag really quick. I'll be back with a car to pick you up in a few minutes."

"Okay. I'll be ready."

As Lucy left the house to go to her apartment above the security building, Kiara went into her bathroom. She packed the toiletries she used each day into the bag she'd bought to hold them for the trip to the hospital, then went to pack a few more items of clothing, just in case they ended up hanging around the hotel for a couple of days.

She wasn't sure why she'd decided that going to Coeur d'Alene was the best decision right then, but there was just something in her gut that told her it was time to go. If she was wrong, there was nothing lost.

Once she was confident that she had everything, Kiara sat on the edge of her bed for a moment, feeling the familiar tightening return for the second time since she'd entered her room.

She gazed down at her phone, wishing she could send a message to Angie or Julian. However, without knowing what was going on, she didn't think it was a good idea to raise the alarm with both of them being so far away.

If the contractions or whatever they were ended up being insignificant, she would have worried them—especially Angie—for no reason.

If they did end up being significant, maybe she'd text them. But there wasn't anything they could do, even if it was really labor. It would be better to just not bother them until all was said and done.

Angie would only worry, being so far away. And Julian... well, he hadn't planned to be there for the birth, anyway.

"Ready to go?" Lucy asked from the doorway a few minutes later.

Kiara nodded and got to her feet. Lucy picked up her bag, and after detouring to the kitchen to fill a water bottle, Kiara followed her out to the vehicle. It was one of the smaller SUVs, but thankfully, just as comfortable as the larger ones.

"How are the contractions?" Lucy asked as she guided the SUV away from the house. "Getting any stronger?"

"Not really." Kiara rubbed her stomach, then sighed. "I'm probably overreacting."

"It's better safe than sorry," Lucy said.

"Do you remember how your mom's labors started?" Kiara asked.

"I remember the last one most clearly. It was with my brother, Davy. She was overdue with him, and her water broke."

"Was she overdue with all her pregnancies?"

"Nope. Only me and Davy were overdue. Two of the others came within a day of their due date. The other three were early to varying degrees, with one early by over three weeks."

"And she had that one at home?" Kiara asked.

She was worried that since she was over two weeks away from her due date, the baby might be too small. All the measurements the doctor had taken over recent weeks had shown that he was growing well, even a little ahead.

"Yep. She was perfectly healthy and didn't need any time in the hospital."

"So if I *am* in labor, he might still be okay?"

"I'm sure he'll be fine," Lucy said. "But even if he has to stay in the hospital, it likely won't be for long."

Kiara hoped Lucy was right, because as time passed, she was beginning to think she was going to be delivering her baby soon.

After they had dinner at the hotel, Kiara decided to take a shower and lay down. But as she got undressed, she experienced a mighty gush of water. Staring in shock at the puddle of water on the floor, Kiara knew her pains were about to get intense.

~*~

Julian dragged himself out of bed and went to the small, attached bathroom to splash water on his face. He'd crashed in the bedroom as soon as they'd taken off after refueling.

It had been ten stressful days in Singapore, but the operation had finally been secured, and they were on their way back to the

US. It was the first time he'd dealt with corporate espionage, and he hoped and prayed it was the last time too.

Leaving the bedroom at the back of the plane, he found that most of the rest of his team were also sleeping. Elijah, however, was awake and sitting at the small boardroom table, his Bible open in front of him. He looked up as Julian sat down in the chair across from him.

"Have you slept at all?" Julian asked.

"Yep. I've only been awake for about twenty minutes."

"How far are we from New York? Do you know?"

"I don't."

When Tracy, the flight attendant, approached them, she told them they had two hours before they'd begin their descent into New York City.

After giving them the information, she asked if they wanted anything to eat. She listed off what was available, and both he and Elijah asked for the full breakfast option. Julian also asked for a cup of coffee, feeling an intense need for caffeine.

Julian was so grateful that Elijah had come along with the team on the trip. The man had been a steady calming influence throughout the highly stressful time. And he'd been there for a life-changing moment for Julian.

During the times when Julian wasn't tied up with Sean and the team at the R&D division, he and Elijah had had some deep conversations about the questions Julian had about the sermons he'd heard.

Elijah had been incredibly patient with Julian's questions, never making him feel stupid for not knowing the answers that probably seemed basic to someone who'd learned about the Bible his whole life. Instead, he'd shared more about his own journey of faith, how he'd come to believe, and the ways his relationship with God had transformed his life.

And midway through their time in Singapore, amid the most intense situation he'd ever dealt with, Julian had finally made the decision to commit his life to God. He hadn't felt an immediate change in himself, but he'd prayed each day for wisdom as he dealt with the security breach.

And he believed that God had answered that prayer.

They were leaving Singapore with the situation resolved. The people who'd tried to steal the information on the FemPulse were in custody. From what they could tell, they'd managed to contain the breach before the most confidential information had been obtained. Sean's diligence and keen observation skills had caught things early on, for which Julian was grateful.

"What are your plans when we get back?" Elijah asked after Tracy had brought them mugs of coffee.

Julian wrapped his hands around the warm mug, savoring the heat against his palms. "First, I have to brief Duncan on everything, then I need to get back to Kiara. I've been away too long."

He hadn't told her yet that they'd left Singapore. His plan was to let her know once he had an idea of how long he'd have to stay in New York. He hoped that it would only take a day or two for him to handle the meetings he needed to have there.

"She's getting close to her due date, isn't she?"

"It's about two weeks away, if everything goes according to schedule." Julian took a sip of his coffee, wincing slightly as the heat hit his tongue. "But from what I've read, babies rarely follow schedules."

Elijah smiled. "True. My sister's first came three weeks early, and her second was two weeks late. You just never know."

"I've been thinking about something you said earlier," Julian said after Tracy had brought them their breakfast. "About how becoming a Christian doesn't instantly fix all your problems, but it gives you a different perspective on them."

Elijah nodded, his expression thoughtful. "It's true. My life hasn't been perfect or easy. You know that. After all, we met in rehab. My dad was never one to admit that he needed God's help. Because I struggled a lot, I always felt like I was a failure. One of the things I've had to learn is that I need God's help. And then I have to accept that God is there to walk with me through the difficult times. Through the times of temptation. It is with His strength that I can get through them. They are no longer insurmountable."

Julian ran a hand through his hair, the edges still damp from splashing his face. "I think that's what I'm starting to understand. I can't do it all by myself. All these years, I've been carrying everything alone because I thought it was what I deserved. The guilt about Angela's kidnapping, my struggles with alcohol, the pressure from work. It's exhausting."

"Well, now you need to turn to God when you're struggling," Elijah said. "And don't be afraid to ask me to pray for you. I want to do that for you."

"I appreciate that," Julian said with a smile. "I want to do that for you too, but as a new Christian, I feel like I don't have as much pull with God as you do."

Elijah chuckled. "That's not how it works. You're a child of God now. New or old, He will hear our prayers."

"Will you let me know if I can pray for you too then?"

"I will," Elijah said. "How are you feeling about Kiara and the baby? I've been praying for you and her."

Julian took a bite of his eggs Benedict, buying himself some time before answering. "To be honest, I'm not sure how I feel. Sometimes it doesn't seem real. Like I'm married and will soon be a dad."

"Are you still wondering if the baby is yours?"

Julian shook his head. "Now that I've gotten to know Kiara more, I don't think she'd do that. She had nothing to gain by lying.

Duncan has set her up financially, so she'll never want for anything, whether we're married or not."

"Are you still planning to end the marriage?"

Wasn't that the question of the hour? "I don't feel as certain about that as I once did. My feelings for Kiara have... changed. But I don't know how Kiara feels."

"You should give your marriage a chance," Elijah said.

"How do I even do that?" Julian asked.

Elijah didn't answer right away, but eventually, he said, "To be honest, I don't have an answer to that. But I do think that perhaps spending more time with her is a good place to start. Take care of her. Help her. You have an opportunity to do that since she's in a place where she needs help. Both now and after the baby is born."

"I told her that I didn't think I needed to be in the delivery room."

"And how did she react to that?"

"She didn't, so I thought it was fine."

"Perhaps one of the best ways to give things a chance between you two is for you both to talk it out."

The conversation ended there because a couple of the guys from the security team joined them. Over the next hour, the rest of the team woke up and were served breakfast.

At one point, Anthony settled into the chair beside Julian. "Are we staying in New York?"

"I think so," Julian said, giving Tracy a smile of thanks as she refilled his coffee. "I need to spend some time talking to Duncan."

Anthony looked away. "I think we should continue straight on to Coeur d'Alene."

Julian stared at his bodyguard, alarm growing at Anthony's words. "What's going on?"

"Kiara asked that no one be told, but Lucy thought you should know."

Fear flooded Julian. "What's happened?"

"Kiara is in labor."

"It's too early."

Anthony shrugged. "Regardless, she's in the hospital in Coeur d'Alene."

"She didn't want me to know?"

"She didn't want anyone to know. Angela doesn't know either."

"And she's in New York with Jude, isn't she?"

Anthony nodded. "I'm not going to pass the information on to them."

Julian lifted his mug and took a sip. He needed to be in Idaho. He wanted to be there for Kiara and to meet his son. Whether that meant he arrived in time for the birth or shortly after, he just needed to be there.

"Make the arrangements for us to fly to Coeur d'Alene as soon as we land in New York."

They were supposed to arrive in New York early in the morning, so if they left as soon as possible after landing, they'd be in Idaho around noon considering the time difference.

"And make sure there's a car waiting to take us to the hospital as soon as we land."

"Will do."

"That's exciting," Elijah said as Anthony walked away, his focus on his phone.

"She's early."

"Not too early, though," Elijah told him. "My sister's son was three weeks early, and he was fine."

Julian hoped that was the case. He wanted to message her, but if Lucy was the only person with Kiara, he didn't want her to get upset that Lucy had spilled the beans.

He knew Duncan would expect to meet with him, so he had to somehow explain why he was going straight to the estate instead of staying in New York, even for just a day.

After some thought, he tapped out a message.

I'm going to head right on to the estate. With Kiara being this close to her due date, I want to be available to her. I'll set up a time to video chat with you once I'm there.

Julian was once again grateful for how their money made life easier because once they landed, they quickly switched planes. After the luggage was sorted out, they took off for Coeur d'Alene.

The five-hour flight seemed to stretch on forever. Anthony remained in contact with Lucy, so they knew that Kiara was still laboring.

When they landed, there were two SUVs waiting with additional security team members. One SUV took the luggage and the security team members back to the estate, while Julian, Anthony, and Elijah got in the other one and headed to the hospital.

Julian had told Elijah he didn't have to hang around at the hospital, but he said he would keep Anthony company while they waited for the baby to make his appearance.

Going against Anthony's instructions to wait for him, Julian practically bolted from the SUV when they arrived at the hospital, leaving Anthony and Elijah to handle the parking details. His heart hammered against his ribs as he strode through the automatic doors into the main lobby.

"I need to find my wife," he told the receptionist, his voice tight with urgency. "Kiara Burke. She's in labor."

The woman tapped on her computer. "Yes, she's in the maternity ward on the third floor. Take the elevators to your right."

Julian nodded his thanks and headed for the elevators, punching the button repeatedly as if that might make it arrive faster. The wait felt interminable, each second stretching into eternity. When the doors finally opened, he stepped inside and jabbed at the third-floor button.

His mind raced with a thousand thoughts as the elevator climbed. What if he was too late? What if something had gone wrong? Why hadn't Kiara wanted him to know?

The doors slid open, and Julian stepped into a quiet hallway. A sign pointed him toward the maternity ward, and he followed it, his footsteps quickening. At the nurse's station, he stopped, trying to control his breathing.

"I'm looking for Kiara Burke," he said to the nurse behind the counter. "I'm Julian Burke, her husband."

The nurse checked her computer. "She's in Room 312. She's still in active labor."

Relief washed over him. He hadn't missed the birth. "Thank you."

Julian followed the room numbers until he found 312. He paused outside the door, suddenly uncertain. He'd told Kiara he didn't want to be in there with her. What if she hadn't wanted him there to begin with?

But he couldn't just stand in the hallway—he needed to see her, to make sure she was alright. If she didn't want him there, he'd go... but only as far as the waiting room.

Gently pushing the door open, Julian stepped inside.

The room was dimly lit, with soft beeping from monitors filling the silence. Lucy stood by the bed, holding Kiara's hand. When she saw Julian, her eyes widened in surprise.

"Julian," she said quietly.

Kiara's head turned toward him, her face flushed and damp with perspiration. Her hair was pulled back in a messy ponytail, curls escaping around her face. She looked exhausted but beautiful.

"You're here," she whispered, her voice cracking slightly.

Julian moved to the bed, his throat tight with emotion. "I'm here."

Lucy let go of her hand and stepped back from the bed. "I'll go check in with Anthony."

Julian nodded, his gaze on Kiara. "How are you doing?"

She lifted her hand to brush a curl back from her face. "I think I'm okay. All things considered."

"Are you okay with me being here?"

Before she could answer, he saw her eyes flutter closed, and she began to breathe heavily. Realizing what was happening, Julian reached out and took her hand, which had curled into a tight fist. As soon as he took her hand, she loosened her fingers and gripped his.

He had no idea what to do, so he just stood there, offering her support with soft words of encouragement.

Finally, she relaxed, the tension going out of her body as she inhaled and then let out a long breath. He waited for her eyes to open, and when they did, she looked right at him.

"I'm fine with you being here," she said. "I'm just surprised. I didn't know you were coming home today."

"I wasn't sure if I was going to come today or in a couple of days, but then a little bird told us what was going on," he said. "And I knew I wanted to be here."

A tired smile crossed Kiara's face. "A little bird, huh? A Lucy bird?"

"Well, she didn't tell me," Julian said. "She told Anthony, and he decided to tell me."

Her eyes fluttered closed again, but it didn't seem like another contraction was coming just yet because she didn't tense up.

"I'm glad you came."

Julian smiled, then turned as the nurse approached him with a wheeled stool. He settled down on it, Kiara's hand still in his, prepared to stay right at her side until their son entered the world.

CHAPTER TWENTY-SEVEN

The contraction eased, and Kiara slumped back against the pillows, her grip on Julian's hand loosening slightly. She kept hold of it though, because she was afraid she was imagining that he was there with her.

Her heart had raced with surprise when she saw him beside her bed. She'd been certain that she would be laboring with Lucy as her support. But now, there he was, sitting beside her bed, his green eyes filled with concern.

"How long have you been in labor?" Julian asked, his thumb gently stroking the back of her hand.

"Since yesterday afternoon," she said, her voice raspy from exhaustion. "My water broke just after six o'clock yesterday. That's when Lucy brought me in."

Julian frowned. "You've been at this for over eighteen hours?"

"I think I read something about first babies taking their time." She tried to smile, but it felt weak even to her. "Even if he is coming early."

"Have you considered any sort of pain relief?" he asked. "An epidural?"

They had offered it, but she felt like she should try to push through the pain without it. Unfortunately, she was exhausted, which made it harder to deal with the pain. It felt like forever since she'd had any sleep.

"I don't know." She shifted on the bed, trying to get comfortable.

"Do you want to get out of bed and walk for a bit?" the nurse asked from where she was checking the monitors. "We can unhook you."

Kiara knew that walking was a good idea, so she nodded. The nurse removed the monitor belt, then helped her to her feet.

"Dad, if she has a contraction while you're walking, let her lean on you," the nurse said. "Follow her lead."

Kiara glanced at Julian when the nurse called him dad and saw a rather bemused look on his face. When their gazes met, he grinned and then offered her his arm.

She shuffled out the door beside him, grateful that Julian kept his pace slow. They'd only gone a few steps when another contraction started.

When she stopped walking, Julian stepped in front of her. "The nurse said to lean on me."

Kiara had seen videos of how to do that, but she didn't know if Julian would understand. But then the pain became too much, and she couldn't focus.

She reached for his shoulders, then pressed her forehead to his chest. His arms went around her, his hands resting gently on her back.

Without even thinking about it, Kiara swayed back and forth, breathing deeply as the contraction peaked, dragged out, then ebbed. When it finally released its hold on her, Kiara took one more deep breath and then straightened.

"Okay?" Julian asked as he looked down at her, concern in his eyes. He still had his hands resting on her back.

She nodded, then moved to take his arm again so they could continue to walk.

"How was your flight?" she asked as they walked, eager for a bit of distraction.

"It was fine," he said. "It was nice not to have to travel commercially in either direction, which I usually do when flying to Singapore."

"Why didn't you this time?"

"With so many of us in the travel party, it was easier to take a private jet. Plus, we were going on such short notice that we needed to have some time to review what was happening and come up with a game plan. That would have been impossible to do on a commercial flight."

Another contraction started, so they stopped again, and this time, once they were in position again, Julian rested his cheek against the top of her head and swayed with her.

Though she'd been prepared to go through the labor with Lucy, Kiara was so grateful that Julian had decided to come to the hospital when he'd heard that she was in labor. As the pain subsided, it occurred to her that perhaps he hadn't intended to stay at the hospital.

"I didn't mean for you to get roped into labor support," Kiara said as they turned the corner to another hallway.

"You didn't rope me into anything," Julian replied. "I'm here because I want to be."

"Well, you can leave at any time," Kiara told him. "I'm sure you're exhausted."

Julian stopped walking and stepped in front of her so they were facing each other. He reached out and took her hands.

"You are also exhausted, so there's no reason I should get to rest when you can't. I'm here for the long haul. Right to the end."

Kiara clung to his hands, unfathomably grateful that he was there supporting her. "Why did you change your mind about being here?"

"I was already reconsidering my decision to not be in the delivery room before I heard you were in labor," he said. "So when Anthony told me, I knew I wanted to be here with you."

She looked away from him, her gaze going down the hallway. "I'm glad you're here. It makes it feel a little... easier."

Julian let go of her hand and touched her cheek. She couldn't keep from looking back at him. "We're in this together, and I'm glad I can be here to help you however you need."

Before she could respond, pain gripped her belly. Working together, they got into position again.

Though Kiara wanted to parse through all the emotions that Julian's words brought up in her heart, she couldn't. Her focus needed to be on bringing their son into the world.

Julian was by her side, and would be until the birth, and that was all that mattered right then.

They walked for awhile, pausing for each contraction, but then Kiara was just too tired to keep going, so they returned to the room. Once she was back in bed, Kiara just wanted to sleep, but almost immediately, she had another contraction to deal with.

Weariness had lowered her emotional defenses, and before she could stop them, tears began to fall. It felt like too much, and she just couldn't keep dealing with the painful contractions.

"Why don't you get the epidural, sweetheart?" Julian spoke softly as he bent close to her after the contraction ended. "Maybe then you can get some rest."

Trying to wipe the tears from her cheeks, Kiara nodded. "I am so tired."

Julian smoothed a hand over her hair, then pressed a kiss to her forehead. "I'll let them know."

It all moved quickly after that, and soon, Kiara was able to fully relax, knowing that she didn't have to breathe through or endure any more painful contractions.

"Try to sleep," Julian said. "I'm going to talk to Anthony and then I'll be back."

Kiara nodded, sleep already pulling at her. She didn't know how long she'd be able to nap, but she wanted to rest up enough to have the energy needed for the final push.

When she opened her eyes next, Julian was sitting beside the bed in a chair that reclined. His head was turned toward her, but he was sound asleep. Kiara took the opportunity to study him.

She still couldn't believe that he was there, and not because he'd felt obliged but because he *wanted* to be there. It gave her hope that he would want to be an active parent in their child's life.

Julian's hair was mussed, like he'd been running his fingers through it, and his clothes were wrinkled from travel. There were dark circles under his eyes that spoke of the strain of the past couple of weeks and his exhaustion. Yet he'd chosen to stay with her, to be part of this experience despite his initial reluctance.

A nurse came in quietly to check the monitors.

"How are you feeling?" she whispered, noticing Julian was asleep.

"Better," Kiara replied softly. "How much longer do you think?"

The nurse checked something on the monitor. "Your contractions are looking good. Regular and strong. The doctor will be in soon to check your progress, then we'll have a better idea of how it's going."

After the nurse left, Kiara shifted slightly, trying to find a more comfortable position without disturbing Julian. The movement must have been enough, though, because his eyes fluttered open. For a moment, he looked disoriented, then his gaze settled on her, and his expression softened.

"Hey," he said, his voice rough with sleep. "How are you doing?"

"Better," Kiara said. "The epidural helped a lot."

Julian straightened in his chair, wincing slightly as he rolled his shoulders. "How long was I out?"

"I don't know. I just woke up myself." Kiara watched as he stretched his arms above his head. "The nurse said the doctor will be in soon to check my progress."

Julian nodded and ran a hand through his hair, making it stand up even more. He looked younger somehow, with his rumpled appearance and the softness in his eyes that hadn't been there when they'd first met.

"Are you hungry?" he asked. "I could see if they have anything I could get for you."

Before Kiara could answer, Doctor Misha walked in. There had been a chance that another doctor might have had to deliver her baby. But thankfully, it had worked out for Doctor Misha to be there.

After greeting them, she said, "Let's see how we're progressing."

Julian stood and moved to Kiara's side, taking hold of her hand. She squeezed his fingers as the doctor examined her, grateful for his steady presence.

"Well," Doctor Misha said, removing her gloves. "You're ten centimeters dilated and fully effaced. Great job!" She smiled warmly. "Let's get ready for you to push."

After the doctor left, Kiara felt a surge of nervous excitement. "It's really happening," she whispered, looking up at Julian. "He's almost here."

The atmosphere in the room changed. Julian stayed by her side, and together they watched as the nurse prepared things.

The nurse went to the monitor and stood there for a minute, then turned to her. "When the next contraction starts, let's try to push."

It took a little bit for Kiara to get the hang of pushing, but thankfully, she managed to figure it out and push with the contractions. The nurse was good about coaching her, and Julian was right there, holding her hand and offering words of encouragement.

She didn't know what she would have done without him.

~ * ~

Julian was in awe of Kiara's strength and focus. He'd never thought much about childbirth and all that it entailed, so it was a bit of a shock how intense it was. He was relieved that Kiara had agreed to the epidural, because he couldn't imagine how painful this final stretch would be without it.

"You're doing great," the nurse said as Kiara slumped back against the bed after a contraction. "You've gotten the hang of it."

For some reason, Julian had assumed that once Kiara started pushing, the baby would come right away. Unfortunately, that wasn't the case.

It took about an hour of pushing before the nurse said, "I can see his head. You can do it."

Over the next twenty minutes, the pushing grew more intense, and soon the doctor was back in the room with them.

Kiara focused intently on her pushing, and Julian did what he could to encourage her.

"That's it," the doctor said from her place at the end of the bed. "Here he comes. Keep pushing."

Kiara let out a groan and then slumped back against the elevated portion of the bed behind her. Julian stared in shock as he saw the baby in the doctor's hands.

"He's here," she announced as she lifted the baby onto Kiara's stomach.

The nurse covered the baby with a blanket and gently rubbed him. He let out a squawk and began to cry.

"It's okay, baby," Kiara said softly as she lifted a hand to touch his cheek. "It's okay."

Julian bent close, his head near Kiara's as they looked at their son. He had a lot of dark hair, which was pressed wetly against his head.

After several minutes, the doctor said, "Do you want to cut the cord, Julian?"

He glanced at Kiara. "Can I?"

"Of course."

Feeling a bit overwhelmed, Julian moved closer to the doctor and took the scissors she held out to him. He followed the directions and soon the cord was cut.

Over the next several minutes, the doctor continued to work on Kiara, while the nurse carried the baby to a nearby infant warming bed.

"Go with him," Kiara said as she watched the woman move away from them.

Before he did as she instructed, he turned his attention fully on Kiara and bent down to rest his forehead on hers. "You did so great. I can't even begin to tell you how amazing you are."

Emotions were flowing through him in a way that Julian had never experienced before. He felt closer to Kiara than he'd ever felt to another person, and in that moment, he knew that he wanted to keep that closeness.

Though she looked exhausted, she managed a smile for him. "I couldn't have done it without you."

Julian appreciated her saying that, but he knew that she would have been strong enough to do it on her own. He was just glad he'd come to his senses, so she hadn't had to.

Straightening, he went to where the nurse was taking care of the baby and stared down at his son. His *son.* He never would have imagined himself having this moment.

Wanting to capture it, Julian pulled out his phone and took several pictures of the baby while the nurse completed the post-birth routine on him. Once he was all wrapped up, she made like she was going to hand him to Julian.

"Uhhhh." He took a step back. "I've never held a baby before."

"Then it's about time you start, Daddy."

Returning his phone to his pocket, he allowed the nurse to place the baby in his arms. She guided him back to the bed where Kiara waited, her eyes shining as she smiled at them.

"Here's your mommy, little guy," he said, shifting close to give the baby to Kiara.

She took him with more ease than Julian had and bent to kiss the knit cap that now covered his head. "Welcome to the world, baby."

"Did you decide on a name for him?"

Kiara looked up at him and smiled. "His name is Theodore Julian Burke."

Julian stared at her. "You're naming him after me?"

"Yes. Unless you'd rather that I didn't."

"No, that's fine," Julian said. "I just... I never thought you'd consider that."

"I thought we could call him Theo or TJ."

"I like TJ," Julian said, pulling out his phone again. "Can I take a picture to send to Angela?"

She nodded, but before he could do that, the nurse came and offered to take a picture of the three of them.

"Do you want me to let the family know he's here?" Julian asked. "Or did you want to wait?"

"You can let them know," she said. "And maybe let Lucy know, too."

When the nurse mentioned she was going to help Kiara get the baby latched on to nurse, Julian excused himself from the room. He wasn't sure that Kiara would be comfortable with him being around while that was going on.

"He's here!" Julian announced as he walked into the waiting room.

The three jumped to their feet and came to congratulate him. Julian showed them the pictures as he gave them the details, including the name.

"That's a great name," Elijah said, thumping him on the back. "Congratulations, man."

"I don't deserve the congratulations," Julian told him. "I did nothing compared to what Kiara did. She was amazing."

Lucy smiled at him. "I'm glad you made it in time for the birth. She never said anything about having just me with her, but I know she was happy to see you."

Julian was glad to hear that, but he wished that he'd told her sooner that he wanted to be there for her. She shouldn't have had to worry about going through something like that on her own.

"I need to let the family know," Julian said as he took his phone back. "And I can only imagine the response that's going to get."

"You'd better let Angela know first," Lucy told him. "I think Kiara would want that."

Julian agreed, and rather than send out a group message, he opened one to just Angela.

Meet your nephew! Theodore Julian Burke, aka TJ. He arrived a few minutes ago weighing 7 lbs 12 ounces and measuring 20.5 inches. He's perfect.

To the message, he attached a couple of pictures. One close-up of TJ and the other of Kiara holding TJ.

"I need to get back to Kiara," he said. "Once everything is settled, you can come meet the baby."

The trio returned to their seats as Julian left the waiting room.

When he got back to the room, Kiara was sitting up, the baby cradled close to her. He hesitated for a moment, but when Kiara looked up and smiled at him, he approached the bed.

"How are you feeling?" he asked as he sat down on the chair he'd used off and on throughout the labor. "Did he feed okay?"

"So far, so good," Kiara said, looking down at TJ. "My milk hasn't come in yet, but he seems to be doing fine."

Julian had no idea what that meant, but if Kiara was happy, he was happy.

His phone rang, and he glanced down to see a video call request. "It's Angela. Are you up for a chat?"

He still hadn't sent an announcement to anyone else, but that could wait. It was important for Kiara to be able to connect with her sister.

At Kiara's nod, he accepted the call and handed the phone to her.

"Kiki!" Angela exclaimed. "Why didn't you tell me you were in labor?"

"Well, there was nothing you could do since you weren't here," Kiara said.

"Julian was there?" Angela asked. "I thought he was coming to New York."

"Lucy told Anthony I was in labor, so Julian decided to come here instead of staying in New York."

"Oh, I'm glad he was there," Angela said. "And oh, Kiki. The baby looks so precious. I'm so happy for you!"

"I'm happy too," Kiara said, glancing at Julian for a moment. "Though I'm also tired. It was a long labor."

"You'll have to tell me all about it when I get home."

"When might that be?" Kiara asked.

"I'm not sure, but if Duncan and Elizabeth decide to return home sooner, I'll come with them, even if Jude has to stay longer."

They chatted for a few more minutes, then Kiara ended the call after promising she'd call Angela again later.

"Thank you," Kiara said as she handed the phone back to Julian.

"I'm going to send a message to Duncan and Annie now so we might get a couple more calls," Julian said. "Are you up for that?"

"I am." Kiara smiled. "I know people have been excited about the baby, so I want them to see him."

"Would you rather wait until after you're done feeding him?"

"I think he's done," Kiara said, looking down at the baby. "He's fallen asleep."

Julian shifted to give Kiara some privacy as she situated herself, and he took the opportunity to send the same message to Duncan and Annie that he'd sent to Angela. The responses were immediate, as he had expected.

Duncan: *Congratulations to you and Kiara! The name is perfect. I can't wait to meet Theodore Julian. Love to you all there.*

Julian stared at the words. *Love.*

His gaze shifted to where Kiara cuddled TJ close. Her gown was back in place, and the baby slept contentedly in her arms. Kiara also looked content.

Emotions swept through Julian, and the strongest one was love. He might not have been sure that was what it was before, but now he knew.

These two had become his world. His home. His everything.

Even before meeting his son, he'd already been feeling that way about Kiara, but he hadn't known how to label it. Now he did.

But how did Kiara feel? She'd never given him any indication that she had any sort of feelings beyond friendship for him.

She hadn't rejected the little moments of affection when he'd reacted naturally and without putting too much thought into it. She'd hugged him. She'd allowed him close enough to kiss her, even if it had just been on the forehead. So she didn't seem to be opposed to the affection.

He didn't know how to prove to her that he loved her or how to prove that he was worthy of her love, but he was going to figure it out.

At one point, he'd accepted that an end date to their marriage was inevitable, but he no longer wanted that.

Julian prayed that God would give him the words that would help him keep his family together because he now believed that

He'd brought them together. They might have had a rocky start, but that didn't mean it had to stay rocky.

Elijah had told him that God could create beauty out of something ugly. That comment had been regarding the ugliness of his life prior to getting sober, but Julian thought that it could apply to the situation with Kiara, too.

Their relationship might have started out mired in alcohol and poor decisions, but that didn't have to continue to define it.

However, their marriage could only end up somewhere beautiful if Kiara also wanted that.

CHAPTER TWENTY-EIGHT

Julian was excited to get to the room and see Kiara and the baby. The night before, she'd sent him to the hotel Anthony booked for their group. They'd all be staying in Coeur d'Alene until Kiara and TJ were discharged and able to go home.

He'd wanted to stay at the hospital with her, but Kiara had assured him that she'd be fine. In the end, she'd convinced him that he needed a decent place to sleep, which wasn't the hospital. The hospital room she had was nice, with big windows and comfortable furniture, but it wasn't really conducive to sleeping on, especially given his height.

Lucy had stayed at the hospital, so once Julian and Anthony got there, he'd send her to the hotel to sleep, and Anthony would take over the security duty. It wasn't a high-risk place security-wise, so Anthony could handle it on his own. Elijah was also coming back with them and would act as a second set of eyes for Anthony.

"I'll send Lucy out," Julian said as the men reached the waiting room.

Anthony gave him a nod, then he and Elijah went to the chairs and sat down. Julian headed for Kiara's room, eager to hear how the night had gone for them.

"Good morning," Julian said as he stepped into the room.

Kiara was seated in one of the chairs at the table near the window, with the baby in her arms. Lucy was in the chair across from Kiara and got to her feet when she saw him.

"Good morning," Kiara said with a smile.

Julian turned to Lucy. "You're welcome to return to the hotel and get some rest."

"Sounds good." She looked over at Kiara. "I'll see you later."

Realizing that Kiara was nursing TJ, Julian sat down in the chair Lucy had vacated, rather than get close to the baby.

"How was your night?" he asked.

"It was okay," she said. "I really don't understand what people mean when they say they slept like a baby like it's a good thing because this baby was awake every two hours to feed."

"How is the feeding going?"

"The nurses seem to think it's going well. They said his latch is good." Kiara looked down at the baby and gently cupped his head. "I'm sore, but they say that's normal."

"Are you in a lot of pain overall?" Julian asked, not wanting to specifically name parts of her body.

"I'm in some pain, but the painkillers I'm taking keep it manageable."

"You did such an incredible job," Julian said. "I don't think I would have done as well handling that level of pain."

Kiara gave him a weary smile. "I wasn't sure I could do it, but I didn't really have a choice."

"It sounds like Duncan and Elizabeth are going to come home in a few days, so Angela will likely come with them. They want to give you some time to adjust before they show up."

"I appreciate that," Kiara said. "I think we're going to be discharged tomorrow."

Julian noticed some papers on the table and leaned forward to look at them. Picking them up, he skimmed over what was written on the paper.

"Do we need to fill these out for his birth certificate?" Julian asked. "I can do that for you if you'd like."

"I think we need to wait until after the test."

Julian looked up at Kiara. "Test? Is something wrong with the baby?"

"No. Not that kind of test," she said, then hesitated briefly. "The paternity test."

Julian frowned. "We don't need to do that. I believe that he's mine."

"I want the test," Kiara said, her gaze dropping to the papers in Julian's hands.

"Why? If I believe that he's my son, why do we need the paternity test?"

"I just... I want it."

Julian stared down at the papers, trying to figure out what to do. He would have thought that she'd be happy that he trusted her and believed what she said about what had happened. Her response didn't make any sense.

"Is this a joke?" he asked, frustration rising inside him for some inexplicable reason. Her insistence on having the test done just felt wrong. Like the closeness he'd thought they were developing was all an illusion. "Is the test going to show he's *not* my son, and all of this will have been for nothing?"

"No! Of course not," Kiara said. "It's not that. I just want the test done."

Julian put the papers back on the table and got to his feet. His unreasonable frustration felt overwhelming, and he was afraid of what he might say.

"I'll be back," he said, his voice tight.

Walking out, he didn't know where to go, so he ended up in the waiting room. Lucy wasn't there, but both men got to their feet as he approached.

"Is everything okay?" Anthony asked, obviously reading his upset expression.

"No."

Julian dropped into a chair. Elijah sat down beside him, while Anthony remained standing a few feet away.

"What happened?" Elijah asked. "You were only in there for a few minutes."

"She told me she wants a paternity test," he said. "I don't understand *why.*"

"So you're upset she wants the paternity test? You don't want it?"

"I believe that she told the truth about what happened between us," Julian said. "I believe TJ is my son. I don't need a paternity test to prove that, and I just don't understand why she's insisting on one. It doesn't make any sense. I want it to make sense. To understand why she wants this."

"And she hasn't explained her reasoning?" Elijah asked.

Julian shook his head. "She just kept saying she wants it."

"Why is it a big deal that she wants the test?"

Julian sat in silence for a minute, trying to get a handle on his frustration. "I guess I thought we were getting closer. To me, that means that we shouldn't need the paternity test. Her wanting this test makes it seem like she doesn't feel the same way."

He leaned forward and braced his elbows on his knees as he dragged his fingers through his hair. Julian knew he was overreacting. He knew he was being unreasonable.

"So your reaction has more to do with what having the test done represents between the two of you than actually having the test done."

"Yeah." Julian sighed heavily. "I guess so."

"I think you need to just let her get the test done," Elijah advised. "Given what you've told me, she's probably dealing with some uncertainty right now. The marriage was only supposed to last until after the baby was born, right? So maybe she's just trying to protect her son. If you go on to have another family, she'll want to make sure that legally, you've taken responsibility for TJ."

Something inside Julian recoiled at Elijah's words. He didn't want another family. He wanted the one he already had.

"I need to apologize and get this sorted out," he said.

"Yes, you do," Elijah agreed. "Let me pray with you before you go back and talk to her."

Julian hadn't even thought about praying regarding the situation. He still needed to get used to that being an option for him.

Bowing his head, he felt Elijah's hand on his back.

"Dear Heavenly Father, we come to you today asking for wisdom for Julian as he and Kiara make this decision about the test. I pray that you will be with them both as they talk, that their communication will be clear so that there is no misunderstanding. In Jesus' name."

Julian lifted his head and glanced over at Elijah. "Thank you."

Elijah smiled. "You're welcome."

Pushing to his feet, Julian ran a hand through his hair to make sure it wasn't standing up in all directions. He felt strangely nervous about approaching Kiara, but Elijah was right. They needed to talk this through, and he needed to apologize.

When he returned to the room, Kiara was back in her bed, the baby sleeping in the curve of her arm. She looked up and watched him approach her with wary eyes.

He pulled a chair over to the bed. Lowering himself into it, he let out a sigh.

Looking at her, he tried to smile reassuringly. "I'm sorry. I shouldn't have reacted the way I did to you saying you still wanted to go ahead with the paternity test. I want you to know that I believe you that TJ is mine. I don't need the test to tell me that. However, if it's what you want... if it's what you *need,* I'll make arrangements for it."

He was still hoping that she'd agree that they didn't need it, but she didn't. This time, however, he managed to keep his emotions under control.

"Can we go ahead and fill out the birth certificate information, though?" Julian asked. "Or do we have to wait for the results?"

Kiara stared at him for a long moment, then she nodded. "The nurse said it would be easier if we had it completed before we left the hospital, even though they can't insist that we do it."

Julian got up and went to the table. He sat down in front of the papers he'd left there earlier. But before he did anything else, he made a phone call to his lawyer to have him arrange for someone to come to the hospital and take the samples for the test.

"Hopefully, we'll get someone here this afternoon," Julian said as he hung up. "But let's get this filled out."

It didn't take too long, and in the process, he discovered some new information.

"Your birthday is coming up," Julian observed as he wrote the date in the space provided. "Did they name you Kiara Noelle because you were born in December?"

"I assume so," she said. "But I don't know for sure because I last talked to my parents when I was eight, and at that age, I didn't know that Noelle was associated with Christmas. All I knew was that I didn't get very much for my birthday because it was so close to Christmas. Plus, I only heard my middle name when I was in trouble, so it wasn't a positive thing."

As he continued to fill out the form, Julian wondered what he could do to make her birthday special for her that year.

"When is your birthday?" Kiara asked.

Julian looked up and said, "February."

"Valentine's Day?"

He rolled his eyes. "Yeah. Unfortunately."

"Seriously?" she asked with a grin.

"Yes. Seriously."

"We didn't celebrate your birthday earlier this year, though."

"Oh, my family knows that I don't celebrate, and if I get even a hint that there's going to be a party, I will definitely be a no-show."

"So you're the birthday Grinch."

Julian chuckled. "I guess you could call me that."

He was glad that they seemed to have moved past the earlier tension he'd caused by his reaction. Looking back on it, he wasn't happy with how easily his frustration had risen. He realized that he didn't like the uncertain position he'd ended up in with Kiara. Coming off two weeks of another stressful situation, he'd just been too close to the edge.

It had brought to light the fact that it was possible that Kiara wasn't feeling about him and their marriage the way he was. He'd never thought he'd need to prove to someone that he could be trusted. That he was worth loving. But if that was what it took to get Kiara to give their marriage... to give them... a chance, he'd do whatever he had to.

Because he loved her and wanted her by his side forever.

It was a totally foreign concept to him. He'd never felt that way about anyone else, and he didn't want to mess things up. So for now, he'd show his love for her by taking care of her and TJ as best he could.

"Okay. I've got this all filled out." He got up with the papers and moved to the bed. "Do you want to look them over?"

"Sure. Want to hold TJ while I do that?"

"Uh... yes. Yes, I do. I just hope I don't break him."

"You won't," Kiara assured him.

Julian carefully took the baby, who was wrapped up like a little burrito. He sat down on the chair beside the bed while Kiara picked up the papers he'd set on her lap.

The baby's eyes fluttered open, and he looked in Julian's direction.

"Hey there, buddy," Julian said softly. "How're you doing? Are you being good to Mommy?"

Never in a million years had he envisioned a moment like this, holding his son as he sat near the woman who had managed to capture his heart. They might have had a little blip, but they'd moved past it, and Julian hoped that when the results for the paternity test came back, they could put it all behind them.

~ * ~

Kiara moved the bassinet closer to the side of the bed she slept on. She was feeling emotional and anxious about the first night at home with the baby.

She'd finished feeding him, he had a clean diaper on and was wrapped up like the nurses had shown her. She, on the other hand, hadn't even had a shower and still needed to brush her teeth and do her skin care.

But she was too tired to do all three, so she'd settled on what she considered the most important. Brushing her teeth.

Leaving her bathroom door open, she quickly brushed her teeth, then took an extra moment to wipe her face with a wet washcloth before putting on some moisturizer. But that was as good as it was going to get.

Back in the dimly lit bedroom, she sank down on the edge of the bed. As she watched TJ sleep, she wondered if she was going to hear him when he cried. She was so tired that she was afraid that being back in the comfort of her own bed would make her sleep too soundly.

A light knock on her open door drew her attention. She looked over to see Julian standing there in a pair of pajama pants and a T-shirt. Even dressed casually, he managed to look handsome and put together. Meanwhile, she still looked nine months pregnant, her hair was frizzy, and she was wearing a T-shirt that might have baby drool on the shoulder.

"Can I come in?" he asked, waiting just outside the door until she nodded. "I want to propose something to you. You're welcome to say no, and I won't be upset, but I don't want you to feel like you have to do everything with the baby."

"There's not much you can do at this point," she said.

"I know, but I still want to help you." He came to stand next to the bassinet and looked down at TJ with a smile. "I want to do my part."

"So what are you proposing?" At this point, she'd consider pretty much anything if it helped her take care of TJ.

"Let me sleep in here with the two of you," he said, shifting his weight from one foot to the other. "Then when he wakes up, I can help you by getting him out of the bassinet and changing his diaper if necessary while you get ready to feed him."

"You want to change his diaper?" Kiara could hardly believe what she was hearing.

"*Want* might be a strong word when it comes to changing diapers. However, it's not when it comes to helping you. I *want* to help you."

Kiara hadn't imagined that he'd want to pitch in, especially with diaper changes.

"Well?" he prodded.

"You're sure you want to sleep in here? I have a feeling it's going to be a pretty fractured night."

"That's fine," Julian said. "I told Duncan I was going to take the next week off. I'll still do some work, but if I need to catch a nap during the day, I can."

"Okay," she said. "I'd appreciate the help."

The designer had chosen a king-size bed for her room, so there was plenty of space for Julian on the far side of the bed. Still, it was weird to share a bed with someone who wasn't Angie. They'd always shared a bed growing up.

But she and Julian were married, so if things had been different, they would have already been spending nights together.

"I have a nightlight on, so I hope that doesn't bother you."

"It won't," Julian assured her as he walked around to the other side of the bed.

She carefully maneuvered herself into the bed, then pulled the bassinet right up against the mattress. The meds she'd taken a short time earlier had kicked in, and the pain was more of a dull ache.

With a sigh, she laid down on her right side, facing the baby, then pulled the comforter up over herself. She felt the bed shift as Julian settled himself.

Reaching out, she snapped off the lamp that was on her side of the bed. The room didn't plunge into darkness like it usually did because of the nightlight, which cast a soft light near the floor.

"Goodnight," Julian said.

"Goodnight."

Kiara hadn't been sure she'd be able to fall asleep because of worrying about the baby, and then with Julian sharing the bed, but as soon as she closed her eyes, sleep claimed her.

It felt like just minutes had passed when the soft cries of the baby woke her. She glanced at the clock and saw that two hours had passed since she'd climbed into bed.

Julian stirred beside her, then flung the comforter off himself. He was a shadowy figure as he came around the bed to the bassinet.

Moving it out of the way, he held out his hand to her. Kiara was grateful for the help in getting to her feet. Julian then bent to lift TJ from the bassinet.

"Hey, buddy," he said. "You're okay."

"Can you bring him here?" Kiara said, moving toward the change table that she'd set up in the room.

Julian carried him over, then laid him down on the change table pad. "Show me what to do so that next time I can do it myself."

Over the next few minutes, Kiara showed Julian how to unwrap the little boy, then unfasten his sleeper.

"The nurse said to keep him covered as much as you can, or you might end up with him peeing all over you."

Julian chuckled. "I'd rather that didn't happen."

She walked him through cleaning the baby, then putting the new diaper on him. Julian fastened the sleeper, not hesitating at all to do everything Kiara had shown him.

Through it all, TJ fussed, but Julian didn't seem to be stressed by it.

"Do you need to use the bathroom or anything?" he asked.

"Yes, I'll be right back."

When she returned a couple of minutes later, Julian was standing with the baby in his arms, gently swaying. TJ had settled a little but was still fussing. Soft music played from the Bluetooth system, and Julian had turned on the gas fireplace that was opposite the large bed.

Kiara sat down in the rocker she'd chosen that had wide arms and was comfortable. It was the same as the one in the nursery. She'd gotten two of them, knowing she'd probably start off nursing in the bedroom since the baby wouldn't be sleeping in the nursery right away.

Julian bent to put the baby in her arms, then stepped back. "Do you need anything? Water? Food?"

She glanced over and saw that she'd forgotten to bring her water bottle into the bedroom earlier. "I could use some water. I think my water bottle is in the kitchen."

Julian left the room, and Kiara focused on getting the baby latched on. As he settled into nursing, Kiara let out a sigh and rested her head back. She had to admit it was nice to have Julian there helping her. And the ambiance he'd set with the music and the fireplace was soothing, enabling her to relax as TJ nursed.

After Julian returned with her water bottle, he settled on the bed, his back against the headboard and his phone in hand.

Midway through the feed, she maneuvered TJ into a position to burp him. She gave a small cheer, and Julian chuckled when the baby let out a burp that seemed too big for his small body.

Despite being exhausted, Kiara felt a sense of contentment. With Julian there, it felt like they were truly a family. She didn't feel like she was alone in dealing with their new baby. It was more than she could ever have hoped for.

Over the next two weeks, Julian proved that that first night wasn't an anomaly. Each night at bedtime, he'd join Kiara in her bedroom, and he'd keep an eye on the baby while she prepared for bed. He'd stepped up and taken an active role in caring for TJ.

During the day, Julian encouraged Kiara to nap at least once. He had food delivered from the main house, so she never had to cook a meal for them.

All in all, it meant that she didn't have to do anything but care for TJ. She was able to just enjoy being a new mom, and she was very grateful for that since she knew that wasn't the case for all new mothers.

And for those two weeks, Kiara put the thought that divorce was imminent now that TJ was born, out of her mind. The paternity test had proven that Julian was TJ's father. She'd known that would be the result. But with legalities such as the divorce looming, she wanted to make sure that it was official who TJ's father was.

Kiara knew she should broach the subject with Julian, just so she'd know when the divorce was coming, but she couldn't do it. She found it much easier to imagine that Julian had decided that he wanted to stay married so that they could raise their son together, the way they'd cared for him together over the past two weeks.

Living in delusion might not be the best choice, but Kiara found that it was easier to keep her emotions under control if she imagined that Julian was there for her as much as he was for TJ.

Each time she settled with TJ in her arms to feed him, she prayed that that would be the outcome. Unfortunately, her faith struggled to be strong enough to believe it was actually possible.

CHAPTER TWENTY-NINE

Julian pulled the UTV to a stop by the back door of the main house. He got out and went around to open Kiara's door. After helping her out, he opened the rear door to unlatch TJ's car seat.

Kiara held the door leading into the mudroom for him, allowing Julian to carry the car seat into the warmth of the house. Right away, they could smell the turkey that was on the menu for their Thanksgiving dinner.

"Where's my grandson?" Duncan asked as he came into the mudroom.

Julian set the car seat down on one of the benches and carefully unbuckled him. He'd gotten more adept at handling the baby, but he still always erred on the side of caution.

"Here you go," Julian said as he lifted TJ and turned toward his dad who eagerly took and cradled the baby in his arms.

"Hello there," Duncan cooed in a way that made everyone present grin.

"You don't get to hog him, Dad," Annie announced from the doorway. "We all get a turn."

Duncan kept hold of TJ as he left the mudroom, brushing past all the women clamoring to see him. They followed Duncan like he was the Pied Piper.

Julian turned to Kiara and helped her with her coat. "I think we could probably leave, and no one would even notice."

Kiara laughed. "Yeah. We're not significant anymore."

Julian hung up both of their coats, then they left the mudroom. Knowing the family would gather in the living room first, they headed in that direction.

Elijah wasn't there, having flown out to New York City a week ago to spend the Thanksgiving holiday with his mom's family.

The past two weeks had passed in a blur of sleepless nights, diapers, and some of the most precious memories Julian had ever had. He and Kiara had fallen into a good schedule, working together so that neither of them was overwhelmed.

Of course, they'd also had help from Elizabeth, Angela, and Annie. Nearly every day, Angela had been at their place for an hour or so, often bringing treats for them.

Julian directed Kiara to a loveseat, then waited for her to sit before settling down beside her. Benji was seated in an armchair near Julian, staring morosely at the fireplace.

"What's up with you, buddy?" Julian asked as he leaned over to tap him on the shoulder.

Benji had been away at college for the past couple of months, but he'd flown home for Thanksgiving.

"Amelia broke up with me," he muttered.

"What?" The question came in a chorus from everyone there.

"Yeah. She's decided that I'm a distraction, and she needs to focus on the Olympics."

"That makes sense."

"Duncan!" Elizabeth turned to her husband. "How can you say that?"

"Whenever you're trying to achieve something that requires a lot of time and energy, it's best not to have other things fracturing your focus." Duncan looked at Benji. "I'm sorry you're hurt, Son, but from what you've said, she's devoted a lot of time to her skating. Going to the Olympics is a huge commitment, so it only makes sense that she'd need to end things with you if she feels she can't give a relationship the time it deserves."

"I don't demand that she spend time with me," Benji said. "In fact, my being away at college means she doesn't even have to worry about finding time for dates."

"But in the back of her mind will be the thought that she needs to keep in contact with you. That she still needs to make time in her day for you."

Benji glared at Duncan before shifting his attention back to the fire.

Julian didn't know what to say. Technically, Duncan was correct, but Julian didn't want to pile on Benji. Also, he'd never experienced what his half-brother was dealing with, so he didn't know what to say to make the guy feel better.

"Your dad is right," Cole said. "When you're striving for something, it can be hard to juggle a relationship too."

"You had a high-performance career and girlfriends," Benji pointed out.

"True," Cole agreed. "But none were serious until I got to the end of my career. It would have been hard to have had a serious relationship with Annie when I was just starting out."

"Excuse me."

The new voice had everyone looking at the entrance to the room. Mrs. Stevens stood there with a smile. "Dinner is served."

"Thank you," Elizabeth said as she got to her feet.

Mrs. Stevens and her daughters were there to prepare and serve the Thanksgiving dinner for them, then they'd have the rest of the weekend off.

Everyone went into the dining room and found their seats. There was a name card at each place setting, not that there was much confusion over who sat where. They always took the same seats when they were at the table. The name cards were just to add to the fall decor that adorned the table.

Duncan handed the baby to Kiara, then took his seat at the head of the table. TJ was still sleeping, and if his pattern was anything to go by, he should continue to sleep for a little while longer.

At Duncan's request, Cole said a prayer of thanks for the food, then the meal began. The meal was a bit more informal than previous Thanksgiving dinners had been. Julian felt it was a good sign that his dad was relaxing his high standards for family meals.

As the food circled the table, Julian put some from each dish onto Kiara's plate and then his own. He didn't miss the looks, combined with smirks, from his sisters, but he ignored them.

After putting some turkey on Kiara's plate, he cut it up, then moved the plate back in front of her.

"Thanks," she said with a smile. "I've figured out how to eat with one hand, but cutting food up is still a struggle."

"It was nice of Julian to do that for you," Elizabeth said.

"We've discovered that things work well when the non-baby-holding parent helps the baby-holding one."

"You've developed a good partnership," Annie observed. "Will you do that for me, babe?"

Cole chuckled. "I can hardly say no. Julian has set a high standard for postpartum fatherhood."

"You're welcome," Julian said, shooting Annie a grin.

Julian had never enjoyed Thanksgiving dinner. It was usually tense, and he hated that at some point, he'd have to share what he was thankful for. He'd been sure it was Elizabeth's idea, and the only thing he ever said he was thankful for was whatever alcoholic beverage he was drinking.

That would not be the case this year. He had a long list of things he planned to share, and alcohol was nowhere on that list.

He wasn't the only person who had experienced a lot of changes over the past year, so he had a feeling that that portion of the evening would end up taking longer than usual.

The food was amazing. Now that he wasn't numbing himself and his taste buds with copious amounts of alcohol, he could appreciate how delicious it was.

"Why don't we move to the family room?" Elizabeth suggested after they'd finished their dessert. "I've asked Mrs. Stephens to prepare some coffee and hot chocolate for us there."

Julian took the baby from Kiara, then they walked with the others to the family room. One of Mrs. Stephens' daughters was in the room, setting up the drinks on the buffet that was arranged against the wall.

Annie spoke to her for a moment, asking about her son, then she began to pour the hot drinks for everyone. Kiara set the diaper bag down by her feet but didn't take the baby from Julian.

He was glad. While he'd wanted to show Kiara his love by helping her out, the truth was, he truly enjoyed helping with TJ. And he now had a complete understanding of Duncan's protectiveness when it came to his children.

Looking down at his son, Julian was convinced he'd go after anyone who even looked at TJ the wrong way.

"I'm so happy to see how our family has expanded this year," Elizabeth said, a warm smile on her face. "It is so wonderful to have new spouses, and now, a new grandchild join us. So much to be thankful for."

"As we've done each year, let's take some time to share what we're thankful for," Duncan said, then looked to his right where Cole sat with Annie. "Would you like to start, Cole?"

"I would *love* to start," he said.

As people shared over the next little while, Julian wasn't surprised by anything that was said. And he was sure that people wouldn't be surprised by what he shared when it was his turn.

When it got to Benji, the young man muttered, "Not feeling very thankful today, to be honest. Maybe next year."

No one forced him to say anything. Julian certainly understood the struggle to voice thankfulness when someone was at a low point in their life.

"Like Elizabeth said, there is much to be thankful for," Kiara began. "And I feel especially thankful this year, starting with you, Duncan."

Duncan focused his attention on Kiara, his expression stoic.

"You took me into your family when you didn't have to. You and Elizabeth gave me a place to belong, and I am so very thankful for that. I'm also so thankful for Angie. She's always been the bright spot in my world, and I'm glad that I didn't lose her this year."

"Never!" Angela said as she leaned over and touched Kiara's hand. "I will always be there for you."

"I know, and I'm very thankful for that. You also have been a big encouragement in helping me understand and accept Jesus into my heart, for which I'm grateful. I'm also thankful for Julian and the way he's stepped up to help me with TJ. He's gone above and beyond, and I don't take it for granted at all." She smiled at him. "I'm thankful to God for... uh... for having you in my life. I couldn't have done this without you."

Julian had so much he wanted to say to her, but they weren't things to be shared in public like this. And maybe not even just yet. At first, their conversations had circled around TJ and taking care of him, but then, they'd realized they had each given their hearts to God.

With them both being new to the faith, they'd had several talks about what it meant. They were some of the deepest conversations they'd ever had, and in those moments, Julian felt that they were forging a lasting connection. One that was stronger and deeper than any he'd shared before.

"In years past, I haven't been very happy to participate in this tradition at Thanksgiving," Julian said when it was his turn. "So buckle up, because tonight I'm making up for lost time."

Everyone laughed. Well, everyone except Benji, but Julian didn't think anything or anyone would get a smile out of his brother.

"First, I want to thank you, Dad." Duncan's eyes widened at the name Julian used because it wasn't something Julian had called him in a lot of years. "I was so angry with you for forcing me to go to rehab and for telling me I needed to get married. Neither were something I wanted. But in the end, they turned out to be the best things that could have happened to me." He turned to look at Angela. "Thank you for forgiving me for what happened. You had every right not to, and yet you did. Thank you. Even though he's not currently here, I want to say I'm also thankful for Elijah. Meeting him in rehab was a blessing as he led me to God and has encouraged me to view things in my life through a different lens."

He shifted in his chair so he could see Kiara more fully. "And I want you to know how thankful I am for you. You have been such an encouragement to me as I've navigated some uncharted waters, and I'm beyond thankful that you are TJ's mom. He might not know it yet, but one day, he's going to be as thankful that you're his mom as I am."

Kiara's eyes had widened as he'd talked, and he could see the emotion in them. For a moment, he almost continued talking, but he didn't need an audience for what else he wanted to share.

"This has been incredible," Duncan said, reaching over to take Elizabeth's hand in his. "I am so thankful to have my family all together again. And I'm thankful for the spouses who have joined the family, and of course, our Theodore Julian. His birth is the culmination of a wonderful year."

There were murmurs of agreement from all present.

Once everyone had shared—including Jude, who had been surprisingly emotional in his brief speech—Elizabeth thanked them all for being there.

Benji took that as signaling the end of the evening and got to his feet. "I'm going to my room. I'll see you guys tomorrow."

Elizabeth's expression was sad as she watched her son leave the room. "First heartbreak is always so hard."

Julian wouldn't know, but there was a chance he'd find out soon if Kiara didn't feel the same way that he did. Which was why he was still a bit uncertain about sharing everything in his heart, even as he planned to show Kiara that he wanted their marriage to continue.

When TJ started to fuss, Julian turned to Kiara. "Did you want to leave?"

She gently bounced the baby and offered him a pacifier. He took it, but Julian knew from experience that his calmness would only last for a few minutes.

"I think maybe we should go home," she said.

Julian was happy to agree. He had enjoyed the time with his family, but he also really enjoyed the quiet evening hours with Kiara and TJ.

He got to his feet, then took TJ from Kiara. "I'll go put him in his car seat."

There was snow lazily drifting down from the sky as they left the house and got into the UTV. It made Julian even more eager to get home.

~ * ~

Kiara had no problem going out with TJ, but she was also relieved to get back to the house, especially since TJ was fussing. She would much rather deal with that in the privacy of their home.

Julian carried the car seat from the garage into the house. He put it on the kitchen counter and worked to free the baby from the straps and blanket covering him while Kiara took off her coat and boots.

"Here you go," Julian said, handing her the baby.

She headed for the bedroom, where she lay TJ on the changing table. When his little face scrunched up, she bent over him to kiss his forehead.

"You're okay, lovey," she murmured. "Let's just change your diaper."

She'd never thought about how much she'd enjoy being a mother, but she really did. Her love for TJ grew every day, and she couldn't imagine her life without the little boy.

As she changed TJ's diaper and put him in a sleeper, Kiara could see bits of her and Julian in him. So far, he favored her in the coloring of his hair and skin. However, his eyes were lighter than hers with a hint of green, and she was pretty sure that he had Julian's nose. He was beautiful.

His fussing increased to crying by the time she'd finished changing him. She picked him up and went to the chair she used for nursing. He frantically latched on, and she had to force herself to relax.

When Julian came into the room with her water bottle a short time later, he had changed into the pajama pants and T-shirt he usually slept in. He came and set the bottle beside her, then went around to his side of the bed.

This had quickly become her favorite part of the day. TJ nursed longer now, and she was comfortable in her chair. Usually they talked or watched something on TV. That night, the television remained dark, so she assumed they would be talking.

"Have you thought much about the future?" Julian asked from where he was seated on the bed. He was leaning against the headboard, his legs stretched out, ankles crossed.

Kiara's stomach sank, even though she'd known that this discussion had been coming. Her hope had been that she'd have more than just two weeks following TJ's birth before the subject of their divorce came up.

She'd told herself that sharing the night hours with him meant nothing more than he was being a supportive co-parent. But it had been hard not to feel that he was also there because he cared about her and wanted to help her.

Things had been going so well that she'd actually begun to hope that maybe there was a chance for them. And now she realized that perhaps she'd made a huge mistake.

"To be honest, I haven't been too focused on it," she said slowly. "TJ has kind of taken up most of my thoughts."

Julian nodded as a small smile crossed his face. "He is pretty demanding for such a little body."

Kiara looked down at him, lying so peacefully in her arms as he nursed. Unbidden, an image of Julian with another family and TJ there with him came into focus in her mind.

The pain in her heart that followed was intense, and tears stung her eyes.

"Kiara," Julian said.

She couldn't look at him. Couldn't let him see the hurt inside her. How could she explain what she was feeling right then?

"Yeah?" She busied herself burping TJ, then transferring him to the other side.

Silence was heavy in the room. He didn't respond. She didn't look at him. It felt like a standoff of some sort.

From the corner of her eye, she saw Julian slide off the bed. Her heart sank, thinking he was leaving the room.

Instead, he came to where she sat and sank down on the carpeted floor in front of her, crossing his legs. For a moment, she just stared at his legs, thinking of how it was a position she'd never seen him in before. It was easier to focus on that.

"Kiara. I didn't mean to upset you. I just wanted to figure out where your thoughts might be regarding our future."

"I didn't realize that there was any option other than the one we agreed on when we got married."

"So you still want a divorce?" Julian asked.

Kiara looked up at him then. "I wasn't aware I had a choice."

Julian frowned. "What?"

"When we agreed to marry, I understood that divorce was inevitable. You said that that was what we were going to do, so I've always assumed that was where we were going to end up."

"So why are you so emotional now that I want to talk about the future?"

Kiara looked back down at TJ and tried to formulate a response. "I guess I'm just sad that the way things have been for the past two weeks is going to end. It's been nice parenting TJ together, and I'll miss that."

"What if I tell you that I didn't bring this up in order for us to settle on a date for the divorce?" Julian said.

Kiara focused on him again. "You want to put it off? For how long?"

"I don't want to put off the divorce," Julian said. "I want to cancel any plans we had for it. I'm not interested in getting divorced. I know it was my plan when we got married, but a lot has changed over the past several months."

Kiara couldn't argue with that, but even if she'd wanted to, she wouldn't have been able to because he'd left her speechless. And confused.

So he didn't want a divorce? Where did that leave them? He wasn't telling her that he loved her, so was this a business type of arrangement?

And if that was the case, was she interested in staying with him under those circumstances? Could she stay, knowing she loved him, when he might view their marriage completely differently?

"So what do you say?" Julian asked, his expression serious. "Would you be willing to turn this from a temporary marriage into a permanent one?"

Though there was still a shadow of hesitancy in her heart, there was a practical side of her that accepted that it would be better for TJ if they stayed married. Julian had proven to be a good man... a good father... and he treated her very well, even though he didn't love her.

The situation could definitely be worse.

"Yes. I would."

Julian smiled, his eyes lighting up. He got to his feet, then leaned over to kiss her forehead. TJ let out a squawk, and Kiara lifted the light blanket enough to see that he was no longer latched.

She covered herself, then moved him out from under the blanket.

"Do you want me to burp him?" Julian offered.

"Sure."

She handed TJ to him, then took a moment to pull herself together before getting up from her chair. While Julian took care of him for a few minutes, Kiara went into the bathroom to get ready for the night.

It took her a little longer than usual to change and do her nighttime routine because she spent a few minutes staring at the mirror, asking herself if she'd made the right decision. But even if it might be better for herself to tell Julian she'd changed her mind, she wouldn't do it because of TJ.

Because they hadn't eaten their Thanksgiving dinner until seven, it was already after ten. Kiara had no idea if it was Julian's normal time to sleep, but he'd gone to bed around this time with her and TJ without comment for the past two weeks.

When she returned to the bedroom, he handed TJ back to her, and she carried him to the change table where she swaddled him. He was already half asleep, so he drifted off quickly as she cradled him close, swaying gently.

Moving slowly, Kiara bent to put him in the bassinet beside the bed. After she'd set him down, she stood by the bassinet, holding her breath and waiting to see if he'd protest. Sometimes he did. Sometimes he didn't.

Thankfully, that night, he stayed asleep.

Kiara was uncertain how to react then. She didn't know if the decision they'd just made would change how things were between them.

However, just like every other night over the past two weeks, Julian turned off the music and the gas fireplace, leaving just the soft glow of the nightlight. He slid beneath the covers on his side as she did on hers.

As silence settled between them, Kiara suddenly felt Julian's hand take hers, reaching across the empty space between them.

"Goodnight, Kiara," he said, giving her fingers a gentle squeeze.

Tension slid away as Kiara kept hold of his hand. "Goodnight."

CHAPTER THIRTY

"Thanks for the lift," Julian said as he got out of the SUV.

After helping get Julian's luggage from the back of the vehicle up to the porch, Anthony climbed into the front seat with the security team member who had met them at the helicopter. Julian stood and watched as they pulled away before turning to the door.

He'd been gone for five days, and he was thrilled to be back at the estate. Back home.

If the trip to their Iceland offices hadn't already been on the calendar as an annual event, he would have gladly ditched it. However, Julian knew he couldn't abandon his responsibilities at the company, just because he'd rather stay home with his wife and son.

He opened the front door, then picked up his bags and carried them into the house. The warmth was a welcome respite from the chill of the December air. With just under two weeks until Christmas, winter had truly arrived, covering the estate in a blanket of snow.

Closing the door, he spotted Kiara coming toward him from the kitchen, a smile on her face. Abandoning his bags by the door, he moved to take her into his arms.

"I missed you," he said as he wrapped his arms around her.

"I missed you too."

Kiara had her arms tight around his waist, and Julian made no move to release her, leaving it up to her when she wanted to end the hug. As far as he was concerned, it could last forever.

Moving back a bit, she looked up at him, and Julian couldn't help but lean forward to place a kiss on her forehead.

Kiara closed her eyes, then drew a breath and pressed her forehead to his shoulder, her curls tickling his chin. Julian smoothed a hand down her back to her waist, letting his palm linger there.

She was soft and warm, and while she once had smelled of vanilla and florals, she now smelled faintly of baby powder and... home.

The two weeks that had passed since Thanksgiving had been wonderful. For the first couple of days, he had seen wariness in Kiara. Uncertainty. As if she didn't quite know how things were going to go, now that they'd changed the terms of their relationship.

Though he wouldn't have pursued anything physical right away, Julian was glad that they had restrictions put on them because she was still recovering from the birth. It meant they could just focus on getting to know each other even more deeply and also be affectionate with no further expectations.

When TJ began to fuss, apparently having had enough of being ignored, Kiara stepped back, but before she moved away, she went up on her tiptoes and kissed his cheek. "I'm glad you're home."

There was nothing that could have wiped the smile from Julian's face as he followed her to the kitchen where TJ lay in a small, wheeled bassinet. "There's my boy."

"Did you want some coffee or something to eat?" Kiara asked. "Angie and I made some gingerbread cookies yesterday."

"Is it either or?" Julian asked as he scooped TJ up and cradled him in his arms. "Can I have both? Because I'd love both."

Kiara chuckled. "Of course."

"So how's it been while I was away?"

They'd spoken every day while he was gone, and she'd told him everything was fine. However, he thought that perhaps she'd just been saying that so he didn't feel bad that he wasn't there to help her.

"We survived," Kiara said as she poured coffee into two mugs. That was a clue right there, as she usually limited her coffee intake.

"But we both really, really missed you. The nights were lonely when he woke up, and it was just the two of us."

"Well, I'm home for awhile, so we can share those nighttime responsibilities again."

"I'm very glad." She put the coffee mugs and a plate of cookies on a tray. "How did the trip go?"

"It went well," he said as they walked from the kitchen to the living room, where she set the tray on the coffee table. "I saw my mom."

"Oh, yeah?" Kiara looked up at him. "How did that go?"

"Better than I thought it would. We went out for dinner last night." Julian settled into the chair Kiara usually used to nurse TJ because it would allow him to rock the baby while they talked. "Her first question was when were we going to get divorced."

Kiara set a mug on the end table beside him, as well as a napkin with a couple of cookies on it. "Then you had to disappoint her."

"And I was very happy to do so."

After picking up her mug and a cookie for herself, Kiara sat down on the couch facing him, tucking a leg underneath her. "So what did she say when you told her there was no divorce happening?"

Julian rolled his eyes. "She said never say never."

Kiara's brows lifted at that. "So it doesn't matter if you're happy? It's more important to her that you're married to someone she approves of?"

"That's about it." He looked down at TJ. "And then when I showed her a picture of him, she said that he looked *just* like me."

"Is she color-blind?"

"If only," Julian said. "I think she just sees what she wants to see, because anyone with eyes can see that he is a good mix of the two of us."

"That's what I've always thought."

Julian took a bite of the cookie. "Oooh. These are delicious. I hope you made lots."

"Well, we did," Kiara said. "However, we made up containers of the cookies to give away."

"I guess that means you'll need to make more."

"You're not the first one to tell us that," Kiara said with a laugh. "So we have another baking day planned."

"Perfect."

They continued to chat, and Julian gave her more details about his trip. But there were a couple of things he didn't tell her. He didn't mention his trip to a jeweler, or the many phone calls he'd had with Annie and Elizabeth.

When TJ began to fuss, Julian stood up so Kiara could take the chair. Once she was seated, he handed her the baby. She picked up the blanket she used to cover herself and quickly got the baby feeding.

"While you feed him, I'm going to take my bags to the room and change."

He had picked up his bags and was heading to his suite when Kiara said, "Julian."

Stopping, he turned to face her. "Yeah?"

She stared at him for a moment, then looked down at TJ. "There's... uh... there's room in the closet in my suite. If you'd... you know."

Julian grinned. He'd been wondering when, or even if, Kiara would feel comfortable combining their living spaces. It wasn't something he had planned to force on her.

"Just so I'm clear before I say yes," Julian began. "You want me to move my things into your room?"

"Yes. If that's what you want. You're already sleeping there every night. I mean, unless you plan to stop doing that. Which would be okay too."

Julian left his bags and walked back to her. Placing his hands on the armrests on either side of Kiara, Julian bent forward. She tipped her head back and stared up at him.

"I want, Kiara," he said. "When I said I didn't want a divorce, it didn't mean that I wanted to keep parts of our lives separate. I want us to combine our lives in every way. I'm not rushing it, but just know that that's where I'm hoping we'll eventually end up. So anytime you ask me something that moves us in that direction, I will always say yes."

The smile she gave him was a little shy, a little flirty. "Okay. I'm glad to hear that."

"Good." Julian leaned closer and gave her a quick kiss, this time, on her lips. "Now, I'm going to take my bags to our room."

His heart was light as he walked toward the room they'd share from now on. Even when TJ eventually moved to the nursery and was sleeping through the night, this would be their room. And the fact that she'd been the one to initiate this step filled him with so much hope.

He'd come to love her so much. And though he wanted to know that she felt the same way about him, he didn't want her to feel any pressure whatsoever. Which was why he had yet to tell her that he loved her.

He came from a place of wealth, power and experience, and while she was good at standing up for herself, he wasn't sure she'd say no to him when the future she wanted for TJ might be impacted.

The moment they'd just shared, however, made him think that she did have feelings for him. Maybe telling her he loved her wouldn't be the pressure he'd thought it might be.

He hung his garment bag up in the closet, then put his suitcase on the luggage rack and opened it. When he found the clothes he wanted to change into, he swapped outfits.

After checking that one of the chest of drawers in the large walk-in closet was empty, Julian unpacked a few things. Just enough to hide the small velvet box he'd brought back with him. That had to stay hidden for a couple more days.

~ * ~

Kiara was so happy to have Julian home. With him gone for five days, she'd realized how much she missed him. And not just because of the help he gave her.

The house had been so quiet with just her and TJ, especially in the evenings. During the day, Angie had come over to hang out with her for a couple of hours. But when evening came, it was just the two of them.

Though she understood that travel was a large part of Julian's job, it didn't mean that she enjoyed his absences. She wouldn't do anything to make Julian feel bad for having to be away, but she wanted to make sure he knew she missed him.

The first night he was home again, he fell right back into the routine they'd established prior to him leaving. And in the dark of the night when TJ woke up, she was no longer alone.

Her birthday was looming the next day, and as with most years, she wasn't exactly looking forward to it. She wasn't dreading it either, really. Even if her birthday was as forgettable that year as it had been in past years, she didn't really care because she had so many things to be thankful for.

And Christmas was just around the corner, and she knew that it wasn't going to be forgettable. Already there was talk of all the presents that would be under the tree for TJ, who would have no memory of any of it.

"Are you ready to go?" Julian asked as he walked out of the bedroom.

He was dressed for dinner at the main house, wearing black slacks and a long-sleeved, dark green button-down shirt. His hair was styled, and he looked very handsome.

She'd gotten ready first, then sat down to nurse TJ while Julian got ready. Hopefully, this feeding would hold the baby over for a while so that she didn't have to nurse him again as soon as they arrived.

"Yes. I think he's done for now."

Julian came over to where she sat and bent to take the baby from her. "Does he need to burp?"

"I burped him already, so he should be okay."

As she got to her feet, Julian smiled. "You look beautiful. Very festive."

Heat crept into Kiara's cheeks. "Thank you. You're as handsome as ever. Our outfits go well together."

She'd chosen a red satin blouse with long full sleeves that had cuffs at the wrist and a bow at the neck. The bodice was fitted and flared out over the straight black skirt she wore.

As Julian put TJ in his car seat, Kiara pulled on her heeled boots. The diaper bag was fully stocked, sitting on the counter. Once they had their coats on, they transferred everything to the UTV in the garage, then Julian helped Kiara into her seat before sliding behind the wheel.

"Did I tell you that I've settled on a car?" Julian asked.

"Really?" They'd talked about getting a vehicle now that Julian was spending more time at the estate. He wanted his own set of wheels.

"When we get home later, I'll show you the pictures and tell you more about it."

He'd asked her opinion, but since she knew nothing about cars, she'd deferred to him. Kiara was sure that he'd pick the best vehicle for their family.

As usual, when they arrived at the house, TJ was quickly claimed by someone. Duncan was a little slow that day, so he lost out to Annie.

Julian took Kiara's hand as they followed the others to the living room. Everyone was there that night except for Benji, who wouldn't be home until the next week.

Kiara hoped that his heart was healing from the breakup with Amelia. She'd met the girl a couple of times when she'd come to see Annie, who helped design and sew her skating costumes.

Amelia had come across as sweet, if a little reserved. Kiara admired her for going after such a lofty goal as the Olympics, even at the cost of her own heartbreak.

Julian led Kiara to the loveseat and sat down beside her, still holding her hand.

When Kiara glanced at Angie, she was beaming at her. They'd talked about what was happening between Kiara and Julian, and Angie was completely on board with it, so happy that her sister had also found happiness in her life.

And even though Julian hadn't yet told her he loved her, it was clear that he cared for her, and that was enough for Kiara. She prayed each night that their relationship would always be a positive thing and would be honoring to God. She hoped that Julian wanted the same thing.

Angie had shared about how she and Jude read the Bible and prayed together each day. That wasn't something that she and Julian had done, but maybe that would come as they both continued to grow in their faith.

"Dinner is served," Mrs. Stevens announced.

It smelled like they were having roast beef, which Kiara was thrilled about. It was one of her favorite meals.

Once they were standing, Julian offered her his arm. They were the last to leave the living room, while Annie walked ahead of them with Cole, still holding TJ.

"When you get tired of holding him, Annie, just hand him back," Kiara said.

"I'll never get tired of him," Annie told her. "And I'm looking forward to seeing how well Cole does in preparing my plate tonight. We'll see if he's learned anything from Julian."

As they walked into the formal dining room, Kiara's eyes widened and her steps slowed. The room had previously been decorated for Christmas, but all those decorations had been removed and replaced with different ones.

The room had been turned into a whimsical wonderland with cream-colored glittery tulle intertwined with gold ribbon draped around the windows and other surfaces. The decor on the table carried on the cream and gold-colored theme.

There was a beautiful floral arrangement made of red and cream roses with lots of greenery. Warm-toned fairy lights were woven throughout all the greenery in the room.

It was all so beautiful. And confusing. Until her gaze landed on a pile of presents stacked on a small table set under the window. Was this for her...?

When she looked up at Julian, he smiled at her. "Surprise!"

Everyone joined in with Julian, and Kiara was overwhelmed. She immediately started crying as she realized that these people thought enough of her to not just plan a simple birthday dinner. They'd gone to the trouble of decorating the room, buying her presents, and surprising her.

"Hey, sweetheart." Julian wrapped his arms around her. "I didn't mean to make you cry."

"They're good tears," Kiara heard Angie say. "She's just a little overwhelmed."

"And my hormones are still in an uproar," Kiara said with a sniff. "Not fair!"

Julian chuckled. "Sorry, my love. I should have taken that into account."

"It's fine." She looked up at him from within the circle of his arms. "In fact, it's perfect. Thank you."

Julian ushered her around the table to her chair. Once everyone was seated, Jude was the one to say grace before they ate, including thanking God for Kiara.

"Oh, it *is* roast beef," Kiara said as the dishes of food were brought to the table. "It's my favorite."

"That's why it's on the table," Angie said. "These are all your favorites."

So much time and attention had gone into this meal, and Kiara was struggling to grasp it all. Angie had always tried to make her birthday special, just like Kiara had tried to do the same for Angie. However, they'd always been constrained by their budget.

There had definitely been no elaborate decorations. Nor had there been roast beef dinners. And the pile of gifts had usually been a pile of one.

This was just so much, and Kiara refused to take it for granted. She had a man who cared for her, a healthy baby, and a brand-new family. Even without the meal and the presents, this would be the best birthday she'd ever had.

Following the meal of roast beef and all the fixings, Mrs. Stevens brought in a beautifully decorated cake with several candles on it. There weren't enough to represent every year of her life, but there were enough to make them a challenge to blow out. It was a rich chocolate cake with a silky buttercream frosting. So decadent.

Then came the gifts. Kiara needed nothing, but still the gifts were things that she loved and which spoke of the family's love for her.

Elizabeth and Duncan had given her a matching set of diamond earrings, a necklace, and a bracelet. She'd never had anything so beautiful and expensive.

Annie and Cole gave her an ankle length, black woolen cape with fur trim. She never would have bought it for herself, but it really appealed to her sense of romance, for some reason.

Angie and Jude's gift to her was a gorgeous copy of her favorite book, which was *Anne of Green Gables.* This book had painted page edges and a gilded cover. It was a far, far cry from the worn paperback she'd read as a girl.

"Thank you so much, everyone," Kiara said when the table was empty of gifts. "I don't have the words to describe what this means to me. This has already been a wonderful year, but now I can't wait to see what the Lord has planned for me in the year ahead."

"You actually have one more gift," Angie said.

"What?" Kiara glanced around. "I absolutely don't need anything more. You were all more than generous."

"Don't you want a gift from your husband?" she asked.

She hadn't even realized that she hadn't opened anything from Julian. He'd already given her so much that she didn't need or expect an actual gift from him.

Julian pushed his chair back from the table, then bent down on one knee beside her. Kiara frowned, confused by what was happening. If they hadn't already been married, she might have thought he was proposing.

"When we got engaged," Julian began, "it wasn't the most romantic moment. In fact, it wasn't romantic at all. Now that we've decided to make a go of our marriage, I don't want you to have missed out on the romance of a proposal. As well as receiving an engagement ring."

Kiara stared at him in shock as he pulled out a small box and opened it. Inside was a beautiful diamond ring.

"I'm not going to ask you to marry me because we've already passed that point," Julian said as he reached for her hand. "But what I do want to do at this moment, as I give you this ring, is to pledge my love to you. I love you, Kiara, and I want you to know that I am so thankful to God that you are my wife."

He *loved* her? Tears came to her eyes again. So maybe there was one gift he could give her, and he had.

"I love you too, Julian." The relief she felt at finally being able to say those words to him was immense. "And I couldn't ask for a better husband or a better father for TJ."

He slid the ring on her finger, then leaned forward and gently cupped her face as he kissed her.

They'd kissed twice before. Once at their wedding, and once the night he'd come home, but this one lingered just a little longer and was filled with emotion and promise.

"You and me forever, my love," Julian murmured.

Forever...

At one time in her life, forever hadn't felt like a positive thing because she and Angie had been stuck in a situation that wasn't very good. Now, though, forever was a promise she wanted and embraced with all her heart.

EPILOGUE

Julian was smiling before he even reached the steps to the front porch. No matter what was beyond the door—crying children, stressed wife—none of it could dim the happiness he felt at being home.

"Hello!" he called out as he stepped into the house. "Anyone home?"

He set his luggage down, then closed the door behind him.

"Daddy! Daddy! Daddy!"

Three-year-old TJ came flying from the direction of the nursery, already in his pajamas. Dark curls bouncing and arms stretched wide, he ran straight to Julian, who scooped him up and held him tight.

"How are you doing, buddy?" Julian asked as he lifted his hand for a high five.

TJ's little hand smacked Julian's, and he grinned. "Good."

"Where's Mama?"

"She's feedin' Soph."

Julian carried TJ to the nursery, where Kiara was seated with ten-month-old Sophia Grace standing on her lap, waving her hands with excitement when she spotted him. Julian set TJ down, then went over to where Kiara sat.

Smiling, he bent down to give Kiara a kiss before taking the baby from her. He nuzzled Sophia's neck and blew a raspberry on her skin, making her laugh with her whole body.

Kiara got to her feet and wrapped her arms around him. "I'm so glad you're home."

Julian gave her a one-armed hug, holding her close to his side. "And I'm so glad to be home. I missed you."

"Can we sit?" she asked.

"Of course." Julian needed the reconnection as much as she apparently did.

He handed Sophia back to her, then sank down into the chair Kiara had just vacated. Once he was situated, he drew Kiara down into his lap, wrapping his arm around her waist and Sophia. TJ scrambled up onto the wide arm of the chair, a book in his hand.

"We're reading, Daddy," TJ announced. "Do you want to read with us?"

"You bet, buddy." Contentment flooded Julian as TJ focused on opening the book to the first page.

He'd been in New York with Duncan for the past four days for meetings, and as with every trip he took away from the estate, he'd missed his family tremendously.

Once TJ had the book open to the right page, he held it so Julian could read it. The story was one that TJ frequently asked for, so he knew parts of it and recited them along with Julian.

Like Kiara, the boy loved books, but he also loved building things and playing with his cars. His personality was reserved with people he didn't know well, but on the estate, he was well acquainted with everyone, whether they were family or employees.

Sophia Grace had arrived a couple of months after TJ turned two. She was a smiley baby, who happily interacted with everyone. And like TJ, she had Kiara's coloring and dark curls.

Once the story was finished, Julian took over getting TJ into bed, while Kiara changed Sophia's diaper and snapped her into a sleeper. Together, they said prayers with each of the kids, then tucked them in. Not every bedtime went so smoothly, but it was as if the kids knew that their parents needed them to settle quickly that night.

As the house quieted, Kiara went to the kitchen while Julian put his bags in the bedroom and changed out of his traveling clothes.

Over the years, they'd developed a schedule where they usually waited to eat supper until after the kids went to bed. It was time for them to unwind from the day and spend time together.

Julian still traveled quite a bit, but when he wasn't traveling, he was at the estate. After some discussions, Duncan had decided to have an office building built near the security building, and he and Julian used that for work when they were home. The staff they'd had in New York had been given the opportunity to move, and most had agreed to transfer, and now they lived in Serenity and commuted to the estate each day.

It was the best of both worlds for him and Duncan. These days, his dad was loath to leave the estate and his grandchildren—five so far. Angie and Jude had a girl and a boy, each close in age to their kids. Annie and Cole had just one, a boy, but Annie was pregnant with child number two. They'd just recently let the family know that the baby was a boy. Julian hoped the kids would grow up to be great friends since they all lived so close together.

Once he'd changed, Julian left the bedroom and went to find Kiara. She stood with her back to him, and he didn't hesitate to step up behind her and wrap his arms around her.

Immediately, she turned to face him, lifting her face for his kiss. With over three years of married life behind them, Julian could only marvel at how their intimacy had deepened. Not just physically, but also emotionally and spiritually. He'd never had a relationship like it before, and he never wanted to have it with anyone but Kiara.

"Missed you, love," Julian murmured as he held her close.

"I missed you too," she told him. "Always."

They stood for another minute, sharing soft kisses and affectionate touches.

"We'd better pick this up later," Kiara said as she squeezed him tight. "Or the food will be cold."

Julian gave her one more kiss, then let her go. "I would hate to ruin the delicious meal you've made."

Together, they got their dinner on the table and sat down. Julian said a prayer of thanks for the food, as well as thanking God for bringing him safely home to his family again. As they ate, they shared what had happened during the days they'd been apart.

They'd spoken each day, but because of the time difference while he'd been in New York, it had been challenging to have long conversations. Plus, TJ loved to video chat with him, which inevitably took up most of the time they had available to chat.

After they were done eating, they cleaned up the dishes together. Julian locked up the house and then turned off the lights. Holding hands, they made their way to the bedroom. Most evenings, they preferred to hang out there once the kids had gone to bed, and they'd finished their dinner.

When Kiara had gotten pregnant with Sophia, they'd made some changes to the house. They'd ended up moving Kiara's library across to one of the rooms in the other suite. Even though Julian had an office close by, they'd left the one he'd originally set up as an office in the house. The bedroom Julian had initially used was now a guest room, though they'd never used it for anyone. Kiara's library became TJ's room, while the nursery was now Sophia's.

If they decided to have more kids—which seemed likely—they'd have to rearrange again. But for the time being, the house was set up perfectly for them.

Kiara helped him unpack his bags, then they sat down together at the bistro style table they'd bought for their room. It was where they sat for their devotions each night.

They'd tried to do it in the mornings, but the kids were too unpredictable with their wake-up times. So, evenings had ended up working better. And there were days when Julian came home so stressed that it was only the thought of getting to this point in the day that kept him from losing his mind.

"Did you see Ben?" Kiara asked, using the name Benji had taken on once he'd gone to college.

"Yes, Dad and I had dinner with him our first night in New York."

"How's he doing?"

"Pretty good, I think."

"Is there any chance he'll come back to live here?"

"I don't think so," Julian said. "He seems happy living in New York City."

"Anything we need to pray about for him?" Kiara asked as she opened the prayer journal they kept.

"Since he's in his last year of college, he and Dad have been trying to figure out where to plug him into the company."

"Is that what Ben wants?"

"I think so, but only if it's something he actually feels he'll be able to truly contribute to and not just because he has the Burke name."

"Any woman in his life?"

Julian grinned, not surprised that Kiara had asked about that. The women in the family seemed determined to keep track of Ben's dating life.

"He said he's been dating someone for a couple of months now," Julian said. "But I don't think it's very serious. He's dealing with what I dealt with when it came to dating."

"Too many beautiful women?"

Julian chuckled. "No. Just never knowing the true motives of someone."

"Well, if Prince William can find someone who wasn't after his crown, I think Ben can find someone who sees him for the great guy he is."

"Never mind Prince William," Julian said. "I found a wonderfully beautiful woman who wasn't after my money."

Kiara smiled at him. "You have such a way with words."

"Only for you, love," Julian said. "Only for you."

Over the past three years, she'd become everything to him. Best friend. Partner. Lover. Confidant. He'd never thought he would find all that in a woman, and yet he had.

Elijah was his other best friend. He'd ended up moving to Idaho after purchasing a home nearby, so they hung out together frequently. They were accountability partners for their sobriety, but they also met with a group of other men for a Bible study.

Over the last few years, Julian had worked hard to find a balance in his life. Kiara and Elijah had been a big help with that, and he was grateful for their input and support.

At the end of their devotions, Julian took Kiara's hand as she closed her eyes and began to pray. She prayed for Ben, for the family, for the courage to keep raising their kids with wisdom even when days were tough and patience ran thin.

Julian loved to listen to her. There was a tone in her voice when she prayed—unpolished, real, unselfconscious. It had taken him a while to pray aloud with confidence, but it had seemed to come much easier to Kiara.

Spending that time together, studying the Bible and praying, filled him with gratitude for everything they'd built.

They finished their time of prayer with "amen" but didn't immediately release each other's hands, enjoying the connection after having been apart.

The man he had been four years ago had been a wreck. It might not have been visible to the world, and he might have denied it, but he had been falling apart.

Though he and Kiara had made a decision that wasn't God-honoring, God had still brought something beautiful out of the mess.

As Julian held Kiara's hand, his thumb found her pulse and lingered. The kids were quiet on the baby monitors—another gift of the estate, everything wired and safe.

For a moment, he just looked at their hands, fingers intertwined.

He remembered when he'd been afraid of this, of being known and needed in any real way. Now it was everything. He liked knowing that Kiara depended on him. That she knew she *could* depend on him. For support. For protection. For love. She deserved it all and more.

Julian could see the lines at the corners of Kiara's eyes, the tiredness that came from wrangling a toddler and a baby by herself for a few days. He thought about how she'd never once complained, even when days were hard and she went to bed exhausted.

But regardless of how tired she might look, she was still the most beautiful woman he knew.

There was no need for words as they prepared for bed, then crawled beneath the covers, just soaking in the closeness they shared.

Julian of four years ago had not seen value in faith, a home, children, and a woman who loved and supported him. However, for present-day Julian, the most important things to him were within those four walls, especially the woman he held in his arms.

The woman who had brought love into his life. Who had seen him at his worst and still stood by him. In her arms, he'd found love and a home. In God, he'd found peace and contentment.

"I love you," he murmured.

Kiara laid with her head on his shoulder. Reaching up, she touched his cheek. "I love you too."

Julian turned his head and pressed a kiss into her palm, thanking God for once again bringing him back to his family. To Kiara.

~*~ *The End* ~*~

ABOUT THE AUTHOR

Kimberly Rae Jordan is a USA Today bestselling author of Christian romances. Many years ago, her love of reading Christian romance morphed into a desire to write stories of love, faith, and family, and thus began a journey that would lead her to places Kimberly never imagined she'd go.

In addition to being a writer, she is also a wife and mother, which means Kimberly spends her days straddling the line between real life in a house on the prairies of Canada and the imaginary world her characters live in. Though caring for her husband and four kids and working on her stories takes up a large portion of her day, Kimberly also enjoys reading and looking at craft ideas that she will likely never attempt to make.

As she continues to pen heartwarming stories of love, faith, and family, Kimberly hopes that readers of all ages will enjoy the journeys her characters take in each book. She has no plan to stop writing the stories God places on her heart and looks forward to where her journey will take her in the years to come

www.ingramcontent.com/pod-product-compliance
Lightning Source LLC
LaVergne TN
LVHW041105080826
845145LV00007B/1691

* 9 7 8 1 9 8 8 4 0 9 9 0 0 *